Thr...
The Chr...
by (...

The Magician's Nephew

The Lion, the Witch and the Wardrobe

The Horse and His Boy

Illustrated by Pauline Baynes

Collins
An imprint of HarperCollinsPublishers

The Chronicles of Narnia
are all available from Collins

in reading order
The Magician's Nephew
The Lion, the Witch and the Wardrobe
The Horse and His Boy
Prince Caspian
The Voyage of the *Dawn Treader*
The Silver Chair
The Last Battle

CONTENTS

This three-in-one edition first published in
Great Britain by Collins 1996
1 3 5 7 9 10 8 6 4 2

Collins is an imprint of HarperCollins*Publishers* Ltd,
77-85 Fulham Palace Road,
Hammersmith, London W6 8JB.

ISBN 0 00 675286-1

The author and illustrator assert the moral right to
be identified as the author and illustrator
of this work.

Printed and bound in Great Britain by Caledonian
International Book Manufacturing Ltd,
Glasgow, G64

The Magician's Nephew

To The Kilmer Family

The Magician's Nephew was first published
in Great Britain by The Bodley Head 1955
First published by Collins 1980

CHAPTER ONE

THE WRONG DOOR

THIS is a story about something that happened long ago when your grandfather was a child. It is a very important story because it shows how all the comings and goings between our own world and the land of Narnia first began.

In those days Mr Sherlock Holmes was still living in Baker Street and the Bastables were looking for treasure in the Lewisham Road. In those days, if you were a boy you had to wear a stiff Eton collar every day, and schools were usually nastier than now. But meals were nicer; and as for sweets, I won't tell you how cheap and good they were, because it would only make your mouth water in vain. And in those days there lived in London a girl called Polly Plummer.

She lived in one of a long row of houses which were all joined together. One morning she was out in the back garden when a boy scrambled up from the garden next door and put his face over the wall. Polly was very surprised because up till now there had never been any children in that house, but only Mr Ketterley and Miss Ketterley, a brother and sister, old bachelor and old maid, living together. So she looked up, full of curiosity. The face of the strange boy was very grubby. It could hardly have been grubbier if he had first rubbed his hands in the earth, and then had a good cry, and then dried his face with his hands. As a matter of fact, this was very nearly what he had been doing.

"Hullo," said Polly.

"Hullo," said the boy. "What's your name?"

"Polly," said Polly. "What's yours?"

"Digory," said the boy.

"I say, what a funny name!" said Polly.

"It isn't half so funny as Polly," said Digory.

"Yes it is," said Polly.

"No, it isn't," said Digory.

"At any rate I *do* wash my face," said Polly, "Which is what you need to do; especially after —" and then she stopped. She had been going to say "After you've been blubbing," but she thought that wouldn't be polite.

"Alright, I have then," said Digory in a much louder voice, like a boy who was so miserable that he didn't care who knew he had been crying. "And so would you," he went on, "if you'd lived all your life in the country and had a pony, and a river at the bottom of the garden, and then been brought to live in a beastly Hole like this."

"London isn't a Hole," said Polly indignantly. But the boy was too wound up to take any notice of her, and he went on —

"And if your father was away in India — and you had to come and live with an Aunt and an Uncle who's mad (who would like that?) — and if the reason was that they were looking after your Mother — and if your Mother was ill and was going to — going to — die." Then his face went the wrong sort of shape as it does if you're trying to keep back your tears.

"I didn't know. I'm sorry," said Polly humbly. And then, because she hardly knew what to say, and also to turn Digory's mind to cheerful subjects, she asked:

"Is Mr Ketterley really mad?"

"Well either he's mad," said Digory, "or there's some other mystery. He has a study on the top floor and Aunt Letty says I must never go up there. Well, that looks fishy to begin with. And then there's another thing. Whenever he tries to say anything to me at meal times — he never even tries to talk to *her* — she always shuts him up. She says, "Don't worry the boy, Andrew" or "I'm sure Digory doesn't want to hear about *that*" or else "Now, Digory, wouldn't you like to go out and play in the garden?"

"What sort of things does he try to say?"

"I don't know. He never gets far enough. But there's more than that. One night — it was last night in fact — as I was going past the foot of the attic-stairs on my way to bed (and I don't much care for going past them either) I'm sure I heard a yell."

"Perhaps he keeps a mad wife shut up there."

"Yes, I've thought of that."

"Or perhaps he's a coiner."

"Or he might have been a pirate, like the man at the beginning of *Treasure Island*, and be always hiding from his old shipmates."

"How exciting!" said Polly, "I never knew your house was so interesting."

"You may think it interesting," said Digory. "But you wouldn't like it if you had to sleep there. How would you like to lie awake listening for Uncle Andrew's step to come creeping along the passage to your room? And he has such awful eyes."

That was how Polly and Digory got to know one another: and as it was just the beginning of the summer holidays and neither of them was going to the sea that year, they met nearly every day.

Their adventures began chiefly because it was one of the wettest and coldest summers there had been for years. That drove them to do indoor things: you might say, indoor exploration. It is wonderful how much exploring you can do with a stump of candle in a big house, or in a row of houses. Polly had discovered long ago that if you opened a certain little door in the box-room attic of her house you would find the cistern and a dark place behind it which you could get into by a little careful climbing. The dark place was like a long tunnel with brick wall on one side and sloping roof on the other. In the roof there were little chunks of light between the slates. There was no floor in this tunnel: you had to step from rafter to rafter, and between them there was only plaster. If you stepped on this you would find yourself falling through the ceiling of the room below. Polly had used the bit of the tunnel just beside the cistern as a smugglers' cave. She had brought up bits of old packing cases and the seats of broken kitchen chairs, and things of that sort, and spread them across from rafter

to rafter so as to make a bit of floor. Here she kept a cash-box containing various treasures, and a story she was writing and usually a few apples. She had often drunk a quiet bottle of ginger-beer in there: the old bottles made it look more like a smugglers' cave.

Digory quite liked the cave (she wouldn't let him see the story) but he was more interested in exploring.

"Look here," he said. "How long does this tunnel go on for? I mean, does it stop where your house ends?"

"No," said Polly. "The walls don't go out to the roof. It goes on. I don't know how far."

"Then we could get the length of the whole row of houses."

"So we could," said Polly, "And oh, I say!"

"What?"

"We could get *into* the other houses."

"Yes, and get taken up for burglars! No thanks."

"Don't be so jolly clever. I was thinking of the house beyond yours."

"What about it?"

"Why, it's the empty one. Daddy says it's always been empty since we came here."

"I suppose we ought to have a look at it then," said Digory. He was a good deal more excited than you'd have thought from the way he spoke. For of course he was thinking, just as you would have been, of all the reasons why the house might have been empty so long. So was Polly. Neither of them said the word "haunted". And both felt that once the thing had been suggested, it would be feeble not to do it.

"Shall we go and try it now?" said Digory.

"Alright," said Polly.

"Don't if you'd rather not," said Digory.

"I'm game if you are," said she.

"How are we to know we're in the next house but one?"

They decided they would have to go out into the box-room and walk across it taking steps as long as the steps from one rafter to the next. That would give them an idea of how many rafters went to a room. Then they would allow about four more for the passage between the two attics in Polly's house, and then the same number for the maid's bedroom as for the box-room. That would give them the length of the house. When they had done that distance twice they would be at the end of Digory's house;

any door they came to after that would let them into an attic of the empty house.

"But I don't expect it's really empty at all," said Digory.

"What do you expect?"

"I expect someone lives there in secret, only coming in and out at night, with a dark lantern. We shall probably discover a gang of desperate criminals and get a reward. It's all rot to say a house would be empty all those years unless there was some mystery."

"Daddy thought it must be the drains," said Polly.

"Pooh! Grown-ups are always thinking of uninteresting explanations," said Digory. Now that they were talking by daylight in the attic instead of by candlelight in the Smugglers' Cave it seemed much less likely that the empty house would be haunted.

When they had measured the attic they had to get a pencil and do a sum. They both got different answers to it at first, and even when they agreed I am not sure they got it right. They were in a hurry to start on the exploration.

"We mustn't make a sound," said Polly as they climbed in again behind the cistern. Because it was such an important occasion they took a candle each (Polly had a good store of them in her cave).

It was very dark and dusty and draughty and they stepped from rafter to rafter without a word except when they whispered to one another, "We're opposite *your* attic now" or "this must be halfway through *our* house". And neither of them stumbled and the candles didn't go out, and at last they came where they could see a little door in the brick wall on their right. There was no bolt or handle on this side of it, of course, for the door had been made for getting in, not for getting out; but there was a catch (as there often is on the inside of a

cupboard door) which they felt sure they would be able to
turn.

"Shall I?" said Digory.

"I'm game if you are," said Polly, just as she had said
before. Both felt that it was becoming very serious, but
neither would draw back. Digory pushed round the catch
with some difficultly. The door swung open and the
sudden daylight made them blink. Then, with a great

shock, they saw that they were looking, not into a deserted attic, but into a furnished room. But it seemed empty enough. It was dead silent. Polly's curiosity got the better of her. She blew out her candle and stepped out into the strange room, making no more noise than a mouse.

It was shaped, of course, like an attic, but furnished as a sitting-room. Every bit of the walls was lined with shelves and every bit of the shelves was full of books. A fire was burning in the grate (you remember that it was a very cold wet summer that year) and in front of the fire-place with its back towards them was a high-backed armchair. Between the chair and Polly, and filling most of the middle of the room, was a big table piled with all sorts of things — printed books, and books of the sort you write in, and ink bottles and pens and sealing-wax and a microscope. But what she noticed first was a bright red wooden tray with a number of rings on it. They were in pairs — a yellow one and a green one together, then a little space, and then another yellow one and another green one. They were no bigger than ordinary rings, and no one could help noticing them because they were so bright. They were the most beautiful shiny little things you can imagine. If Polly had been a very little younger she would have wanted to put one in her mouth.

The room was so quiet that you noticed the ticking of the clock at once. And yet, as she now found, it was not absolutely quiet either. There was a faint — a very, very faint — humming sound. If Hoovers had been invented in those days Polly would have thought it was the sound of a Hoover being worked a long way off — several rooms away and several floors below. But it was a nicer sound than that, a more musical tone: only so faint that you could hardly hear it.

"It's alright; there's no one here," said Polly over her shoulder to Digory. She was speaking above a whisper now. And Digory came out, blinking and looking extremely dirty – as indeed Polly was too.

"This is no good," he said. "It's not an empty house at all. We'd better bunk before anyone comes."

"What do you think those are?" said Polly, pointing at the coloured rings.

"Oh come *on*," said Digory. "The sooner –"

He never finished what he was going to say for at that moment something happened. The high-backed chair in front of the fire moved suddenly and there rose up out of it – like a pantomime demon coming up out of a trapdoor – the alarming form of Uncle Andrew. They were not in the empty house at all; they were in Digory's house and in the forbidden study! Both children said "O-o-oh" and realized their terrible mistake. They felt they ought to have known all along that they hadn't gone nearly far enough.

Uncle Andrew was tall and very thin. He had a long clean-shaven face with a sharply-pointed nose and extremely bright eyes and a great tousled mop of grey hair.

Digory was quite speechless, for Uncle Andrew looked a thousand times more alarming than he had ever looked before. Polly was not so frightened yet; but she soon was. For the very first thing Uncle Andrew did was to walk across to the door of the room, shut it, and turn the key in the lock. Then he turned round, fixed the children with his bright eyes, and smiled, showing all his teeth.

"There!" he said. "Now my fool of a sister can't get at you!"

It was dreadfully unlike anything a grown-up would be expected to do. Polly's heart came into her mouth, and she and Digory started backing towards the little door they had come in by. Uncle Andrew was too quick for them. He got behind them and shut that door too and stood in front of it. Then he rubbed his hands and made his knuckles crack. He had very long, beautifully white, fingers.

"I am delighted to see you," he said. "Two children are just what I wanted."

"Please, Mr Ketterley," said Polly. "It's nearly my dinner time and I've got to go home. Will you let us out, please?"

"Not just yet," said Uncle Andrew. "This is too good an opportunity to miss. I wanted two children. You see, I'm in the middle of a great experiment. I've tried it on a guinea-pig and it seemed to work. But then a guinea-pig can't tell you anything. And you can't explain to it how to come back."

"Look here, Uncle Andrew," said Digory, "it really is dinner time and they'll be looking for us in a moment. You must let us out."

"Must?" said Uncle Andrew.

Digory and Polly glanced at one another. They dared not say anything, but the glances meant "Isn't this dreadful?" and "We must humour him."

"If you let us go for our dinner now," said Polly, "we could come back after dinner."

"Ah, but how do I know that you would?" said Uncle Andrew with a cunning smile. Then he seemed to change his mind.

"Well, well," he said, "if you really must go, I suppose you must. I can't expect two youngsters like you to find it much fun talking to an old buffer like me." He sighed and went on. "You've no idea how lonely I sometimes am. But no matter. Go to your dinner. But I must give you a present before you go. It's not every day that I see a little girl in my dingy old study; especially, if I may say so, such a very attractive young lady as yourself."

Polly began to think he might not really be mad after all.

"Wouldn't you like a ring, my dear?" said Uncle Andrew to Polly.

"Do you mean one of those yellow or green ones?" said Polly. "How lovely!"

"Not a green one," said Uncle Andrew. "I'm afraid I can't give the green ones away. But I'd be delighted to give you any of the yellow ones: with my love. Come and try one on."

Polly had now quite got over her fright and felt sure that the old gentleman was not mad; and there was certainly something strangely attractive about those bright rings. She moved over to the tray.

"Why! I declare," she said. "That humming noise gets louder here. It's almost as if the rings were making it."

"What a funny fancy, my dear," said Uncle Andrew with a laugh. It sounded a very natural laugh, but Digory had seen an eager, almost a greedy, look on his face.

"Polly! Don't be a fool!" he shouted. "Don't touch them."

It was too late. Exactly as he spoke, Polly's hand went out to touch one of the rings. And immediately, without a flash or a noise or a warning of any sort, there was no Polly. Digory and his Uncle were alone in the room.

CHAPTER TWO

DIGORY AND HIS UNCLE

IT was so sudden, and so horribly unlike anything that had ever happened to Digory even in a nightmare, that he let out a scream. Instantly Uncle Andrew's hand was over his mouth. "None of that!" he hissed in Digory's ear. "If you start making a noise your Mother'll hear it. And you know what a fright might do to her."

As Digory said afterwards, the horrible meanness of getting at a chap in *that* way, almost made him sick. But of course he didn't scream again.

"That's better," said Uncle Andrew. "Perhaps you couldn't help it. It *is* a shock when you first see someone vanish. Why, it gave even me a turn when the guinea-pig did it the other night."

"Was that when you yelled?" asked Digory.

"Oh, you heard *that*, did you? I hope you haven't been spying on me?"

"No, I haven't," said Digory indignantly. "But what's happened to Polly?"

"Congratulate me, my dear boy," said Uncle Andrew, rubbing his hands. "My experiment has succeeded. The little girl's gone – vanished – right out of the world."

"What have you done to her?"

"Sent her to – well – to another place."

"What *do* you mean?" asked Digory.

Uncle Andrew sat down and said, "Well, I'll tell you all about it. Have you ever heard of old Mrs Lefay?"

"Wasn't she a great-aunt or something?" said Digory.

"Not exactly," said Uncle Andrew. "She was my godmother. That's her, there, on the wall."

Digory looked and saw a faded photograph: it showed the face of an old woman in a bonnet. And he could now remember that he had once seen a photo of the same face in an old drawer, at home, in the country. He had asked his Mother who it was and Mother had not seemed to want to talk about the subject much. It was not at all a nice face, Digory thought, though of course with those early photographs one could never really tell.

"Was there — wasn't there — something wrong about her, Uncle Andrew?" he asked.

"Well," said Uncle Andrew with a chuckle, "it depends what you call *wrong*. People are so narrow-minded. She certainly got very queer in later life. Did very unwise things. That was why they shut her up."

"In an asylum, do you mean?"

"Oh no, no, no," said Uncle Andrew in a shocked voice. "Nothing of that sort. Only in prison."

"I say!" said Digory. "What had she done?"

"Ah, poor woman," said Uncle Andrew. "She had been very unwise. There were a good many different things. We needn't go into all that. She was always very kind to me."

"But look here, what has all this got to do with Polly? I do wish you'd —"

"All in good time, my boy," said Uncle Andrew. "They let old Mrs Lefay out before she died and I was one of the very few people whom she would allow to see her in her last illness. She had got to dislike ordinary, ignorant people, you understand. I do myself. But she and I were interested in the same sort of things. It was only a few days before her death that she told me to go to an old bureau in her house and open a secret drawer and bring her a little box that I would find there. The moment I picked up that box I could tell by the pricking in my fingers that I held some great secret in my hands. She gave it me and made me promise that as soon as she was dead I would burn it, unopened, with certain ceremonies. That promise I did not keep."

"Well, then, it was jolly rotten of you," said Digory.

"Rotten?" said Uncle Andrew with a puzzled look.

"Oh, I see. You mean that little boys ought to keep their promises. Very true: most right and proper, I'm sure, and I'm very glad you have been taught to do it. But of course you must understand that rules of that sort, however excellent they may be for little boys – and servants – and women – and even people in general, can't possibly be expected to apply to profound students and great thinkers and sages. No, Digory. Men like me, who possess hidden wisdom, are freed from common rules just as we are cut off from common pleasures. Ours, my boy, is a high and lonely destiny."

As he said this he sighed and looked so grave and noble and mysterious that for a second Digory really thought he was saying something rather fine. But then he remembered the ugly look he had seen on his Uncle's face the moment before Polly had vanished: and all at once he saw through Uncle Andrew's grand words. "All it means," he said to himself, "Is that he thinks he can do anything he likes to get anything he wants."

"Of course," said Uncle Andrew, "I didn't dare to open the box for a long time, for I knew it might contain something highly dangerous. For my godmother was a *very* remarkable woman. The truth is, she was one of the last mortals in this country who had fairy blood in her. (She said there had been two others in her time. One was a duchess and the other was a charwoman.) In fact, Digory, you are now talking to the last man (possibly) who really had a fairy godmother. There! That'll be something for you to remember when you are an old man yourself."

"I bet she was a bad fairy," thought Digory; and added out loud. "But what about Polly?"

"How you do harp on that!" said Uncle Andrew. "As if that was what mattered! My first task was of course to study the box itself. It was very ancient. And I knew enough even then to know that it wasn't Greek, or Old Egyptian, or Babylonian, or Hittite, or Chinese. It was older than any of those nations. Ah – that was a great day when I at last found out the truth. The box was Atlantean; it came from the lost island of Atlantis. "That meant it was centuries older than any of the stone-age things they dig up in Europe. And it wasn't a rough, crude thing like them either. For in the very dawn of time Atlantis was already a great city with palaces and temples and learned men."

He paused for a moment as if he expected Digory to say something. But Digory was disliking his Uncle more every minute, so he said nothing.

"Meanwhile," continued Uncle Andrew, "I was learning a good deal in other ways (it wouldn't be proper to explain them to a child) about Magic in general. That meant that I came to have a fair idea what sort of things might be in the box. By various tests I narrowed down the possibilities. I had to get to know some – well, some devilish queer people, and go through some very disagreeable experiences. That was what turned my head grey. One doesn't become a magician for nothing. My health broke down in the end. But I got better. And at last I actually *knew*."

Although there was not really the least chance of anyone overhearing them, he leaned forward and almost whispered as he said:

"The Atlantean box contained something that had been brought from another world when our world was only just beginning."

"What?" asked Digory, who was now interested in spite of himself.

"Only dust," said Uncle Andrew. "Fine, dry dust. Nothing much to look at. Not much to show for a lifetime of toil, you might say. Ah, but when I looked at that dust (I took jolly good care not to touch it) and thought that every grain had once been in another world – I don't mean another planet, you know; they're part of our world and you could get to them if you went far enough – but a really Other World – another Nature – another universe – somewhere you would never reach even if you travelled through the space of this universe for ever and ever – a world that could be reached only by Magic – well!" Here Uncle Andrew rubbed his hands till his knuckles cracked like fireworks.

"I knew," he went on, "that if only you could get it into the right form, that dust would draw you back to the place it had come from. But the difficulty was to get it into the right form. My earlier experiments were all failures. I tried them on guinea-pigs. Some of them only died. Some exploded like little bombs —"

"It was a jolly cruel thing to do," said Digory who had once had a guinea-pig of his own.

"How you do keep getting off the point!" said Uncle Andrew. "That's what the creatures were for. I'd bought them myself. Let me see — where was I? Ah yes. At last I succeeded in making the rings: the yellow rings. But now a new difficulty arose. I was pretty sure, now, that a yellow ring would send any creature that touched it into the Other Place. But what would be the good of that if I couldn't get them back to tell me what they had found there?"

"And what about *them*?" said Digory. "A nice mess they'd be in if they couldn't get back!"

"You will keep on looking at everything from the wrong point of view," said Uncle Andrew with a look of impatience. "Can't you understand that the thing is a great experiment? The whole point of sending anyone into the Other Place is that I want to find out what it's like."

"Well why didn't you go yourself then?"

Digory had hardly ever seen anyone so surprised and offended as his Uncle did at this simple question. "Me? Me?" he exclaimed. "The boy must be mad! A man at my time of life, and in my state of health, to risk the shock and the dangers of being flung suddenly into a different universe? I never heard anything so preposterous in my life! Do you realize what you're saying? Think what Another World means — you might meet anything — anything."

"And I suppose you've sent Polly into it then," said Digory. His cheeks were flaming with anger now. "And all I can say," he added, "even if you are my Uncle — is that you've behaved like a coward, sending a girl to a place you're afraid to go to yourself."

"Silence, sir!" said Uncle Andrew, bringing his hand down on the table. "I will not be talked to like that by a little, dirty, schoolboy. You don't understand. I am the great scholar, the magician, the adept, who is *doing* the experiment. Of course I need subjects to do it *on*. Bless my soul, you'll be telling me next that I ought to have asked the guinea-pigs' permission before I used *them*! No great wisdom can be reached without sacrifice. But the idea of my going myself is ridiculous. It's like asking a general to fight as a common soldier. Supposing I got killed, what would become of my life's work?"

"Oh, do stop jawing," said Digory. "Are you going to bring Polly back?"

"I was going to tell you, when you so rudely interrupted me," said Uncle Andrew, "that I did at last find out a way of doing the return journey. The green rings draw you back."

"But Polly hasn't got a green ring."

"No," said Uncle Andrew with a cruel smile.

"Then she can't get back," shouted Digory. "And it's exactly the same as if you'd murdered her."

"She can get back," said Uncle Andrew, "if someone else will go after her, wearing a yellow ring himself and taking two green rings, one to bring himself back and one to bring her back."

And now of course Digory saw the trap in which he was caught: and he stared at Uncle Andrew, saying nothing, with his mouth wide open. His cheeks had gone very pale.

"I hope," said Uncle Andrew presently in a very high and mighty voice, just as if he were a perfect Uncle who had given one a handsome tip and some good advice, "I *hope*, Digory, you are not given to showing the white feather. I should be very sorry to think that anyone of our family had not enough honour and chivalry to go to the aid of – er – a lady in distress."

"Oh shut up!" said Digory. "If you had any honour and all that, you'd be going yourself. But I know you won't. Alright. I see I've got to go. But you *are* a beast. I suppose you planned the whole thing, so that she'd go without knowing it and then I'd have to go after her."

"Of course," said Uncle Andrew with his hateful smile.

"Very well. I'll go. But there's one thing I jolly well mean to say first. I didn't believe in Magic till today. I see now it's real. Well if it is, I suppose all the old fairy tales are more or less true. And you're simply a wicked, cruel magician like the ones in the stories. Well, I've never read a story in which people of that sort weren't paid out in the end, and I bet you will be. And serve you right."

Of all the things Digory had said this was the first that really went home. Uncle Andrew started and there came over his face a look of such horror that, beast though he was, you could almost feel sorry for him. But a second later he smoothed it all away and said with a rather forced laugh, "Well, well, I suppose that is a natural thing for a child to think – brought up among women, as you have been. Old wives' tales, eh? I don't think you need worry about *my* danger, Digory. Wouldn't it be better to worry about the danger of your little friend? She's been gone some time. If there are any dangers Over There – well, it would be a pity to arrive a moment too late."

"A lot *you* care," said Digory fiercely. "But I'm sick of this jaw. What have I got to do?"

"You really must learn to control that temper of yours, my boy," said Uncle Andrew coolly. "Otherwise you'll grow up like your Aunt Letty. Now. Attend to me."

He got up, put on a pair of gloves, and walked over to the tray that contained the rings.

"They only work," he said, "if they're actually touching your skin. Wearing gloves, I can pick them up – like this – and nothing happens. If you carried one in your pocket nothing would happen: but of course you'd have to be careful not to put your hand in your pocket and touch it by accident. The moment you touch a yellow ring, you vanish out of this world. When you are in the Other Place I expect – of course this hasn't been tested yet, but I *expect* – that the moment you touch a green ring you vanish out of that world and – I expect – reappear in this. Now. I take these two greens and drop them into your right-hand pocket. Remember very carefully which pocket the greens are in. G for green and R for right. G.R. you see: which are the first two letters of green. One for you and one for the little girl. And now you pick up a yellow one for yourself. I should put it on – on your finger – if I were you. There'll be less chance of dropping it."

Digory had almost picked up the yellow ring when he suddenly checked himself.

"Look here," he said. "What about Mother? Supposing she asks where I am?"

"The sooner you go, the sooner you'll be back," said Uncle Andrew cheerfully.

"But you don't really know whether I can get back."

Uncle Andrew shrugged his shoulders, walked across to the door, unlocked it, threw it open, and said:

"Oh very well then. Just as you please. Go down and have your dinner. Leave the little girl to be eaten by wild animals or drowned or starved in Otherworld or lost there for good, if that's what you prefer. It's all one to me. Perhaps before tea time you'd better drop in on Mrs Plummer and explain that she'll never see her daughter again; because you were afraid to put on a ring."

"By gum," said Digory, "don't I just wish I was big enough to punch your head!"

Then he buttoned up his coat, took a deep breath, and picked up the ring. And he thought then, as he always thought afterwards too, that he could not decently have done anything else.

CHAPTER THREE

THE WOOD BETWEEN THE WORLDS

UNCLE ANDREW and his study vanished instantly. Then, for a moment, everything became muddled. The next thing Digory knew was that there was a soft green light coming down on him from above, and darkness below. He didn't seem to be standing on anything, or sitting, or lying. Nothing appeared to be touching him. "I believe I'm in water," said Digory. "Or *under* water." This frightened him for a second, but almost at once he could feel that he was rushing upwards. Then his head suddenly came out into the air and he found himself scrambling ashore, out on to smooth grassy ground at the edge of a pool.

As he rose to his feet he noticed that he was neither dripping nor panting for breath as anyone would expect after being under water. His clothes were perfectly dry. He was standing by the edge of a small pool – not more than ten feet from side to side – in a wood. The trees grew close together and were so leafy that he could get no glimpse of the sky. All the light was green light that came through the leaves: but there must have been a very strong sun overhead, for this green daylight was bright and warm. It was the quietest wood you could possibly imagine. There were no birds, no insects, no animals, and no wind. You could almost feel the trees growing. The pool he had just got out of was not the only pool. There were dozens of others – a pool every few yards as far as his eyes could reach. You could almost feel the trees drinking the water up with their roots. This wood was very much alive. When he tried to describe it afterwards

Digory always said, "It was a *rich* place: as rich as plumcake."

The strangest thing was that, almost before he had looked about him, Digory had half forgotten how he had come there. At any rate, he was certainly not thinking about Polly, or Uncle Andrew, or even his Mother. He was not in the least frightened, or excited, or curious. If anyone had asked him "Where did you come from?" he would probably have said, "I've always been here." That was what it felt like — as if one had always been in that place and never been bored although nothing had ever happened. As he said long afterwards, "It's not the sort of place where things happen. The trees go on growing, that's all."

After Digory had looked at the wood for a long time he noticed that there was a girl lying on her back at the foot of a tree a few yards away. Her eyes were nearly shut but not quite, as if she were just between sleeping and waking. So he looked at her for a long time and said nothing. And at last she opened her eyes and looked at him for a long time and she also said nothing. Then she spoke, in a dreamy, contented sort of voice.

"I think I've seen you before," she said.

"I rather think so too," said Digory. "Have you been here long?"

"Oh, always," said the girl. "At least – I don't know – a very long time."

"So have I," said Digory.

"No you haven't, said she. "I've just seen you come up out of that pool."

"Yes, I suppose I did," said Digory with a puzzled air, "I'd forgotten."

Then for quite a long time neither said any more.

"Look here," said the girl presently, "I wonder did we ever really meet before? I had a sort of idea – a sort of picture in my head – of a boy and a girl, like us – living somewhere quite different – and doing all sorts of things. Perhaps it was only a dream."

"I've had that same dream, I think," said Digory. "About a boy and a girl, living next door – and something about crawling among rafters. I remember the girl had a dirty face."

"Aren't you getting it mixed? In my dream it was the boy who had the dirty face."

"I can't remember the boy's face," said Digory:

and then added, "Hullo! What's that?"

"Why! it's a guinea-pig," said the girl. And it was — a fat guinea-pig, nosing about in the grass. But round the middle of the guinea-pig there ran a tape, and, tied on to it by the tape, was a bright yellow ring.

"Look! look," cried Digory, "The ring! And look! You've got one on your finger. And so have I."

The girl now sat up, really interested at last. They stared very hard at one another, trying to remember. And then, at exactly the same moment, she shouted out "Mr Ketterley" and he shouted out "Uncle Andrew", and they knew who they were and began to remember the whole story. After a few minutes hard talking they had got it straight. Digory explained how beastly Uncle Andrew had been.

"What do we do now?" said Polly. "Take the guinea-pig and go home?"

"There's no hurry," said Digory with a huge yawn.

"I think there is," said Polly. "This place is too quiet. It's so — so dreamy. You're almost asleep. If we once give in to it we shall just lie down and drowse for ever and ever."

"It's very nice here," said Digory.

"Yes, it is," said Polly. "But we've got to get back." She stood up and began to go cautiously towards the guinea-pig. But then she changed her mind.

"We might as well leave the guinea-pig," she said. "It's perfectly happy here, and your uncle will only do something horrid to it if we take it home."

"I bet he would," answered Digory. "Look at the way

he's treated *us*. By the way, how *do* we get home?"

"Go back into the pool, I expect."

They came and stood together at the edge looking down into the smooth water. It was full of the reflection of the green, leafy branches; they made it look very deep.

"We haven't any bathing things," said Polly.

"We shan't need them, silly," said Digory. "We're going in with our clothes on. Don't you remember it didn't wet us on the way up?"

"Can you swim?"

"A bit. Can you?"

"Well – not much."

"I don't think we shall need to swim," said Digory "We want to go *down*, don't we?"

Neither of them much liked the idea of jumping into that pool, but neither said so to the other. They took hands and said "One – Two – Three – Go" and jumped. There was a great splash and of course they closed their eyes. But when they opened them again they found they were still standing, hand in hand, in the green wood, and hardly up to their ankles in water. The pool was apparently only a couple of inches deep. They splashed back on to the dry ground.

"What on earth's gone wrong?" said Polly in a frightened voice; but not quite so frightened as you might expect, because it is hard to feel really frightened in that wood. The place is too peaceful.

"Oh! I know," said Digory, "Of course it won't work. We're still wearing our yellow rings. They're for the outward journey, you know. The green ones take you home. We must change rings. Have you got pockets? Good. Put your yellow ring in your left. I've got two greens. Here's one for you."

They put on their green rings and came back to the pool. But before they tried another jump Digory gave a long "O-o-oh!"

"What's the matter?" said Polly.

"I've just had a really wonderful idea," said Digory. "What are all the other pools?"

"How do you mean?"

"Why, if we can get back to our own world by jumping into *this* pool, mightn't we get somewhere else by jumping into one of the others? Supposing there was a world at the bottom of every pool."

"But I thought we were already in your Uncle Andrew's Other World or Other Place or whatever he called it. Didn't you say —"

"Oh bother Uncle Andrew," interrupted Digory. "I don't believe he knows anything about it. He never had the pluck to come here himself. He only talked of *one* Other World. But suppose there were dozens?"

"You mean, this wood might be only one of them?"

"No, I don't believe this wood is a world at all. I think it's just a sort of in-between place."

Polly looked puzzled. "Don't you see?" said Digory. "No, do listen. Think of our tunnel under the slates at home. It isn't a room in any of the houses. In a way, it isn't really part of any of the houses. But once you're in the tunnel you can go along it and come into any of the houses in the row. Mightn't this wood be the same? — a place that isn't in any of the worlds, but once you've found that place you can get into them all."

"Well, even if you can —" began Polly, but Digory went on as if he hadn't heard her.

"And of course that explains everything," he said. "That's why it is so quiet and sleepy here. Nothing ever happens here. Like at home. It's in the houses that people talk, and do things, and have meals. Nothing goes on in the in-between places, behind the walls and above the ceilings and under the floor, or in our own tunnel. But when you come out of our tunnel you may find yourself in *any* house. I think we can get out of this place into jolly well Anywhere! We don't need to jump back into the same pool we came up by. Or not just yet."

"The Wood between the Worlds," said Polly dreamily. "It sounds rather nice."

"Come on," said Digory. "Which pool shall we try?"

"Look here," said Polly, "I'm not going to try any new pool till we've made sure that we *can* get back by the old one. We're not even sure if it'll work yet."

"Yes," said Digory. "And get caught by Uncle Andrew and have our rings taken away before we've had any fun. No thanks."

"Couldn't we just go part of the way down into our own pool," said Polly. "Just to see if it works. Then if it does, we'll change rings and come up again before we're really back in Mr Ketterley's study."

"Can we go *part* of the way down?"

"Well, it took time coming up. I suppose it'll take a little time going back."

Digory made rather a fuss about agreeing to this, but he had to in the end because Polly absolutely refused to do any exploring in new worlds until she had made sure about getting back to the old one. She was quite as brave as he about some dangers (wasps, for instance) but she was not so interested in finding out things nobody had ever heard of before; for Digory was the sort of person who wants to know everything, and when he grew up he became the famous Professor Kirke who comes into other books.

After a good deal of arguing they agreed to put on their green rings ("Green for safety," said Digory, "so you can't help remembering which is which") and hold hands and jump. But as soon as they seemed to be getting back to Uncle Andrew's study, or even to their own world, Polly was to shout "Change" and they would slip off their greens and put on their yellows. Digory wanted to be the one who shouted "Change" but Polly wouldn't agree.

They put on the green rings, took hands, and once more shouted "One – Two – Three – Go". This time it worked. It is very hard to tell you what it felt like, for everything happened so quickly. At first there were bright lights moving about in a black sky; Digory always thinks these were stars and even swears that he saw Jupiter quite close – close enough to see its moon. But almost at once there were rows and rows of roofs and chimney pots about them, and they could see St Paul's and knew they were looking at London. But you could see through the walls of all the houses. Then they could see Uncle Andrew, very vague and shadowy, but getting clearer and more solid-looking all the time, just as if he were coming into focus. But before he became quite real Polly shouted "Change", and they did change, and our world faded away like a dream, and the green light above grew stronger and stronger, till their heads came out of the pool and they scrambled ashore. And there was the wood all about them, as green and bright and still as ever. The whole thing had taken less than a minute.

"There!" said Digory. "That's alright. Now for the adventure. Any pool will do. Come on. Let's try that one."

"Stop!" said Polly. "Aren't we going to mark *this* pool?"

They stared at each other and turned quite white as they realized the dreadful thing that Digory had just been going to do. For there were any number of pools in the wood, and the pools were all alike and the trees were all alike, so that if they had once left behind the pool that led to our own world without making some sort of landmark, the chances would have been a hundred to one against their ever finding it again.

Digory's hand was shaking as he opened his penknife and cut out a long strip of turf on the bank of the pool. The soil (which smelled nice) was of a rich reddish brown and showed up well against the green. "It's a good thing *one* of us has some sense," said Polly.

"Well don't keep on gassing about it," said Digory. "Come along, I want to see what's in one of the other pools." And Polly gave him a pretty sharp answer and he said something even nastier in reply. The quarrel lasted for several minutes but it would be dull to write it all down. Let us skip on to the moment at which they stood with beating hearts and rather scared faces on the edge of the unknown pool with their yellow rings on and held hands and once more said "One – Two – Three – Go!"

Splash! Once again it hadn't worked. This pool, too, appeared to be only a puddle. Instead of reaching a new world they only got their feet wet and splashed their legs for the second time that morning (if it was a morning: it seems to be always the same time in the Wood between the Worlds).

"Blast and botheration!" exclaimed Digory. "What's gone wrong now? We've put our yellow rings on all right. He said yellow for the outward journey."

Now the truth was that Uncle Andrew, who knew nothing about the Wood between the Worlds, had quite a wrong idea about the rings. The yellow ones weren't "outward" rings and the green ones weren't "homeward" rings; at least, not in the way he thought. The stuff of which both were made had all come from the wood. The stuff in the yellow rings had the power of drawing you into the wood; it was stuff that wanted to get back to its own place, the in-between place. But the stuff in the green rings is stuff that is trying to get out of its own place: so that a green ring would take you out of the wood into a world. Uncle Andrew, you see, was working with things he did not really understand; most magicians are. Of course Digory did not realize the truth quite clearly either, or not till later. But when they had talked it over, they decided to try their green rings on the new pool, just to see what happened.

"I'm game if you are," said Polly. But she really said this because, in her heart of hearts, she now felt sure that neither kind of ring was going to work at all in the new pool, and so there was nothing worse to be afraid of than another splash. I am not quite sure that Digory had not the same feeling. At any rate, when they had both put on their greens and come back to the edge of the water, and taken hands again, they were certainly a good deal more cheerful and less solemn than they had been the first time.

"One – Two – Three – Go!" said Digory. And they jumped.

CHAPTER FOUR

THE BELL AND THE HAMMER

THERE was no doubt about the Magic this time. Down and down they rushed, first through darkness and then through a mass of vague and whirling shapes which might have been almost anything. It grew lighter. Then suddenly they felt that they were standing on something solid. A moment later everything came into focus and they were able to look about them.

"What a queer place!" said Digory.

"I don't like it," said Polly with something like a shudder.

What they noticed first was the light. It wasn't like sunlight, and it wasn't like electric light, or lamps, or candles, or any other light they had ever seen. It was a dull, rather red light, not at all cheerful. It was steady and did not flicker. They were standing on a flat paved surface and buildings rose all around them. There was no roof overhead; they were in a sort of courtyard. The sky was extraordinarily dark — a blue that was almost black. When you had seen that sky you wondered that there should be any light at all.

"It's very funny weather here," said Digory. "I wonder if we've arrived just in time for a thunderstorm; or an eclipse."

"I don't like it," said Polly.

Both of them, without quite knowing why, were talking in whispers. And though there was no reason why they should still go on holding hands after their jump, they didn't let go.

The walls rose very high all round that courtyard. They

had many great windows in them, windows without glass, through which you saw nothing but black darkness. Lower down there were great pillared arches, yawning blackly like the mouths of railway tunnels. It was rather cold.

The stone of which everything was built seemed to be red, but that might only be because of the curious light. It was obviously very old. Many of the flat stones that paved the courtyard had cracks across them. None of them fitted closely together and the sharp corners were all worn off. One of the arched doorways was half filled up with rubble. The two children kept on turning round and round to look at the different sides of the courtyard. One reason was that they were afraid of somebody — or something — looking out of those windows at them when their backs were turned.

"Do you think anyone lives here?" said Digory at last, still in a whisper.

"No," said Polly. "It's all in ruins. We haven't heard a sound since we came."

"Let's stand still and listen for a bit," suggested Digory.

They stood still and listened, but all they could hear was the thump-thump of their own hearts. This place was at least as quiet as the Wood between the Worlds. But it was a different kind of quietness. The silence of the Wood had been rich and warm (you could almost hear the trees growing) and full of life: this was a dead, cold, empty silence. You couldn't imagine anything growing in it.

"Let's go home," said Polly.

"But we haven't seen anything yet," said Digory. "Now we're here, we simply must have a look round."

"I'm sure there's nothing at all interesting here."

"There's not much point in finding a magic ring that

lets you into other worlds if you're afraid to look at them
when you've got there."

"Who's talking about being afraid?" said Polly, letting
go of Digory's hand.

"I only thought you didn't seem very keen on exploring
this place."

"I'll go anywhere you go."

"We can get away the moment we want to," said
Digory. "Let's take off our green rings and put them in
our right-hand pockets. All we've got to do is to remember that our yellow are in our left-hand pockets. You can
keep your hand as near your pocket as you like, but don't
put it in or you'll touch your yellow and vanish."

They did this and went quietly up to one of the big
arched doorways which led into the inside of the building.
And when they stood on the threshold and could look in,
they saw it was not so dark inside as they had thought at
first. It led into a vast, shadowy hall which appeared
to be empty; but on the far side there was a row of pillars
with arches between them and through those arches
there streamed in some more of the same tired-looking
light. They crossed the hall, walking very carefully for
fear of holes in the floor or of anything lying about that
they might trip over. It seemed a long walk. When they
had reached the other side they came out through the
arches and found themselves in another and larger
courtyard.

"That doesn't look very safe," said Polly, pointing at a
place where the wall bulged outward and looked as if it
were ready to fall over into the courtyard. In one place a
pillar was missing between two arches and the bit that
came down to where the top of the pillar ought to have
been hung there with nothing to support it. Clearly, the

place had been deserted for hundreds, perhaps thousands, of years.

"If it's lasted till now, I suppose it'll last a bit longer," said Digory. "But we must be very quiet. You know a noise sometimes brings things down — like an avalanche in the Alps."

They went on out of that courtyard into another doorway, and up a great flight of steps and through vast rooms that opened out of one another till you were dizzy with the mere size of the place. Every now and then they thought they were going to get out into the open and see what sort of country lay around the enormous palace. But each time they only got into another courtyard. They must have been magnificent places when people were still living there. In one there had once been a fountain. A great stone monster with wide-spread wings stood with its mouth open and you could still see a bit of piping at the back of its mouth, out of which the water used to pour. Under it was a wide stone basin to hold the water; but it was as dry as a bone. In other places there were the dry sticks of some sort of climbing plant which had wound itself round the pillars and helped to pull some of them down. But it had died long ago. And there were no ants or spiders or any of the other living things you expect to see in a ruin; and where the dry earth showed between the broken flagstones there was no grass or moss.

It was all so dreary and all so much the same that even Digory was thinking they had better put on their yellow rings and get back to the warm, green, living forest of the In-between place, when they came to two huge doors of some metal that might possibly be gold. One stood a little ajar. So of course they went to look in. Both started back and drew a long breath: for here at last was something worth seeing.

For a second they thought the room was full of people – hundreds of people, all seated, and all perfectly still. Polly and Digory, as you may guess, stood perfectly still themselves for a good long time, looking in. But presently they decided that what they were looking at could not be real people. There was not a movement nor the sound of a breath among them all. They were like the most wonderful waxworks you ever saw.

This time Polly took the lead. There was something in this room which interested her more than it interested Digory: all the figures were wearing magnificent clothes. If you were interested in clothes at all, you could hardly help going in to see them closer. And the blaze of their colours made this room look, not exactly cheerful, but at

any rate rich and majestic after all the dust and emptiness of the others. It had more windows, too, and was a good deal lighter.

I can hardly describe the clothes. The figures were all robed and had crowns on their heads. Their robes were of crimson and silvery grey and deep purple and vivid green: and there were patterns, and pictures of flowers and strange beasts, in needlework all over them. Precious stones of astonishing size and brightness stared from their crowns and hung in chains round their necks and peeped out from all the places where anything was fastened.

"Why haven't these clothes all rotted away long ago?" asked Polly.

"Magic," whispered Digory. "Can't you feel it? I bet this whole room is just stiff with enchantments. I could feel it the moment we came in."

"Any one of these dresses would cost hundreds of pounds," said Polly.

But Digory was more interested in the faces, and indeed these were well worth looking at. The people sat in their stone chairs on each side of the room and the floor was left free down the middle. You could walk down and look at the faces in turn.

"They were *nice* people, I think," said Digory.

Polly nodded. All the faces they could see were certainly nice. Both the men and women looked kind and wise, and they seemed to come of a handsome race. But after the children had gone a few steps down the room they came to faces that looked a little different. These were very solemn faces. You felt you would have to mind your P's and Q's, if you ever met living people who looked like that. When they had gone a little further, they found themselves among faces they didn't like: this was about the middle of the room. The faces here looked very strong and proud and happy, but they looked cruel. A little further on they looked crueller. Further on again, they were still cruel but they no longer looked happy. They were even despairing faces: as if the people they belonged to had done dreadful things and also suffered dreadful things. The last figure of all was the most interesting — a woman even more richly dressed than the others, very tall (but every figure in that room was taller than the people of our world), with a look of such fierceness and pride that it took your breath away. Yet she was beautiful too. Years afterwards when he was an old man, Digory said he had never in all his life known a woman so beautiful. It is only fair to add that Polly always said she couldn't see anything specially beautiful about her.

This woman, as I said, was the last: but there were plenty of empty chairs beyond her, as if the room had been intended for a much larger collection of images.

"I do wish we knew the story that's behind all this," said Digory. "Let's go back and look at that table sort of thing in the middle of the room."

The thing in the middle of the room was not exactly a table. It was a square pillar about four feet high and on it there rose a little golden arch from which there hung a little golden bell; and beside this there lay a little golden hammer to hit the bell with.

"I wonder . . . I wonder . . . I wonder . . ." said Digory.

"There seems to be something written here," said Polly, stooping down and looking at the side of the pillar.

"By gum, so there is," said Digory. "But of course we shan't be able to read it."

"Shan't we? I'm not so sure," said Polly.

They both looked at it hard and, as you might have expected, the letters cut in the stone were strange. But now a great wonder happened: for, as they looked, though the shape of the strange letters never altered, they found that they could understand them. If only Digory had remembered what he himself had said a few minutes ago, that this was an enchanted room, he might have guessed that the enchantment was beginning to work. But he was too wild with curiosity to think about that. He was longing more and more to know what was written on the pillar. And very soon they both knew. What it said was something like this – at least this is the sense of it though the poetry, when you read it there, was better:

Make your choice, adventurous Stranger;
Strike the bell and bide the danger,
Or wonder, till it drives you mad,
What would have followed if you had.

"No fear!" said Polly. "We don't want any danger."

"Oh but don't you see it's no good!" said Digory. "We can't get out of it now. We shall always be wondering what else would have happened if we had struck the bell. I'm not going home to be driven mad by always thinking of that. No fear!"

"Don't be so silly," said Polly. "As if anyone would! What does it matter what would have happened?"

"I expect anyone who's come as far as this is bound to go on wondering till it sends him dotty. That's the Magic of it, you see. I can feel it beginning to work on me already."

"Well I don't," said Polly crossly. "And I don't believe you do either. You're just putting it on."

"That's all *you* know," said Digory. "It's because you're a girl. Girls never want to know anything but gossip and rot about people getting engaged."

"You looked exactly like your Uncle when you said that," said Polly.

"Why can't you keep to the point?" said Digory. "What we're talking about is –"

"How exactly like a man!" said Polly in a very grown-up voice; but she added hastily, in her real voice, "And don't say I'm just like a woman, or you'll be a beastly copy-cat."

"I should never dream of calling a kid like you a woman," said Digory loftily.

"Oh, I'm a kid, am I?" said Polly who was now in a

real rage. "Well you needn't be bothered by having a kid with you any longer then. I'm off. I've had enough of this place. And I've had enough of you too — you beastly, stuck-up, obstinate pig!"

"None of that!" said Digory in a voice even nastier than he meant it to be; for he saw Polly's hand moving to her pocket to get hold of her yellow ring. I can't excuse what he did next except by saying that he was very sorry for it afterwards (and so were a good many other people). Before Polly's hand reached her pocket, he grabbed her wrist, leaning across with his back against her chest. Then, keeping her other arm out of the way with his other elbow, he leaned forward, picked up the hammer, and struck the golden bell a light, smart tap. Then he let her go and they fell apart staring at each other and breathing hard. Polly was just beginning to cry, not with fear, and not even because he had hurt her wrist quite badly, but with furious anger. Within two seconds, however, they had something to think about that drove their own quarrels quite out of their minds.

As soon as the bell was struck it gave out a note, a sweet note such as you might have expected, and not very loud. But instead of dying away again, it went on; and as it went on it grew louder. Before a minute had passed it was twice as loud as it had been to begin with. It was soon so loud that if the children had tried to speak (but they weren't thinking of speaking now — they were just standing with their mouths open) they would not have heard one another. Very soon it was so loud that they could not have heard one another even by shouting. And still it grew: all on one note, a continuous sweet sound, though the sweetness had something horrible about it, till all the air in that great room was throbbing with it and they could feel the stone floor trembling under their feet. Then at last it began to be mixed with another sound, a vague, disastrous noise which sounded first like the roar of a distant train, and then like the crash of a falling tree. They heard something like great weights falling. Finally, with a sudden rush and thunder, and a shake that nearly flung them off their feet, about a quarter of the roof at one end of the room fell in, great blocks of masonry fell all round them, and the walls rocked. The noise of the bell stopped. The clouds of dust cleared away. Everything became quiet again.

It was never found out whether the fall of the roof was due to Magic or whether that unbearably loud sound from the bell just happened to strike the note which was more than those crumbling walls could stand.

"There! I hope you're satisfied now," panted Polly.

"Well, it's all over, anyway," said Digory.

And both thought it was; but they had never been more mistaken in their lives.

CHAPTER FIVE

THE DEPLORABLE WORD

THE children were facing one another across the pillar where the bell hung, still trembling, though it no longer gave out any note. Suddenly they heard a soft noise from the end of the room which was still undamaged. They turned quick as lightning to see what it was. One of the robed figures, the furthest-off one of all, the woman whom Digory thought so beautiful, was rising from its chair. When she stood up they realized that she was even taller than they had thought. And you could see at once, not only from her crown and robes, but from the flash of her eyes and the curve of her lips, that she was a great queen. She looked round the room and saw the damage and saw the children, but you could not guess from her face what she thought of either or whether she was surprised. She came forward with long, swift strides.

"Who has awaked me? Who has broken the spell?" she asked.

"I think it must have been me," said Digory.

"You!" said the Queen, laying her hand on his shoulder – a white, beautiful hand, but Digory could feel that it was strong as steel pincers. "You? But you are only a child, a common child. Anyone can see at a glance that you have no drop of royal or noble blood in your veins. How did such as you dare to enter this house?"

"We've come from another world; by Magic," said Polly, who thought it was high time the Queen took some notice of her as well as of Digory.

"Is this true?" said the Queen, still looking at Digory and not giving Polly even a glance.

"Yes, it is," said he.

The Queen put her other hand under his chin and forced it up so that she could see his face better. Digory tried to stare back but he soon had to let his eyes drop. There was something about hers that overpowered him.

After she had studied him for well over a minute, she let go of his chin and said:

"You are no magician. The mark of it is not on you. You must be only the servant of a magician. It is on another's Magic that you have travelled here."

"It was my Uncle Andrew," said Digory.

At the moment, not in the room itself but from somewhere very close, there came, first a rumbling, then a creaking, and then a roar of falling masonry, and the floor shook.

"There is great peril here," said the Queen. "The whole palace is breaking up. If we are not out of it in a few minutes we shall be buried under the ruin." She spoke as calmly as if she had been merely mentioning the time of day. "Come," she added, and held out a hand to each of the children. Polly, who was disliking the Queen and feeling rather sulky, would not have let her hand be taken if she could have helped it. But though the Queen spoke so calmly, her movements were as quick as thought. Before Polly knew what was happening her left hand had been caught in a hand so much larger and stronger than her own that she could do nothing about it.

"This is a terrible woman," thought Polly. "She's strong enough to break my arm with one twist. And now that she's got my left hand I can't get at my yellow ring. If I tried to stretch across and get my right hand into my left pocket I mightn't be able to reach it, before she asked me what I was doing. Whatever happens we mustn't let her know about the rings. I do hope Digory has the sense to keep his mouth shut. I wish I could get a word with him alone."

The Queen led them out of the Hall of Images into a long corridor and then through a whole maze of halls and stairs and courtyards. Again and again they heard parts of the great palace collapsing, sometimes quite close to them. Once a huge arch came thundering down only a moment after they had passed through it. The Queen was walking quickly — the children had to trot to keep up with her — but she showed no sign of fear. Digory thought, "She's wonderfully brave. And strong. She's what I call a Queen! I do hope she's going to tell us the story of this place."

She did tell them certain things as they went along:

"That is the door to the dungeons," she would say, or "That passage leads to the principal torture chambers," or "This was the old banqueting hall where my great-grandfather bade seven hundred nobles to a feast and killed them all before they had drunk their fill. They had had rebellious thoughts."

They came at last into a hall larger and loftier than any they had yet seen. From its size and from the great doors at the far end, Digory thought that now at last they must be coming to the main entrance. In this he was quite right. The doors were dead black, either ebony or some black metal which is not found in our world. They were fastened with great bars, most of them too high to reach and all too heavy to lift. He wondered how they would get out.

The Queen let go of his hand and raised her arm. She drew herself up to her full height and stood rigid. Then she said something which they couldn't understand (but it sounded horrid) and made an action as if she were throwing something towards the doors. And those high and heavy doors trembled for a second as if they were made of silk and then crumbled away till there was nothing left of them but a heap of dust on the threshold.

"Whew!" whistled Digory.

"Has your master magician, your uncle, power like mine?" asked the Queen, firmly seizing Digory's hand again. "But I shall know later. In the meantime, remember what you have seen. This is what happens to things, and to people, who stand in my way."

Much more light than they had yet seen in that country was pouring in through the now empty doorway, and when the Queen led them out through it they were not

surprised to find themselves in the open air. The wind
that blew in their faces was cold, yet somehow stale. They
were looking from a high terrace and there was a great
landscape out below them.

Low down and near the horizon hung a great, red sun,
far bigger than our sun. Digory felt at once that it was
also older than ours: a sun near the end of its life, weary
of looking down upon that world. To the left of the sun,
and higher up, there was a single star, big and bright.
Those were the only two things to be seen in the dark sky;
they made a dismal group. And on the earth, in every
direction, as far as the eye could reach, there spread a vast

city in which there was no living thing to be seen. And all
the temples, towers, palaces, pyramids, and bridges cast
long, disastrous-looking shadows in the light of that
withered sun. Once a great river had flowed through the
city, but the water had long since vanished, and it was
now only a wide ditch of grey dust.

"Look well on that which no eyes will ever see again,"
said the Queen. "Such was Charn, that great city, the city
of the King of Kings, the wonder of the world, perhaps of
all worlds. Does your uncle rule any city as great as this,
boy?"

"No," said Digory. He was going to explain that Uncle
Andrew didn't rule any cities, but the Queen went on:

"It is silent now. But I have stood here when the whole
air was full of the noises of Charn; the trampling of feet,
the creaking of wheels, the cracking of the whips and the
groaning of slaves, the thunder of chariots, and the
sacrificial drums beating in the temples. I have stood here
(but that was near the end) when the roar of battle went
up from every street and the river of Charn ran red." She
paused and added, "All in one moment one woman
blotted it out for ever."

"Who?" said Digory in a faint voice; but he had
already guessed the answer.

"I," said the Queen. "I, Jadis the last Queen, but the
Queen of the World."

The two children stood silent, shivering in the cold
wind.

"It was my sister's fault," said the Queen. "She drove
me to it. May the curse of all the Powers rest upon her
forever! At any moment I was ready to make peace – yes
and to spare her life too, if only she would yield me the
throne. But she would not. Her pride has destroyed the

whole world. Even after the war had begun, there was a
solemn promise that neither side would use Magic. But
when she broke her promise, what could I do? Fool! As if
she did not know that I had more Magic than she! She
even knew that I had the secret of the Deplorable Word.
Did she think — she was always a weakling — that I would
not use it?"

"What was it?" said Digory.

"That was the secret of secrets," said the Queen Jadis.
"It had long been known to the great kings of our race
that there was a word which, if spoken with the proper
ceremonies, would destroy all living things except the one
who spoke it. But the ancient kings were weak and soft-
hearted and bound themselves and all who should come
after them with great oaths never even to seek after the
knowledge of that word. But I learned it in a secret place
and paid a terrible price to learn it. I did not use it until
she forced me to it. I fought to overcome her by every
other means. I poured out the blood of my armies like
water —"

"Beast!" muttered Polly.

"The last great battle," said the Queen, "raged for
three days here in Charn itself. For three days I looked
down upon it from this very spot. I did not use my power
till the last of my soldiers had fallen, and the accursed
woman, my sister, at the head of her rebels was halfway
up those great stairs that lead up from the city to the
terrace. Then I waited till we were so close that we could
see one another's faces. She flashed her horrible, wicked
eyes upon me and said, "Victory." "Yes," said I, "Victory, but not yours." Then I spoke the Deplorable Word.
A moment later I was the only living thing beneath the
sun."

"But the people?" gasped Digory.

"What people, boy?" asked the Queen.

"All the ordinary people," said Polly, "who'd never done you any harm. And the women, and the children, and the animals."

"Don't you understand?" said the Queen (still speaking to Digory). "I was the Queen. They were all *my* people. What else were they there for but to do my will?"

"It was rather hard luck on them, all the same," said he.

"I had forgotten that you are only a common boy. How should you understand reasons of State? You must learn, child, that what would be wrong for you or for any of the common people is not wrong in a great Queen such as I. The weight of the world is on our shoulders. We must be freed from all rules. Ours is a high and lonely destiny."

Digory suddenly remembered that Uncle Andrew had used exactly the same words. But they sounded much grander when Queen Jadis said them; perhaps because Uncle Andrew was not seven feet tall and dazzlingly beautiful.

"And what did you do then?" said Digory.

"I had already cast strong spells on the hall where the images of my ancestors sit. And the force of those spells was that I should sleep among them, like an image myself, and need neither food nor fire, though it were a thousand years, till one came and struck the bell and awoke me."

"Was it the Deplorable Word that made the sun like that?" asked Digory.

"Like what?" said Jadis.

"So big, so red, and so cold."

"It has always been so," said Jadis. "At least, for

hundreds of thousands of years. Have you a different sort of sun in your world?"

"Yes, it's smaller and yellower. And it gives a good deal more heat."

The Queen gave a long drawn "A-a-ah!" And Digory saw on her face that same hungry and greedy look which he had lately seen on Uncle Andrew's. "So," she said, "yours is a younger world."

She paused for a moment to look once more at the deserted city — and if she was sorry for all the evil she had done there, she certainly didn't show it — and then said:

"Now, let us be going. It is cold here at the end of all the ages."

"Going where?" asked both the children.

"Where?" repeated Jadis in surprise. "To your world, of course."

Polly and Digory looked at each other, aghast. Polly had disliked the Queen from the first; and even Digory, now that he had heard the story, felt that he had seen quite as much of her as he wanted. Certainly, she was not at all the sort of person one would like to take home. And if they did like, they didn't know how they could. What they wanted was to get away themselves: but Polly couldn't get at her ring and of course Digory couldn't go without her. Digory got very red in the face and stammered.

"Oh — oh — our world. I d-didn't know you wanted to go there."

"What else were you sent here for if not to fetch me?" asked Jadis.

"I'm sure you wouldn't like our world at all," said Digory. "It's not her sort of place, is it Polly? It's very dull; not worth seeing, really."

"It will soon be worth seeing when I rule it," answered the Queen.

"Oh, but you can't," said Digory. "It's not like that. They wouldn't let you, you know."

The Queen gave a contemptuous smile. "Many great kings," she said, "thought they could stand against the House of Charn. But they all fell, and their very names are forgotten. Foolish boy! Do you think that I, with my beauty and my Magic, will not have your whole world at my feet before a year has passed? Prepare your incantations and take me there at once."

"This is perfectly frightful," said Digory to Polly.

"Perhaps you fear for this Uncle of yours," said Jadis. "But if he honours me duly, he shall keep his life and his throne. I am not coming to fight against *him*. He must be a very great Magician, if he has found how to send you here. Is he King of your whole world or only of part?"

"He isn't King of anywhere," said Digory.

"You are lying," said the Queen. "Does not Magic always go with the royal blood? Who ever heard of common people being Magicians? I can see the truth whether you speak it or not. Your Uncle is the great King and the great Enchanter of your world. And by his art he has seen the shadow of my face, in some magic mirror or some enchanted pool; and for the love of my beauty he has made a potent spell which shook your world to its foundations and sent you across the vast gulf between world and world to ask my favour and to bring me to him. Answer me: is that not how it was?"

"Well, not *exactly*," said Digory.

"Not exactly," shouted Polly. "Why, it's absolute bosh from beginning to end."

"Minions!" cried the Queen, turning in rage upon Polly

and seizing her hair, at the very top of her head where it hurts most. But in so doing she let go of both the children's hands. "Now," shouted Digory; and "Quick!" shouted Polly. They plunged their left hands into their pockets. They did not even need to put the rings on. The moment they touched them, the whole of that dreary world vanished from their eyes. They were rushing upward and a warm green light was growing nearer overhead.

CHAPTER SIX

THE BEGINNING OF UNCLE ANDREW'S TROUBLES

"Let go! Let go!" screamed Polly.

"I'm not touching you!" said Digory.

Then their heads came out of the pool and, once more, the sunny quietness of the Wood between the Worlds was all about them, and it seemed richer and warmer and more peaceful than ever after the staleness and ruin of the place they had just left. I think that, if they had been given the chance, they would again have forgotten who they were and where they came from and would have lain down and enjoyed themselves, half asleep, listening to the growing of the trees. But this time there was something that kept them as wide-awake as possible: for as soon as they had got out on to the grass, they found that they were not alone. The Queen, or the Witch (whichever you like to call her) had come up with them, holding on fast by Polly's hair. That was why Polly had been shouting out "Let go!"

This proved, by the way, another thing about the rings which Uncle Andrew hadn't told Digory because he didn't know it himself. In order to jump from world to world by one of those rings you don't need to be wearing or touching it yourself; it is enough if you are touching someone who is touching it. In that way they work like a magnet; and everyone knows that if you pick up a pin with a magnet, any other pin which is touching the first pin will come too.

Now that you saw her in the wood, Queen Jadis looked different. She was much paler than she had been; so pale that hardly any of her beauty was left. And she was stooped and seemed to be finding it hard to breathe, as if the air of that place stifled her. Neither of the children felt in the least afraid of her now.

"Let go! Let go of my hair," said Polly. "What do you mean by it?"

"Here! Let go of her hair. At once," said Digory.

They both turned and struggled with her. They were stronger than she and in a few seconds they had forced her to let go. She reeled back, panting, and there was a look of terror in her eyes.

"Quick, Digory!" said Polly. "Change rings and into the home pool."

"Help! Help! Mercy!" cried the Witch in a faint voice, staggering after them. "Take me with you. You cannot mean to leave me in this horrible place. It is killing me."

"It's a reason of State," said Polly spitefully. "Like when you killed all those people in your own world. Do be quick, Digory." They had put on their green rings, but Digory said:

"Oh bother! What *are* we to do?" He couldn't help feeling a little sorry for the Queen.

"Oh don't be such an ass," said Polly. "Ten to one she's only shamming. Do come *on*." And then both children plunged into the home pool. "It's a good thing we made that mark," thought Polly. But as they jumped Digory felt that a large cold finger and thumb had caught him by the ear. And as they sank down and the confused shapes of our own world began to appear, the grip of that finger and thumb grew stronger. The Witch was apparently recovering her strength. Digory struggled and kicked, but it was not of the least use. In a moment they found themselves in Uncle Andrew's study; and there was

Uncle Andrew himself, staring at the wonderful creature that Digory had brought back from beyond the world.

And well he might stare. Digory and Polly stared too. There was no doubt that the Witch had got over her faintness; and now that one saw her in our own world, with ordinary things around her, she fairly took one's breath away. In Charn she had been alarming enough: in London, she was terrifying. For one thing, they had not realized till now how very big she was. "Hardly human" was what Digory thought when he looked at her; and he may have been right, for some say there is giantish blood in the royal family of Charn. But even her height was nothing compared with her beauty, her fierceness, and her wildness. She looked ten times more alive than most of the people one meets in London. Uncle Andrew was bowing and rubbing his hands and looking, to tell the truth, extremely frightened. He seemed a little shrimp of a creature beside the Witch. And yet, as Polly said afterwards, there was a sort of likeness between her face and his, something in the expression. It was the look that all wicked Magicians have, the "Mark" which Jadis had said she could not find in Digory's face. One good thing about seeing the two together was that you would never again be afraid of Uncle Andrew, any more than you'd be afraid of a worm after you had met a rattlesnake or afraid of a cow after you had met a mad bull.

"Pooh!" thought Digory to himself. "*Him* a Magician! Not much. Now *she's* the real thing."

Uncle Andrew kept on rubbing his hands and bowing. He was trying to say something very polite, but his mouth had gone all dry so that he could not speak. His "experiment" with the rings, as he called it, was turning out more successful than he liked: for though he had dabbled in Magic for years he had always left all the dangers (as far as one can) to other people. Nothing at all like this had ever happened to him before.

Then Jadis spoke; not very loud, but there was something in her voice that made the whole room quiver.

"Where is the Magician who has called me into this world?"

"Ah – ah – Madam," gasped Uncle Andrew, "I am most honoured – highly gratified – a most unexpected pleasure – if only I had had the opportunity of making any preparations – I – I –"

"Where is the Magician, Fool?" said Jadis.

"I – I am, Madam. I hope you will excuse any – er –

liberty these naughty children may have taken. I assure
you, there was no intention —"

"You?" said the Queen in a still more terrible voice.
Then, in one stride, she crossed the room, seized a great
handful of Uncle Andrew's grey hair and pulled his head

back so that his face looked up into hers. Then she
studied his face as she had studied Digory's face in the
palace of Charn. He blinked and licked his lips nervously
all the time. At last she let him go: so suddenly that he
reeled back against the wall.

"I see," she said scornfully, "you are a Magician — of a
sort. Stand up, dog, and don't sprawl there as if you were
speaking to your equals. How do you come to know
Magic? *You* are not of royal blood, I'll swear."

"Well — ah — not perhaps in the strict sense,"

stammered Uncle Andrew. "Not exactly royal, Ma'am. The Ketterleys are, however, a very old family. An old Dorsetshire family, Ma'am."

"Peace," said the Witch. "I see what you are. You are a little, peddling Magician who works by rules and books. There is no real Magic in your blood and heart. Your kind was made an end of in my world a thousand years ago. But here I shall allow you to be my servant."

"I should be most happy – delighted to be of any service – a p-pleasure, I assure you."

"Peace! You talk far too much. Listen to your first task. I see we are in a large city. Procure for me at once a chariot or a flying carpet or a well-trained dragon, or whatever is usual for royal and noble persons in your land. Then bring me to places where I can get clothes and jewels and slaves fit for my rank. Tomorrow I will begin the conquest of the world."

"I – I – I'll go and order a cab at once," gasped Uncle Andrew.

"Stop," said the Witch, just as he reached the door. "Do not dream of treachery. My eyes can see through walls and into the minds of men. They will be on you wherever you go. At the first sign of disobedience I will lay such spells on you that anything you sit down on will feel like red hot iron and whenever you lie in a bed there will be invisible blocks of ice at your feet. Now go."

The old man went out, looking like a dog with its tail between its legs.

The children were now afraid that Jadis would have something to say to them about what had happened in the wood. As it turned out, however, she never mentioned it either then or afterwards. I think (and Digory thinks too) that her mind was of a sort which cannot remember that

quiet place at all, and however often you took her there
and however long you left her there, she would still know
nothing about it. Now that she was left alone with the
children, she took no notice
of either of them. And that
was like her too. In Charn
she had taken no notice of
Polly (till the very end)
because Digory was the one
she wanted to make use of.
Now that she had Uncle
Andrew, she took no notice
of Digory. I expect most
witches are like that. They
are not interested in things
or people unless they can
use them; they are terribly
practical. So there was
silence in the room for a
minute or two. But you could tell by the way Jadis tapped
her foot on the floor that she was growing impatient.

Presently she said, as if to herself, "What is the old fool
doing? I should have brought a whip." She stalked out
of the room in pursuit of Uncle Andrew without one
glance at the children.

"Whew!" said Polly, letting out a long breath of relief.
"And now I must get home. It's frightfully late. I shall
catch it."

"Well do, do come back as soon as you can," said
Digory. "This is simply ghastly, having her here. We must
make some sort of plan."

"That's up to your Uncle now," said Polly. "It was he
who started all this messing about with Magic."

"All the same, you will come back, won't you? Hang it all, you can't leave me alone in a scrape like this."

"I shall go home by the tunnel," said Polly rather coldly. "That'll be the quickest way. And if you want me to come back, hadn't you better say you're sorry?"

"Sorry?" exclaimed Digory. "Well now, if that isn't just like a girl! What have I done?"

"Oh nothing of course," said Polly sarcastically. "Only nearly screwed my wrist off in that room with all the wax-works, like a cowardly bully. Only struck the bell with the hammer, like a silly idiot. Only turned back in the wood so that she had time to catch hold of you before we jumped into our own pool. That's all."

"Oh," said Digory, very surprised. "Well, alright, I'll say I'm sorry. And I really am sorry about what happened in the waxworks room. There: I've said I'm sorry. And now, do be decent and come back. I shall be in a frightful hole if you don't."

"I don't see what's going to happen to you. It's Mr Ketterley who's going to sit on red hot chairs and have ice in his bed, isn't it?"

"It isn't that sort of thing," said Digory. "What I'm bothered about is Mother. Suppose that creature went into her room. She might frighten her to death."

"Oh, I see," said Polly in rather a different voice. "Alright. We'll call it Pax. I'll come back – if I can. But I must go now." And she crawled through the little door into the tunnel; and that dark place among the rafters which had seemed so exciting and adventurous a few hours ago, seemed quite tame and homely now.

We must now go back to Uncle Andrew. His poor old heart went pit-a-pat as he staggered down the attic stairs and he kept on dabbing at his forehead with a handkerchief. When he reached his bedroom, which was the floor below, he locked himself in. And the very first thing he did was to grope in his wardrobe for a bottle and a wine-glass which he always kept hidden there where Aunt Letty could not find them. He poured himself out a glassful of some nasty, grown-up drink and drank it off at one gulp. Then he drew a deep breath.

"Upon my word," he said to himself. "I'm dreadfully shaken. Most upsetting! And at my time of life!"

He poured out a second glass and drank it too; then he began to change his clothes. You have never seen such clothes, but I can remember them. He put on a very high, shiny, stiff collar of the sort that made you hold your chin up all the time. He put on a white waistcoat with a pattern on it and arranged his gold watch chain across the front. He put on his best frock-coat, the one he kept for weddings and funerals. He got out his best tall hat and polished it up. There was a vase of flowers (put there by Aunt Letty) on his dressing table; he took one and put it in his button-hole. He took a clean handkerchief (a lovely one such as you couldn't buy today) out of the little left-hand drawer and put a few drops of scent on it. He took his eye-glass, with the thick black ribbon, and screwed it into his eye; then he looked at himself in the mirror.

Children have one kind of silliness, as you know, and grown-ups have another kind. At this moment Uncle Andrew was beginning to be silly in a very grown-up way. Now that the Witch was no longer in the same room with him he was quickly forgetting how she had frightened him and thinking more and more of her wonderful beauty. He kept on saying to himself, "A dem fine woman, sir, a dem fine woman. A superb creature." He had also somehow managed to forget that it was the children who had got hold of this "superb creature": he felt as if he himself by his Magic had called her out of unknown worlds.

"Andrew, my boy," he said to himself as he looked in the glass, "you're a devilish well preserved fellow for your age. A distinguished-looking man, sir."

You see, the foolish old man was actually beginning to imagine the Witch would fall in love with him. The two drinks probably had something to do with it, and so had his best clothes. But he was, in any case, as vain as a peacock; that was why he had become a Magician.

He unlocked the door, went downstairs, sent the housemaid out to fetch a hansom (everyone had lots of servants in those days) and looked into the drawing-room. There, as he expected, he found Aunt Letty. She was busily mending a mattress. It lay on the floor near the window and she was kneeling on it.

"Ah, Letitia my dear," said Uncle Andrew, "I – ah – have to go out. Just lend me five pounds or so, there's a good gel." ("Gel" was the way he pronounced girl.)

"No, Andrew dear," said Aunty Letty in her firm, quiet voice, without looking up from her work. "I've told you times without number that I *will not* lend you money."

"Now pray don't be troublesome, my dear gel," said Uncle Andrew. "It's most important. You will put me in a deucedly awkward position if you don't."

"Andrew," said Aunt Letty, looking him straight in the face, "I wonder *you* are not ashamed to ask *me* for money."

There was a long, dull story of a grown-up kind behind these words. All you need to know about it is that Uncle Andrew, what with "managing dear Letty's business matters for her", and never doing any work, and running up large bills for brandy and cigars (which Aunt Letty had paid again and again) had made her a good deal poorer than she had been thirty years ago.

"My dear gel," said Uncle Andrew, "you don't understand. I shall have some quite unexpected expenses today. I have to do a little entertaining. Come now, don't be tiresome."

"And who, pray, are *you* going to entertain, Andrew?" asked Aunt Letty.

"A – a most distinguished visitor has just arrived."

"Distinguished fiddlestick!" said Aunt Letty. "There hasn't been a ring at the bell for the last hour."

At that moment the door was suddenly flung open. Aunt Letty looked round and saw with amazement that an enormous woman, splendidly dressed, with bare arms and flashing eyes, stood in the doorway. It was the Witch.

CHAPTER SEVEN

WHAT HAPPENED AT THE FRONT DOOR

"Now, slave, how long am I to wait for my chariot?" thundered the Witch. Uncle Andrew cowered away from her. Now that she was really present, all the silly thoughts he had had while looking at himself in the glass were oozing out of him. But Aunt Letty at once got up from her knees and came over to the centre of the room.

"And who is this young person, Andrew, may I ask?" said Aunt Letty in icy tones.

"Distinguished foreigner — v-very important p-person," he stammered.

"Rubbish!" said Aunt Letty, and then, turning to the Witch, "Get out of my house this moment, you shameless hussy, or I'll send for the police." She thought the Witch must be someone out of a circus and she did not approve of bare arms.

"What woman is this?" said Jadis. "Down on your knees, minion, before I blast you."

"No strong language in this house *if* you please, young woman," said Aunt Letty.

Instantly, as it seemed to Uncle Andrew, the Queen towered up to an even greater height. Fire flashed from her eyes: she flung out her arm with the same gesture and the same horrible-sounding words that had lately turned the palace-gates of Charn to dust. But nothing happened except that Aunt Letty, thinking that those horrible words were meant to be ordinary English, said:

"I thought as much. The woman is drunk. Drunk! She can't even speak clearly."

It must have been a terrible moment for the Witch

when she suddenly realized that her power of turning
people into dust, which had been quite real in her own
world, was not going to work in ours. But she did not
lose her nerve even for a second. Without wasting a
thought on her disappointment, she lunged forward,

caught Aunt Letty round the neck and the knees, raised
her high above her head as if she had been no heavier
than a doll, and threw her across the room. While Aunt
Letty was still hurtling through the air, the housemaid
(who was having a beautifully exciting morning) put her
head in at the door and said, "If you please, sir, the
'ansom's come."

"Lead on, Slave," said the Witch to Uncle Andrew. He began muttering something about "regrettable violence — must really protest", but at a single glance from Jadis he became speechless. She drove him out of the room and out of the house; and Digory came running down the stairs just in time to see the front door close behind them.

"Jiminy!" he said. "She's loose in London. And with Uncle Andrew. I wonder what on earth is going to happen now."

"Oh, Master Digory," said the housemaid (who was really having a wonderful day), "I think Miss Ketterley's hurt herself somehow." So they both rushed into the drawing-room to find out what had happened.

If Aunt Letty had fallen on bare boards or even on the carpet, I suppose all her bones would have been broken: but by great good luck she had fallen on the mattress. Aunt Letty was a very tough old lady: aunts often were in those days. After she had had some *sal volatile* and sat still for a few minutes, she said there was nothing the matter with her except a few bruises. Very soon she was taking charge of the situation.

"Sarah," she said to the housemaid (who had never had such a day before), "go around to the police station at once and tell them there is a dangerous lunatic at large. I will take Mrs Kirke's lunch up myself." Mrs Kirke was, of course, Digory's mother.

When Mother's lunch had been seen to, Digory and Aunt Letty had their own. After that he did some hard thinking.

The problem was how to get the Witch back to her own world, or at any rate out of ours, as soon as possible. Whatever happened, she must not be allowed to go rampaging about the house. Mother must not see her.

And, if possible, she must not be allowed to go rampaging about London either. Digory had not been in the drawing-room when she tried to "blast" Aunt Letty, but he had seen her "blast" the gates at Charn: so he knew her terrible powers and did not know that she had lost any of them by coming into our world. And he knew she meant to conquer our world. At the present moment, as far as he could see, she might be blasting Buckingham Palace or the Houses of Parliament: and it was almost certain that quite a number of policemen had by now been reduced to little heaps of dust. And there didn't seem to be anything he could do about that. "But the rings seem to work like magnets," thought Digory. "If I can only touch her and then slip on my yellow, we shall both go into the Wood between the Worlds. I wonder will she go all faint again there? Was that something the place does to her, or was it only the shock of being pulled out of her own world? But I suppose I'll have to risk that. And how am I to find the beast? I don't suppose Aunt Letty would let me go out, not unless I said where I was going. And I haven't got more than twopence. I'd need any amount of money for buses and trams if I went looking all over London. Anyway, I haven't the faintest idea where to look. I wonder if Uncle Andrew is still with her."

It seemed in the end that the only thing he could do was to wait and hope that Uncle Andrew and the Witch would come back. If they did, he must rush out and get hold of the Witch and put on his yellow Ring before she had a chance to get into the house. This meant that he must watch the front door like a cat watching a mouse's hole; he dared not leave his post for a moment. So he went into the dining-room and "glued his face" as they say, to the

window. It was a bow-window from which you could see
the steps up to the front door and see up and down the
street, so that no one could reach the front door without
your knowing. "I wonder what Polly's doing?" thought
Digory.

He wondered about this a good deal as the first slow
half-hour ticked on. But you need not wonder, for I am
going to tell you. She had got home late for her dinner,
with her shoes and stockings very wet. And when they
asked her where she had been and what on earth she had
been doing, she said she had been out with Digory Kirke.
Under further questioning she said she had got her feet
wet in a pool of water, and that the pool was in a wood.
Asked where the wood was, she said she didn't know.
Asked if it was in one of the parks, she said truthfully
enough that she supposed it might be a sort of park. From
all of this Polly's mother got the idea that Polly had gone
off, without telling anyone, to some part of London she
didn't know, and gone into a strange park and amused
herself jumping into puddles. As a result she was told that
she had been very naughty indeed and that she wouldn't
be allowed to play with "that Kirke boy" any more if
anything of the sort ever happened again. Then she was
given dinner with all the nice parts left out and sent to
bed for two solid hours. It was a thing that happened to
one quite often in those days.

So while Digory was staring out of the dining-room
window, Polly was lying in bed, and both were thinking
how terribly slowly the time could go. I think, myself, I
would rather have been in Polly's position. She had only
to wait for the end of her two hours: but every few
minutes Digory would hear a cab or a baker's van or a
butcher's boy coming round the corner and think "Here

she comes", and then find it wasn't. And in between these false alarms, for what seemed hours and hours, the clock ticked on and one big fly — high up and far out of reach — buzzed against the window. It was one of those houses that get very quiet and dull in the afternoon and always seem to smell of mutton.

During his long watching and waiting one small thing happened which I shall have to mention because something important came of it later on. A lady called with some grapes for Digory's Mother; and as the dining-room door was open, Digory couldn't help overhearing Aunt Letty and the lady as they talked in the hall.

"What lovely grapes!" came Aunt Letty's voice. "I'm sure if anything could do her good these would. But poor, dear little Mabel! I'm afraid it would need fruit from the land of youth to help her now. Nothing in *this* world will do much." Then they both lowered their voices and said a lot more that he could not hear.

If he had heard that bit about the land of youth a few days ago he would have thought Aunt Letty was just talking without meaning anything in particular, the way grown-ups do, and it wouldn't have interested him. He almost thought so now. But suddenly it flashed upon his mind that he now knew (even if Aunt Letty didn't) that there really were other worlds and that he himself had been in one of them. At that rate there might be a real Land of Youth somewhere. There might be almost anything. There might be fruit in some other world that would really cure his mother! And oh, oh — Well, you know how it feels if you begin hoping for something that you want desperately badly; you almost fight against the hope because it is too good to be true; you've been disappointed so often before. That was how Digory felt. But it was no good trying to throttle this hope. It might — really, really, it just might be true. So many odd things had happened already. And he had the magic rings. There must be worlds you could get to through every pool in the wood. He could hunt through them all. And then — *Mother well again*. Everything right again. He forgot all about watching for the Witch. His hand was already going into the pocket where he kept the yellow ring, when all at once he heard a sound of galloping.

"Hullo! What's that?" thought Digory. "Fire-engine? I wonder what house is on fire. Great Scott, it's coming here. Why, it's Her."

I needn't tell you who he meant by *Her*.

First came the hansom. There was no one in the driver's seat. On the roof — not sitting, but standing on the roof — swaying with superb balance as it came at full speed round the corner with one wheel in the air — was Jadis the Queen of Queens and the Terror of Charn. Her teeth were bared, her eyes shone like fire, and her long hair streamed out behind her like a comet's tail. She was flogging the horse without mercy. Its nostrils were wide and red and its sides were spotted with foam. It galloped madly up to the front door, missing the lamp-post by an inch, and then reared up on its hind legs. The hansom crashed into the lamp-post and shattered into several pieces. The Witch, with a magnificent jump, had sprung clear just in time and landed on the horse's back. She settled herself astride and leaned forward, whispering things in its ear. They must have been things meant not to quiet it but to madden it. It was on its hind legs again in a moment, and its neigh was like a scream; it was all hoofs and teeth and eyes and tossing mane. Only a splendid rider could have stayed on its back.

Before Digory had recovered his breath a good many
other things began to happen. A second hansom dashed
up close behind the first: out of it there jumped a fat man
in a frock-coat and a policeman. Then came a third hansom with two more policemen in it. After it, came about
twenty people (mostly errand boys) on bicycles, all ringing their bells and letting out cheers and cat-calls. Last of

all came a crowd of people on foot: all very hot with
running, but obviously enjoying themselves. Windows
shot up in all the houses of that street and a housemaid or
a butler appeared at every front door. They wanted to see
the fun.

Meanwhile an old gentleman had begun to struggle
shakily out of the ruins of the first hansom. Several people
rushed forward to help him; but as one pulled him one
way and another another, perhaps he would have got out
quite as quickly on his own. Digory guessed that the old
gentleman must be Uncle Andrew but you couldn't see his
face; his tall hat had been bashed down over it.

Digory rushed out and joined the crowd.

"That's the woman, that's the woman," cried the fat

man, pointing at Jadis. "Do your duty, Constable.
Hundreds and thousands of pounds' worth she's taken
out of my shop. Look at that rope of pearls round her
neck. That's mine. And she's given me a black eye too,
what's more."

"That she 'as, guv'nor," said one of the crowd. "And as
lovely a black eye as I'd wish to see. Beautiful bit of
work that must 'ave been. Gor! ain't she strong then!"

"You ought to put a nice raw beefsteak on it, Mister,
that's what it wants," said a butcher's boy.

"Now then," said the most important of the policemen,
"what's all this 'ere?"

"I tell you she —" began the fat man, when someone
else called out:

"Don't let the old cove in the cab get away. 'E put 'er
up to it."

The old gentleman, who was certainly Uncle Andrew,
had just succeeded in standing up and was rubbing his
bruises. "Now then," said the policeman, turning to him,
"What's all this?"

"Womfle — pomfy — shomf," came Uncle Andrew's
voice from inside the hat.

"None of that now," said the policeman sternly. "You'll find this is no laughing matter. Take that 'at off, see?"

This was more easily said than done. But after Uncle Andrew had struggled in vain with the hat for some time, two other policemen seized it by the brim and forced it off.

"Thank you, thank you," said Uncle Andrew in a faint voice. "Thank you. Dear me, I'm terribly shaken. If someone could give me a small glass of brandy —"

"Now you attend to me, if you please," said the policeman, taking out a very large note book and a very small pencil. "Are you in charge of that there young woman?"

"Look out!" called several voices, and the policeman jumped a step backwards just in time. The horse had aimed a kick at him which would probably have killed him. Then the Witch wheeled the horse round so that she faced the crowd and its hind-legs were on the footpath. She had a long, bright knife in her hand and had been busily cutting the horse free from the wreck of the hansom.

All this time Digory had been trying to get into a position from which he could touch the Witch. This wasn't at all easy because, on the side nearest to him, there were too many people. And in order to get round to the other side he had to pass between the horse's hoofs and the railings of the "area" that surrounded the house; for the Ketterleys' house had a basement. If you know anything about horses, and especially if you had seen what a state that horse was in at the moment, you will realize that this was a ticklish thing to do. Digory knew lots about horses, but he set his teeth and got ready to make a dash for it as soon as he saw a favourable moment.

A red-faced man in a bowler hat had now shouldered his way to the front of the crowd.

"Hi! P'leeceman," he said, "that's my 'orse what she's sitting on, same as it's my cab what she's made matchwood of."

"One at a time, please, one at a time," said the policeman.

"But there ain't no time," said the Cabby. "I know that 'orse better'n you do. 'Tain't an ordinary 'orse. 'Is father was a hofficer's charger in the cavalry, 'e was. And if the young woman goes on hexcitin' 'im, there'll be murder done. 'Ere, let me get at him."

The policeman was only to glad to have a good reason for standing further away from the horse. The Cabby took a step nearer, looked up at Jadis, and said in a not unkindly voice:

"Now, Missie, let me get at 'is 'ead, and just you get off. You're a Lidy, and you don't want all these roughs going for you, do you? You want to go 'ome and 'ave a nice cup of tea and a lay down quiet like; then you'll feel ever so much better." At the same time he stretched out his hand towards the horse's head with the words, "Steady, Strawberry, old boy. Steady now."

Then for the first time the Witch spoke.

"Dog!" came her cold, clear voice, ringing loud above all the other noises. "Dog, unhand our royal charger. We are the Empress Jadis."

CHAPTER EIGHT

THE FIGHT AT THE LAMP-POST

"Ho! Hempress, are you? We'll see about that," said a voice. Then another voice said, "Three cheers for the Hempress of Colney 'Atch" and quite a number joined in. A flush of colour came into the Witch's face and she bowed ever so slightly. But the cheers died away into roars of laughter and she saw that they had only been making fun of her. A change came over her expression and she changed the knife to her left hand. Then, without warning, she did a thing that was dreadful to see. Lightly, easily, as if it were the most ordinary thing in the world, she stretched up her right arm and wrenched off one of the cross-bars of the lamp-post. If she had lost some magical powers in our world, she had not lost her strength; she could break an iron bar as if it were a stick of barley-sugar. She tossed her new weapon up in the air, caught it again, brandished it, and urged the horse forward.

"Now's my chance," thought Digory. He darted between the horse and the railings and began going forward. If only the brute would stay still for a moment he might catch the Witch's heel. As he rushed, he heard a sickening crash and a thud. The Witch had brought the bar down on the chief policeman's helmet: the man fell like a nine-pin.

"Quick, Digory. This *must* be stopped," said a voice beside him. It was Polly, who had rushed down the moment she was allowed out of bed.

"You *are* a brick," said Digory. "Hold on to me tight. You'll have to manage the ring. Yellow, remember. And don't put it on till I shout."

There was a second crash and another policeman crumpled up. There came an angry roar from the crowd: "Pull her down. Get a few paving-stones. Call out the Military." But most of them were getting as far away as they could. The Cabby, however, obviously the bravest as well as the kindest person present, was keeping close to the horse, dodging this way and that to avoid the bar, but still trying to catch Strawberry's head.

The crowd booed and bellowed again. A stone whistled over Digory's head. Then came the voice of the Witch, clear like a great bell, and sounding as if, for once, she were almost happy.

"Scum! You shall pay dearly for this when I have conquered your world. Not one stone of your city will be left. I will make it as Charn, as Felinda, as Sorlois, as Bramandin."

Digory as last caught her ankle. She kicked back with her heel and hit him in the mouth. In his pain he lost hold. His lip was cut and his mouth full of blood. From somewhere very close by came the voice of Uncle Andrew in a sort of trembling scream. "Madam — my dear young lady — for heaven's sake — compose yourself." Digory made a second grab at her heel, and was again shaken off. More men were knocked down by the iron bar. He made a third grab: caught the heel: held on like grim death, shouting to Polly "Go!" then — Oh, thank goodness. The angry, frightened faces had vanished. The angry, frightened voices were silenced. All except Uncle Andrew's. Close beside Digory in the darkness, it was wailing on "Oh, oh, is this delirium? Is it the end? I can't bear it. It's not fair. I never meant to be a Magician. It's all a misunderstanding. It's all my godmother's fault; I must protest against this.

In my state of health too. A very old Dorsetshire family."

"Bother!" thought Digory. 'We didn't want to bring *him* along. My hat, what a picnic. Are you there, Polly?"

"Yes, I'm here. Don't keep on shoving."

"I'm not," began Digory, but before he could say anything more, their heads came out into the warm, green sunshine of the wood. And as they stepped out of the pool Polly cried out:

"Oh look! We've brought the old horse with us too. *And* Mr Ketterley. *And* the Cabby. This is a pretty kettle of fish!"

As soon as the Witch saw that she was once more in the wood she turned pale and bent down till her face touched the mane of the horse. You could see she felt deadly sick. Uncle Andrew was shivering. But Strawberry, the horse, shook his head, gave a cheerful whinny, and seemed to feel better. He became quiet for the first time since Digory had seen him. His ears, which had been laid flat back on his skull, came into their proper position, and the fire went out of his eyes.

"That's right, old boy," said the Cabby, slapping Strawberry's neck. "That's better. Take it easy."

Strawberry did the most natural thing in the world. Being very thirsty (and no wonder) he walked slowly across to the nearest pool and stepped into it to have a drink. Digory was still holding the Witch's heel and Polly was holding Digory's hand. One of the Cabby's hands was on Strawberry; and Uncle Andrew, still very shaky, had just grabbed on the Cabby's other hand.

"Quick," said Polly, with a look at Digory. "Greens!"

So the horse never got his drink. Instead, the whole party found themselves sinking into darkness. Strawberry neighed; Uncle Andrew whimpered. Digory said, "That was a bit of luck."

There was a short pause. Then Polly said, "Oughtn't we to be nearly there now?"

"We do seem to be somewhere," said Digory. "At least I'm standing on something solid."

"Why, so am I, now that I come to think of it," said Polly. "But why's it so dark? I say, do you think we got into the wrong Pool?"

"Perhaps this *is* Charn," said Digory. "Only we've got back in the middle of the night."

"This is not Charn," came the Witch's voice. "This is an empty world. This is Nothing."

And really it was uncommonly like Nothing. There were no stars. It was so dark that they couldn't see one another at all and it made no difference whether you kept your eyes shut or open. Under their feet there was a cool, flat something which might have been earth, and was certainly not grass or wood. The air was cold and dry and there was no wind.

"My doom has come upon me," said the Witch in a voice of horrible calmness.

"Oh don't say that," babbled Uncle Andrew. "My dear young lady, pray don't say such things. It can't be as bad as that. Ah – Cabman – my good man – you don't happen to have a flask about you? A drop of spirits is just what I need."

"Now then, now then," came the Cabby's voice, a good firm, hardy voice. "Keep cool everyone, that's what I say. No bones broken, anyone? Good. Well there's something to be thankful for straight away, and more than anyone could expect after falling all that way. Now, if we've fallen down some diggings – as it might be for a new station on the Underground – someone will come and get us out presently, see! And if we're dead – which I don't deny it might be – well, you got to remember that worse things 'appen at sea and a chap's got to die sometime. And there ain't nothing to be afraid of if a chap's led a decent life. And if you ask me, I think the best thing we could do to pass the time would be sing a 'ymn."

And he did. He struck up at once a harvest thanksgiving hymn, all about crops being "safely gathered in". It was not very suitable to a place which felt as if nothing had ever grown there since the beginning of time, but it was the one he could remember best. He had a fine voice and the children joined in; it was very cheering. Uncle Andrew and the Witch did not join in.

Towards the end of the hymn Digory felt someone plucking at his elbow and from a general smell of brandy and cigars and good clothes he decided that it must be Uncle Andrew. Uncle Andrew was cautiously pulling him away from the others. When they had gone a little distance, the old man put his mouth so close to Digory's ear that it tickled, and whispered:

"Now, my boy. Slip on your ring. Let's be off."

But the Witch had very good ears. "Fool!" came her voice and she leaped off the horse. "Have you forgotten that I can hear men's thoughts? Let go the boy. If you attempt treachery I will take such vengeance upon you as never was heard of in all worlds from the beginning."

"And," added Digory, "if you think I'm such a mean pig as to go off and leave Polly – and the Cabby – and the horse – in a place like this, you're well mistaken."

"You are a very naughty and impertinent little boy," said Uncle Andrew.

"Hush!" said the Cabby. They all listened.

In the darkness something was happening at last. A voice had begun to sing. It was very far away and Digory found it hard to decide from what direction it was coming. Sometimes it seemed to come from all directions at once. Sometimes he almost thought it was coming out of the earth beneath them. Its lower notes were deep enough to be the voice of the earth herself. There were no words. There was hardly even a tune. But it was, beyond comparison, the most beautiful noise he had ever heard. It was so beautiful he could hardly bear it. The horse seemed to like it too; he gave the sort of whinney a horse would give if, after years of being a cab-horse, it found itself back in the old field where it had played as a foal, and saw someone whom it remembered and loved coming across the field to bring it a lump of sugar.

"Gawd!" said the Cabby. "Ain't it lovely?"

Then two wonders happened at the same moment. One was that the voice was suddenly joined by other voices; more voices than you could possibly count. They were in harmony with it, but far higher up the scale: cold, tingling, silvery voices. The second wonder was that the blackness overhead, all at once, was blazing with stars. They didn't come out gently one by one, as they do on a summer evening. One moment there had been nothing but darkness; next moment a thousand, thousand points of light leaped out – single stars, constellations, and planets, brighter and bigger than any in our world. There were no clouds. The new stars and the new voices began at exactly the same time. If you had seen and heard it, as Digory did, you would have felt quite certain that it was the stars themselves which were singing, and that it was the First Voice, the deep one, which had made them appear and made them sing.

"Glory be!" said the Cabby. "I'd ha' been a better man all my life if I'd known there were things like this."

The Voice on the earth was now louder and more triumphant; but the voices in the sky, after singing loudly with it for a time, began to get fainter. And now something else was happening.

Far away, and down near the horizon, the sky began to turn grey. A light wind, very fresh, began to stir. The sky, in that one place, grew slowly and steadily paler. You could see shapes of hills standing up dark against it. All the time the Voice went on singing.

There was soon light enough for them to see one another's faces. The Cabby and the two children had open mouths and shining eyes; they were drinking in the sound, and they looked as if it reminded them of something. Uncle Andrew's mouth was open too, but not open with joy. He looked more as if his chin had simply dropped away from the rest of his face. His shoulders were stopped and his knees shook. He was not liking the Voice. If he could have got away from it by creeping into a rat's hole, he would have done so. But the Witch looked as if, in a way, she understood the music better than any of them. Her mouth was shut, her lips were pressed together, and her fists were clenched. Ever since the song began she had felt that this whole world was filled with a Magic different from hers and stronger. She hated it. She would have smashed that whole world, or all worlds, to pieces, if it would only stop the singing. The horse stood with its ears well forward, and twitching. Every now and then it snorted and stamped the ground. It no longer looked like a tired old cab-horse; you could now well believe that its father had been in battles.

The eastern sky changed from white to pink and from pink to gold. The Voice rose and rose, till all the air was shaking with it. And just as it swelled to the mightiest and most glorious sound it had yet produced, the sun arose.

Digory had never seen such a sun. The sun above the ruins of Charn had looked older than ours: this looked younger. You could imagine that it laughed for joy as it came up. And as its beams shot across the land the travellers could see for the first time what sort of place they were in. It was a valley through which a broad, swift river wound its way, flowing eastward towards the sun. Southward there were mountains, northward there were lower hills. But it was a valley of mere earth, rock and water; there was not a tree, not a bush, not a blade of grass to be seen. The earth was of many colours: they were fresh, hot and vivid. They made you feel excited; until you saw the Singer himself, and then you forgot everything else.

It was a Lion. Huge, shaggy, and bright, it stood facing the risen sun. Its mouth was wide open in song and it was about three hundred yards away.

"This is a terrible world," said the Witch. "We must fly at once. Prepare the Magic."

"I quite agree with you, Madam," said Uncle Andrew. "A most disagreeable place. Completely uncivilized. If only I were a younger man and had a gun —"

"Garn!" said the Cabby. "You don't think you could shoot '*im*, do you?"

"And who *would*?" said Polly.

"Prepare the Magic, old fool," said Jadis.

"Certainly, Madam," said Uncle Andrew cunningly. "I must have both the children touching me. Put on your homeward ring at once, Digory." He wanted to get away without the Witch.

"Oh, it's *rings*, is it?" cried Jadis. She would have had her hands in Digory's pocket before you could say knife, but Digory grabbed Polly and shouted out:

"Take care. If either of you come half an inch nearer, we two will vanish and you'll be left here for good. Yes: I have a ring in my pocket that will take Polly and me home. And look! My hand is just ready. So keep your distance. I'm sorry about you (he looked at the Cabby) and about the horse, but I can't help that. As for you two (he looked at Uncle Andrew and the Queen), you're both magicians, so you ought to enjoy living together."

"'Old your noise, everyone," said the Cabby. "I want to listen to the moosic."

For the song had now changed.

CHAPTER NINE

THE FOUNDING OF NARNIA

THE Lion was pacing to and fro about that empty land and singing his new song. It was softer and more lilting than the song by which he had called up the stars and the sun; a gentle, rippling music. And as he walked and sang the valley grew green with grass. It spread out from the Lion like a pool. It ran up the sides of the little hills like a wave. In a few minutes it was creeping up the lower slopes of the distant mountains, making that young world every moment softer. The light wind could now be heard ruffling the grass. Soon there were other things besides grass. The higher slopes grew dark with heather. Patches of rougher and more bristling green appeared in the valley. Digory did not know what they were until one began coming up quite close to him. It was a little, spiky thing that threw out dozens of arms and covered these arms with green and grew larger at the rate of about an inch every two seconds. There were dozens of these things all round him now. When they were nearly as tall as himself he saw what they were. "Trees!" he exclaimed.

The nuisance of it, as Polly said afterwards, was that you weren't left in peace to watch it all. Just as Digory said "Trees!" he had to jump because Uncle Andrew had sidled up to him again and was going to pick his pocket. It wouldn't have done Uncle Andrew much good if he had succeeded, for he was aiming at the right-hand pocket because he still thought the green rings were "homeward" rings. But of course Digory didn't want to lose either.

"Stop!" cried the Witch. "Stand back. No, further back. If anyone goes within ten paces of either of the children, I will knock out his brains." She was poising in her hand the iron bar that she had torn off the lamp-post, ready to throw it. Somehow no one doubted that she would be a very good shot.

"So!" she said. "You would steal back to your own world with the boy and leave me here."

Uncle Andrew's temper at last got the better of his fears. "Yes, Ma'am, I would," he said. "Most undoubtedly I would. I should be perfectly in my rights. I have been most shamefully, most abominably treated. I have done my best to show you such civilities as were in my power. And what has been my reward? You have robbed — I must repeat the word — *robbed* a highly respectable jeweller. You have insisted on my entertaining you to an exceedingly expensive, not to say ostentatious, lunch, though I was obliged to pawn my watch and chain in order to do so (and let me tell you, Ma'am, that none of our family have been in the habit of frequenting pawnshops, except my cousin Edward, and he was in the Yeomanry). During that indigestible meal — I'm feeling the worse for it at this very moment — your behaviour and conversation attracted the unfavourable attention of everyone present. I feel I have been publicly disgraced. I shall never be able to show my face in that restaurant again. You have assaulted the police. You have stolen —"

"Oh stow it, Guv'nor, do stow it," said the Cabby. "Watchin' and listenin's the thing at present; not talking."

There was certainly plenty to watch and to listen to. The tree which Digory had noticed was now a full-grown beech whose branches swayed gently above his head. They stood on cool, green grass, sprinkled with daisies and buttercups. A little way off, along the river bank, willows were growing. On the other side tangles of flowering currant, lilac, wild rose, and rhododendron closed them in. The horse was tearing up delicious mouthfuls of new grass.

All this time the Lion's song, and his stately prowl, to and fro, backwards and forwards, was going on. What was rather alarming was that at each turn he came a little nearer. Polly was finding the song more and more interesting because she thought she was beginning to see the connection between the music and the things that were happening. When a line of dark firs sprang up on a ridge about a hundred yards away she felt that they were connected with a series of deep, prolonged notes which the Lion had sung a second before. And when he burst into a rapid series of lighter notes she was not surprised to see primroses suddenly appearing in every direction. Thus, with an unspeakable thrill, she felt quite certain that all the things were coming (as she said) "out of the Lion's head". When you listened to his song you heard the things he was making up: when you looked round you, you saw them. This was so exciting that she had no time to be afraid. But Digory and the Cabby could not help feeling a bit nervous as each turn of the Lion's walk brought him nearer. As for Uncle Andrew, his teeth were chattering, but his knees were shaking so that he could not run away.

Suddenly the Witch stepped boldly out towards the Lion. It was coming on, always singing, with a slow, heavy pace. It was only twelve yards away. She raised her arm and flung the iron bar straight at its head.

Nobody, least of all Jadis, could have missed at that range. The bar struck the Lion fair between the eyes. It glanced off and fell with a thud in the grass. The Lion

came on. Its walk was neither slower nor faster than
before; you could not tell whether it even knew it had
been hit. Though its soft pads made no noise, you could
feel the earth shake beneath their weight.

The Witch shrieked and ran: in a few moments she was
out of sight among the trees. Uncle Andrew turned to do
likewise, tripped over a root, and fell flat on his face in a

little brook that ran down to join the river. The children
could not move. They were not even quite sure that they
wanted to. The Lion paid no attention to them. Its huge
red mouth was open, but open in song not in a snarl. It
passed by them so close that they could have touched its
mane. They were terribly afraid it would turn and look at
them, yet in some queer way they wished it would. But
for all the notice it took of them they might just as well
have been invisible and unsmellable. When it had passed

them and gone a few paces further it turned, passed them again, and continued its march eastward.

Uncle Andrew, coughing and spluttering, picked himself up.

"Now, Digory," he said, "we've got rid of that woman, and the brute of a lion is gone. Give me your hand and put on your ring at once."

"Keep off," said Digory, backing away from him. "Keep clear of him, Polly. Come over here beside me. Now I warn you, Uncle Andrew, don't come one step nearer, we'll just vanish."

"Do what you're told this minute, sir," said Uncle Andrew. "You're an extremely disobedient, ill-behaved little boy."

"No fear," said Digory. "We want to stay and see what happens. I thought you wanted to know about other worlds. Don't you like it now you're here?"

"Like it!" exclaimed Uncle Andrew. "Just look at the state I'm in. And it was my best coat and waistcoat, too." He certainly was a dreadful sight by now: for of course, the more dressed up you were to begin with, the worse you look after you've crawled out of a smashed hanson-cab and fallen into a muddy brook. "I'm not saying," he added, "that this is not a most interesting place. If I were a younger man, now – perhaps I could get some lively young fellow to come here first. One of those big-game hunters. Something might be made of this country. The climate is delightful. I never felt such air. I believe it would have done me good if – if circumstances had been more favourable. If only we'd had a gun."

"Guns be blowed," said the Cabby. "I think I'll go and see if I can give Strawberry a rub down. That horse 'as more sense than some 'umans as I could mention." He walked back to Strawberry and began making the hissing noises that grooms make.

"Do you still think *that* Lion could be killed by a gun?" asked Digory. "He didn't mind the iron bar much."

"With all her faults," said Uncle Andrew, "that's a plucky gel, my boy. It was a spirited thing to do." He rubbed his hands and cracked his knuckles, as if he were once more forgetting how the Witch frightened him whenever she was really there.

"It was a wicked thing to do," said Polly. "What harm had he done her?"

"Hullo! What's that?" said Digory. He had darted forward to examine something only a few yards away. "I say, Polly," he called back. "Do come and look."

Uncle Andrew came with her; not because he wanted to see but because he wanted to keep close to the children — there might be a chance of stealing their rings. But when he saw what Digory was looking at, even he began to take an interest. It was a perfect little model of a lamp-post, about three feet high but lengthening, and thickening in proportion, as they watched it; in fact growing just as the trees had grown.

"It's alive too — I mean, it's lit," said Digory. And so it was; though of course, the brightness of the sun made the little flame in the lantern hard to see unless your shadow fell on it.

"Remarkable, most remarkable," muttered Uncle Andrew. "Even I never dreamt of Magic like this. We're in a world where everything, even a lamp-post, comes to life and grows. Now I wonder what sort of seed a lamp-post grows from?"

"Don't you see?" said Digory. "This is where the bar fell — the bar she tore off the lamp-post at home. It sank into the ground and now it's coming up as a young lamp-post." (But not so very young now; it was as tall as Digory while he said this.)

"That's it! Stupendous, stupendous," said Uncle Andrew, rubbing his hands harder than ever. "Ho, ho! They laughed at my Magic. That fool of a sister of mine thinks I'm a lunatic. I wonder what they'll say now? I have discovered a world where everything is bursting with life and growth. Columbus, now, they talk about Columbus. But what was America to this? The commercial possibilities of this country are unbounded. Bring a few old bits of scrap iron here, bury 'em, and up they come as brand new railway engines, battleships, anything you please. They'll cost nothing, and I can sell 'em at full prices in England. I shall be a millionaire. And then the climate! I feel years younger already. I can run it as a health resort. A good sanatorium here might be worth twenty thousand a year. Of course I shall have to let a few people into the secret. The first thing is to get that brute shot."

"You're just like the Witch," said Polly. "All you think of is killing things."

"And then as regards oneself," Uncle Andrew continued, in a happy dream. "There's no knowing how long I might live if I settled here. And that's a big consideration when a fellow has turned sixty. I shouldn't be surprised if I never grew a day older in this country! Stupendous! The land of youth!"

"Oh!" cried Digory. "The land of youth! Do you think it really is?" For of course he remembered what Aunt Letty had said to the lady who brought the grapes, and that sweet hope rushed back upon him. "Uncle Andrew", he said, "do you think there's anything here that would cure Mother?"

"What are you talking about?" said Uncle Andrew. "This isn't a chemist's shop. But as I was saying –"

"You don't care twopence about her," said Digory savagely. "I thought you might; after all, she's your sister as well as my Mother. Well, no matter. I'm jolly well going to ask the Lion himself if he can help me." And he turned and walked briskly away. Polly waited for a moment and then went after him.

"Here! Stop! Come back! The boy's gone mad," said Uncle Andrew. He followed the children at a cautious distance behind; for he didn't want to get too far away from the green rings or too near the Lion.

In a few minutes Digory came to the edge of the wood and there he stopped. The Lion was singing still. But now the song had once more changed. It was more like what we should call a tune, but it was also far wilder. It made you want to run and jump and climb. It made you want to shout. It made you want to rush at other people and either hug them or fight them. It made Digory hot and red in the face. It had some effect on Uncle Andrew, for Digory could hear him saying, "A spirited gel, sir. It's a pity about her temper, but a dem fine woman all the same, a dem fine woman." But what the song did to the two humans was nothing compared with what it was doing to the country.

Can you imagine a stretch of grassy land bubbling like water in a pot? For that is really the best description of what was happening. In all directions it was swelling into humps. They were of very different sizes, some no bigger than mole-hills, some as big as wheel-barrows, two the size of cottages. And the humps moved and swelled till they burst, and the crumbled earth poured out of them, and from each hump there came out an animal. The moles came out just as you might see a mole come out in England. The dogs came out, barking the moment their heads were free, and struggling as you've seen them do when they are getting through a narrow hole in a hedge. The stags were the queerest to watch, for of course the antlers came up a long time before the rest of them, so at first Digory thought they were trees. The frogs, who all came up near the river, went straight into it with a plop-plop and a loud croaking. The panthers, leopards and things of that sort, sat down at once to wash the loose earth off their hind quarters and then stood up against the trees to sharpen their front claws. Showers of birds came out of the trees. Butterflies fluttered. Bees got to work on the flowers as if they hadn't a second to lose. But the greatest moment of all was when the biggest hump broke like a small earthquake and out came the sloping back, the large, wise head, and the four baggy-trousered legs of an elephant. And now you could hardly hear the song of the Lion; there was so much cawing, cooing, crowing, braying, neighing, baying, barking, lowing, bleating, and trumpeting.

But though Digory could no longer hear the Lion, he could see it. It was so big and so bright that he could not take his eyes off it. The other animals did not appear to be afraid of it. Indeed, at that very moment, Digory heard the sound of hoofs from behind; a second later the old cab-horse trotted past him and joined the other beasts. (The air had apparently suited him as well as it had suited Uncle Andrew. He no longer looked like the poor, old slave he had been in London; he was picking up his feet and holding his head erect.) And now, for the first time, the Lion was quite silent. He was going to and fro among the animals. And every now and then he would go up to two of them (always two at a time) and touch their noses with his. He would touch two beavers among all the beavers, two leopards among all the leopards, one stag and one deer among all the deer, and leave the rest. Some sorts of animal he passed over altogether. But the pairs

which he had touched instantly left their own kinds and
followed him. At last he stood still and all the creatures
whom he had touched came and stood in a wide circle
around him. The others whom he had not touched began
to wander away. Their noises faded gradually into the
distance. The chosen beasts who remained were now

utterly silent, all with their eyes fixed intently upon the
Lion. The cat-like ones gave an occasional twitch of the
tail but otherwise all were still. For the first time that day
there was complete silence, except for the noise of
running water. Digory's heart beat wildly; he knew something very solemn was going to be done. He had not forgotten about his Mother; but he knew jolly well that,
even for her, he couldn't interrupt a thing like this.

The Lion, whose eyes never blinked, stared at the
animals as hard as if he was going to burn them up with
his mere stare. And gradually a change came over them.
The smaller ones – the rabbits, moles and such-like –
grew a good deal larger. The very big ones – you noticed
it most with the elephants – grew a little smaller. Many

animals sat up on their hind legs. Most put their heads on one side as if they were trying very hard to understand. The Lion opened his mouth, but no sound came from it; he was breathing out, a long, warm breath; it seemed to sway all the beasts as the wind sways a line of trees. Far overhead from beyond the veil of blue sky which hid them the stars sang again; a pure, cold, difficult music. Then there came a swift flash like fire (but it burnt nobody) either from the sky or from the Lion itself, and every drop of blood tingled in the children's bodies, and the deepest, wildest voice they had ever heard was saying:

"Narnia, Narnia, Narnia, awake. Love. Think. Speak. Be walking trees. Be talking beasts. Be divine waters."

CHAPTER TEN

THE FIRST JOKE AND OTHER MATTERS

It was of course the Lion's voice. The children had long felt sure that he could speak: yet it was a lovely and terrible shock when he did.

Out of the trees wild people stepped forth, gods and goddesses of the wood; with them came Fauns and Satyrs and Dwarfs. Out of the river rose the river god with his Naiad daughters. And all these and all the beasts and birds in their different voices, low or high or thick or clear, replied:

"Hail, Aslan. We hear and obey. We are awake. We love. We think. We speak. We know."

"But please, we don't know very much yet," said a nosey and snorty kind of voice. And that really did make the children jump, for it was the cab-horse who had spoken.

"Good old Strawberry," said Polly. "I *am* glad he was one of the ones picked out to be a Talking Beast." And the Cabby, who was now standing beside the children, said, "Strike me pink. I always did say that 'oss 'ad a lot of sense, though."

"Creatures, I give you yourselves," said the strong, happy voice of Aslan. "I give to you forever this land of Narnia. I give you the woods, the fruits, the rivers. I give you the stars and I give you myself. The Dumb Beasts whom I have not chosen are yours also. Treat them gently and cherish them but do not go back to their ways lest you cease to be Talking Beasts. For out of them you were taken and into them you can return. Do not so."

"No, Aslan, we won't, we won't," said everyone. But one perky jackdaw added in a loud voice, "No fear!" and everyone else had finished just before he said it so that his words came out quite clear in a dead silence; and perhaps you have found out how awful that can be — say, at a party. The Jackdaw became so embarrassed that it hid its head under its wings as if it was going to sleep. And all the other animals began making various queer noises

which are their ways of laughing and which, of course, no one has ever heard in our world. They tried at first to repress it, but Aslan said:

"Laugh and fear not, creatures. Now that you are no longer dumb and witless, you need not always be grave. For jokes as well as justice come in with speech."

So they all let themselves go. And there was such merriment that the Jackdaw himself plucked up courage again and perched on the cab-horse's head, between its ears, clapping its wings, and said:

"Aslan! Aslan! Have I made the first joke? Will everybody always be told how I made the first joke?"

"No, little friend," said the Lion. "You have not *made* the first joke; you have only *been* the first joke." Then everyone laughed more than ever; but the Jackdaw didn't mind and laughed just as loud till the horse shook its head and the Jackdaw lost its balance and fell off, but remembered its wings (they were still new to it) before it reached the ground.

"And now," said Aslan, "Narnia is established. We must next take thought for keeping it safe. I will call some of you to my council. Come hither to me, you the chief Dwarf, and you the River-god, and you Oak and the He-Owl, and both the Ravens and the Bull-Elephant. We must talk together. For though the world is not five hours old an evil has already entered it."

The creatures he had named came forward and he turned away eastward with them. The others all began talking, saying things like "*What* did he say had entered the world? – A Neevil – What's a Neevil? – No, he didn't say a Neevil, he said a weevil – Well, what's that?"

"Look here," said Digory to Polly, "I've got to go after him – Aslan, I mean, the Lion. I must speak to him."

"Do you think we can?" said Polly. "I wouldn't dare."

"I've got to," said Digory. "It's about Mother. If anyone could give me something that would do her good, it would be him."

"I'll come along with you," said the Cabby. "I liked the looks of '*im*. And I don't reckon these other beasts will go for us. And I want a word with old Strawberry."

So all three of them stepped out boldly – or as boldly as

they could — towards the assembly of animals. The
creatures were so busy talking to one another and making
friends that they didn't notice the three humans until they
were very close; nor did they hear Uncle Andrew, who

was standing trembling in his buttoned boots a good way
off and shouting (but by no means at the top of his voice).

"Digory! Come back! Come back at once when you're
told. I forbid you to go a step further."

When at last they were right in among the animals, the
animals all stopped talking and stared at them.

"Well?" said the He-Beaver at last, "what, in the name of Aslan, are these?"

"Please," began Digory in rather a breathless voice, when a Rabbit said, "They're a kind of large lettuce, that's my belief."

"No, we're not, honestly we're not," said Polly hastily. "We're not at all nice to eat."

"There!" said the Mole. "They can talk. Who ever heard of a talking lettuce?"

"Perhaps they're the Second Joke," suggested the Jackdaw.

A Panther, which had been washing its face, stopped for a moment to say, "Well, if they are, they're nothing like so good as the first one. At least, *I* don't see anything very funny about them." It yawned and went on with its wash.

"Oh, please," said Digory. "I'm in such a hurry. I want to see the Lion."

All this time the Cabby had been trying to catch Strawberry's eye. Now he did. "Now, Strawberry, old boy," he said. "You know me. You ain't going to stand there and say as you don't know me."

"What's the Thing talking about, Horse?" said several voices.

"Well," said Strawberry very slowly, "I don't exactly know, I think most of us don't know much about anything yet. But I've a sort of idea I've seen a thing like this before. I've a feeling I lived somewhere else — or was something else — before Aslan woke us all up a few minutes ago. It's all very muddled. Like a dream. But there were things like these three in the dream."

"What?" said the Cabby. "Not know me? Me what used to bring you a hot mash of an evening when you was out of sorts? Me what rubbed you down proper? Me what never forgot to put your cloth on you if you was standing in the cold? I wouldn't 'ave thought it of you, Strawberry."

"It *does* begin to come back," said the Horse thoughtfully. "Yes. Let me think now, let me think. Yes, you used to tie a horrid black thing behind me and then hit me to make me run, and however far I ran this black thing would always be coming rattle-rattle behind me."

"We 'ad our living to earn, see," said the Cabby. "Yours the same as mine. And if there 'adn't been no work and no whip there'd 'ave been no stable, no hay, no mash, and no oats. For you did get a taste of oats when I could afford 'em, which no one can deny."

"Oats?" said the Horse, pricking up his ears. "Yes, I remember something about that. Yes, I remember more and more. You were always sitting up somewhere behind, and I was always running in front, pulling you and the black thing. I know I did all the work."

"Summer, I grant you," said the Cabby. " 'Ot work for you and a cool seat for me. But what about winter, old boy, when you was keeping yourself warm and I was sitting up there with my feet like ice and my nose fair pinched off me with the wind, and my 'ands that numb I couldn't 'ardly 'old the reins?"

"It was a hard, cruel country," said Strawberry. "There was no grass. All hard stones."

"Too true, mate, too true!" said the Cabby. "A 'ard world it was. I always did say those paving-stones weren't fair on any 'oss. That's Lunn'on, that is. I didn't like it no more than what you did. You were a country 'oss, and I was a country man. Used to sing in the choir, I did, down at 'ome. But there wasn't a living for me there."

"Oh please, please," said Digory. "Could we get on? The Lion's getting further and further away. And I do want to speak to him so dreadfully badly."

"Look 'ere, Strawberry," said the Cabby. "This young gen'leman 'as something on his mind that he wants to talk to the Lion about; 'im you call Aslan. Suppose you was to let 'im ride on your back (which 'e'd take it very kindly) and trot 'im over to where the Lion is. And me and the little girl will be following along."

"Ride?" said Strawberry. "Oh, I remember now. That means sitting on my back. I remember there used to be a little one of you two-leggers who used to do that long ago. He used to have little hard, square lumps of some white stuff that he gave me. They tasted – oh, wonderful, sweeter than grass."

"Ah, that'd be sugar," said the Cabby.

"Please, Strawberry," begged Digory, "do, do let me get up and take me to Aslan."

"Well, I don't mind," said the Horse. "Not for once in a way. Up you get."

"Good old Strawberry," said the Cabby. "'Ere, young 'un, I'll give you a lift." Digory was soon on Strawberry's back, and quite comfortable, for he had ridden bare-back before on his own pony.

"Now, do gee up, Strawberry," he said.

"You don't happen to have a bit of that white stuff about you, I suppose?" said the Horse.

"No. I'm afraid I haven't," said Digory.

"Well, it can't be helped," said Strawberry, and off they went.

At that moment a large Bulldog, who had been sniffing and staring very hard, said:

"Look. Isn't there another of these queer creatures –

over there, beside the river, under the trees?"

Then all the animals looked and saw Uncle Andrew, standing very still among the rhododendrons and hoping he wouldn't be noticed.

"Come on!" said several voices. "Let's go and find out." So, while Strawberry was briskly trotting away with Digory in one direction (and Polly and the Cabby were following on foot) most of the creatures rushed towards Uncle Andrew with roars, barks, grunts, and various noises of cheerful interest.

We must now go back a bit and explain what the whole scene had looked like from Uncle Andrew's point of view. It had not made at all the same impression on him as on the Cabby and the children. For what you see and hear depends a good deal on where you are standing: it also depends on what sort of person you are.

Ever since the animals had first appeared, Uncle Andrew had been shrinking further and further back into the thicket. He watched them very hard of course; but he wasn't really interested in seeing what they were doing, only in seeing whether they were going to make a rush at him. Like the Witch, he was dreadfully practical. He simply didn't notice that Aslan was choosing one pair out of every kind of beasts. All he saw, or thought he saw, was a lot of dangerous wild animals walking vaguely about. And he kept on wondering why the other animals didn't run away from the big Lion.

When the great moment came and the Beasts spoke, he missed the whole point; for a rather interesting reason. When the Lion had first begun singing, long ago when it was still quite dark, he had realized that the noise was a song. And he had disliked the song very much. It made him think and feel things he did not want to think and feel. Then, when the sun rose and he saw that the singer was a lion ("*only* a lion," as he said to himself) he tried his hardest to make believe that it wasn't singing and never had been singing – only roaring as any lion might in a zoo in our own world. "Of course it can't really have been singing," he thought, "I must have imagined it. I've been letting my nerves get out of order. Who ever heard of a lion singing?" And the longer and more beautiful the Lion sang, the harder Uncle Andrew tried to make himself believe that he could hear nothing but roaring. Now the trouble about trying to make yourself stupider than you really are is that you very often succeed. Uncle Andrew did. He soon did hear nothing but roaring in Aslan's song. Soon he couldn't have heard anything else even if he had wanted to. And when at last the Lion spoke and said, "Narnia awake," he didn't hear any words: he heard only a snarl. And when the Beasts spoke in answer, he heard only barkings, growlings, bayings, and howlings. And when they laughed – well, you can imagine. That was worse for Uncle Andrew than anything that had happened yet. Such a horrid, bloodthirsty din of hungry and angry brutes he had never heard in his life. Then, to his utter rage and horror, he saw the other three humans actually walking out into the open to meet the animals.

"The fools!" he said to himself. "Now those brutes will eat the rings along with the children and I'll never be able to get home again. What a selfish little boy that Digory is! And the others are just as bad. If they want to throw away their own lives, that's their business. But what about *me*? They don't seem to think of that. No one thinks of *me*."

Finally, when a whole crowd of animals came rushing towards him, he turned and ran for his life. And now anyone could see that the air of that young world was really doing the old gentleman good. In London he had been far too old to run: now, he ran at a speed which would have made him certain to win the hundred yards' race at any Prep school in England. His coat-tails flying out behind him were a fine sight. But of course it was no use. Many of the animals behind him were swift ones; it was the first run they had ever taken in their lives and they were all longing to use their new muscles. "After him! After him!" they shouted. "Perhaps he's that Neevil! Tally-ho! Tantivy! Cut him off! Round him up! Keep it up! Hurrah!"

In a very few minutes some of them got ahead of him. They lined up in a row and barred his way. Others hemmed him in from behind. Wherever he looked he saw terrors. Antlers of great elks and the huge face of an elephant towered over him. Heavy, serious-minded bears and boars grunted behind him. Cool-looking leopards and panthers with sarcastic faces (as he thought) stared at him and waved their tails. What struck him most of all was the number of open mouths. The animals had really opened their mouths to pant; he thought they had opened their mouths to eat him.

Uncle Andrew stood trembling and swaying this way and that. He had never liked animals at the best of times, being usually rather afraid of them; and of course years of doing cruel experiments on animals had made him hate and fear them far more.

"Now, sir," said the Bulldog in his business-like way, "are you animal, vegetable, or mineral?" That was what it really said; but all Uncle Andrew heard was "Gr-r-r-arrh-ow!"

CHAPTER ELEVEN

DIGORY AND HIS UNCLE ARE
BOTH IN TROUBLE

You may think the animals were very stupid not to see at once that Uncle Andrew was the same kind of creature as the two children and the Cabby. But you must remember that the animals knew nothing about clothes. They thought that Polly's frock and Digory's Norfolk suit and the Cabby's bowler hat were as much parts of them as their own fur and feathers. They wouldn't have known even that those three were all of the same kind if they hadn't spoken to them and if Strawberry had not seemed to think so. And Uncle Andrew was a great deal taller than the children and a good deal thinner than the Cabby. He was all in black except for his white waistcoat (not very white by now), and the great grey mop of his hair (now very wild indeed) didn't look to them like anything they had seen in the three other humans. So it was only natural that they should be puzzled. Worst of all, he didn't seem to be able to talk.

He had tried to. When the Bulldog spoke to him (or, as he thought, first snarled and then growled at him) he held out his shaking hand and gasped "Good Doggie, then, poor old fellow." But the beasts could not understand him any more than he could understand them. They didn't hear any words: only a vague sizzling noise. Perhaps it was just as well they didn't, for no dog that I ever knew, least of all a Talking Dog of Narnia, likes being called a Good Doggie then; any more than you would like being called My Little Man.

Then Uncle Andrew dropped down in a dead faint.

"There!" said a Warthog, "it's only a tree. I always thought so." (Remember, they had never yet seen a faint or even a fall.)

The Bulldog, who had been sniffing Uncle Andrew all over, raised its head and said, "It's an animal. Certainly an animal. And probably the same kind as those other ones."

"I don't see that," said one of the Bears. "An animal wouldn't just roll over like that. We're animals and *we* don't roll over. We stand up. Like this." He rose to his hind legs, took a step backwards, tripped over a low branch and fell flat on his back.

"The Third Joke, the Third Joke, the Third Joke!" said the Jackdaw in great excitement.

"I still think it's a sort of tree," said the Warthog.

"If it's a tree," said the other Bear, "there might be a bees' nest in it."

"I'm sure it's not a tree," said the Badger. "I had a sort of idea it was trying to speak before it toppled over."

"That was only the wind in its branches," said the Warthog.

"You surely don't mean," said the Jackdaw to the Badger, "that you think its a *talking* animal! It didn't say any words."

"And yet, you know," said the Elephant (the She-Elephant, of course; her husband, as you remember, had been called away by Aslan). "And yet, you know, it might be an animal of some kind. Mightn't the whitish lump at this end be a sort of face? And couldn't those holes be eyes and a mouth? No nose, of course. But then – ahem – one mustn't be narrow-minded. Very few of us have what could exactly be called a Nose." She squinted down the length of her own trunk with pardonable pride.

"I object to that remark very strongly," said the Bulldog.

"The Elephant is quite right," said the Tapir.

"I tell you what!" said the Donkey brightly, "perhaps it's an animal that can't talk but thinks it can."

"Can it be made to stand up?" said the Elephant thoughtfully. She took the limp form of Uncle Andrew gently in her trunk and set him up on end: upside down, unfortunately, so that two half-sovereigns, three half-crowns, and a sixpence fell out of his pocket. But it was no use. Uncle Andrew merely collapsed again.

"There!" said several voices. "It isn't an animal at all. It's not alive."

"I tell you, it *is* an animal," said the Bulldog. "Smell it for yourself."

"Smelling isn't everything," said the Elephant.

"Why," said the Bulldog, "if a fellow can't trust his nose, what is he to trust?"

"Well, his brains perhaps," she replied mildly.

"I object to that remark very strongly," said the Bulldog.

"Well, we must do something about it," said the Elephant. "Because it may be the Neevil, and it must be shown to Aslan. What do most of us think? Is it an animal or something of the tree kind?"

"Tree! Tree!" said a dozen voices.

"Very well," said the Elephant. "Then, if it's a tree it wants to be planted. We must dig a hole."

The two Moles settled that part of the business pretty quickly. There was some dispute as to which way up Uncle Andrew ought to be put into the hole, and he had a very narrow escape from being put in head foremost. Several animals said his legs must be his branches and therefore the grey, fluffy thing (they meant his head) must be his root. But then others said that the forked end of him was the muddier and that it spread out more, as roots ought to do. So finally he was planted right way up. When they had patted down the earth it came up above his knees.

"It looks dreadfully withered," said the Donkey.

"Of course it wants some watering," said the Elephant. "I think I *might* say (meaning no offence to anyone present) that, perhaps, for *that* sort of work, my kind of nose –"

"I object to that remark very strongly," said the Bulldog. But the Elephant walked quietly to the river, filled her trunk with water, and came back to attend to Uncle Andrew. The sagacious animal went on doing this till gallons of water had been squirted over him, and water was running out of the skirts of his frock-coat as if he had been for a bath with all his clothes on. In the end it revived him. He awoke from his faint. What a wakening it was! But we must leave him to think over his wicked deed (if he was likely to do anything so sensible) and turn to more important things.

Strawberry trotted on with Digory on his back till the noise of the other animals died away, and now the little group of Aslan and his chosen councillors was quite close. Digory knew that he couldn't possibly break in on so solemn a meeting, but there was no need to do so. At a word from Aslan, the He-Elephant, the Ravens, and all the rest of them drew aside. Digory slipped off the horse and found himself face to face with Aslan. And Aslan was bigger and more beautiful amd more brightly golden and more terrible than he had thought. He dared not look into the great eyes.

"Please — Mr Lion — Aslan — Sir," said Digory, "could you — may I — please, will you give me some magic fruit of this country to make Mother well?"

He had been desperately hoping that the Lion would say "Yes"; he had been horribly afraid it might say "No". But he was taken aback when it did neither.

"This is the Boy," said Aslan, looking, not at Digory, but at his councillors. "This is the Boy who did it."

"Oh dear," thought Digory, "what have I done now?"

"Son of Adam," said the Lion. "There is an evil Witch abroad in my new land of Narnia. Tell these good Beasts how she came here."

A dozen different things that he might say flashed through Digory's mind, but he had the sense to say nothing except the exact truth.

"I brought her, Aslan," he answered in a low voice.

"For what purpose?"

"I wanted to get her out of my own world back into her own. I thought I was taking her back to her own place."

"How came she to be in your world, Son of Adam?"

"By — by Magic."

The Lion said nothing and Digory knew that he had not told enough.

"It was my Uncle, Aslan," he said. "He sent us out of our own world by magic rings, at least I had to go because he sent Polly first, and then we met the Witch in a place called Charn and she just held on to us when —"

"You *met* the Witch?" said Aslan in a low voice which had the threat of a growl in it.

"She woke up," said Digory wretchedly. And then, turning very white, "I mean, I woke her. Because I wanted to know what would happen if I struck a bell. Polly didn't want to. It wasn't her fault. I — I fought her. I know I shouldn't have. I think I was a bit enchanted by the writing under the bell."

"Do you?" asked Aslan; still speaking very low and deep.

"No," said Digory. "I see now I wasn't. I was only pretending."

There was a long pause. And Digory was thinking all the time, "I've spoiled everything. There's no chance of getting anything for Mother now."

When the Lion spoke again, it was not to Digory.

"You see, friends," he said, "that before the new, clean world I gave you is seven hours old, a force of evil has already entered it; waked and brought hither by this son of Adam." The Beasts, even Strawberry, all turned their eyes on Digory till he felt that he wished the ground would swallow him up. "But do not be cast down," said Aslan, still speaking to the Beasts. "Evil will come of that evil, but it is still a long way off, and I will see to it that the worst falls upon myself. In the meantime, let us take such order that for many hundred years yet this shall be a merry land in a merry world. And as Adam's race has done the harm, Adam's race shall help to heal it. Draw near, you other two."

The last words were spoken to Polly and the Cabby who had now arrived. Polly, all eyes and mouth, was staring at Aslan and holding the Cabby's hand rather tightly. The Cabby gave one glance at the Lion, and took off his bowler hat: no one had yet seen him without it. When it was off, he looked younger and nicer, and more like a countryman and less like a London cabman.

"Son," said Aslan to the Cabby. "I have known you long. Do you know me?"

"Well, no, sir," said the Cabby. "Leastways, not in an ordinary manner of speaking. Yet I feel somehow, if I may make so free, as 'ow we've met before."

"It is well," said the Lion. "You know better than you think you know, and you shall live to know me better yet. How does this land please you?"

"It's a fair treat, sir," said the Cabby.

"Would you like to live here always?"

"Well you see sir, I'm a married man," said the Cabby. "If my wife was here neither of us would ever want to go back to London, I reckon. We're both country folks really."

Aslan threw up his shaggy head, opened his mouth, and uttered a long, single note; not very loud, but full of power. Polly's heart jumped in her body when she heard it. She felt sure that it was a call, and that anyone who heard that call would want to obey it and (what's more) would be able to obey it, however many worlds and ages lay between. And so, though she was filled with wonder, she was not really astonished or shocked when all of a sudden a young woman, with a kind, honest face stepped out of nowhere and stood beside her. Polly knew at once that it was the Cabby's wife, fetched out of our world not by any tiresome magic rings, but quickly, simply and sweetly as a bird flies to its nest. The young woman had apparently been in the middle of a washing day, for she wore an apron, her sleeves were rolled up to the elbow, and there were soapsuds on her hands. If she had had time to put on her good clothes (her best hat had imitation cherries on it) she would have looked dreadful; as it was, she looked rather nice.

Of course she thought she was dreaming. That was why she didn't rush across to her husband and ask him what on earth had happened to them both. But when she looked at the Lion she didn't feel quite so sure it was a

dream, yet for some reason she did not appear to be very frightened. Then she dropped a little half curtsey, as some country girls still knew how to do in those days. After that, she went and put her hand in the Cabby's and stood there looking round her a little shyly.

"My children," said Aslan, fixing his eyes on both of them, "you are to be the first King and Queen of Narnia."

The Cabby opened his mouth in astonishment, and his wife turned very red.

"You shall rule and name all these creatures, and do justice among them, and protect them from their enemies when enemies arise. And enemies will arise, for there is an evil Witch in this world."

The Cabby swallowed hard two or three times and cleared his throat.

"Begging your pardon, sir," he said, "and thanking you very much I'm sure (which my Missus does the same) but I ain't no sort of a chap for a job like that. I never 'ad much eddycation, you see."

"Well," said Aslan, "can you use a spade and a plough and raise food out of the earth?"

"Yes, sir, I could do a bit of that sort of work: being brought up to it, like."

"Can you rule these creatures kindly and fairly, remembering that they are not slaves like the dumb beasts of the world you were born in, but Talking Beasts and free subjects?"

"I see that, sir," replied the Cabby. "I'd try to do the square thing by them all."

"And would you bring up your children and grandchildren to do the same?"

"It'd be up to me to try, sir. I'd do my best: wouldn't we, Nellie?"

"And you wouldn't have favourites either among your own children or among the other creatures or let any hold another under or use it hardly?"

"I never could abide such goings on, sir, and that's the truth. I'd give 'em what for if I caught 'em at it," said the Cabby. (All through this conversation his voice was growing slower and richer. More like the country voice he must have had as a boy and less like the sharp, quick voice of a cockney.)

"And if enemies came against the land (for enemies will arise) and there was war, would you be the first in the charge and the last in the retreat?"

"Well, sir," said the Cabby very slowly, "a chap don't exactly know till he's been tried. I dare say I might turn out ever such a soft 'un. Never did no fighting except with my fists. I'd try – that is, I 'ope I'd try – to do my bit."

"Then," said Aslan, "You will have done all that a King should do. Your coronation will be held presently. And you and your children and grandchildren shall be blessed, and some will be Kings of Narnia, and others will be Kings of Archenland which lies yonder over the Southern Mountains. And you, little Daughter (here he turned to Polly) are welcome. Have you forgiven the Boy for the violence he did you in the Hall of Images in the desolate palace of accursed Charn?"

"Yes, Aslan, we've made it up," said Polly.

"That is well," said Aslan. "And now for the Boy himself."

CHAPTER TWELVE

STRAWBERRY'S ADVENTURE

DIGORY kept his mouth very tight shut. He had been growing more and more uncomfortable. He hoped that, whatever happened, he wouldn't blub or do anything ridiculous.

"Son of Adam," said Aslan. "Are you ready to undo the wrong that you have done to my sweet country of Narnia on the very day of its birth?"

"Well, I don't see what I can do," said Digory. "You see, the Queen ran away and —"

"I asked, are you ready?" said the Lion.

"Yes," said Digory. He had had for a second some wild idea of saying "I'll try to help you if you'll promise to help my Mother," but he realized in time that the Lion was not at all the sort of person one could try to make bargains with. But when he had said "Yes," he thought of his Mother, and he thought of the great hopes he had had, and how they were all dying away, and a lump came in his throat and tears in his eyes, and he blurted out:

"But please, please — won't you — can't you give me something that will cure Mother?" Up till then he had been looking at the Lion's great feet and the huge claws on them; now, in his despair, he looked up at its face. What he saw surprised him as much as anything in his whole life. For the tawny face was bent down near his own and (wonder of wonders) great shining tears stood in the Lion's eyes. They were such big, bright tears compared with Digory's own that for a moment he felt as if the Lion must really be sorrier about his Mother than he was himself.

"My son, my son," said Aslan. "I know. Grief is great. Only you and I in this land know that yet. Let us be good to one another. But I have to think of hundreds of years in the life of Narnia. The Witch whom you have brought into this world will come back to Narnia again. But it need not be yet. It is my wish to plant in Narnia a tree that she will not dare to approach, and that tree will protect Narnia from her for many years. So this land shall have a long, bright morning before any clouds come over the sun. You must get me the seed from which that tree is to grow."

"Yes, sir," said Digory. He didn't know how it was to be done but he felt quite sure now that he would be able to do it. The Lion drew a deep breath, stooped its head even lower and gave him a Lion's kiss. And at once Digory felt that new strength and courage had gone into him.

"Dear son," said Aslan, "I will tell you what you must do. Turn and look to the West and tell me what do you see?"

"I see terribly big mountains, Aslan," said Digory, "I see this river coming down cliffs in a waterfall. And beyond the cliff there are high green hills with forests. And beyond those there are higher ranges that look almost black. And then, far away, there are big snowy mountains all heaped up together – like pictures of the Alps. And behind those there's nothing but the sky."

"You see well," said the Lion. "Now the land of Narnia ends where the waterfall comes down, and once you have reached the top of the cliffs you will be out of Narnia and into the Western Wild. You must journey through those mountains till you find a green valley with a blue lake in it, walled round by mountains of ice. At the end of the lake there is a steep, green hill. On the top of that hill there is a garden. In the centre of that garden is a tree. Pluck an apple from that tree and bring it back to me."

"Yes, sir," said Digory again. He hadn't the least idea of how he was to climb the cliff and find his way among all the mountains, but he didn't like to say that for fear it would sound like making excuses. But he did say, "I hope, Aslan, you're not in a hurry. I shan't be able to get there and back very quickly."

"Little son of Adam, you shall have help," said Aslan. He then turned to the Horse who had been standing quietly beside them all this time, swishing his tail to keep the flies off, and listening with his head on one side as if the conversation were a little difficult to understand.

"My dear," said Aslan to the Horse, "would you like to be a winged horse?"

You should have seen how the Horse shook its mane and how its nostrils widened, and the little tap it gave the ground with one back hoof. Clearly it would very much like to be a winged horse. But it only said:

"If you wish, Aslan – if you really mean – I don't know why it should be me – I'm not a very clever horse."

"Be winged. Be the father of all flying horses," roared Aslan in a voice that shook the ground. "Your name is Fledge."

The horse shied, just as it might have shied in the old, miserable days when it pulled a hansom. Then it roared. It strained its neck back as if there were a fly biting its shoulders and it wanted to scratch them. And then, just as the beasts had burst out of the earth, there burst out from the shoulders of Fledge wings that spread and grew, larger than eagles', larger than swans', larger than angels' wings in church windows. The feathers shone chestnut colour and copper colour. He gave a great sweep with them and leaped into the air. Twenty feet above Aslan and Digory he snorted, neighed, and curvetted. Then, after circling once round them, he dropped to the earth, all four hoofs together, looking awkward and surprised, but extremely pleased.

"Is it good, Fledge?" said Aslan.

"It is very good, Aslan," said Fledge.

"Will you carry this little son of Adam on your back to the mountain-valley I spoke of?"

"What? Now? At once?" said Strawberry — or Fledge, as we must now call him — "Hurrah! Come on little one, I've had things like you on my back before.

Long, long ago. When there were green fields; and
sugar."

"What are the two daughters of Eve whispering
about?" said Aslan, turning very suddenly on Polly and
the Cabby's wife, who had in fact been making friends.

"If you please, sir," said Queen Helen (for that is what
Nellie the cabman's wife now was), "I think the little girl
would love to go too, if it weren't no trouble."

"What does Fledge say about that?" asked the Lion.

"Oh, I don't mind two, not when they're little ones,"
said Fledge. "But I hope the Elephant doesn't want to
come as well."

The Elephant had no such wish, and the new King of
Narnia helped both the children up: that is, he gave
Digory a rough heave and set Polly as gently and daintily
on the horse's back as if she were made of china and
might break. "There they are, Strawberry — Fledge, I
should say. This is a rum go."

"Do not fly too high," said Aslan. "Do not try to go
over the tops of the great ice-mountains. Look out for the
valleys, the green places, and fly through them. There will
always be a way through. And now, begone with my
blessing."

"Oh Fledge!" said Digory, leaning forward to pat the
Horse's glossy neck. "This *is* fun. Hold on to me tight,
Polly."

Next moment the country dropped away beneath them,
and whirled round as Fledge, like a huge pigeon, circled
once or twice before setting off on his long westward flight.
Looking down, Polly could hardly see the King and the
Queen, and even Aslan himself was only a bright yellow
spot on the green grass. Soon the wind was in their faces
and Fledge's wings settled down to a steady beat.

All Narnia, many-coloured with lawns and rocks and heather and different sorts of trees, lay spread out below them, the river winding through it like a ribbon of quicksilver. They could already see over the tops of the low hills which lay northward on their right; beyond those hills a great moorland sloped gently up and up to the horizon. On their left the mountains were much higher, but every now and then there was a gap when you could see, between steep pine woods, a glimpse of the southern lands that lay beyond them, looking blue and far away.

"That'll be where Archenland is," said Polly.

"Yes, but look ahead!" said Digory.

For now a great barrier of cliffs rose before them and they were almost dazzled by the sunlight dancing on the great waterfall by which the river roars and sparkles down into Narnia itself from the high western lands in which it rises. They were flying so high already that the thunder of those falls could only just be heard as a small, thin sound, but they were not yet high enough to fly over the top of the cliffs.

"We'll have to do a bit of zig-zagging here," said Fledge. "Hold on tight."

He began flying to and fro, getting higher at each turn. The air grew colder, and they heard the call of eagles far below them.

"I say, look back! Look behind," said Polly.

There they could see the whole valley of Narnia stretched out to where, just before the eastern horizon, there was a gleam of the sea. And now they were so high that they could see tiny-looking jagged mountains appearing beyond the northwest moors, and plains of what looked like sand far in the south.

"I wish we had someone to tell us what all those places are," said Digory.

"I don't suppose they're anywhere yet," said Polly. "I mean, there's no one there, and nothing happening. The world only began today."

"No, but people *will* get there," said Digory. "And then they'll have histories, you know."

"Well, it's a jolly good thing they haven't now," said Polly. "Because nobody can be made to learn it. Battles and dates and all that rot."

Now they were over the top of the cliffs and in a few minutes the valley land of Narnia had sunk out of sight behind them. They were flying over a wild country of steep hills and dark forests, still following the course of the river. The really big mountains loomed ahead. But the sun was now in the travellers' eyes and they couldn't see things very clearly in that direction. For the sun sank lower and lower till the western sky was all like one great furnace full of melted gold; and it set at last behind a jagged peak which stood up against the brightness as sharp and flat as if it were cut out of cardboard.

"It's none too warm up here," said Polly.

"And my wings are beginning to ache," said Fledge. There's no sign of the valley with a Lake in it, like what Aslan said. What about coming down and looking out for a decent spot to spend the night in? We shan't reach that place tonight."

"Yes, and surely it's about time for supper?" said Digory.

So Fledge came lower and lower. As they came down nearer to the earth and among the hills, the air grew warmer and after travelling so many hours with nothing to listen to but the beat of Fledge's wings, it was nice to

hear the homely and earthy noises again – the chatter of
the river on its stony bed and the creaking of trees in the
light wind. A warm, good smell of sun-baked earth and
grass and flowers came up to them. At last Fledge
alighted. Digory rolled off and helped Polly to dismount.
Both were glad to stretch their stiff legs.

The valley in which they had come down was in the
heart of the mountains; snowy heights, one of them
looking rose-red in the reflections of the sunset, towered
above them.

"I *am* hungry," said Digory.

"Well, tuck in," said Fledge, taking a big mouthful of
grass. Then he raised his head, still chewing and with bits
of grass sticking out on each side of his mouth like
whiskers, and said, "Come on, you two. Don't be shy.
There's plenty for us all."

"But we can't eat grass," said Digory.

"H'm, h'm," said Fledge, speaking with his mouth full.
"Well – h'm – don't know quite what you'll do then.
Very good grass too."

Polly and Digory stared at one another in dismay.

"Well, I *do* think someone might have arranged about
our meals," said Digory.

"I'm sure Aslan would have, if you'd asked him," said
Fledge.

"Wouldn't he know without being asked?" said Polly.

"I've no doubt he would," said the Horse (still with
his mouth full). "But I've a sort of idea he likes to be
asked."

"But what on earth are we to do?" asked Digory.

"I'm sure I don't know," said Fledge. "Unless you try
the grass. You might like it better than you think."

"Oh, don't be silly," said Polly, stamping her foot. "Of

course humans can't eat grass, any more than you could eat a mutton chop."

"For goodness' sake don't talk about chops and things," said Digory. "It only makes it worse."

Digory said that Polly had better take herself home by ring and get something to eat there; he couldn't himself because he had promised to go straight on his message for Aslan, and, if once he showed up again at home, anything might happen to prevent his getting back. But Polly said she wouldn't leave him, and Digory said it was jolly decent of her.

"I say," said Polly, "I've still got the remains of that bag of toffee in my jacket. It'll be better than nothing."

"A lot better," said Digory, "But be careful to get your hand into your pocket without touching your ring."

This was a difficult and delicate job but they managed it in the end. The little paper bag was very squashy and sticky when they finally got it out, so that it was more a question of tearing the bag off the toffees than of getting the toffees out of the bag. Some grown-ups (you know how fussy they can be about that sort of thing) would rather have gone without supper altogether than eaten those toffees. There were nine of them all told. It was Digory who had the bright idea of eating four each and planting the ninth; for, as he said, "if the bar off the lamp-post turned into a little light-tree, why shouldn't this turn into a toffee-tree?" So they dibbled a small hole in the turf and buried the piece of toffee. Then they ate the other pieces, making them last as long as they could. It was a poor meal, even with all the paper they couldn't help eating as well.

When Fledge had quite finished his own excellent supper he lay down. The children came and sat one on each side of him leaning against his warm body, and when he had spread a wing over each they were really quite snug. As the bright young stars of that new world came out they talked over everything: how Digory had hoped to get something for his Mother and how, instead of that, he had been sent on this message. And they repeated to one another all the signs by which they would

know the places they were looking for – the blue lake and the hill with a garden on top of it. The talk was just beginning to slow down as they got sleepy, when suddenly Polly sat up wide awake and said "Hush!"

Everyone listened as hard as they could.

"Perhaps it was only the wind in the trees," said Digory presently.

"I'm not so sure," said Fledge. "Anyway – wait! There it goes again. By Aslan, it *is* something."

The horse scrambled to its feet with a great noise and a great unheaval; the children were already on theirs. Fledge trotted to and fro, sniffing and whinnying. The children tip-toed this way and that, looking behind every bush and tree. They kept on thinking they saw things, and there was one time when Polly was perfectly certain she had seen a tall, dark figure gliding quickly away in a westerly direction. But they caught nothing and in the end Fledge lay down again and the children re-snuggled (if that is the right word) under his wings. They went to sleep at once. Fledge stayed awake much longer moving his ears to and fro in the darkness and sometimes giving a little shiver with his skin as if a fly had lighted on him: but in the end he too slept.

CHAPTER THIRTEEN

AN UNEXPECTED MEETING

"Wake up, Digory, wake up, Fledge," came the voice of Polly. "It *has* turned into a toffee tree. And it's the loveliest morning."

The low early sunshine was streaming through the wood and the grass was grey with dew and the cobwebs were like silver. Just beside them was a little, very dark-wooded tree, about the size of an apple tree. The leaves were whitish and rather papery, like the herb called honesty, and it was loaded with little brown fruits that looked rather like dates.

"Hurrah!" said Digory. "But I'm going to have a dip first." He rushed through a flowering thicket or two down to the river's edge. Have you ever bathed in a mountain river that is running in shallow cataracts over red and blue and yellow stones with the sun on it? It is as good as the sea: in some ways almost better. Of course, he had to dress again without drying but it was well worth it. When he came back, Polly went down and had her bathe; at least she said that was what she'd been doing, but we know she was not much of a swimmer and perhaps it is best not to ask too many questions. Fledge visited the river too but he only stood in midstream, stooping down for a long drink of water and then shaking his mane and neighing several times.

Polly and Digory got to work on the toffee-tree. The fruit was delicious; not exactly like toffee – softer for one thing, and juicy – but like fruit which reminded one of toffee. Fledge also made an excellent breakfast; he tried one of the toffee fruits and liked it but said he felt more like grass at that hour in the morning. Then with some difficulty the children got on his back and the second journey began.

It was even better than yesterday, partly because every one was feeling so fresh, and partly because the newly risen sun was at their backs and, of course, everything looks nicer when the light is behind you. It was a wonderful ride. The big snowy mountains rose above them in every direction. The valleys, far beneath them, were so green, and all the streams which tumbled down from the glaciers into the main river were so blue, that it was like flying over gigantic pieces of jewellery. They would have liked this part of the adventure to go on longer than it did. But quite soon they were all sniffing the air and saying "What is it?" and "Did you smell something?" and "Where's it coming from?" For a heavenly smell, warm and golden, as if from all the most delicious fruits and flowers of the world, was coming up to them from somewhere ahead.

"It's coming from that valley with the lake in it," said Fledge.

"So it is," said Digory. "And look! There's a green hill at the far end of the lake. And look how blue the water is."

"It must be the Place," said all three.

Fledge came lower and lower in wide circles. The icy peaks rose up higher and higher above. The air came up warmer and sweeter every moment, so sweet that it almost brought the tears to your eyes. Fledge was now gliding with his wings spread out motionless on each side, and his hoofs pawing for the ground. The steep green hill was rushing towards them. A moment later he alighted on its slope, a little awkwardly. The children rolled off, fell without hurting themselves on the warm, fine grass, and stood up panting a little.

They were three-quarters of the way up the hill, and set out at once to climb to the top. (I don't think Fledge could have managed this without his wings to balance him and to give him the help of a flutter now and then.) All round the very top of the hill ran a high wall of green turf. Inside the wall trees were growing. Their branches hung out over the wall; their leaves showed not only green but also blue and silver when the wind stirred them. When the travellers reached the top they walked nearly all the way round it outside the green wall before they found the gates: high gates of gold, fast shut, facing due east.

Up till now I think Fledge and Polly had had the idea that they would go in with Digory. But they thought so no longer. You never saw a place which was so obviously private. You could see at a glance that it belonged to someone else. Only a fool would dream of going in unless he had been sent there on very special business. Digory himself understood at once that the others wouldn't and couldn't come in with him. He went forward to the gates alone.

When he had come close up to them he saw words written on the gold with silver letters; something like this:

> *Come in by the gold gates or not at all,*
> *Take of my fruit for others or forbear,*
> *For those who steal or those who climb my wall*
> *Shall find their heart's desire and find despair.*

"*Take of my fruit for others,*" said Digory to himself. "Well, that's what I'm going to do. It means I mustn't eat any myself, I suppose. I don't know what all that jaw in the last line is about. *Come in by the gold gates.* Well who'd want to climb a wall if he could get in by a gate! But how do the gates open?" He laid his hand on them and instantly they swung apart, opening inwards, turning on their hinges without the least noise.

Now that he could see into the place it looked more private than ever. He went in very solemnly, looking about him. Everything was very quiet inside. Even the fountain which rose near the middle of the garden made only the faintest sound. The lovely smell was all round him: it was a happy place but very serious.

He knew which was the right tree at once, partly because it stood in the very centre and partly because the great silver apples with which it was loaded shone so and cast a light of their own down on the shadowy places where the sunlight did not reach. He walked straight across to it, picked an apple, and put it in the breast pocket of his Norfolk jacket. But he couldn't help looking at it and smelling it before he put it away.

It would have been better if he had not. A terrible thirst and hunger came over him and a longing to taste that fruit. He put it hastily into his pocket; but there were plenty of others. Could it be wrong to taste one? After all, he thought, the notice on the gate might not have been exactly an order; it might have been only a piece of advice — and who cares about advice? Or even if it were an order, would he be disobeying it by eating an apple? He had already obeyed the part about taking one "for others".

While he was thinking of all this he happened to look up through the branches towards the top of the tree. There, on a branch above his head, a wonderful bird was roosting. I say "roosting" because it seemed almost asleep; perhaps not quite. The tiniest slit of one eye was open. It was larger than an eagle, its breast saffron, its head crested with scarlet, and its tail purple.

"And it just shows," said Digory afterwards when he was telling the story to the others, "that you can't be too careful in these magical places. You never know what may be watching you." But I think Digory would not have taken an apple for himself in any case. Things like Do Not Steal were, I think, hammered into boys' heads a good deal harder in those days than they are now. Still, we can never be certain.

Digory was just turning to go back to the gates when he stopped to have one last look around. He got a terrible shock. He was not alone. There, only a few yards away from him, stood the Witch. She was just throwing away the core of an apple which she had eaten. The juice was darker than you would expect and had made a horrid stain round her mouth. Digory guessed at once that she must have climbed in over the wall. And he began to see that there might be some sense in that last line about getting your heart's desire and getting despair along with it. For the Witch looked stronger and prouder than ever, and even, in a way, triumphant; but her face was deadly white, white as salt.

All this flashed through Digory's mind in a second; then he took to his heels and ran for the gates as hard as he could pelt; the Witch after him. As soon as he was out, the gates closed behind him of their own accord. That gave him the lead but not for long. By the time he had reached the others and was shouting out "Quick, get on, Polly! Get up, Fledge", the Witch had climbed the wall, or vaulted over it, and was close behind him again.

"Stay where you are," cried Digory, turning round to face her, "or we'll all vanish. Don't come an inch nearer."

"Foolish boy," said the Witch. "Why do you run from me? I mean you no harm. If you do not stop and listen to me now, you will miss some knowledge that would have made you happy all your life."

"Well I don't want to hear it, thanks," said Digory. But he did.

"I know what errand you have come on," continued the Witch. "For it was I who was close beside you in the woods last night and heard all your counsels. You have plucked fruit in the garden yonder. You have it in your pocket now. And you are going to carry it back, untasted, to the Lion; for *him* to eat, for *him* to use. You simpleton! Do you know what that fruit is? I will tell you. It is the apple of youth, the apple of life. I know, for I have tasted it; and I feel already such changes in myself that I know I shall never grow old or die. Eat it, Boy, eat it; and you and I will both live forever and be king and queen of this whole world — or of your world, if we decide to go back there."

"No thanks," said Digory, "I don't know that I care much about living on and on after everyone I know is dead. I'd rather live an ordinary time and die and go to Heaven."

"But what about this Mother of yours whom you pretend to love so?"

"What's she got to do with it?" said Digory.

"Do you not see, Fool, that one bite of that apple would heal her? You have it in your pocket. We are here by ourselves and the Lion is far away. Use your Magic and go back to your own world. A minute later you can be at your Mother's bedside, giving her the fruit. Five minutes later you will see the colour coming back to her face. She will tell you the pain is gone. Soon she will tell you she feels stronger. Then she will fall asleep — think of that; hours of sweet natural sleep, without pain, without drugs. Next day everyone will be saying how wonderfully she has recovered. Soon she will be quite well again. All will be well again. Your home will be happy again. You will be like other boys."

"Oh!" gasped Digory as if he had been hurt, and put his hand to his head. For he now knew that the most terrible choice lay before him.

"What has the Lion ever done for you that you should

be his slave?" said the Witch. "What can he do to you once you are back in your own world? And what would your Mother think if she knew that you *could* have taken her pain away and given her back her life and saved your Father's heart from being broken, and that you *wouldn't* — that you'd rather run messages for a wild animal in a strange world that is no business of yours?"

"I — I don't think he is a wild animal," said Digory in a dried-up sort of voice. "He is — I don't know —"

"Then he is something worse," said the Witch. "Look what he has done to you already; look how heartless he has made you. That is what he does to everyone who listens to him. Cruel, pitiless boy! you would let your own Mother die rather than —"

"Oh shut up," said the miserable Digory, still in the same voice. "Do you think I don't see? But I — I promised."

"Ah, but you didn't know what you were promising. And no one here can prevent you."

"Mother herself," said Digory, getting the words out with difficulty, "wouldn't like it — awfully strict about keeping promises — and not stealing — and all that sort of thing. *She'd* tell me not to do it — quick as anything — if she was here."

"But she need never know," said the Witch, speaking more sweetly than you would have thought anyone with so fierce a face could speak. "You wouldn't tell her how you'd got the apple. Your Father need never know. No one in your world need know anything about this whole story. You needn't take the little girl back with you, you know."

That was where the Witch made her fatal mistake. Of course Digory knew that Polly could get away by her own ring as easily as he could get away by his. But apparently the Witch didn't know this. And the meanness of the suggestion that he should leave Polly behind suddenly made all the other things the Witch had been saying to him sound false and hollow. And even in the midst of all his misery, his head suddenly cleared, and he said (in a different and much louder voice):

"Look here; where do *you* come into all this? Why are *you* so precious fond of *my* Mother all of a sudden? What's it got to do with you? What's your game?"

"Good for you, Digs," whispered Polly in his ear. "Quick! Get away *now*." She hadn't dared to say anything all through the argument because, you see, it wasn't *her* Mother who was dying.

"Up then," said Digory, heaving her on to Fledge's back and then scrambling up as quickly as he could. The horse spread its wings.

"Go then, Fools," called the Witch. "Think of me, Boy, when you lie old and weak and dying, and remember how you threw away the chance of endless youth! It won't be offered you again."

They were already so high that they could only just hear her. Nor did the Witch waste any time gazing up at them; they saw her set off northward down the slope of the hill.

They had started early that morning and what happened in the garden had not taken very long, so that Fledge and Polly both said they would easily get back to Narnia before nightfall. Digory never spoke on the way back, and the others were shy of speaking to him. He was very sad and he wasn't even sure all the time that he had done the right thing; but whenever he remembered the shining tears in Aslan's eyes he became sure.

All day Fledge flew steadily with untiring wings; eastward with the river to guide him, through the mountains and over the wild wooded hills, and then over the great waterfall and down, and down, to where the woods of Narnia were darkened by the shadow of the mighty cliff, till at last, when the sky was growing red with sunset behind them, he saw a place where many creatures were gathered together by the riverside. And soon he could see Aslan himself in the midst of them. Fledge glided down, spread out his four legs, closed his wings, and landed cantering. Then he pulled up. The children dismounted. Digory saw all the animals, dwarfs, satyrs, nymphs, and other things drawing back to the left and right to make way for him. He walked up to Aslan, handed him the apple and said:

"I've brought you the apple you wanted, sir."

CHAPTER FOURTEEN

THE PLANTING OF THE TREE

"WELL done," said Aslan in a voice that made the earth shake. Then Digory knew that all the Narnians had heard those words and that the story of them would be handed down from father to son in that new world for hundreds of years and perhaps forever. But he was in no danger of feeling conceited for he didn't think about it at all now that he was face to face with Aslan. This time he found he could look straight into the Lion's eyes. He had forgotten his troubles and felt absolutely content.

"Well done, son of Adam," said the Lion again. "For this fruit you have hungered and thirsted and wept. No hand but yours shall sow the seed of the Tree that is to be the protection of Narnia. Throw the apple towards the river bank where the ground is soft."

Digory did as he was told. Everyone had grown so quiet that you could hear the soft thump where it fell into the mud.

"It is well thrown," said Aslan. "Let us now proceed to the Coronation of King Frank of Narnia and Helen his Queen."

The children now noticed these two for the first time. They were dressed in strange and beautiful clothes, and from their shoulders rich robes flowed out behind them to where four dwarfs held up the King's train and four river-nymphs the Queen's. Their heads were bare; but Helen had let her hair down and it made a great improvement in her appearance. But it was neither hair nor clothes that made them look so different from their old selves. Their faces had a new expression, especially the King's. All the sharpness and cunning and quarrelsomeness which he had picked up as a London cabby seemed to have been washed away, and the courage and kindness which he had always had were easier to see. Perhaps it was the air of the young world that had done it, or talking with Aslan, or both.

"Upon my word," whispered Fledge to Polly. "My old master's been changed nearly as much as I have! Why, he's a real master now."

"Yes, but don't buzz in my ear like that," said Polly. "It tickles so."

"Now," said Aslan, "some of you undo that tangle you have made with those trees and let us see what we shall find there."

Digory now saw that where four trees grew close together their branches had all been laced together or tied together with switches so as to make a sort of cage. The two Elephants with their trunks and a few dwarfs with their little axes soon got it all undone. There were three things inside. One was a young tree that seemed to be made of gold; the second was a young tree that seemed to be made of silver; but the third was a miserable object in muddy clothes, sitting hunched up between them.

"Gosh!" whispered Digory. "Uncle Andrew!"

To explain all this we must go back a bit. The Beasts, you remember, had tried planting and watering him. When the watering brought him to his senses, he found himself soaking wet, buried up to his thighs in earth (which was quickly turning into mud) and surrounded by more wild animals than he had ever dreamed of in his life before. It is perhaps not surprising that he began to scream and howl. This was in a way a good thing, for it at last persuaded everyone (even the Warthog) that he

was alive. So they dug him up again (his trousers were in
a really shocking state by now). As soon as his legs were
free he tried to bolt, but one swift curl of the Elephant's
trunk round his waist soon put an end to that. Everyone
now thought he must be safely kept somewhere till Aslan
had time to come and see him and say what should be

done about him. So they made a sort of cage or coop all
round him. They then offered him everything they could
think of to eat.

The Donkey collected great piles of thistles and threw
them in, but Uncle Andrew didn't seem to care about
them. The Squirrels bombarded him with volleys of nuts,
but he only covered his head with his hands and tried to
keep out of the way. Several birds flew to and fro

diligently dropping worms on him. The Bear was especially kind. During the afternoon he found a wild bees' nest and instead of eating it himself (which he would very much like to have done) this worthy creature brought it back to Uncle Andrew. But this was in fact the worst failure of all. The Bear lobbed the whole sticky mass over the top of the enclosure and unfortunately it hit Uncle Andrew slap in the face (not all the bees were dead). The Bear, who would not at all have minded being hit in the face by a honeycomb himself, could not understand why Uncle Andrew staggered back, slipped, and sat down. And it was sheer bad luck that he sat down on the pile of thistles. "And anyway," as the Warthog said, "quite a lot of honey has got into the creature's mouth and that's bound to have done it some good." They were really getting quite fond of their strange pet and hoped that Aslan would allow them to keep it. The cleverer ones were quite sure by now that at least some of the noises which came out of his mouth had a meaning. They christened him Brandy because he made that noise so often.

In the end, however, they had to leave him there for the night. Aslan was busy all that day instructing the new King and Queen and doing other important things, and could not attend to "poor old Brandy". What with the nuts, pears, apples, and bananas that had been thrown in to him, he did fairly well for supper; but it wouldn't be true to say that he passed an agreeable night.

"Bring out that creature," said Aslan. One of the Elephants lifted Uncle Andrew in its trunk and laid him at the Lion's feet. He was too frightened to move.

"Please, Aslan," said Polly, "could you say something to – to unfrighten him? And then could you say

something to prevent him from ever coming back here
again?"

"Do you think he *wants* to?" said Aslan.

"Well, Aslan," said Polly, "he might send someone else.
He's so excited about the bar off the lamp-post growing
into a lamp-post tree and he thinks —"

"He thinks great folly, child," said Aslan. "This world
is bursting with life for these few days because the song
with which I called it into life still hangs in the air and
rumbles in the ground. It will not be so for long. But I
cannot tell that to this old sinner, and I cannot comfort
him either; he has made himself unable to hear my voice.
If I spoke to him, he would hear only growlings and
roarings. Oh Adam's sons, how cleverly you defend
yourselves against all that might do you good! But I will
give him the only gift he is still able to receive."

He bowed his great head rather sadly, and breathed
into the Magician's terrified face. "Sleep," he said. "Sleep
and be separated for some few hours from all the
torments you have devised for yourself." Uncle Andrew
immediately rolled over with closed eyes and began
breathing peacefully.

"Carry him aside and lay him down," said Aslan.
"Now, dwarfs! Show your smith-craft. Let me see you
make two crowns for your King and Queen."

More Dwarfs than you could dream of rushed forward
to the Golden Tree. They had all its leaves stripped off,
and some of its branches torn off too, before you could
say Jack Robinson. And now the children could see that it
did not merely look golden but was of real, soft gold. It
had of course sprung up from the half-sovereigns which
had fallen out of Uncle Andrew's pocket when he was
turned upside down; just as the silver had grown up from

the half-crowns. From nowhere, as it seemed, piles of dry brushwood for fuel, a little anvil, hammers, tongs, and bellows were produced. Next moment (how those dwarfs loved their work!) the fire was blazing, the bellows were roaring, the gold was melting, the hammers were clinking. Two Moles, whom Aslan had set to dig (which was what they liked best) earlier in the day, poured out a pile of

precious stones at the dwarfs' feet. Under the clever fingers of the little smiths two crowns took shape — not ugly, heavy things like modern European crowns, but light, delicate, beautifully shaped circles that you could really wear and look nicer by wearing. The King's was set with rubies and the Queen's with emeralds.

When the crowns had been cooled in the river Aslan made Frank and Helen kneel before him and he placed the crowns on their heads. Then he said, "Rise up King and Queen of Narnia, father and mother of many kings that shall be in Narnia and the Isles and Archenland. Be just and merciful and brave. The blessing is upon you."

Then everyone cheered or bayed or neighed or

trumpeted or clapped its wings and the royal pair stood looking solemn and a little shy, but all the nobler for their shyness. And while Digory was still cheering he heard the deep voice of Aslan beside him, saying:

"Look!"

Everyone in that crowd turned its head, and then everyone drew a long breath of wonder and delight. A little way off, towering over their heads, they saw a tree which had certainly not been there before. It must have grown up silently, yet swiftly as a flag rises when you pull it up on a flagstaff, while they were all busied about the coronation. Its spreading branches seemed to cast a light rather than a shade, and silver apples peeped out like stars from under every leaf. But it was the smell which came from it, even more than the sight, that had made everyone draw in their breath. For a moment one could hardly think about anything else.

"Son of Adam," said Aslan, "you have sown well. And you, Narnians, let it be your first care to guard this Tree, for it is your Shield. The Witch of whom I told you has fled far away into the North of the world; she will live on there, growing stronger in dark Magic. But while that Tree flourishes she will never come down into Narnia. She dare not come within a hundred miles of the Tree, for its smell, which is joy and life and health to you, is death and horror and despair to her."

Everyone was staring solemnly at the Tree when Aslan suddenly swung round his head (scattering golden gleams of light from his mane as he did so) and fixed his large eyes on the children. "What is it, children?" he said, for he caught them in the very act of whispering and nudging one another.

"Oh – Aslan, sir," said Digory, turning red, "I forgot to

tell you. The Witch has already eaten one of those apples, one of the same kind that Tree grew from." He hadn't really said all he was thinking, but Polly at once said it for him (Digory was always much more afraid than she of looking a fool.)

"So we thought, Aslan," she said, "that there must be some mistake, and she can't really mind the smell of those apples."

"Why do you think that, Daughter of Eve?" asked the Lion.

"Well, she ate one."

"Child," he replied, "that is why all the rest are now a horror to her. That is what happens to those who pluck and eat fruits at the wrong time and in the wrong way. The fruit is good, but they loathe it ever after."

"Oh I see," said Polly. "And I suppose because she took it in the wrong way it won't work for her. I mean it won't make her always young and all that?"

"Alas," said Aslan, shaking his head. "It will. Things always work according to their nature. She has won her heart's desire; she has unwearying strength and endless days like a goddess. But length of days with an evil heart is only length of misery and already she begins to know it. All get what they want; they do not always like it."

"I — I nearly ate one myself, Aslan," said Digory. "Would I —"

"You would, child," said Aslan. "For the fruit always works — it must work — but it does not work happily for any who pluck it at their own will. If any Narnian, un-bidden, had stolen an apple and planted it here to protect Narnia, it would have protected Narnia. But it would have done so by making Narnia into another strong and cruel empire like Charn, not the kindly land I mean it to be. And the Witch tempted you to do another thing, my son, did she not?"

"Yes, Aslan. She wanted me to take an apple home to Mother."

"Understand, then, that it would have healed her; but not to your joy or hers. The day would have come when both you and she would have looked back and said it would have been better to die in that illness."

And Digory could say nothing, for tears choked him and he gave up all hopes of saving his Mother's life; but at the same time he knew that the Lion knew what would have happened, and that there might be things more terrible even than losing someone you love by death. But now Aslan was speaking again, almost in a whisper:

"That is what *would* have happened, child, with a stolen apple. It is not what will happen now. What I give you now will bring joy. It will not, in your world, give endless life, but it will heal. Go. Pluck her an apple from the Tree."

For a second Digory could hardly understand. It was as if the whole world had turned inside out and upside down. And then, like someone in a dream, he was walking across to the Tree, and the King and Queen were cheering him and all the creatures were cheering too. He plucked the apple and put it in his pocket. Then he came back to Aslan.

"Please," he said, "may we go home now?" He had forgotten to say "Thank you", but he meant it, and Aslan understood.

CHAPTER FIFTEEN

THE END OF THIS STORY AND THE BEGINNING OF ALL THE OTHERS

"You need no rings when I am with you," said the voice of Aslan. The children blinked and looked about them. They were once more in the Wood between the Worlds; Uncle Andrew lay on the grass, still asleep; Aslan stood beside them.

"Come," said Aslan, "it is time that you went back. But there are two things to see to first; a warning, and a command. Look here, children."

They looked and saw a little hollow in the grass, with a grassy bottom, warm and dry.

"When you were last here," said Aslan, "that hollow was a pool, and when you jumped into it you came to the world where a dying sun shone over the ruins of Charn. There is no pool now. That world is ended, as if it had never been. Let the race of Adam and Eve take warning."

"Yes, Aslan," said both the children. But Polly added, "But we're not quite as bad as that world, are we, Aslan?"

"Not yet, Daughter of Eve," he said. "Not yet. But you are growing more like it. It is not certain that some wicked one of your race will not find out a secret as evil as the Deplorable Word and use it to destroy all living things. And soon, very soon, before you are an old man and an old woman, great nations in your world will be ruled by tyrants who care no more for joy and justice and mercy than the Empress Jadis. Let your world beware. That is the warning. Now for the command. As soon as you can, take from this Uncle of yours his magic rings and bury them so that no one can use them again."

Both the children were looking up into the Lion's face as he spoke these words. And all at once (they never knew exactly how it happened) the face seemed to be a sea of tossing gold in which they were floating, and such a sweetness and power rolled about them and over them and entered them that they felt they had never really been happy or wise or good, or even alive and awake, before. And the memory of that moment stayed with them always, so that as long as they both lived, if ever they were sad or afraid or angry, the thought of all that golden goodness, and the feeling that it was still there, quite close, just round some corner or just behind some door, would come back and make them sure, deep down inside, that all was well. Next minute all three of them (Uncle Andrew now awake) came tumbling into the noise, heat, and hot smells of London.

They were on the pavement outside the Ketterleys' front door, and except that the Witch, the Horse, and the Cabby were gone, everything was exactly as they had left it. There was the lamp-post, with one arm missing; there was the wreck of the hansom cab; and there was the crowd. Everyone was still talking and people were kneeling beside the damaged policeman, saying things like, "He's coming round" or "How do you feel now, old chap?" or "The Ambulance will be here in a jiffy."

"Great Scott!" thought Digory, "I believe the whole adventure's taken no time at all."

Most people were wildly looking round for Jadis and the horse. No one took any notice of the children for no one had seen them go or noticed them coming back. As for Uncle Andrew, what between the state of his clothes and the honey on his face, he could not have been recognized by anyone. Fortunately the front door of the house was open and the housemaid was standing in the doorway staring at the fun (what a day that girl was having!) so the children had no difficulty in bustling Uncle Andrew indoors before anyone asked any questions.

He raced up the stairs before them and at first they were very afraid he was heading for his attic and meant to hide his remaining magic rings. But they needn't have bothered. What he was thinking about was the bottle in his wardrobe, and he disappeared at once into his bedroom and locked the door. When he came out again (which was not for a long time) he was in his dressing-gown and made straight for the bathroom.

"Can you get the other rings, Poll?" said Digory. "I want to go to Mother."

"Right. See you later," said Polly and clattered up the attic stairs.

Then Digory took a minute to get his breath, and then went softly into his Mother's room. And there she lay, as he had seen her lie so many other times, propped up on the pillows, with a thin, pale face that would make you cry to look at. Digory took the Apple of Life out of his pocket.

And just as the Witch Jadis had looked different when you saw her in our world instead of in her own, so the fruit of that mountain garden looked different too. There were of course all sorts of coloured things in the bedroom; the coloured counterpane on the bed, the wallpaper, the sunlight from the window, and Mother's pretty, pale blue dressing jacket. But the moment Digory took the Apple out of his pocket, all those things seemed to have scarcely any colour at all. Every one of them, even

the sunlight, looked faded and dingy. The brightness of
the Apple threw strange lights on the ceiling. Nothing else
was worth looking at: you couldn't look at anything else.
And the smell of the Apple of Youth was as if there was a
window in the room that opened on Heaven.

"Oh, darling, how lovely," said Digory's Mother.

"You will eat it, won't you? Please," said Digory.

"I don't know what the Doctor would say," she
answered. "But really – I almost feel as if I could."

He peeled it and cut it up and gave it to her piece by
piece. And no sooner had she finished it than she smiled
and her head sank back on the pillow and she was asleep:
a real, natural, gentle sleep, without any of those nasty
drugs, which was, as Digory knew, the thing in the whole
world that she wanted most. And he was sure now that
her face looked a little different. He bent down and kissed

her very softly and stole out of the room with a beating heart; taking the core of the apple with him. For the rest of that day, whenever he looked at the things about him, and saw how ordinary and unmagical they were, he hardly dared to hope; but when he remembered the face of Aslan he did hope.

That evening he buried the core of the Apple in the back garden.

Next morning when the Doctor made his usual visit, Digory leaned over the banisters to listen. He heard the Doctor come out with Aunt Letty and say:

"Miss Ketterley, this is the most extraordinary case I have known in my whole medical career. It is — it is like a miracle. I wouldn't tell the little boy anything at present; we don't want to raise any false hopes. But in my opinion —" then his voice became too low to hear.

That afternoon he went down the garden and whistled their agreed secret signal for Polly (she hadn't been able to get back the day before).

"What luck?" said Polly, looking over the wall. "I mean, about your Mother?"

"I think — I *think* it is going to be alright," said Digory. "But if you don't mind I'd really rather not talk about it yet. What about the rings?"

"I've got them all," said Polly. "Look, it's alright, I'm wearing gloves. Let's bury them."

"Yes, let's. I've marked the place where I buried the core of the Apple yesterday."

Then Polly came over the wall and they went together to the place. But, as it turned out, Digory need not have marked the place. Something was already coming up. It was not growing so that you could see it grow as the new trees had done in Narnia; but it was already well above ground. They got a trowel and buried all the magic rings, including their own ones, in a circle round it.

About a week after this it was quite certain that Digory's Mother was getting better. About a fortnight later she was able to sit out in the garden. And a month later that whole house had become a different place. Aunt Letty did everything that Mother liked; windows were opened, frowsy curtains were drawn back to brighten up the rooms, there were new flowers everywhere, and nicer things to eat, and the old piano was tuned and Mother took up her singing again, and had such games with Digory and Polly that Aunt Letty would say "I declare, Mabel, you're the biggest baby of the three."

When things go wrong, you'll find they usually go on getting worse for some time; but when things once start going right they often go on getting better and better. After about six weeks of this lovely life there came a long letter from Father in India, which had wonderful news in it. Old Great-Uncle Kirke had died and this meant, apparently, that Father was now very rich. He was going to retire and come home from India forever and ever. And the great big house in the country, which Digory had heard of all his life and never seen would now be their home; the big house with the suits of armour, the stables, the kennels, the river, the park, the hot-houses, the vineries, the woods, and the mountains behind it. So that Digory felt just as sure as you that they were all going to live happily ever after. But perhaps you would like to know just one or two things more.

Polly and Digory were always great friends and she came nearly every holidays to stay with them at their beautiful house in the country; and that was where she learned to ride and swim and milk and bake and climb.

In Narnia the Beasts lived in great peace and joy and neither the Witch nor any other enemy came to trouble that pleasant land for many hundred years. King Frank and Queen Helen and their children lived happily in Narnia and their second son became King of Archenland. The boys married nymphs and the girls married wood-gods and river-gods. The lamp-post which the Witch had planted (without knowing it) shone day and night in the Narnian forest, so that the place where it grew came to be called Lantern Waste; and when, many years later, another child from our world got into Narnia, on a snowy night, she found the light still burning. And that adventure was, in a way, connected with the ones I have just been telling you.

It was like this. The tree which sprang from the Apple that Digory planted in the back garden, lived and grew into a fine tree. Growing in the soil of our world, far out of the sound of Aslan's voice and far from the young air of Narnia, it did not bear apples that would revive a dying woman as Digory's Mother had been revived, though it did bear apples more beautiful than any others in England, and they were extremely good for you, though not fully magical. But inside itself, in the very sap of it, the tree (so to speak) never forgot that other tree in Narnia to which it belonged. Sometimes it would move mysteriously when there was no wind blowing: I think that when this happened there were high winds in Narnia and the English tree quivered because, at that moment, the Narnia tree was rocking and swaying in a strong south-western gale. However, that might be, it was proved later that there was still magic in its wood. For when Digory was quite middle-aged (and he was a famous learned man, a Professor, and a great traveller by that time) and the Ketterleys' old house belonged to him, there was a great storm all over the south of England which blew the tree down. He couldn't bear to have it simply chopped up for firewood, so he had part of the timber made into a wardrobe, which he put in his big house in the country. And though he himself did not discover the magic properties of that wardrobe, someone else did. That was the beginning of all the comings and goings between Narnia and our world, which you can read of in other books.

When Digory and his people went to live in the big country house, they took Uncle Andrew to live with them; for Digory's Father said, "We must try to keep the old fellow out of mischief, and it isn't fair that poor Letty should have him always on her hands." Uncle Andrew never tried any Magic again as long as he lived. He had learned his lesson, and in his old age he became a nicer and less selfish old man than he had ever been before. But he always liked to get visitors alone in the billiard-room and tell them stories about a mysterious lady, a foreign royalty, with whom he had driven about London. "A devilish temper she had," he would say. "But she was a dem fine woman, sir, a dem fine woman."

The Lion, the Witch and the Wardrobe

To Lucy Barfield

My dear Lucy,
I wrote this story for you, but when I began it I had not realized that girls grow quicker than books. As a result you are already too old for fairytales, and by the time it is printed and bound you will be older still. But some day you will be old enough to start reading fairytales again. You can then take it down from some upper shelf, dust it, and tell me what you think of it. I shall probably be too deaf to hear, and too old to understand, a word you say, but I shall still be

your affectionate Godfather,

C. S. LEWIS

CHAPTER ONE

LUCY LOOKS INTO A WARDROBE

ONCE there were four children whose names were Peter, Susan, Edmund and Lucy. This story is about something that happened to them when they were sent away from London during the war because of the air-raids. They were sent to the house of an old Professor who lived in the heart of the country, ten miles from the nearest railway station and two miles from the nearest post office. He had no wife and he lived in a very large house with a housekeeper called Mrs Macready and three servants. (Their names were Ivy, Margaret and Betty, but they do not come into the story much.) He himself was a very old man with shaggy white hair which grew over most of his face as well as on his head, and they liked him almost at once; but on the first evening when he came out to meet them at the front door he was so odd-looking that Lucy (who was the youngest) was a little afraid of him, and Edmund (who was the next youngest) wanted to laugh and had to keep on pretending he was blowing his nose to hide it.

As soon as they had said good night to the Professor and gone upstairs on the first night, the boys came into the girls' room and they all talked it over.

"We've fallen on our feet and no mistake," said Peter. "This is going to be perfectly splendid. That old chap will let us do anything we like."

"I think he's an old dear," said Susan.

"Oh, come off it!" said Edmund, who was tired

and pretending not to be tired, which always made him bad-tempered. "Don't go on talking like that."

"Like what?" said Susan; "and anyway, it's time you were in bed."

"Trying to talk like Mother," said Edmund. "And who are you to say when I'm to go to bed? Go to bed yourself."

"Hadn't we all better go to bed?" said Lucy. "There's sure to be a row if we're heard talking here."

"No there won't," said Peter. "I tell you this is the sort of house where no one's going to mind what we do. Anyway, they won't hear us. It's about ten minutes' walk from here down to that dining-room, and any amount of stairs and passages in between."

"What's that noise?" said Lucy suddenly. It was a far larger house than she had ever been in before and the thought of all those long passages and rows of doors leading into empty rooms was beginning to make her feel a little creepy.

"It's only a bird, silly," said Edmund.

"It's an owl," said Peter. "This is going to be a wonderful place for birds. I shall go to bed now. I say, let's go and explore tomorrow. You might find anything in a place like this. Did you see those mountains as we came along? And the woods? There might be eagles. There might be stags. There'll be hawks."

"Badgers!" said Lucy.

"Foxes!" said Edmund.

"Rabbits!" said Susan.

But when next morning came there was a steady

rain falling, so thick that when you looked out of the window you could see neither the mountains nor the woods nor even the stream in the garden.

"Of course it *would* be raining!" said Edmund. They had just finished their breakfast with the Professor and were upstairs in the room he had set apart for them – a long, low room with two windows looking out in one direction and two in another.

"Do stop grumbling, Ed," said Susan. "Ten to one it'll clear up in an hour or so. And in the meantime we're pretty well off. There's a wireless and lots of books."

"Not for me," said Peter; "I'm going to explore in the house."

Everyone agreed to this and that was how the adventures began. It was the sort of house that you never seem to come to the end of, and it was full of unexpected places. The first few doors they tried led only into spare bedrooms, as everyone had expected that they would; but soon they came to a very long room full of pictures and there they found a suit of armour; and after that was a room all hung with green, with a harp in one corner; and then came three steps down and five steps up, and then a kind of little upstairs hall and a door that led out on to a balcony, and then a whole series of rooms that led into each other and were lined with books – most of them very old books and some bigger than a Bible in a church. And shortly after that they looked into a room that was quite empty except for one big wardrobe; the sort that has a looking-glass in the door. There was nothing else in the room at all except a dead blue-bottle on the window-sill.

"Nothing there!" said Peter, and they all trooped out again – all except Lucy. She stayed behind because she thought it would be worth while trying the door of the wardrobe, even though she felt almost sure that it would be locked. To her surprise

it opened quite easily, and two moth-balls dropped out.

Looking into the inside, she saw several coats hanging up – mostly long fur coats. There was nothing Lucy liked so much as the smell and feel of fur. She immediately stepped into the wardrobe and got in among the coats and rubbed her face against them, leaving the door open, of course, because she knew that it is very foolish to shut oneself into any wardrobe. Soon she went further in and found that

there was a second row of coats hanging up behind
the first one. It was almost quite dark in there and
she kept her arms stretched out in front of her so as
not to bump her face into the back of the wardrobe.
She took a step further in — then two or three steps —
always expecting to feel woodwork against the tips
of her fingers. But she could not feel it.

"This must be a simply enormous wardrobe!"
thought Lucy, going still further in and pushing the
soft folds of the coats aside to make room for her.
Then she noticed that there was something crunching under her feet. "I wonder is that more moth-
balls?" she thought, stooping down to feel it with
her hand. But instead of feeling the hard, smooth
wood of the floor of the wardrobe, she felt something soft and powdery and extremely cold. "This is
very queer," she said, and went on a step or two
further.

Next moment she found that what was rubbing
against her face and hands was no longer soft fur
but something hard and rough and even prickly.
"Why, it is just like branches of trees!" exclaimed
Lucy. And then she saw that there was a light ahead
of her; not a few inches away where the back of the
wardrobe ought to have been, but a long way off.
Something cold and soft was falling on her. A
moment later she found that she was standing in the
middle of a wood at night-time with snow under her
feet and snowflakes falling through the air.

Lucy felt a little frightened, but she felt very
inquisitive and excited as well. She looked back over
her shoulder and there, between the dark tree-

trunks, she could still see the open doorway of the wardrobe and even catch a glimpse of the empty room from which she had set out. (She had, of course, left the door open, for she knew that it is a

very silly thing to shut oneself into a wardrobe.) It seemed to be still daylight there. "I can always get back if anything goes wrong," thought Lucy. She began to walk forward, *crunch-crunch* over the snow and through the wood towards the other light. In about ten minutes she reached it and found it was a lamp-post. As she stood looking at it, wondering why there was a lamp-post in the middle of a wood and wondering what to do next, she heard a pitter patter of feet coming towards her. And soon after that a very strange person stepped out from among the trees into the light of the lamp-post.

He was only a little taller than Lucy herself and he carried over his head an umbrella, white with snow. From the waist upwards he was like a man, but his legs were shaped like a goat's (the hair on them was glossy black) and instead of feet he had goat's hoofs. He also had a tail, but Lucy did not notice this at first because it was neatly caught up over the arm that held the umbrella so as to keep it from trailing in the snow. He had a red woollen muffler round his neck and his skin was rather reddish too. He had a strange, but pleasant little face, with a short pointed beard and curly hair, and out of the hair there stuck two horns, one on each side of his forehead. One of his hands, as I have said, held the umbrella: in the other arm he carried several brown-paper parcels. What with the parcels and the snow it looked just as if he had been doing his Christmas shopping. He was a Faun. And when he saw Lucy he gave such a start of surprise that he dropped all his parcels.

"Goodness gracious me!" exclaimed the Faun.

CHAPTER TWO

WHAT LUCY FOUND THERE

"GOOD EVENING," said Lucy. But the Faun was so busy picking up its parcels that at first it did not reply. When it had finished it made her a little bow.

"Good evening, good evening," said the Faun. "Excuse me — I don't want to be inquisitive — but should I be right in thinking that you are a Daughter of Eve?"

"My name's Lucy," said she, not quite understanding him.

"But you are — forgive me — you are what they call a girl?" said the Faun.

"Of course I'm a girl," said Lucy.

"You are in fact Human?"

"Of course I'm human," said Lucy, still a little puzzled.

"To be sure, to be sure," said the Faun. "How stupid of me! But I've never seen a Son of Adam or a Daughter of Eve before. I am delighted. That is to say —" and then it stopped as if it had been going to say something it had not intended but had remembered in time. "Delighted, delighted," it went on. "Allow me to introduce myself. My name is Tumnus."

"I am very pleased to meet you, Mr Tumnus," said Lucy.

"And may I ask, O Lucy Daughter of Eve," said Mr Tumnus, "how you have come into Narnia?"

"Narnia? What's that?" said Lucy.

"This is the land of Narnia," said the Faun, "where

we are now; all that lies between the lamp-post and the great castle of Cair Paravel on the eastern sea. And you – you have come from the wild woods of the west?"

"I – I got in through the wardrobe in the spare room," said Lucy.

"Ah!" said Mr Tumnus in a rather melancholy voice, "if only I had worked harder at geography when I was a little Faun, I should no doubt know all about those strange countries. It is too late now."

"But they aren't countries at all," said Lucy, almost laughing. "It's only just back there – at least – I'm not sure. It is summer there."

"Meanwhile," said Mr Tumnus, "it is winter in Narnia, and has been for ever so long, and we shall both catch cold if we stand here talking in the snow. Daughter of Eve from the far land of Spare Oom where eternal summer reigns around the bright city of War Drobe, how would it be if you came and had tea with me?"

"Thank you very much, Mr Tumnus," said Lucy. "But I was wondering whether I ought to be getting back."

"It's only just round the corner," said the Faun, "and there'll be a roaring fire – and toast – and sardines – and cake."

"Well, it's very kind of you," said Lucy. "But I shan't be able to stay long."

"If you will take my arm, Daughter of Eve," said Mr Tumnus, "I shall be able to hold the umbrella over both of us. That's the way. Now – off we go."

And so Lucy found herself walking through the

wood arm in arm with this strange creature as if they had known one another all their lives.

They had not gone far before they came to a place where the ground became rough and there were rocks all about and little hills up and little hills down. At the bottom of one small valley Mr Tumnus turned suddenly aside as if he were going to walk straight into an unusually large rock, but at the last moment Lucy found he was leading her into the entrance of a cave. As soon as they were inside she found herself blinking in the light of a wood fire. Then Mr Tumnus stooped and took a flaming piece of wood out of the fire with a neat little pair of tongs, and lit a lamp. "Now we shan't be long," he said, and immediately put a kettle on.

Lucy thought she had never been in a nicer place. It was a little, dry, clean cave of reddish stone with a carpet on the floor and two little chairs ("one for me and one for a friend," said Mr Tumnus) and a table and a dresser and a mantelpiece over the fire and above that a picture of an old Faun with a grey beard. In one corner there was a door which Lucy thought must lead to Mr Tumnus's bedroom, and on one wall was a shelf full of books. Lucy looked at these while he was setting out the tea things. They had titles like *The Life and Letters of Silenus* or *Nymphs and Their Ways* or *Men, Monks and Gamekeepers; a Study in Popular Legend* or *Is Man a Myth?*

"Now, Daughter of Eve!" said the Faun.

And really it was a wonderful tea. There was a nice brown egg, lightly boiled, for each of them, and then sardines on toast, and then buttered toast, and then

toast with honey, and then a sugar-topped cake. And
when Lucy was tired of eating the Faun began to talk.
He had wonderful tales to tell of life in the forest. He
told about the midnight dances and how the Nymphs
who lived in the wells and the Dryads who lived in the
trees came out to dance with the Fauns; about long
hunting parties after the milk-white stag who could
give you wishes if you caught him; about feasting and
treasure-seeking with the wild Red Dwarfs in deep
mines and caverns far beneath the forest floor; and
then about summer when the woods were green and

old Silenus on his fat donkey would come to visit them, and sometimes Bacchus himself, and then the streams would run with wine instead of water and the whole forest would give itself up to jollification for weeks on end. "Not that it isn't always winter now," he added gloomily. Then to cheer himself up he took out from its case on the dresser a strange little flute that looked as if it were made of straw and began to play. And the tune he played made Lucy want to cry and laugh and dance and go to sleep all at the same time. It must have been hours later when she shook herself and said:

"Oh, Mr Tumnus – I'm so sorry to stop you, and I do love that tune – but really, I must go home. I only meant to stay for a few minutes."

"It's no good *now*, you know," said the Faun, laying down its flute and shaking its head at her very sorrowfully.

"No good?" said Lucy, jumping up and feeling rather frightened. "What do you mean? I've got to go home at once. The others will be wondering what has happened to me." But a moment later she asked, "Mr Tumnus! Whatever is the matter?" for the Faun's brown eyes had filled with tears and then the tears began trickling down its cheeks, and soon they were running off the end of its nose; and at last it covered its face with its hands and began to howl.

"Mr Tumnus! Mr Tumnus!" said Lucy in great distress. "Don't! Don't! What is the matter? Aren't you well? Dear Mr Tumnus, do tell me what is wrong." But the Faun continued sobbing as if its heart would break. And even when Lucy went over

and put her arms round him and lent him her handkerchief, he did not stop. He merely took the handkerchief and kept on using it, wringing it out with both hands whenever it got too wet to be any more use, so that presently Lucy was standing in a damp patch.

"Mr Tumnus!" bawled Lucy in his ear, shaking him. "Do stop. Stop it at once! You ought to be ashamed of yourself, a great big Faun like you. What on earth are you crying about?"

"Oh – oh – oh!" sobbed Mr Tumnus, "I'm crying because I'm such a bad Faun."

"I don't think you're a bad Faun at all," said Lucy. "I think you are a very good Faun. You are the nicest Faun I've ever met."

"Oh – oh – you wouldn't say that if you knew," replied Mr Tumnus between his sobs. "No, I'm a bad Faun. I don't suppose there ever was a worse Faun since the beginning of the world."

"But what have you done?" asked Lucy.

"My old father, now," said Mr Tumnus; "that's his picture over the mantelpiece. He would never have done a thing like this."

"A thing like what?" said Lucy.

"Like what I've done," said the Faun. "Taken service under the White Witch. That's what I am. I'm in the pay of the White Witch."

"The White Witch? Who is she?"

"Why, it is she that has got all Narnia under her thumb. It's she that makes it always winter. Always winter and never Christmas; think of that!"

"How awful!" said Lucy. "But what does she pay *you* for?"

"That's the worst of it," said Mr Tumnus with a deep groan. "I'm a kidnapper for her, that's what I am. Look at me, Daughter of Eve. Would you believe that I'm the sort of Faun to meet a poor innocent child in the wood, one that had never done me any harm, and pretend to be friendly with it, and invite it home to my cave, all for the sake of lulling it asleep and then handing it over to the White Witch?"

"No," said Lucy. "I'm sure you wouldn't do anything of the sort."

"But I have," said the Faun.

"Well," said Lucy rather slowly (for she wanted to be truthful and yet not be too hard on him), "well, that was pretty bad. But you're so sorry for it that I'm sure you will never do it again."

"Daughter of Eve, don't you understand?" said the Faun. "It isn't something I *have* done. I'm doing it now, this very moment."

"What do you mean?" cried Lucy, turning very white.

"You are the child," said Tumnus. "I had orders from the White Witch that if ever I saw a Son of Adam or a Daughter of Eve in the wood, I was to catch them and hand them over to her. And you are the first I ever met. And I've pretended to be your friend and asked you to tea, and all the time I've been meaning to wait till you were asleep and then go and tell *Her*."

"Oh, but you won't, Mr Tumnus," said Lucy. "You won't, will you? Indeed, indeed you really mustn't."

"And if I don't," said he, beginning to cry again, "she's sure to find out. And she'll have my tail cut off, and my horns sawn off, and my beard plucked out, and she'll wave her wand over my beautiful cloven hoofs and turn them into horrid solid hoofs like a wretched horse's. And if she is extra and specially angry she'll turn me into stone and I shall be only a statue of a Faun in her horrible house until the four thrones at Cair Paravel are filled – and goodness knows when that will happen, or whether it will ever happen at all."

"I'm very sorry, Mr Tumnus," said Lucy. "But please let me go home."

"Of course I will," said the Faun. "Of course I've got to. I see that now. I hadn't known what Humans were like before I met you. Of course I can't give you up to the Witch; not now that I know you. But we must be off at once. I'll see you back to the lamp-post. I suppose you can find your own way from there back to Spare Oom and War Drobe?"

"I'm sure I can," said Lucy.

"We must go as quietly as we can," said Mr

Tumnus. "The whole wood is full of *her* spies. Even some of the trees are on her side."

They both got up and left the tea things on the table, and Mr Tumnus once more put up his umbrella and gave Lucy his arm, and they went out into the snow. The journey back was not at all like the journey to the Faun's cave; they stole along as quickly as they could, without speaking a word, and Mr Tumnus kept to the darkest places. Lucy was relieved when they reached the lamp-post again.

"Do you know your way from here, Daughter of Eve?" said Tumnus.

Lucy looked very hard between the trees and could just see in the distance a patch of light that looked like daylight. "Yes," she said, "I can see the wardrobe door."

"Then be off home as quick as you can," said the Faun, "and – c-can you ever forgive me for what I meant to do?"

"Why, of course I can," said Lucy, shaking him heartily by the hand. "And I do hope you won't get into dreadful trouble on my account."

"Farewell, Daughter of Eve," said he. "Perhaps I may keep the handkerchief?"

"Rather!" said Lucy, and then ran towards the far off patch of daylight as quickly as her legs would carry her. And presently instead of rough branches brushing past her she felt coats, and instead of crunching snow under her feet she felt wooden boards, and all at once she found herself jumping out of the wardrobe into the same empty room from which the whole adventure had started. She shut the wardrobe door tightly behind her and looked around, panting for breath. It was still raining and she could hear the voices of the others in the passage.

"I'm here," she shouted. "I'm here. I've come back, I'm all right."

CHAPTER THREE

EDMUND AND THE WARDROBE

Lucy ran out of the empty room into the passage and found the other three.

"It's all right," she repeated, "I've come back."

"What on earth are you talking about, Lucy?" asked Susan.

"Why? said Lucy in amazement, "haven't you all been wondering where I was?"

"So you've been hiding, have you?" said Peter. "Poor old Lu, hiding and nobody noticed! You'll have to hide longer than that if you want people to start looking for you."

"But I've been away for hours and hours," said Lucy.

The others all stared at one another.

"Batty!" said Edmund, tapping his head. "Quite batty."

"What do you mean, Lu?" asked Peter.

"What I said," answered Lucy. "It was just after breakfast when I went into the wardrobe, and I've been away for hours and hours, and had tea, and all sorts of things have happened."

"Don't be silly, Lucy," said Susan. "We've only just come out of that room a moment ago, and you were there then."

"She's not being silly at all," said Peter, "she's just making up a story for fun, aren't you, Lu? And why shouldn't she?"

"No, Peter, I'm not," she said. "It's – it's a magic

wardrobe. There's a wood inside it, and it's snowing, and there's a Faun and a Witch and it's called Narnia; come and see."

The others did not know what to think, but Lucy was so excited that they all went back with her into the room. She rushed ahead of them, flung open the door of the wardrobe and cried, "Now! go in and see for yourselves."

"Why, you goose," said Susan, putting her head inside and pulling the fur coats apart, "it's just an ordinary wardrobe; look! there's the back of it."

Then everyone looked in and pulled the coats apart; and they all saw – Lucy herself saw – a perfectly ordinary wardrobe. There was no wood and no snow, only the back of the wardrobe, with hooks on it. Peter went in and rapped his knuckles on it to make sure that it was solid.

"A jolly good hoax, Lu," he said as he came out again; "you have really taken us in, I must admit. We half believed you."

"But it wasn't a hoax at all," said Lucy, "really and truly. It was all different a moment ago. Honestly it was. I promise."

"Come, Lu," said Peter, "that's going a bit far. You've had your joke. Hadn't you better drop it now?"

Lucy grew very red in the face and tried to say something, though she hardly knew what she was trying to say, and burst into tears.

For the next few days she was very miserable. She could have made it up with the others quite easily at any moment if she could have brought herself to say that the whole thing was only a story made up for fun. But Lucy was a very truthful girl and she knew that she was really in the right; and she could not bring herself to say this. The others who thought she was telling a lie, and a silly lie too, made her very unhappy. The two elder ones did this without meaning to do it, but Edmund could be spiteful, and on this occasion he was spiteful. He sneered and jeered at Lucy and kept on asking her if she'd found any other new countries in other cupboards all over the house. What made it worse was that these days ought to have been delightful. The weather was fine and they were out of doors from morning to night, bathing, fishing, climbing trees, and lying in the heather. But Lucy could not properly enjoy any of it. And so things went on until the next wet day.

That day, when it came to the afternoon and there was still no sign of a break in the weather, they decided to play hide-and-seek. Susan was "It" and as soon as the others scattered to hide, Lucy went to the room where the wardrobe was. She did not mean to hide in the wardrobe, because she knew that would only set the others talking again about the whole wretched business. But she did want to have one more look inside it; for by this time she was beginning to wonder herself whether Narnia and the Faun had not been a dream. The house was so large and complicated and full of hiding-places that she thought she would have time to have one look into the wardrobe and then hide somewhere else. But as soon as she reached it she heard steps in the passage outside, and then there was nothing for it but to jump into the wardrobe and hold the

door closed behind her. She did not shut it properly
because she knew that it is very silly to shut oneself into
a wardrobe, even if it is not a magic one.

Now the steps she had heard were those of Edmund;
and he came into the room just in time to see Lucy vanishing into the wardrobe. He at once decided to get
into it himself – not because he thought it a particularly good place to hide but because he wanted to go on
teasing her about her imaginary country. He opened
the door. There were the coats hanging up as usual,
and a smell of mothballs, and darkness and silence,
and no sign of Lucy. "She thinks I'm Susan come to
catch her," said Edmund to himself, "and so she's
keeping very quiet in at the back." He jumped in and

shut the door, forgetting what a very foolish thing this
is to do. Then he began feeling about for Lucy in the
dark. He had expected to find her in a few seconds and
was very surprised when he did not. He decided to open
the door again and let in some light. But he could not

find the door either. He didn't like this at all and began
groping wildly in every direction; he even shouted out,
"Lucy! Lu! Where are you? I know you're here."

There was no answer and Edmund noticed that his
own voice had a curious sound — not the sound you
expect in a cupboard, but a kind of open-air sound. He
also noticed that he was unexpectedly cold; and then
he saw a light.

"Thank goodness," said Edmund, "the door must
have swung open of its own accord." He forgot all
about Lucy and went towards the light, which he
thought was the open door of the wardrobe. But
instead of finding himself stepping out into the spare
room he found himself stepping out from the shadow
of some thick dark fir trees into an open place in the
middle of a wood.

There was crisp, dry snow under his feet and more
snow lying on the branches of the trees. Overhead
there was pale blue sky, the sort of sky one sees on a
fine winter day in the morning. Straight ahead of him

he saw between the tree-trunks the sun, just rising, very red and clear. Everything was perfectly still, as if he were the only living creature in that country. There was not even a robin or a squirrel among the trees, and the wood stretched as far as he could see in every direction. He shivered.

He now remembered that he had been looking for Lucy; and also how unpleasant he had been to her about her "imaginary country" which now turned out not to have been imaginary at all. He thought that she must be somewhere quite close and so he shouted, "Lucy! Lucy! I'm here too — Edmund."

There was no answer.

"She's angry about all the things I've been saying lately," thought Edmund. And though he did not like to admit that he had been wrong, he also did not much like being alone in this strange, cold, quiet place; so he shouted again.

"I say, Lu! I'm sorry I didn't believe you. I see now you were right all along. Do come out. Make it Pax."

Still there was no answer.

"Just like a girl," said Edmund to himself, "sulking somewhere, and won't accept an apology." He looked round him again and decided he did not much like this place, and had almost made up his mind to go home, when he heard, very far off in the wood, a sound of bells. He listened and the sound came nearer and nearer and at last there swept into sight a sledge drawn by two reindeer.

The reindeer were about the size of Shetland ponies and their hair was so white that even the snow hardly looked white compared with them; their branching horns were gilded and shone like something on fire when the sunrise caught them. Their harness was of scarlet leather and covered with bells. On the sledge, driving the reindeer, sat a fat dwarf who would have been about three feet high if he had been standing. He was dressed in polar bear's fur and on his head he wore a red hood with a long gold tassel hanging down from its point; his huge beard covered his knees and served him instead of a rug. But behind him, on a much higher seat in the middle of the sledge sat a very different person – a great lady, taller than any woman that Edmund had ever seen. She also was covered in white fur up to her throat and held a long straight golden wand in her right hand and wore a golden crown on her head. Her face was white – not merely pale, but white like snow or paper or icing-sugar, except for her very red mouth. It was a beautiful face in other respects, but proud and cold and stern.

The sledge was a fine sight as it came sweeping towards Edmund with the bells jingling and the dwarf cracking his whip and the snow flying up on each side of it.

"Stop!" said the Lady, and the dwarf pulled the reindeer up so sharp that they almost sat down. Then they recovered themselves and stood champing their bits and blowing. In the frosty air the breath coming out of their nostrils looked like smoke.

"And what, pray, are you?" said the Lady, looking hard at Edmund.

"I'm – I'm – my name's Edmund," said Edmund rather awkwardly. He did not like the way she looked at him.

The Lady frowned, "Is that how you address a Queen?" she asked, looking sterner than ever.

"I beg your pardon, your Majesty, I didn't know," said Edmund.

"Not know the Queen of Narnia?" cried she. "Ha! You shall know us better hereafter. But I repeat — what are you?"

"Please, your Majesty," said Edmund, "I don't know what you mean. I'm at school — at least I was — it's the holidays now."

CHAPTER FOUR

TURKISH DELIGHT

"BUT what *are* you?" said the Queen again. "Are you a great overgrown dwarf that has cut off its beard?"

"No, your Majesty," said Edmund, "I never had a beard, I'm a boy."

"A boy!" said she. "Do you mean you are a Son of Adam?"

Edmund stood still, saying nothing. He was too confused by this time to understand what the question meant.

"I see you are an idiot, whatever else you may be," said the Queen. "Answer me, once and for all, or I shall lose my patience. Are you human?"

"Yes, your Majesty," said Edmund.

"And how, pray, did you come to enter my dominions?"

"Please, your Majesty, I came in through a wardrobe."

"A wardrobe? What do you mean?"

"I – I opened a door and just found myself here, your Majesty," said Edmund.

"Ha!" said the Queen, speaking more to herself than to him. "A door. A door from the world of men! I have heard of such things. This may wreck all. But he is only one, and he is easily dealt with." As she spoke these words she rose from her seat and looked Edmund full in the face, her eyes flaming; at the same moment she raised her wand. Edmund felt sure that she was going to do something dreadful but he seemed unable to move. Then, just as he gave himself up for lost, she appeared to change her mind.

"My poor child," she said in quite a different voice, "how cold you look! Come and sit with me here on the sledge and I will put my mantle round you and we will talk."

Edmund did not like this arrangement at all but he dared not disobey; he stepped on to the sledge and sat at her feet, and she put a fold of her fur mantle round him and tucked it well in.

"Perhaps something hot to drink?" said the Queen. "Should you like that?"

"Yes please, your Majesty," said Edmund, whose teeth were chattering.

The Queen took from somewhere among her wrappings a very small bottle which looked as if it were made of copper. Then, holding out her arm, she let one drop fall from it on the snow beside the sledge. Edmund saw the drop for a second in mid-air, shining like a diamond. But the moment it touched the snow there was a hissing sound and there stood a jewelled cup full of something that steamed. The dwarf immediately took this and handed it to Edmund with a bow and a smile; not a very nice smile. Edmund felt much better as he began to sip the hot drink. It was something he had never tasted before, very sweet and foamy and creamy, and it warmed him right down to his toes.

"It is dull, Son of Adam, to drink without eating," said the Queen presently. "What would you like best to eat?"

"Turkish Delight, please, your Majesty," said Edmund.

The Queen let another drop fall from her bottle on to the snow, and instantly there appeared a round box, tied with green silk ribbon, which, when opened, turned out to contain several pounds of the best Turkish Delight. Each piece was sweet and light to the very centre and Edmund had never tasted anything more delicious. He was quite warm now, and very comfortable.

While he was eating the Queen kept asking him questions. At first Edmund tried to remember that it is rude to speak with one's mouth full, but soon he forgot about this and thought only of trying to shovel down as much Turkish Delight as he could, and the more he ate the more he wanted to eat, and he never asked himself why the Queen should be so inquisitive. She got him to tell her that he had one brother and two sisters, and that one of his sisters had already been in Narnia and had met a Faun there, and that no one except himself and his brother and his sisters knew anything about Narnia. She seemed especially interested in the fact that there were four of them, and kept on coming back to it. "You are sure there are just four of you?" she asked. "Two Sons of Adam and two Daughters of Eve, neither more nor less?" and Edmund, with his mouth full of Turkish Delight, kept on saying, "Yes, I told you that before," and forgetting to call her "Your Majesty", but she didn't seem to mind now.

At last the Turkish Delight was all finished and Edmund was looking very hard at the empty box and wishing that she would ask him whether he would like some more. Probably the Queen knew quite well what he was thinking; for she knew, though Edmund did not, that this was enchanted Turkish Delight and that anyone who had once tasted it would want more and more of it, and would even, if they were allowed, go on eating it till they killed themselves. But she did not offer him any more. Instead, she said to him,

"Son of Adam, I should so much like to see your brother and your two sisters. Will you bring them to see me?"

"I'll try," said Edmund, still looking at the empty box.

"Because, if you did come again — bringing them with you of course — I'd be able to give you some more Turkish Delight. I can't do it now, the magic will only work once. In my own house it would be another matter."

"Why can't we go to your house now?" said Edmund. When he had first got on to the sledge he had been afraid that she might drive away with him to some unknown place from which he would not be able to get back; but he had forgotten about that fear now.

"It is a lovely place, my house," said the Queen. "I am sure you would like it. There are whole rooms full of Turkish Delight, and what's more, I have no children of my own. I want a nice boy whom I could bring up as a Prince and who would be King of Narnia when I am gone. While he was Prince he would wear a gold crown and eat Turkish Delight all day long; and you are much the cleverest and handsomest young man I've ever met. I think I would like to make you the Prince — some day, when you bring the others to visit me."

"Why not now?" said Edmund. His face had become very red and his mouth and fingers were sticky. He did not look either clever or handsome, whatever the Queen might say.

"Oh, but if I took you there now," said she, "I shouldn't see your brother and your sisters. I very much want to know your charming relations. You are to be the Prince and — later on — the King; that is understood. But you must have courtiers and nobles. I will make your brother a Duke and your sisters Duchesses."

"There's nothing special about *them*," said Edmund, "and, anyway, I could always bring them some other time."

"Ah, but once you were in my house," said the Queen, "you might forget all about them. You would be enjoying yourself so much that you wouldn't want the bother of going to fetch them. No. You must go back to your own country now and come to me another day, *with them*, you understand. It is no good coming without them."

"But I don't even know the way back to my own country," pleaded Edmund. "That's easy," answered the Queen. "Do you see that lamp?" She pointed with her wand and Edmund turned and saw the same lamp-post under which Lucy had met the Faun. "Straight on, beyond that, is the way to the World of Men. And now look the other way' – here she pointed in the opposite direction – "and tell me if you can see two little hills rising above the trees."

"I think I can," said Edmund.

"Well, my house is between those two hills. So next time you come you have only to find the lamp-post and look for those two hills and walk through the wood till you reach my house. But remember – you must bring the others with you. I might have to be very angry with you if you came alone."

"I'll do my best," said Edmund.

"And, by the way," said the Queen, "you needn't tell them about me. It would be fun to keep it a secret between us two, wouldn't it? Make it a surprise for them. Just bring them along to the two hills – a clever boy like you will easily think of some excuse for doing that – and when you come to my house you could just say "Let's see who lives here" or something like that. I am sure that would be best. If your sister has met one of the Fauns, she may have heard strange stories about me – nasty stories that might make her afraid to come to me. Fauns will say anything, you know, and now –"

"Please, please," said Edmund suddenly, "please couldn't I have just one piece of Turkish Delight to eat on the way home?"

"No, no," said the Queen with a laugh, "you must wait till next time." While she spoke, she signalled to the dwarf to drive on, but as the sledge swept away out of sight, the Queen waved to Edmund, calling out, "Next time! Next time! Don't forget. Come soon."

Edmund was still staring after the sledge when he heard someone calling his own name, and looking round he saw Lucy coming towards him from another part of the wood.

"Oh, Edmund!" she cried. "So you've got in too! Isn't it wonderful, and now –"

"All right," said Edmund, "I see you were right and it is a magic wardrobe after all. I'll say I'm sorry if you like. But where on earth have you been all this time? I've been looking for you everywhere."

"If I'd known you had got in I'd have waited for you," said Lucy, who was too happy and excited to notice how snappishly Edmund spoke or how flushed and strange his face was. "I've been having lunch with dear Mr Tumnus, the Faun, and he's very well and the White Witch has done nothing to him for letting me go, so he thinks she can't have found out and perhaps everything is going to be all right after all."

"The White Witch?" said Edmund; "who's she?"

"She is a perfectly terrible person," said Lucy. "She calls herself the Queen of Narnia though she has no right to be queen at all, and all the Fauns and Dryads and Naiads and Dwarfs and Animals – at least all the good ones — simply hate her. And she can turn people into stone and do all kinds of horrible things. And she has made a magic so that it is always winter in Narnia — always winter, but it never gets to Christmas. And she drives about on a sledge, drawn by reindeer, with her wand in her hand and a crown on her head."

Edmund was already feeling uncomfortable from having eaten too many sweets, and when he heard that the Lady he had made friends with was a dangerous witch he felt even more uncomfortable. But he still wanted to taste that Turkish Delight again more than he wanted anything else.

"Who told you all that stuff about the White Witch?" he asked.

"Mr Tumnus, the Faun," said Lucy.

"You can't always believe what Fauns say," said Edmund, trying to sound as if he knew far more about them than Lucy.

"Who said so?" asked Lucy.

"Everyone knows it," said Edmund; "ask anybody you like. But it's pretty poor sport standing here in the snow. Let's go home."

"Yes, let's," said Lucy. "Oh, Edmund, I *am* glad you've got in too. The others will have to believe in Narnia now that both of us have been there. What fun it will be!"

But Edmund secretly thought that it would not be as good fun for him as for her. He would have to admit that Lucy had been right, before all the others, and he felt sure the others would all be on the side of the Fauns and the animals; but he was already more than half on the side of the Witch. He did not know what he would say, or how he would keep his secret once they were all talking about Narnia.

By this time they had walked a good way. Then suddenly they felt coats around them instead of branches and next moment they were both standing outside the wardrobe in the empty room.

"I say," said Lucy, "you do look awful, Edmund. Don't you feel well?"

"I'm all right," said Edmund, but this was not true. He was feeling very sick.

"Come on then," said Lucy, "let's find the others. What a lot we shall have to tell them! And what wonderful adventures we shall have now that we're all in it together."

CHAPTER FIVE

BACK ON THIS SIDE OF THE DOOR

BECAUSE the game of hide-and-seek was still going on, it took Edmund and Lucy some time to find the others. But when at last they were all together (which happened in the long room, where the suit of armour was) Lucy burst out:

"Peter! Susan! It's all true. Edmund has seen it too. There *is* a country you can get to through the wardrobe. Edmund and I both got in. We met one another in there, in the wood. Go on, Edmund; tell them all about it."

"What's all this about, Ed?" said Peter.

And now we come to one of the nastiest things in this story. Up to that moment Edmund had been feeling sick, and sulky, and annoyed with Lucy for being right, but he hadn't made up his mind what to do. When Peter suddenly asked him the question he decided all at once to do the meanest and most spiteful thing he could think of. He decided to let Lucy down.

"Tell us, Ed," said Susan.

And Edmund gave a very superior look as if he were far older than Lucy (there was really only a year's difference) and then a little snigger and said, "Oh, yes, Lucy and I have been playing – pretending that all her story about a country in the wardrobe is true. Just for fun, of course. There's nothing there really."

Poor Lucy gave Edmund one look and rushed out of the room.

Edmund, who was becoming a nastier person every minute, thought that he had scored a great success, and went on at once to say, "There she goes again. What's the matter with her? That's the worst of young kids, they always —"

"Look here," said Peter, turning on him savagely, "shut up! You've been perfectly beastly to Lu ever since she started this nonsense about the wardrobe, and now you go playing games with her about it and setting her off again. I believe you did it simply out of spite."

"But it's all nonsense," said Edmund, very taken aback.

"Of course it's all nonsense," said Peter, "that's just the point. Lu was perfectly all right when we left home, but since we've been down here she seems to be either going queer in the head or else turning into a most frightful liar. But whichever it is, what good do you think you'll do by jeering and nagging at her one day and encouraging her the next?"

"I thought — I thought," said Edmund; but he couldn't think of anything to say.

"You didn't think anything at all," said Peter; "it's just spite. You've always liked being beastly to anyone smaller than yourself; we've seen that at school before now."

"Do stop it," said Susan; "it won't make things any better having a row between you two. Let's go and find Lucy."

It was not surprising that when they found Lucy, a good deal later, everyone could see that she had been crying. Nothing they could say to her made any difference. She stuck to her story and said:

"I don't care what you think, and I don't care what you say. You can tell the Professor or you can write to Mother or you can do anything you like. I know I've met a Faun in there and – I wish I'd stayed there and you are all beasts, beasts."

It was an unpleasant evening. Lucy was miserable and Edmund was beginning to feel that his plan wasn't working as well as he had expected. The two older ones were really beginning to think that Lucy was out of her mind. They stood in the passage talking about it in whispers long after she had gone to bed.

The result was the next morning they decided that they really would go and tell the whole thing to the Professor. "He'll write to Father if he thinks there is really something wrong with Lu," said Peter; "it's getting beyond us." So they went and knocked at the study door, and the Professor said "Come in," and got up and found chairs for them and said he was quite at their disposal. Then he sat listening to them with the tips of his fingers pressed together and never interrupting, till they had finished the whole story. After that he said nothing for quite a long time. Then he cleared his throat and said the last thing either of them expected:

"How do you know," he asked, "that your sister's story is not true?"

"Oh, but –" began Susan, and then stopped. Anyone could see from the old man's face that he was perfectly serious. Then Susan pulled herself together and said, "But Edmund said they had only been pretending."

"That is a point," said the Professor, "which

certainly deserves consideration; very careful consideration. For instance — if you will excuse me for asking the question — does your experience lead you to regard your brother or your sister as the more reliable? I mean, which is the more truthful?"

"That's just the funny thing about it, sir," said Peter. "Up till now, I'd have said Lucy every time."

"And what do you think, my dear?" said the Professor, turning to Susan.

"Well," said Susan, "in general, I'd say the same as Peter, but this couldn't be true — all this about the wood and the Faun."

"That is more than I know," said the Professor, "and a charge of lying against someone whom you have always found truthful is a very serious thing; a very serious thing indeed."

"We were afraid it mightn't even be lying," said Susan; "we thought there might be something wrong with Lucy."

"Madness, you mean?" said the Professor quite coolly. "Oh, you can make your minds easy about that. One has only to look at her and talk to her to see that she is not mad."

"But then," said Susan, and stopped. She had never dreamed that a grown-up would talk like the Professor and didn't know what to think.

"Logic!" said the Professor half to himself. "Why don't they teach logic at these schools? There are only three possibilities. Either your sister is telling lies, or she is mad, or she is telling the truth. You know she doesn't tell lies and it is obvious that she is not mad. For the moment then and unless any further evidence turns up, we must assume that she is telling the truth."

Susan looked at him very hard and was quite sure from the expression on his face that he was not making fun of them.

"But how could it be true, sir?" said Peter.

"Why do you say that?" asked the Professor.

"Well, for one thing," said Peter, "if it was real why doesn't everyone find this country every time they go to the wardrobe? I mean, there was nothing there when we looked; even Lucy didn't pretend there was."

"What has that to do with it?" said the Professor.

"Well, sir, if things are real, they're there all the time."

"Are they?" said the Professor; and Peter did not know quite what to say.

"But there was no time," said Susan. "Lucy had had no time to have gone anywhere, even if there was such a place. She came running after us the very moment we were out of the room. It was less than a minute, and she pretended to have been away for hours."

"That is the very thing that makes her story so likely to be true," said the Professor. "If there really is a door in this house that leads to some other world (and I should warn you that this is a very strange house, and even I know very little about it) — if, I say, she had got into another world, I should not be at all surprised to find that the other world had a separate time of its own; so that however long you stayed there it would never take up any of *our* time. On the other hand, I don't think many girls of her age would invent that idea for themselves. If she had been pretending, she would have hidden for a reasonable time before coming out and telling her story."

"But do you really mean, sir," said Peter, "that

there could be other worlds — all over the place, just round the corner — like that?"

"Nothing is more probable," said the Professor, taking off his spectacles and beginning to polish them, while he muttered to himself, "I wonder what they *do* teach them at these schools."

"But what are we to do?" said Susan. She felt

that the conversation was beginning to get off the point.

"My dear young lady," said the Professor, suddenly looking up with a very sharp expression at both of them, "there is one plan which no one has yet suggested and which is well worth trying."

"What's that?" said Susan.

"We might all try minding our own business," said he. And that was the end of that conversation.

After this things were a good deal better for Lucy. Peter saw to it that Edmund stopped jeering at her, and neither she nor anyone else felt inclined to talk about the wardrobe at all. It had become a rather

alarming subject. And so for a time it looked as if all the adventures were coming to an end; but that was not to be.

This house of the Professor's – which even he knew so little about – was so old and famous that people from all over England used to come and ask permission to see over it. It was the sort of house that is mentioned in guide books and even in histories; and well it might be, for all manner of stories were told about it, some of them even stranger than the one I am telling you now. And when parties of sightseers arrived and asked to see the house, the Professor always gave them permission, and Mrs Macready, the housekeeper, showed them round, telling them about the pictures and the armour, and the rare books in the library. Mrs Macready was not fond of children, and did not like to be interrupted when she was telling visitors all the things she knew. She had said to Susan and Peter almost on the first morning (along with a good many other instructions), "And please remember you're to keep out of the way whenever I'm taking a party over the house."

"Just as if any of us would *want* to waste half the morning trailing round with a crowd of strange grown-ups!" said Edmund, and the other three thought the same. That was how the adventures began for the second time.

A few mornings later Peter and Edmund were looking at the suit of armour and wondering if they could take it to bits when the two girls rushed into the room and said, "Look out! Here comes the Macready and a whole gang with her."

"Sharp's the word," said Peter, and all four made off through the door at the far end of the room. But when they had got out into the Green Room and beyond it, into the Library, they suddenly heard voices ahead of them, and realized that Mrs

Macready must be bringing her party of sightseers up the back stairs – instead of up the front stairs as they had expected. And after that – whether it was that they lost their heads, or that Mrs Macready was trying to catch them, or that some magic in the house had come to life and was chasing them into Narnia – they seemed to find themselves being followed everywhere, until at last Susan said, "Oh bother those trippers! Here – let's get into the Wardrobe Room till they've passed. No one will follow us in there." But the moment they were inside they heard the voices in the passage – and then someone fumbling at the door – and then they saw the handle turning.

"Quick!" said Peter, "there's nowhere else," and flung open the wardrobe. All four of them bundled inside it and sat there, panting, in the dark. Peter held the door closed but did not shut it; for, of course, he remembered, as every sensible person does, that you should never never shut yourself up in a wardrobe.

CHAPTER SIX

INTO THE FOREST

"I wish the Macready would hurry up and take all these people away," said Susan presently, "I'm getting horribly cramped."

"And what a filthy smell of camphor!" said Edmund.

"I expect the pockets of these coats are full of it," said Susan, "to keep away the moths."

"There's something sticking into my back," said Peter.

"And isn't it cold?" said Susan.

"Now that you mention it, it is cold," said Peter, "and hang it all, it's wet too. What's the matter with this place? I'm sitting on something wet. It's getting wetter every minute." He struggled to his feet.

"Let's get out," said Edmund, "they've gone."

"O-o-oh!" said Susan suddenly, and everyone asked her what was the matter.

"I'm sitting against a tree," said Susan, "and look! It's getting light – over there."

"By jove, you're right," said Peter, "and look there – and there. It's trees all round. And this wet stuff is snow. Why, I do believe we've got into Lucy's wood after all."

And now there was no mistaking it and all four children stood blinking in the daylight of a winter day. Behind them were coats hanging on pegs, in front of them were snow-covered trees.

Peter turned at once to Lucy.

"I apologize for not believing you," he said, "I'm sorry. Will you shake hands?"

"Of course," said Lucy, and did.

"And now," said Susan, "what do we do next?"

"Do?" said Peter, "why, go and explore the wood, of course."

"Ugh!" said Susan, stamping her feet, "it's pretty cold. What about putting on some of these coats?"

"They're not ours," said Peter doubtfully.

"I am sure nobody would mind," said Susan; "it isn't as if we wanted to take them out of the house; we shan't take them even out of the wardrobe."

"I never thought of that, Su," said Peter. "Of course, now you put it that way, I see. No one could say you had bagged a coat as long as you leave it in the wardrobe where you found it. And I suppose this whole country is in the wardrobe."

They immediately carried out Susan's very sensible plan. The coats were rather too big for them so that they came down to their heels and looked more like royal robes than coats when they had put them on. But they all felt a good deal warmer and each thought the others looked better in their new get-up and more suitable to the landscape.

"We can pretend we are Arctic explorers," said Lucy.

"This is going to be exciting enough without pretending," said Peter, as he began leading the way forward into the forest. There were heavy darkish clouds overhead and it looked as if there might be more snow before night.

"I say," began Edmund presently, "oughtn't we to

be bearing a bit more to the left, that is, if we are aiming for the lamp-post?" He had forgotten for the moment that he must pretend never to have been in the wood before. The moment the words were out of his mouth he realized that he had given himself away. Everyone stopped; everyone stared at him. Peter whistled.

"So you really were here," he said, "that time Lu said she'd met you in here – and you made out she was telling lies."

There was a dead silence. "Well, of all the poison-ous little beasts –" said Peter, and shrugged his shoulders and said no more. There seemed, indeed, no more to say, and presently the four resumed their journey; but Edmund was saying to himself, "I'll pay you all out for this, you pack of stuck-up, self-satisfied prigs."

"Where *are* we going anyway?" said Susan, chiefly for the sake of changing the subject.

"I think Lu ought to be the leader," said Peter; "goodness knows she deserves it. Where will you take us, Lu?"

"What about going to see Mr Tumnus?" said Lucy. "He's the nice Faun I told you about."

Everyone agreed to this and off they went walking briskly and stamping their feet. Lucy proved a good leader. At first she wondered whether she would be able to find the way, but she recognized an odd-looking tree on one place and a stump in another and brought them on to where the ground became uneven and into the little valley and at last to the very door of Mr Tumnus's cave. But there a terrible surprise awaited them.

The door had been wrenched off its hinges and broken to bits. Inside, the cave was dark and cold and had the damp feel and smell of a place that had not been lived in for several days. Snow had drifted in from the doorway and was heaped on the floor,

mixed with something black, which turned out to be the charred sticks and ashes from the fire. Someone had apparently flung it about the room and then stamped it out. The crockery lay smashed on the floor and the picture of the Faun's father had been slashed into shreds with a knife.

"This is a pretty good wash-out," said Edmund; "not much good coming here."

"What is this?" said Peter, stooping down. He had just noticed a piece of paper which had been nailed through the carpet to the floor.

"Is there anything written on it?" asked Susan.

"Yes, I think there is," answered Peter, "but I can't read it in this light. Let's get out into the open air."

They all went out in the daylight and crowded round Peter as he read out the following words:

The former occupant of these premises, the Faun Tumnus, is under arrest and awaiting his trial on a charge of High Treason against her Imperial Majesty Jadis, Queen of Narnia, Chatelaine of Cair Paravel, Empress of the Lone Islands, etc., also of comforting her said Majesty's enemies, harbouring spies and fraternizing with Humans.
> *signed* MAUGRIM, Captain of the Secret Police,
>> LONG LIVE THE QUEEN!

The children stared at each other.

"I don't know that I'm going to like this place after all," said Susan.

"Who is this Queen, Lu?" said Peter. "Do you know anything about her?"

"She isn't a real queen at all," answered Lucy; "she's a horrible witch, the White Witch. Everyone – all the wood people – hate her. She has made an enchantment over the whole country so that it is always winter here and never Christmas."

"I – I wonder if there's any point in going on," said Susan. "I mean, it doesn't seem particularly safe here and it looks as if it won't be much fun either. And it's getting colder every minute, and we've brought nothing to eat. What about just going home?"

"Oh, but we can't, we can't," said Lucy suddenly; "don't you see? We can't just go home, not after this. It is all on my account that the poor Faun has got into this trouble. He hid me from the Witch and showed me the way back. That's what it means by comforting the Queen's enemies and fraternizing with Humans. We simply must try to rescue him."

"A lot *we* could do! said Edmund, "when we haven't even got anything to eat!"

"Shut up — you!" said Peter, who was still very angry with Edmund. "What do you think, Susan?"

"I've a horrid feeling that Lu is right," said Susan. "I don't want to go a step further and I wish we'd never come. But I think we must try to do something for Mr Whatever-his-name is — I mean the Faun."

"That's what I feel too," said Peter. "I'm worried about having no food with us. I'd vote for going back and getting something from the larder, only there doesn't seem to be any certainty of getting into this country again when once you've got out of it. I think we'll have to go on."

"So do I," said both the girls.

"If only we knew where the poor chap was imprisoned!" said Peter.

They were all still wondering what to do next, when Lucy said, "Look! There's a robin, with such a red breast. It's the first bird I've seen here. I say! — I wonder can birds talk in Narnia? It almost looks as if it wanted to say something to us." Then she turned to the Robin and said, "Please, can you tell us where Tumnus the Faun has been taken to?" As she said this she took a step towards the bird. It at once flew away but only as far as to the next tree. There it perched and looked at them very hard as if it understood all they had been saying. Almost without noticing that they had done so, the four children went a step or two nearer to it. At this the Robin flew away again to the next tree and once more looked at them very hard. (You couldn't have found a robin with a redder chest or a brighter eye.)

"Do you know," said Lucy, "I really believe he means us to follow him."

"I've an idea he does," said Susan. "What do you think, Peter?"

"Well, we might as well try it," answered Peter. The Robin appeared to understand the matter thoroughly. It kept going from tree to tree, always a few yards ahead of them, but always so near that they could easily follow it. In this way it led them on, slightly downhill. Wherever the Robin alighted a little shower of snow would fall off the branch. Presently the clouds parted overhead and the winter sun came out and the snow all around them grew dazzlingly bright. They had been travelling in this way for about half an hour, with the two girls in front, when Edmund said to Peter, "if you're not still too high and mighty to talk to me, I've something to say which you'd better listen to."

"What is it?" asked Peter.

"Hush! Not so loud," said Edmund; "there's no good frightening the girls. But have you realized what we're doing?"

"What?" said Peter, lowering his voice to a whisper.

"We're following a guide we know nothing about. How do we know which side that bird is on? Why shouldn't it be leading us into a trap?"

"That's a nasty idea. Still — a robin, you know. They're good birds in all the stories I've ever read. I'm sure a robin wouldn't be on the wrong side."

"It if comes to that, which *is* the right side? How do we know that the Fauns are in the right and the Queen (yes, I know we've been *told* she's a witch) is in the wrong? We don't really know anything about either."

"The Faun saved Lucy."

"He *said* he did. But how do we know? And there's another thing too. Has anyone the least idea of the way home from here?"

"Great Scott!" said Peter, "I hadn't thought of that."

"And no chance of dinner either," said Edmund.

A DAY WITH THE BEAVERS

WHILE the two boys were whispering behind, both the girls suddenly cried "Oh!" and stopped.

"The robin!" cried Lucy, "the robin. It's flown away." And so it had — right out of sight.

"And now what are we to do?" said Edmund, giving Peter a look which was as much as to say "What did I tell you?"

"Sh! Look!" said Susan.

"What?" said Peter.

"There's something moving among the trees over there to the left."

They all stared as hard as they could, and no one felt very comfortable.

"There it goes again," said Susan presently.

"I saw it that time too," said Peter. "It's still there. It's just gone behind that big tree."

"What is it?" asked Lucy, trying very hard not to sound nervous.

"Whatever it is," said Peter, "it's dodging us. It's something that doesn't want to be seen."

"Let's go home," said Susan. And then, though nobody said it out loud, everyone suddenly realized the same fact that Edmund had whispered to Peter at the end of the last chapter. They were lost.

"What's it like?" said Lucy.

"It's — it's a kind of animal," said Susan; and then, "Look! Look! Quick! There it is."

They all saw it this time, a whiskered furry face

which had looked out at them from behind a tree. But this time it didn't immediately draw back. Instead, the animal put its paw against its mouth just as humans put their finger on their lips when they are signalling to you to be quiet. Then it disappeared again. The children all stood holding their breath.

A moment later the stranger came out from behind the tree, glanced all round as if it were afraid someone was watching, said "Hush", made signs to them to join it in the thicker bit of wood where it was standing, and then once more disappeared.

"I know what it is," said Peter; "it's a beaver. I saw the tail."

"It wants us to go to it," said Susan, "and it is warning us not to make a noise."

"I know," said Peter. "The question is, are we to go to it or not? What do you think, Lu?"

"I think it's a nice beaver," said Lucy.

"Yes, but how do we *know*?" said Edmund.

"Shan't we have to risk it?" said Susan. "I mean,

it's no good just standing here and I feel I want some dinner."

At this moment the Beaver again popped its head out from behind the tree and beckoned earnestly to them.

"Come on," said Peter, "let's give it a try. All keep

close together. We ought to be a match for one beaver if it turns out to be an enemy."

So the children all got close together and walked up to the tree and in behind it, and there, sure enough, they found the Beaver; but it still drew back, saying to them in a hoarse throaty whisper, "Further in, come further in. Right in here. We're not safe in the open!"

Only when it had led them into a dark spot where four trees grew so close together that their boughs met and the brown earth and pine needles could be seen underfoot because no snow had been able to fall there, did it begin to talk to them.

"Are you the Sons of Adam and the Daughters of Eve?" it said.

"We're some of them," said Peter.

"S-s-s-sh!" said the Beaver, "not so loud please. We're not safe even here."

"Why, who are you afraid of?" said Peter. "There's no one here but ourselves."

"There are the trees," said the Beaver. "They're always listening. Most of them are on our side, but there *are* trees that would betray us to *her*; you know who I mean," and it nodded its head several times.

"If it comes to talking about sides," said Edmund, "how do we know you're a friend?"

"Not meaning to be rude, Mr Beaver," added Peter, "but you see, we're strangers."

"Quite right, quite right," said the Beaver. "Here is my token." With these words it held up to them a little white object. They all looked at it in surprise, till suddenly Lucy said, "Oh, of course. It's my handkerchief – the one I gave to poor Mr Tumnus."

"That's right," said the Beaver. "Poor fellow, he got wind of the arrest before it actually happened and handed this over to me. He said that if anything happened to him I must meet you here and take you on to –" Here the Beaver's voice sank into silence and it gave one or two very mysterious nods. Then signalling to the children to stand as close around it as they possibly could, so that their faces were actually tickled by its whiskers, it added in a low whisper –

"They say Aslan is on the move – perhaps has already landed."

And now a very curious thing happened. None of the children knew who Aslan was any more than you do; but the moment the Beaver had spoken these words everyone felt quite different. Perhaps it has sometimes happened to you in a dream that someone says something which you don't understand but in the dream it feels as if it had some enormous meaning – either a terrifying one which turns the whole dream into a nightmare or else a lovely meaning too lovely to put into words, which makes the dream so beautiful that you remember it all your life and are always wishing you could get into that dream again. It was like that now. At the name of Aslan each one of the children felt something jump in its inside. Edmund felt a sensation of mysterious horror. Peter felt suddenly brave and adventurous. Susan felt as if some delicious smell or some delightful strain of music had just floated by her. And Lucy got the feeling you have when you wake up in the morning and realize that it is the beginning of the holidays or the beginning of summer.

"And what about Mr Tumnus," said Lucy; "where is he?"

"S-s-s-sh," said the Beaver, "not here. I must bring you where we can have a real talk and also dinner."

No one except Edmund felt any difficulty about trusting the beaver now, and everyone, including Edmund, was very glad to hear the word "dinner".

They therefore all hurried along behind their new friend who led them at a surprisingly quick pace, and always in the thickest parts of the forest, for over an hour. Everyone was feeling very tired and very hungry when suddenly the trees began to get thinner in front of them and the ground to fall steeply downhill. A minute later they came out under the open sky (the sun was still shining) and found themselves looking down on a fine sight.

They were standing on the edge of a steep, narrow valley at the bottom of which ran – at least it would have been running if it hadn't been frozen – a fairly large river. Just below them a dam had been built across this river, and when they saw it everyone suddenly remembered that of course beavers are always making dams and felt quite sure that Mr Beaver had made this one. They also noticed that he now had a sort of modest expression on his face – the sort of look people have when you are visiting a garden they've made or reading a story they've written. So it was only common politeness when Susan said, "What a lovely dam!" And Mr Beaver didn't say "Hush" this time but "Merely a trifle! Merely a trifle! And it isn't really finished!"

Above the dam there was what ought to have been a deep pool but was now, of course, a level floor of dark green ice. And below the dam, much lower down, was more ice, but instead of being smooth this was all frozen into the foamy and wavy shapes in which the water had been rushing along at the very moment when the frost came. And where the water had been trickling over and spurting through the dam there was now a glittering wall of icicles, as if the side of the dam had been covered all over with flowers and wreaths and festoons of the purest sugar. And out in the middle, and partly on top of the dam was a funny little house shaped rather like an enormous beehive and from a hole in the roof smoke was going up, so that when you saw it (especially if you were hungry) you at once thought of cooking and became hungrier than you were before.

That was what the others chiefly noticed, but Edmund noticed something else. A little lower down the river there was another small river which came down another small valley to join it. And looking up that valley, Edmund could see two small hills, and he was almost sure they were the two hills which the White Witch had pointed out to him when he parted from her at the lamp-post that other day. And then between them, he thought, must be her palace, only a mile off or less. And he thought about Turkish Delight and about being a King ("And I wonder how Peter will like that?" he asked himself) and horrible ideas came into his head.

"Here we are," said Mr Beaver, "and it looks as if Mrs Beaver is expecting us. I'll lead the way. But be careful and don't slip."

The top of the dam was wide enough to walk on, though not (for humans) a very nice place to walk because it was covered with ice, and though the frozen pool was level with it on one side, there was a nasty drop to the lower river on the other. Along this route Mr Beaver led them in single file right out to the middle where they could look a long way up the river and a long way down it. And when they had reached the middle they were at the door of the house.

"Here we are, Mrs Beaver," said Mr Beaver, "I've found them. Here are the Sons and Daughters of Adam and Eve' – and they all went in.

The first thing Lucy noticed as she went in was a

burring sound, and the first thing she saw was a kind-looking old she-beaver sitting in the corner with a thread in her mouth working busily at her sewing machine, and it was from it that the sound came. She stopped her work and got up as soon as the children came in.

"So you've come at last!" she said, holding out both her wrinkled old paws. "At last! To think that ever I should live to see this day! The potatoes are on boiling and the kettle's singing and I daresay, Mr Beaver, you'll get us some fish."

"That I will," said Mr Beaver, and he went out of the house (Peter went with him), and across the ice of the deep pool to where he had a little hole in the ice which he kept open every day with his hatchet. They took a pail with them. Mr Beaver sat down quietly at the edge of the hole (he didn't seem to mind it being so chilly), looked hard into it, then suddenly shot in his paw, and before you could say Jack Robinson had

whisked out a beautiful trout. Then he did it all over again until they had a fine catch of fish.

Meanwhile the girls were helping Mrs Beaver to fill the kettle and lay the table and cut the bread and put the plates in the oven to heat and draw a huge jug of beer for Mr Beaver from a barrel which stood in one corner of the house, and to put on the frying-pan and get the dripping hot. Lucy thought the Beavers had a very snug little home though it was not at all like Mr Tumnus's cave. There were no books or pictures, and instead of beds there were bunks, like on board ship, built into the wall. And there were hams and strings of onions hanging from the roof, and against the walls were gum boots and oilskins and hatchets and pairs of shears and spades and trowels and things for carrying mortar in and fishing-rods and fishing-nets and sacks. And the cloth on the table, though very clean, was very rough.

Just as the frying-pan was nicely hissing Peter and Mr Beaver came in with the fish which Mr Beaver had already opened with his knife and cleaned out in the open air. You can think how good the new-caught fish smelled while they were frying and how the hungry children longed for them to be done and how very much hungrier still they had become before Mr Beaver said, "Now we're nearly ready." Susan drained the potatoes and then put them all back in the empty pot to dry on the side of the range while Lucy was helping Mrs Beaver to dish up the trout, so that in a very few minutes everyone was drawing up their stools (it was all three-legged stools in the Beavers' house except for Mrs Beaver's own special rocking-chair beside the fire) and preparing to enjoy themselves. There was a jug of creamy milk for the children (Mr Beaver stuck to beer) and a great big lump of deep yellow butter in the middle of the table from which everyone took as much as he wanted to go with his potatoes, and all the children thought

– and I agree with them – that there's nothing to beat good freshwater fish if you eat it when it has been alive half an hour ago and has come out of the pan

half a minute ago. And when they had finished the fish Mrs Beaver brought unexpectedly out of the oven a great and gloriously sticky marmalade roll, steaming hot, and at the same time moved the kettle on to the fire, so that when they had finished the marmalade roll the tea was made and ready to be poured out. And when each person had got his (or her) cup of tea, each person shoved back his (or her) stool so as to be able to lean against the wall and gave a long sigh of contentment.

"And now," said Mr Beaver, pushing away his empty beer mug and pulling his cup of tea towards him, "if you'll just wait till I've got my pipe lit up and going nicely – why, now we can get to business. It's snowing again," he added, cocking his eye at the window. "That's all the better, because it means we shan't have any visitors; and if anyone should have been trying to follow you, why he won't find any tracks."

WHAT HAPPENED AFTER DINNER

"AND now," said Lucy, "do please tell us what's happened to Mr Tumnus."

"Ah, that's bad," said Mr Beaver, shaking his head. "That's a very, very bad business. There's no doubt he was taken off by the police. I got that from a bird who saw it done."

"But where's he been taken to?" asked Lucy.

"Well, they were heading northwards when they were last seen and we all know what that means."

"No, *we* don't," said Susan. Mr Beaver shook his head in a very gloomy fashion.

"I'm afraid it means they were taking him to her House," he said.

"But what'll they do to him, Mr Beaver?" gasped Lucy.

"Well," said Mr Beaver, "you can't exactly say for sure. But there's not many taken in there that ever comes out again. Statues. All full of statues they say it is – in the courtyard and up the stairs and in the hall. People she's turned" – (he paused and shuddered) "turned into stone."

"But, Mr Beaver," said Lucy, "can't we – I mean we *must* do something to save him. It's too dreadful and it's all on my account."

"I don't doubt you'd save him if you could, dearie," said Mrs Beaver, "but you've no chance of getting into that House against her will and ever coming out alive."

"Couldn't we have some stratagem?" said Peter. "I mean couldn't we dress up as something, or pretend to be – oh, pedlars or anything – or watch till she was gone out – or – oh, hang it all, there must be *some* way. This Faun saved my sister at his own risk, Mr Beaver. We can't just leave him to be – to be – to have that done to him."

"It's no good, Son of Adam," said Mr Beaver, "no good *your* trying, of all people. But now that Aslan is on the move –"

"Oh, yes! Tell us about Aslan!" said several voices at once; for once again that strange feeling – like the first signs of spring, like good news, had come over them.

"Who is Aslan?" asked Susan.

"Aslan?" said Mr Beaver. "Why, don't you know? He's the King. He's the Lord of the whole wood, but not often here, you understand. Never in my time or my father's time. But the word has reached us that he has come back. He is in Narnia at this moment. He'll settle the White Queen all right. It is he, not you, that will save Mr Tumnus."

"She won't turn him into stone too?" said Edmund.

"Lord love you, Son of Adam, what a simple thing to say!" answered Mr Beaver with a great laugh. "Turn *him* into stone? If she can stand on her two feet and look him in the face it'll be the most she can do and more than I expect of her. No, no. He'll put all to rights as it says in an old rhyme in these parts:

Wrong will be right, when Aslan comes in sight,
At the sound of his roar, sorrows will be no more,
When he bares his teeth, winter meets its death,
And when he shakes his mane, we shall have spring
                                                again.

You'll understand when you see him."

"But shall we see him?" asked Susan.

"Why, Daughter of Eve, that's what I brought you here for. I'm to lead you where you shall meet him," said Mr Beaver.

"Is – is he a man?" asked Lucy.

"Aslan a man!" said Mr Beaver sternly. "Certainly not. I tell you he is the King of the wood and the son of the great Emperor-beyond-the-Sea. Don't you know who is the King of Beasts? Aslan is a lion – *the* Lion, the great Lion."

"Ooh!" said Susan, "I'd thought he was a man. Is he – quite safe? I shall feel rather nervous about meeting a lion."

"That you will, dearie, and no mistake," said Mrs Beaver; "if there's anyone who can appear before Aslan without their knees knocking, they're either braver than most or else just silly."

"Then he isn't safe?" said Lucy.

"Safe?" said Mr Beaver; "don't you hear what Mrs Beaver tells you? Who said anything about safe? 'Course he isn't safe. But he's good. He's the King, I tell you."

"I'm longing to see him," said Peter, "even if I do feel frightened when it comes to the point."

"That's right, Son of Adam," said Mr Beaver, bringing his paw down on the table with a crash that made all the cups and saucers rattle. "And so you shall. Word has been sent that you *are* to meet him, to-morrow if you can, at the Stone Table."

"Where's that?" said Lucy.

"I'll show you," said Mr Beaver. "It's down the river, a good step from here. I'll take you to it!"

"But meanwhile what about poor Mr Tumnus?" said Lucy.

"The quickest way you can help him is by going to meet Aslan," said Mr Beaver, "once he's with us, then we can begin doing things. Not that we don't need you too. For that's another of the old rhymes:

When Adam's flesh and Adam's bone
Sits at Cair Paravel in throne,
The evil time will be over and done.

So things must be drawing near their end now he's come and you've come. We've heard of Aslan coming into these parts before — long ago, nobody can say when. But there's never been any of your race here before."

"That's what I don't understand, Mr Beaver," said Peter, "I mean isn't the Witch herself human?"

"She'd like us to believe it," said Mr Beaver, "and it's on that that she bases her claim to be Queen. But she's no Daughter of Eve. She comes of your father Adam's" — (here Mr Beaver bowed) "your father Adam's first wife, her they called Lilith. And she was one of the Jinn. That's what she comes from on one side. And on the other she comes of the giants. No, no, there isn't a drop of real human blood in the Witch."

"That's why she's bad all through, Mr Beaver," said Mrs Beaver.

"True enough, Mrs Beaver," replied he, "there may be two views about humans (meaning no offence to the present company). But there's no two views about things that look like humans and aren't."

"I've known good Dwarfs," said Mrs Beaver.

"So've I, now you come to speak of it," said her husband, "but precious few, and they were the ones least like men. But in general, take my advice, when you meet anything that's going to be human and isn't yet, or used to be human once and isn't now, or ought to be human and isn't, you keep your eyes on it and feel for your hatchet. And that's why the Witch is always on the lookout for any humans in Narnia. She's been watching for you this many a year, and if she knew there were four of you she'd be more dangerous still."

"What's that to do with it?" asked Peter.

"Because of another prophecy," said Mr Beaver. "Down at Cair Paravel – that's the castle on the sea coast down at the mouth of this river which ought to be the capital of the whole country if all was as it should be – down at Cair Paravel there are four thrones and it's a saying in Narnia time out of mind that when two Sons of Adam and two Daughters of Eve sit in those four thrones, then it will be the end not only of the White Witch's reign but of her life, and that is why we had to be so cautious as we came along, for if she knew about you four, your lives wouldn't be worth a shake of my whiskers!"

All the children had been attending so hard to what Mr Beaver was telling them that they had noticed nothing else for a long time. Then during the moment of silence that followed his last remark, Lucy suddenly said:

"I say – where's Edmund?"

There was a dreadful pause, and then everyone began asking "Who saw him last? How long has he been missing? Is he outside? and then all rushed to the door and looked out. The snow was falling thickly and steadily, the green ice of the pool had vanished under a thick white blanket, and from where the little house

stood in the centre of the dam you could hardly see either bank. Out they went, plunging well over their ankles into the soft new snow, and went round the house in every direction. "Edmund! Edmund!" they called till they were hoarse. But the silently falling snow seemed to muffle their voices and there was not even an echo in answer.

"How perfectly dreadful!" said Susan as they at last came back in despair. "Oh, how I wish we'd never come."

"What on earth are we to do, Mr Beaver?" said Peter.

"Do?" said Mr Beaver, who was already putting on his snow-boots, "do? We must be off at once. We haven't a moment to spare!"

"We'd better divide into four search parties," said Peter, "and all go in different directions. Whoever finds him must come back here at once and —"

"Search parties, Son of Adam?" said Mr Beaver; "what for?"

"Why, to look for Edmund, of course!"

"There's no point in looking for him," said Mr Beaver.

"What do you mean?" said Susan. "He can't be far away yet. And we've got to find him. What do you mean when you say there's no use looking for him?"

"The reason there's no use looking," said Mr Beaver, "is that we know already where he's gone!" Everyone stared in amazement. "Don't you understand?" said Mr Beaver. "He's gone to *her*, to the White Witch. He has betrayed us all."

"Oh, surely — oh, really!" said Susan, "he can't have done that."

"Can't he?" said Mr Beaver, looking very hard at the three children, and everything they wanted to say died on their lips, for each felt suddenly quite certain inside that this was exactly what Edmund had done.

"But will he know the way?" said Peter.

"Has he been in this country before?" asked Mr Beaver. "Has he ever been here alone?"

"Yes," said Lucy, almost in a whisper. "I'm afraid he has."

"And did he tell you what he'd done or who he'd met?"

"Well, no, he didn't," said Lucy.

"Then mark my words," said Mr Beaver, "he has already met the White Witch and joined her side, and been told where she lives. I didn't like to mention it before (he being your brother and all) but the moment I set eyes on that brother of yours I said to myself 'Treacherous'. He had the look of one who has been with the Witch and eaten her food. You can always tell them if you've lived long in Narnia; something about their eyes."

"All the same," said Peter in a rather choking sort of voice, "we'll still have to go and look for him. He is our brother after all, even if he is rather a little beast. And he's only a kid."

"Go to the Witch's House?" said Mrs Beaver. "Don't you see that the only chance of saving either him or yourselves is to keep away from her?"

"How do you mean?" said Lucy.

"Why, all she wants is to get all four of you (she's thinking all the time of those four thrones at Cair Paravel). Once you were all four inside her House her job would be done – and there'd be four new statues in her collection before you'd had time to speak. But she'll keep him alive as long as he's the only one she's got, because she'll want to use him as a decoy; as bait to catch the rest of you with."

"Oh, can *no* one help us?" wailed Lucy.

"Only Aslan," said Mr Beaver, "we must go on and meet him. That's our only chance now."

"It seems to me, my dears," said Mrs Beaver, "that it

is very important to know just *when* he slipped away. How much he can tell her depends on how much he heard. For instance, had we started talking of Aslan before he left? If not, then we may do very well, for she won't know that Aslan has come to Narnia, or that we are meeting him, and will be quite off her guard as far as *that* is concerned."

"I don't remember his being here when we were talking about Aslan —" began Peter, but Lucy interrupted him.

"Oh yes, he was," she said miserably; "don't you remember, it was he who asked whether the Witch couldn't turn Aslan into stone too?"

"So he did, by Jove," said Peter; "just the sort of thing he would say, too!"

"Worse and worse," said Mr Beaver, "and the next thing is this. Was he still here when I told you that the place for meeting Aslan was the Stone Table?"

And of course no one knew the answer to this question.

"Because, if he was," continued Mr Beaver, "then she'll simply sledge down in that direction and get between us and the Stone Table and catch us on our way down. In fact we shall be cut off from Aslan."

"But that isn't what she'll do first," said Mrs Beaver, "not if I know her. The moment that Edmund tells her that we're all here she'll set out to catch us this very night, and if he's been gone about half an hour, she'll be here in about another twenty minutes."

"You're right, Mrs Beaver," said her husband, "we must all get away from here. There's not a moment to lose."

IN THE WITCH'S HOUSE

AND now of course you want to know what had happened to Edmund. He had eaten his share of the dinner, but he hadn't really enjoyed it because he was thinking all the time about Turkish Delight — and there's nothing that spoils the taste of good ordinary food half so much as the memory of bad magic food. And he had heard the conversation, and hadn't enjoyed it much either, because he kept on thinking that the others were taking no notice of him and trying to give him the cold shoulder. They weren't, but he imagined it. And then he had listened until Mr Beaver told them about Aslan and until he had heard the whole arrangement for meeting Aslan at the Stone Table. It was then that he began very quietly to edge himself under the curtain which hung over the door. For the mention of Aslan gave him a mysterious and horrible feeling just as it gave the others a mysterious and lovely feeling.

Just as Mr Beaver had been repeating the rhyme about *Adam's flesh and Adam's bone* Edmund had been very quietly turning the door-handle; and just before Mr Beaver had begun telling them that the White Witch wasn't really human at all but half a Jinn and half a giantess, Edmund had got outside into the snow and cautiously closed the door behind him.

You mustn't think that even now Edmund was quite so bad that he actually wanted his brother and sisters to be turned into stone. He did want Turkish

Delight and to be a Prince (and later a King) and to pay Peter out for calling him a beast. As for what the Witch would do with the others, he didn't want her to be particularly nice to them – certainly not to put them on the same level as himself; but he managed to believe, or to pretend he believed, that she wouldn't do anything very bad to them, "Because," he said to himself, "all these people who say nasty things about her are her enemies and probably half of it isn't true. She was jolly nice to me, anyway, much nicer than they are. I expect she is the rightful Queen really. Anyway, she'll be better than that awful Aslan!" At least, that was the excuse he made in his own mind for what he was doing. It wasn't a very good excuse, however, for deep down inside him he really knew that the White Witch was bad and cruel.

The first thing he realized when he got outside and found the snow falling all round him, was that he had left his coat behind in the Beavers' house. And of course there was no chance of going back to get it now. The next thing he realized was that the daylight was almost gone, for it had been nearly three o'clock when they sat down to dinner and the winter days were short. He hadn't reckoned on this; but he had to make the best of it. So he turned up his collar and shuffled across the top of the dam (luckily it wasn't so slippery since the snow had fallen) to the far side of the river.

It was pretty bad when he reached the far side. It was growing darker every minute and what with that and the snowflakes swirling all round him he could hardly see three feet ahead. And then too there was no road. He kept slipping into deep drifts of snow, and skidding on frozen puddles, and tripping over fallen tree-trunks, and sliding down steep banks, and barking his shins against rocks, till he was wet and cold and bruised all over. The silence and the

loneliness were dreadful. In fact I really think he might have given up the whole plan and gone back and owned up and made friends with the others, if he hadn't happened to say to himself, "When I'm King of Narnia the first thing I shall do will be to make some decent roads." And of course that set him off thinking about being a King and all the other things he would do and this cheered him up a good deal. He had just settled in his mind what sort of palace he would have and how many cars and all about his private cinema and where the principal railways would run and what laws he would make against beavers and dams and was putting the finishing touches to some schemes for keeping Peter in his place, when the weather changed. First the snow stopped. Then a wind sprang up and it became freezing cold. Finally, the clouds rolled away and the moon came out. It was a full moon and, shining on all that snow, it made everything almost as bright as day – only the shadows were rather confusing.

He would never have found his way if the moon hadn't come out by the time he got to the other river – you remember he had seen (when they first arrived at the Beavers') a smaller river flowing into the great one lower down. He now reached this and turned to follow it up. But the little valley down which it came was much steeper and rockier than the one he had just left and much overgrown with bushes, so that he could not have managed it at all in the dark. Even as it was, he got wet through for he had to stoop under branches and great loads of snow came sliding off on to his back. And every time this happened he thought more and more how he hated Peter – just as if all this had been Peter's fault.

But at last he came to a part where it was more level and the valley opened out. And there, on the other side of the river, quite close to him, in the middle of a little plain between two hills, he saw what must be the White Witch's House. And the moon was shining brighter than ever. The House was really a small castle. It seemed to be all towers; little towers with long pointed spires on them, sharp as needles. They looked like huge dunce's caps or sorcerer's caps. And they shone in the moonlight and their long shadows looked strange on the snow. Edmund began to be afraid of the House.

But it was too late to think of turning back now.

He crossed the river on the ice and walked up to the House. There was nothing stirring; not the slightest sound anywhere. Even his own feet made no noise on the deep newly fallen snow. He walked on and on, past corner after corner of the House, and past turret after turret to find the door. He had to go right round

to the far side before he found it. It was a huge arch but the great iron gates stood wide open.

Edmund crept up to the arch and looked inside into the courtyard, and there he saw a sight that nearly made his heart stop beating. Just inside the gate, with the moonlight shining on it, stood an enormous lion crouched as if it was ready to spring. And Edmund stood in the shadow of the arch, afraid to go on and afraid to go back, with his knees knocking together. He stood there so long that his teeth would have been chattering with cold even if they had not been chattering with fear. How long this really lasted I don't know, but it seemed to Edmund to last for hours.

Then at last he began to wonder why the lion was

standing so still – for it hadn't moved one inch since he first set eyes on it. Edmund now ventured a little nearer, still keeping in the shadow of the arch as much as he could. He now saw from the way the lion was standing that it couldn't have been looking at him at all. ("But supposing it turns its head?" thought Edmund.) In fact it was staring at something else – namely a little dwarf who stood with his back to it about four feet away. "Aha!" thought Edmund. "When it springs at the dwarf then will be my chance to escape." But still the lion never moved, nor did the dwarf. And now at last Edmund remembered what the others had said about the White Witch turning people into stone. Perhaps this was only a stone lion. And as soon as he had thought of that he noticed that the lion's back and the top of its head were covered with snow. Of course it must be only a statue! No living animal would have let itself get covered with snow. Then very slowly and with his heart beating as if it would burst, Edmund ventured to go up to the lion. Even now he hardly dared to touch it, but at last he put out his hand, very quickly, and did. It was cold stone. He had been frightened of a mere statue!

The relief which Edmund felt was so great that in spite of the cold he suddenly got warm all over right down to his toes, and at the same time there came into his head what seemed a perfectly lovely idea. "Probably," he thought, "this is the great Lion Aslan that they were all talking about. She's caught him already and turned him into stone. So *that's* the end of all their fine ideas about him! Pooh! Who's afraid of Aslan?"

And he stood there gloating over the stone lion, and presently he did something very silly and childish. He took a stump of lead pencil out of his pocket and scribbled a moustache on the lion's upper lip and then a pair of spectacles on its eyes. Then he said, "Yah! Silly old Aslan! How do you like being a stone? You thought yourself mighty fine, didn't you?" But in spite of the scribbles on it the face of the great stone beast still looked so terrible, and sad, and noble, staring up in the moonlight, that Edmund didn't really get any fun out of jeering at it. He turned away and began to cross the courtyard.

As he got into the middle of it he saw that there were dozens of statues all about – standing here and there rather as the pieces stand on a chess-board when it is half-way through the game. There were stone satyrs, and stone wolves, and bears and foxes and cat-a-mountains of stone. There were lovely stone shapes that looked like women but who were really the spirits of trees. There was the great shape of a centaur and a winged horse and a long lithe creature that Edmund took to be a dragon. They all looked so strange standing there perfectly life-like and also perfectly still, in the bright cold moonlight, that it was eerie work crossing the courtyard. Right in the very middle stood a huge shape like a man, but as tall as a tree, with a fierce face and a shaggy beard and a great club in its right hand. Even though he knew that it was only a stone giant and not a live one, Edmund did not like going past it.

He now saw that there was a dim light showing from a doorway on the far side of the courtyard. He went to it, there was a flight of stone steps going up to an open door. Edmund went up them. Across the threshold lay a great wolf.

"It's all right, it's all right," he kept saying to himself; "it's only a stone wolf. It can't hurt me", and he raised his leg to step over it. Instantly the huge

creature rose, with all the hair bristling along its back, opened a great, red mouth and said in a growling voice:

"Who's there? Who's there? Stand still, stranger, and tell me who you are."

"If you please, sir," said Edmund, trembling so that he could hardly speak, "my name is Edmund, and I'm

the Son of Adam that Her Majesty met in the wood the other day and I've come to bring her the news that my brother and sisters are now in Narnia – quite close, in the Beavers' house. She – she wanted to see them."

"I will tell Her Majesty," said the Wolf. "Meanwhile, stand still on the threshold, as you value your life." Then it vanished into the house.

Edmund stood and waited, his fingers aching with cold and his heart pounding in his chest, and presently the grey wolf, Maugrim, the Chief of the Witch's Secret Police, came bounding back and said, "Come in! Come in! Fortunate favourite of the Queen – or else not so fortunate."

And Edmund went in, taking great care not to tread on the Wolf's paws.

He found himself in a long gloomy hall with many pillars, full, as the courtyard had been, of statues. The one nearest the door was a little faun with a very sad expression on its face, and Edmund couldn't help wondering if this might be Lucy's friend. The only light came from a single lamp and close beside this sat the White Witch.

"I'm come, your Majesty," said Edmund, rushing eagerly forward.

"How dare you come alone?" said the Witch in a terrible voice. "Did I not tell you to bring the others with you?"

"Please, your Majesty," said Edmund, "I've done the best I can. I've brought them quite close. They're in the little house on top of the dam just up the river – with Mr and Mrs Beaver."

A slow cruel smile came over the Witch's face.

"Is this all your news?" she asked.

"No, your Majesty," said Edmund, and proceeded to tell her all he had heard before leaving the Beavers' house.

"What! Aslan?" cried the Queen, "Aslan! Is this true? If I find you have lied to me —"

"Please, I'm only repeating what they said," stammered Edmund.

But the Queen, who was no longer attending to him, clapped her hands. Instantly the same dwarf whom Edmund had seen with her before appeared.

"Make ready our sledge," ordered the Witch, "and use the harness without bells."

CHAPTER TEN

THE SPELL BEGINS TO BREAK

Now we must go back to Mr and Mrs Beaver and the three other children. As soon as Mr Beaver said, "There's no time to lose," everyone began bundling themselves into coats, except Mrs Beaver, who started picking up sacks and laying them on the table and said: "Now, Mr Beaver, just reach down that ham. And here's a packet of tea, and there's sugar, and some matches. And if someone will get two or three loaves out of the crock over there in the corner."

"What *are* you doing, Mrs Beaver?" exclaimed Susan.

"Packing a load for each of us, dearie," said Mrs Beaver very coolly. "You didn't think we'd set out on a journey with nothing to eat, did you?"

"But we haven't time!" said Susan, buttoning the collar of her coat. "She may be here any minute."

"That's what I say," chimed in Mr Beaver.

"Get along with you all," said his wife. "Think it over, Mr Beaver. She can't be here for quarter of an hour at least."

"But don't we want as big a start as we can possibly get," said Peter, "if we're to reach the Stone Table before her?"

"You've got to remember *that*, Mrs Beaver," said Susan. "As soon as she has looked in here and finds we're gone she'll be off at top speed."

"That she will," said Mrs Beaver. "But we can't get

there before her whatever we do, for she'll be on a sledge and we'll be walking."

"Then — have we no hope?" said Susan.

"Now don't you get fussing, there's a dear," said Mrs Beaver, "but just get half a dozen clean handkerchiefs out of the drawer. 'Course we've got a hope. We can't get there *before* her but we can keep under cover and go by ways she won't expect and perhaps we'll get through."

"That's true enough, Mrs Beaver," said her husband. "But it's time we were out of this."

"And don't *you* start fussing either, Mr Beaver," said his wife. "There. That's better. There's five

loads and the smallest for the smallest of us: that's you, my dear," she added, looking at Lucy.

"Oh, do please come on," said Lucy.

"Well, I'm nearly ready now," answered Mrs Beaver at last, allowing her husband to help her into her snow-boots. "I suppose the sewing machine's too heavy to bring?"

"Yes. It *is*," said Mr Beaver. "A great deal too heavy. And you don't think you'll be able to use it while we're on the run, I suppose?"

"I can't abide the thought of that Witch fiddling with it," said Mrs Beaver, "and breaking it or stealing it, as likely as not."

"Oh, please, please, please, do hurry!" said the three children. And so at last they all got outside and Mr Beaver locked the door ("It'll delay her a bit," he said) and they set off, all carrying their loads over their shoulders.

The snow had stopped and the moon had come out when they began their journey. They went in single file – first Mr Beaver, then Lucy, then Peter, then Susan, and Mrs Beaver last of all. Mr Beaver led them across the dam and on to the right bank of the river and then along a very rough sort of path among the trees right down by the river-bank. The sides of the valley, shining in the moonlight, towered up far above them on either hand. "Best keep down here as much as possible," he said. "She'll have to keep to the top, for you couldn't bring a sledge down here."

It would have been a pretty enough scene to look at it through a window from a comfortable armchair; and even as things were, Lucy enjoyed it at first. But as they went on walking and walking – and walking – and as the sack she was carrying felt heavier and heavier, she began to wonder how she was going to keep up at all. And she stopped looking at the dazzling brightness of the frozen river with all its waterfalls of ice and at the white masses of the tree-tops and the great glaring moon and the countless stars and could only watch the little short legs of Mr Beaver going pad-pad-pad-pad through the snow in front of her as if they were never going to stop. Then the moon disappeared and the snow began to fall once more. And at last Lucy was so tired that she was almost asleep and walking at the same time when suddenly she found that Mr Beaver had turned away from the river-bank to the right and was leading them steeply uphill into the very thickest bushes. And then as she came fully awake she found that Mr Beaver was just vanishing into a little hole in the bank which had been almost hidden under the bushes until you were quite on top of it. In fact, by the time she realized what was happening, only his short flat tail was showing.

Lucy immediately stooped down and crawled in after him. Then she heard noises of scrambling and puffing and panting behind her and in a moment all five of them were inside.

"Wherever is this?" said Peter's voice, sounding tired and pale in the darkness. (I hope you know what I mean by a voice sounding pale.)

"It's an old hiding-place for beavers in bad times," said Mr Beaver, "and a great secret. It's not much of a place but we must get a few hours' sleep."

"If you hadn't all been in such a plaguey fuss when we were starting, I'd have brought some pillows," said Mrs Beaver.

It wasn't nearly such a nice cave as Mr Tumnus's, Lucy thought – just a hole in the ground but dry and earthy. It was very small so that when they all lay down they were all a bundle of clothes together, and what with that and being warmed up by their long

walk they were really rather snug. If only the floor of
the cave had been a little smoother! Then Mrs Beaver
handed round in the dark a little flask out of which
everyone drank something – it made one cough and
splutter a little and stung the throat, but it also made
you feel deliciously warm after you'd swallowed it –
and everyone went straight to sleep.

It seemed to Lucy only the next minute (though
really it was hours and hours later) when she woke up
feeling a little cold and dreadfully stiff and thinking
how she would like a hot bath. Then she felt a set of
long whiskers tickling her cheek and saw the cold
daylight coming in through the mouth of the cave.
But immediately after that she was very wide awake
indeed, and so was everyone else. In fact they were all
sitting up with their mouths and eyes wide open
listening to a sound which was the very sound they'd
all been thinking of (and sometimes imagining they
heard) during their walk last night. It was a sound of
jingling bells.

Mr Beaver was out of the cave like a flash the
moment he heard it. Perhaps you think, as Lucy
thought for a moment, that this was a very silly thing
to do? But it was really a very sensible one. He knew
he could scramble to the top of the bank among
bushes and brambles without being seen; and he
wanted above all things to see which way the Witch's
sledge went. The others all sat in the cave waiting
and wondering. They waited nearly five minutes.
Then they heard something that frightened them
very much. They heard voices. "Oh," thought Lucy,
"he's been seen. She's caught him!" Great was their

surprise when a little later, they heard Mr Beaver's voice calling to them from just outside the cave.

"It's all right," he was shouting. "Come out, Mrs Beaver. Come out, Sons and Daughters of Adam. It's all right! It isn't *Her*!" This was bad grammar of course, but that is how beavers talk when they are excited; I mean, in Narnia – in our world they usually don't talk at all.

So Mrs Beaver and the children came bundling out of the cave, all blinking in the daylight, and with earth all over them, and looking very frowsty and unbrushed and uncombed and with the sleep in their eyes.

"Come on!" cried Mr Beaver, who was almost dancing with delight. "Come and see! This is a nasty knock for the Witch! It looks as if her power is already crumbling."

"What *do* you mean, Mr Beaver?" panted Peter as they all scrambled up the steep bank of the valley together.

"Didn't I tell you," answered Mr Beaver, "that she'd made it always winter and never Christmas? Didn't I tell you? Well, just come and see!"

And then they were all at the top and did see.

It *was* a sledge, and it *was* reindeer with bells on their harness. But they were far bigger than the Witch's reindeer, and they were not white but brown. And on the sledge sat a person whom everyone knew the moment they set eyes on him. He was a huge man in a bright red robe (bright as hollyberries) with a hood that had fur inside it and a great white beard that fell like a foamy waterfall over his chest.

Everyone knew him because, though you see people of his sort only in Narnia, you see pictures of them and hear them talked about even in our world – the world on this side of the wardrobe door. But when you really see them in Narnia it is rather different. Some of the pictures of Father Christmas in our world make him look only funny and jolly. But now that the children actually stood looking at him they didn't find it quite like that. He was so big, and so glad, and so real, that they all became quite still. They felt very glad, but also solemn.

"I've come at last," said he. "She has kept me out for a long time, but I have got in at last. Aslan is on the move. The Witch's magic is weakening."

And Lucy felt running through her that deep shiver of gladness which you only get if you are being solemn and still.

"And now," said Father Christmas, "for your presents. There is a new and better sewing machine for you, Mrs Beaver. I will drop it in your house as I pass."

"If you please, sir," said Mrs Beaver, making a curtsey. "It's locked up."

"Locks and bolts make no difference to me," said Father Christmas. "And as for you, Mr Beaver, when you get home you will find your dam finished and mended and all the leaks stopped and a new sluice-gate fitted."

Mr Beaver was so pleased that he opened his mouth very wide and then found he couldn't say anything at all.

"Peter, Adam's Son," said Father Christmas.

"Here, sir," said Peter.

"These are your presents," was the answer, "and they are tools not toys. The time to use them is perhaps near at hand. Bear them well." With these words he handed to Peter a shield and a sword. The shield was the colour of silver and across it there ramped a red lion, as bright as a ripe strawberry at the moment when you pick it. The hilt of the sword was of gold and it had a sheath and a sword belt and everything it needed, and it was just the right size and weight for Peter to use. Peter was silent and solemn as he received these gifts, for he felt they were a very serious kind of present.

"Susan, Eve's Daughter," said Father Christmas. "These are for you," and he handed her a bow and a quiver full of arrows and a little ivory horn. "You must use the bow only in great need," he said, "for I do not mean you to fight in the battle. It does not easily miss. And when you put this horn to your lips and blow it, then, wherever you are, I think help of some kind will come to you."

Last of all he said, "Lucy, Eve's Daughter," and Lucy came forward. He gave her a little bottle of what looked like glass (but people said afterwards that it was made of diamond) and a small dagger. "In this bottle," he said, "there is a cordial made of the juice of one of the fire-flowers that grow in the mountains of the sun. If you or any of your friends is hurt, a few drops of this will restore them. And the dagger is to defend yourself at great need. For you also are not to be in the battle."

"Why, sir?" said Lucy. "I think – I don't know – but I think I could be brave enough."

"That is not the point," he said. "But battles are ugly when women fight. And now" – here he suddenly looked less grave – "here is something for the moment for you all!" and he brought out (I suppose from the big bag at his back, but nobody quite saw him do it) a large tray containing five cups and saucers, a bowl of lump sugar, a jug of cream, and a great big teapot all sizzling and piping hot. Then he cried out "Merry Christmas! Long live the true King!" and cracked his whip, and he and the reindeer and the sledge and all were out of sight before anyone realized that they had started.

Peter had just drawn his sword out of its sheath and was showing it to Mr Beaver, when Mrs Beaver said:

"Now then, now then! Don't stand talking there till the tea's got cold. Just like men. Come and help to carry the tray down and we'll have breakfast. What a mercy I thought of bringing the bread-knife."

So down the steep bank they went and back to the cave, and Mr Beaver cut some of the bread and ham into sandwiches and Mrs Beaver poured out the tea and everyone enjoyed themselves. But long before they had finished enjoying themselves Mr Beaver said, "Time to be moving on now."

CHAPTER ELEVEN

ASLAN IS NEARER

EDMUND meanwhile had been having a most disappointing time. When the dwarf had gone to get the sledge ready he expected that the Witch would start being nice to him, as she had been at their last meeting. But she said nothing at all. And when at last Edmund plucked up his courage to say, "Please, your Majesty, could I have some Turkish Delight? You — you – said –" she answered, "Silence, fool!" Then she appeared to change her mind and said, as if to herself, "And yet it will not do to have the brat fainting on the way," and once more clapped her hands. Another dwarf appeared.

"Bring the human creature food and drink," she said.

The dwarf went away and presently returned bringing an iron bowl with some water in it and an iron plate with a hunk of dry bread on it. He grinned in a repulsive manner as he set them down on the floor beside Edmund and said:

"Turkish Delight for the little Prince. Ha! Ha! Ha!"

"Take it away," said Edmund sulkily. "I don't want dry bread." But the Witch suddenly turned on him with such a terrible expression on her face that he apologized and began to nibble at the bread, though it was so stale he could hardly get it down.

"You may be glad enough of it before you taste bread again," said the Witch.

While he was still chewing away the first dwarf came back and announced that the sledge was ready. The White Witch rose and went out, ordering Edmund to go with her. The snow was again falling as they came into the courtyard, but she took no notice of that and made Edmund sit beside her on the

sledge. But before they drove off she called Maugrim and he came bounding like an enormous dog to the side of the sledge.

"Take with you the swiftest of your wolves and go at once to the house of the Beavers," said the Witch, "and kill whatever you find there. If they are already gone, then make all speed to the Stone Table, but do not be seen. Wait for me there in hiding. I meanwhile must go many miles to the West before I find a place where I can drive across the river. You may overtake these humans before they reach the

Stone Table. You will know what to do if you find them!"

"I hear and obey, O Queen," growled the Wolf, and immediately he shot away into the snow and darkness, as quickly as a horse can gallop. In a few minutes he had called another wolf and was with him down on the dam sniffing at the Beavers' house. But of course they found it empty. It would have been a dreadful thing for the Beavers and the children if the night had remained fine, for the wolves would then have been able to follow their trail – and ten to one would have overtaken them before they had got to the cave. But now that the snow had begun again the scent was cold and even the footprints were covered up.

Meanwhile the dwarf whipped up the reindeer, and the Witch and Edmund drove out under the archway and on and away into the darkness and the cold. This was a terrible journey for Edmund, who had no coat. Before they had been going quarter of an hour all the front of him was covered with snow – he soon stopped trying to shake it off because, as quickly as he did that, a new lot gathered, and he was so tired. Soon he was wet to the skin. And oh, how miserable he was! It didn't look now as if the Witch intended to make him a King. All the things he had said to make himself believe that she was good and kind and that her side was really the right side sounded to him silly now. He would have given anything to meet the others at this moment – even Peter! The only way to comfort himself now was to try to believe that the whole thing was a dream and that he might wake up at any moment. And as they went on, hour after hour, it did come to seem like a dream.

This lasted longer than I could describe even if I wrote pages and pages about it. But I will skip on to the time when the snow had stopped and the morning had come and they were racing along in the daylight. And still they went on and on, with no sound but the everlasting swish of the snow and the creaking of the reindeer's harness. And then at last the Witch said, "What have we here? Stop!" and they did.

How Edmund hoped she was going to say something about breakfast! But she had stopped for quite a different reason. A little way off at the foot of a tree sat a merry party, a squirrel and his wife with their children and two satyrs and a dwarf and an old dog-fox, all on stools round a table. Edmund couldn't quite see what they were eating, but it smelled lovely and there seemed to be decorations of holly and he wasn't at all sure that he didn't see something like a plum pudding. At the moment when the sledge stopped, the Fox, who was obviously the oldest person present, had just risen to its feet, holding a glass in its right paw as if it was going to say something. But when the whole party saw the sledge stopping and who was in it, all the gaiety went out of their faces. The father squirrel stopped eating with his fork half-way to his mouth and one of the satyrs stopped with its fork actually in its mouth, and the baby squirrels squeaked with terror.

"What is the meaning of this?" asked the Witch Queen. Nobody answered.

"Speak, vermin!" she said again. "Or do you want

my dwarf to find you a tongue with his whip? What is the meaning of all this gluttony, this waste, this self-indulgence? Where did you get all these things?"

"Please, your Majesty," said the Fox, "we were given them. And if I might make so bold as to drink your Majesty's very good health – "

"Who gave them to you?" said the Witch.

"F-F-F-Father Christmas," stammered the Fox.

"What?" roared the Witch, springing from the sledge and taking a few strides nearer to the terrified animals. "He has not been here! He cannot have been here! How dare you – but no. Say you have been lying and you shall even now be forgiven."

At that moment one of the young squirrels lost its head completely.

"He has – he has – he has!" it squeaked, beating its little spoon on the table. Edmund saw the Witch bite her lips so that a drop of blood appeared on her white cheek. Then she raised her wand. "Oh, don't, don't, please don't," shouted Edmund, but even while he was shouting she had waved her wand and instantly where the merry party had been there were only statues of creatures (one with its stone fork fixed forever half-way to its stone mouth) seated round a stone table on which there were stone plates and a stone plum pudding.

"As for you," said the Witch, giving Edmund a stunning blow on the face as she re-mounted the sledge, "let that teach you to ask favour for spies and traitors. Drive on!" And Edmund for the first time in this story felt sorry for someone besides himself. It seemed so pitiful to think of those little stone figures sitting there all the silent days and all the dark nights, year after year, till the moss grew on them and at last even their faces crumbled away.

Now they were steadily racing on again. And soon Edmund noticed that the snow which splashed against them as they rushed through it was much wetter than it had been all last night. At the same time he noticed that he was feeling much less cold. It was also becoming foggy. In fact every minute it grew foggier and warmer. And the sledge was not running nearly as well as it had been running up till now. At first he thought this was because the reindeer were tired, but soon he saw that that couldn't be the real reason. The sledge jerked, and skidded and kept on jolting as if it had struck against stones. And however the dwarf whipped the poor reindeer the sledge went slower and slower. There also seemed to be a curious noise all round them, but the noise of their driving and jolting and the dwarf's shouting at the reindeer prevented Edmund from hearing what it was, until suddenly the sledge stuck so fast that it wouldn't go on at all. When that happened there was a moment's silence. And in that silence Edmund could at last listen to the other noise properly. A strange, sweet, rustling, chattering noise – and yet not so strange, for he'd heard it before – if only he could remember where! Then all at once he did remember. It was the noise of running water. All round them though out of sight, there were streams, chattering, murmuring, bubbling, splashing and even (in the distance) roaring. And his heart gave a great leap (though he hardly knew why) when he realized that the frost was over. And much nearer there was a drip-drip-drip from the branches of all the trees. And then, as he looked at one tree he saw a great load of snow slide off it and for the first time since he had entered Narnia he saw the dark green of a fir tree. But he hadn't time to listen or watch any longer, for the Witch said:

"Don't sit staring, fool! Get out and help."

And of course Edmund had to obey. He stepped out into the snow – but it was really only slush by now – and began helping the dwarf to get the sledge out of the muddy hole it had got into. They got it out in the end, and by being very cruel to the reindeer the dwarf managed to get it on the move again, and they drove a little further. And now the snow was really melting in earnest and patches of green grass were beginning to appear in every direction. Unless you have looked at a world of snow as long as Edmund had been looking at it, you will hardly be able to

imagine what a relief those green patches were after the endless white. Then the sledge stopped again.

"It's no good, your Majesty," said the dwarf. "We can't sledge in this thaw."

"Then we must walk," said the Witch.

"We shall never overtake them walking," growled the dwarf. "Not with the start they've got."

"Are you my councillor or my slave?" said the Witch. "Do as you're told. Tie the hands of the human creature behind it and keep hold of the end of the rope. And take your whip. And cut the harness of the reindeer; they'll find their own way home."

The dwarf obeyed, and in a few minutes Edmund found himself being forced to walk as fast as he could with his hands tied behind him. He kept on slipping in the slush and mud and wet grass, and every time he slipped the dwarf gave him a curse and sometimes a flick with the whip. The Witch walked behind the dwarf and kept on saying, "Faster! Faster!"

Every moment the patches of green grew bigger and the patches of snow grew smaller. Every moment more and more of the trees shook off their robes of snow. Soon, wherever you looked, instead of white shapes you saw the dark green of firs or the black prickly branches of bare oaks and beeches and elms. Then the mist turned from white to gold and presently cleared away altogether. Shafts of delicious sunlight struck down on to the forest floor and overhead you could see a blue sky between the tree tops.

Soon there were more wonderful things happening. Coming suddenly round a corner into a glade of silver birch trees Edmund saw the ground covered in all directions with little yellow flowers — celandines. The noise of water grew louder. Presently they actually crossed a stream. Beyond it they found snowdrops growing.

"Mind your own business!" said the dwarf when

he saw that Edmund had turned his head to look at them; and he gave the rope a vicious jerk.

But of course this didn't prevent Edmund from seeing. Only five minutes later he noticed a dozen crocuses growing round the foot of an old tree – gold and purple and white. Then came a sound even more delicious than the sound of the water. Close beside the path they were following a bird suddenly chirped from the branch of a tree. It was answered by the chuckle of another bird a little further off. And then, as if that had been a signal, there was chattering and chirruping in every direction, and then a moment of full song, and within five minutes the whole wood was ringing with birds' music, and wherever Edmund's eyes turned he saw birds alighting on branches, or sailing overhead or chasing one another or having their little quarrels or tidying up their feathers with their beaks.

"Faster! Faster!" said the Witch.

There was no trace of the fog now. The sky became bluer and bluer, and now there were white clouds hurrying across it from time to time. In the wide glades there were primroses. A light breeze sprang up which scattered drops of moisture from the swaying branches and carried cool, delicious scents against the faces of the travellers. The trees began to come fully alive. The larches and birches were covered with green, the laburnums with gold. Soon the beech trees had put forth their delicate, transparent leaves. As the travellers walked under them the light also became green. A bee buzzed across their path.

"This is no thaw," said the dwarf, suddenly stopping. "This is *Spring*. What are we to do? Your winter has been destroyed, I tell you! This is Aslan's doing."

"If either of you mention that name again," said the Witch, "he shall instantly be killed."

CHAPTER TWELVE

PETER'S FIRST BATTLE

WHILE the dwarf and the White Witch were saying this, miles away the Beavers and the children were walking on hour after hour into what seemed a delicious dream. Long ago they had left the coats behind them. And by now they had even stopped saying to one another, "Look! there's a kingfisher," or "I say, bluebells!" or "What was that lovely smell?" or "Just listen to that thrush!" They walked on in silence drinking it all in, passing through patches of warm sunlight into cool, green thickets and out again into wide mossy glades where tall elms raised the leafy roof far overhead, and then into dense masses of flowering currant and among hawthorn bushes where the sweet smell was almost overpowering.

They had been just as surprised as Edmund when they saw the winter vanishing and the whole wood passing in a few hours or so from January to May. They hadn't even known for certain (as the Witch did) that this was what would happen when Aslan came to Narnia. But they all knew that it was her spells which had produced the endless winter; and therefore they all knew when this magic spring began that something had gone wrong, and badly wrong, with the Witch's schemes. And after the thaw had been going on for some time they all realized that the Witch would no longer be able to use her sledge. After that they didn't hurry so much and they allowed themselves more rests and longer ones. They were pretty tired by now of course; but not what I'd call bitterly tired – only slow and feeling very dreamy and quiet inside as one does when one is coming to the end of a long day in the open. Susan had a slight blister on one heel.

They had left the course of the big river some time ago; for one had to turn a little to the right (that meant a little to the south) to reach the place of the Stone Table. Even if this had not been their way they couldn't have kept to the river valley once the thaw began, for with all that melting snow the river was soon in flood – a wonderful, roaring, thundering yellow flood – and their path would have been under water.

And now the sun got low and the light got redder and the shadows got longer and the flowers began to think about closing.

"Not long now," said Mr Beaver, and began leading them uphill across some very deep, springy moss (it felt nice under their tired feet) in a place where only tall trees grew, very wide apart. The climb, coming at the end of the long day, made them all pant and blow. And just as Lucy was wondering whether she could really get to the top without another long rest, suddenly they *were* at the top. And this is what they saw.

They were on a green open space from which you could look down on the forest spreading as far as one could see in every direction – except right ahead. There, far to the East, was something twinkling and moving. "By gum!" whispered Peter to Susan, "the sea!" In the very middle of this open hill-top was the

Stone Table. It was a great grim slab of grey stone supported on four upright stones. It looked very old; and it was cut all over with strange lines and figures that might be the letters of an unknown language. They gave you a curious feeling when you looked at them. The next thing they saw was a pavilion pitched on one side of the open place. A wonderful pavilion it was – and especially now when the light of the setting sun fell upon it – with sides of what looked like yellow silk and cords of crimson and tent-pegs of ivory; and high above it on a pole a banner which bore a red rampant lion fluttering in the breeze which was blowing in their faces from the far-off sea. While they were looking at this they heard a sound of music on their right; and turning in that direction they saw what they had come to see.

Aslan stood in the centre of a crowd of creatures who had grouped themselves round him in the shape of a half-moon. There were Tree-Women there and Well-Women (Dryads and Naiads as they used to be called in our world) who had stringed instruments; it was they who had made the music. There were four great centaurs. The horse part of them was like huge English farm horses, and the man part was like stern but beautiful giants. There was also a unicorn, and a bull with the head of a man, and a pelican, and an eagle, and a great Dog. And next to Aslan stood two leopards of whom one carried his crown and the other his standard.

But as for Aslan himself, the Beavers and the children didn't know what to do or say when they saw him. People who have not been in Narnia

sometimes think that a thing cannot be good and terrible at the same time. If the children had ever thought so, they were cured of it now. For when they tried to look at Aslan's face they just caught a glimpse of the golden mane and the great, royal, solemn, overwhelming eyes; and then they found they couldn't look at him and went all trembly.

"Go on," whispered Mr Beaver.

"No," whispered Peter, "you first."

"No, Sons of Adam before animals," whispered Mr Beaver back again.

"Susan," whispered Peter, "What about you? Ladies first."

"No, you're the eldest," whispered Susan. And of course the longer they went on doing this the more awkward they felt. Then at last Peter realized that it was up to him. He drew his sword and raised it to the salute and hastily saying to the others "Come on. Pull yourselves together," he advanced to the Lion and said:

"We have come – Aslan."

"Welcome, Peter, Son of Adam," said Aslan. "Welcome, Susan and Lucy, Daughters of Eve. Welcome He-Beaver and She-Beaver."

His voice was deep and rich and somehow took the fidgets out of them. They now felt glad and quiet and it didn't seem awkward to them to stand and say nothing.

"But where is the fourth?" asked Aslan.

"He has tried to betray them and joined the White Witch, O Aslan," said Mr Beaver. And then something made Peter say,

"That was partly my fault, Aslan. I was angry with him and I think that helped him to go wrong."

And Aslan said nothing either to excuse Peter or to blame him but merely stood looking at him with his great unchanging eyes. And it seemed to all of them that there was nothing to be said.

"Please – Aslan," said Lucy, "can anything be done to save Edmund?"

"All shall be done," said Aslan. "But it may be harder than you think." And then he was silent again for some time. Up to that moment Lucy had been thinking how royal and strong and peaceful his face looked; now it suddenly came into her head that he looked sad as well. But next minute that expression was quite gone. The Lion shook his mane and clapped his paws together ("Terrible paws," thought Lucy, "if he didn't know how to velvet them!") and said,

"Meanwhile, let the feast be prepared. Ladies, take these Daughters of Eve to the pavilion and minister to them."

When the girls had gone Aslan laid his paw – and though it was velveted it was very heavy – on Peter's shoulder and said, "Come, Son of Adam, and I will show you a far-off sight of the castle where you are to be King."

And Peter with his sword still drawn in his hand went with the Lion to the eastern edge of the hilltop. There a beautiful sight met their eyes. The sun was setting behind their backs. That meant that the whole country below them lay in the evening light – forest and hills and valleys and, winding away like a silver snake, the lower part of the great river. And beyond all this, miles away, was the sea, and beyond the sea the sky, full of clouds which were just turning rose colour with the reflection of the sunset. But just where the land of Narnia met the sea – in fact, at the mouth of the great river – there was something on a little hill, shining. It was shining because it was a castle and of course the sunlight was reflected from all the windows which looked towards Peter and the sunset; but to Peter it looked like a great star resting on the seashore.

"That, O Man," said Aslan, "is Cair Paravel of the four thrones, in one of which you must sit as King. I show it to you because you are the first-born and you will be High King over all the rest."

And once more Peter said nothing, for at that moment a strange noise woke the silence suddenly. It was like a bugle, but richer.

"It is your sister's horn," said Aslan to Peter in a low voice; so low as to be almost a purr, if it is not disrespectful to think of a Lion purring.

For a moment Peter did not understand. Then, when he saw all the other creatures start forward and heard Aslan say with a wave of his paw, "Back! Let the Prince win his spurs," he did understand, and set off running as hard as he could to the pavilion. And there he saw a dreadful sight.

The Naiads and Dryads were scattering in every direction. Lucy was running towards him as fast as her short legs would carry her and her face was as white as paper. Then he saw Susan make a dash for a tree, and swing herself up, followed by a huge grey beast. At first Peter thought it was a bear. Then he saw that it looked like an Alsatian, though it was far too big to be a dog. Then he realized that it was a wolf — a wolf standing on its hind legs, with its front paws against the tree-trunk, snapping and snarling. All the hair on its back stood up on end. Susan had not been able to get higher than the second big branch. One of her legs hung down so that her foot was only an inch or two above the snapping teeth. Peter wondered why she did not get higher or at least take a better grip; then he realized that she was just going to faint and that if she fainted she would fall off.

Peter did not feel very brave; indeed, he felt he was going to be sick. But that made no difference to what he had to do. He rushed straight up to the monster and aimed a slash of his sword at its side. That stroke never reached the Wolf. Quick as lightning it turned round, its eyes flaming, and its mouth wide open in a howl of anger. If it had not been so angry that it simply had to howl it would have got him by the throat at once. As it was — though all this happened too quickly for Peter to think at all — he had just time to duck down and plunge his sword, as hard as he could, between the brute's forelegs into its heart. Then came a horrible, confused moment like something in a nightmare. He was tugging and pulling and the Wolf seemed neither alive nor dead, and its bared teeth knocked against his forehead, and everything was blood and heat and hair. A moment later he found that the monster lay dead and he had drawn his sword out of it and was straightening his back and rubbing the sweat off his face and out of his eyes. He felt tired all over.

Then, after a bit, Susan came down the tree. She and Peter felt pretty shaky when they met and I won't say there wasn't kissing and crying on both sides. But in Narnia no one thinks any the worse of you for that.

"Quick! Quick!" shouted the voice of Aslan. "Centaurs! Eagles! I see another wolf in the thickets. There — behind you. He has just darted away. After him, all of you. He will be going to his mistress. Now is your chance to find the Witch and rescue the fourth Son of Adam." And instantly with a thunder of hoofs and beating of wings a dozen or so of the swiftest creatures disappeared into the gathering darkness.

Peter, still out of breath, turned and saw Aslan close at hand.

"You have forgotten to clean your sword," said Aslan.

It was true. Peter blushed when he looked at the bright blade and saw it all smeared with the Wolf's hair and blood. He stooped down and wiped it quite clean on the grass, and then wiped it quite dry on his coat.

"Hand it to me and kneel, Son of Adam," said Aslan. And when Peter had done so he struck him with the flat of the blade and said, "Rise up, Sir Peter Wolf's-Bane. And, whatever happens, never forget to wipe your sword."

CHAPTER THIRTEEN

DEEP MAGIC FROM THE DAWN OF TIME

Now we must get back to Edmund. When he had been made to walk far further than he had ever known that anybody *could* walk, the Witch at last halted in a dark valley all overshadowed with fir trees and yew trees. Edmund simply sank down and lay on his face doing nothing at all and not even caring what was going to happen next provided they would let him lie still. He was too tired even to notice how hungry and thirsty he was. The Witch and the dwarf were talking close beside him in low tones.

"No," said the dwarf, "it is no use now, O Queen. They must have reached the Stone Table by now."

"Perhaps the Wolf will smell us out and bring us news," said the Witch.

"It cannot be good news if he does," said the dwarf.

"Four thrones in Cair Paravel," said the Witch. "How if only three were filled? That would not fulfil the prophecy."

"What difference would that make now that *He* is here?" said the dwarf. He did not dare, even now, to mention the name of Aslan to his mistress.

"He may not stay long. And then – we would fall upon the three at Cair."

"Yet it might be better," said the dwarf, "to keep this one" (here he kicked Edmund) "for bargaining with."

"Yes! and have him rescued," said the Witch scornfully.

"Then," said the dwarf, "we had better do what we have to do at once."

"I would like to have it done on the Stone Table itself," said the Witch. "That is the proper place. That is where it has always been done before."

"It will be a long time now before the Stone Table can again be put to its proper use," said the dwarf.

"True," said the Witch; and then, "Well, I will begin."

At that moment with a rush and a snarl a Wolf rushed up to them.

"I have seen them. They are all at the Stone Table, with Him. They have killed my captain, Maugrim. I was hidden in the thickets and saw it all. One of the Sons of Adam killed him. Fly! Fly!"

"No," said the Witch. "There need be no flying. Go quickly. Summon all our people to meet me here as speedily as they can. Call out the giants and the werewolves and the spirits of those trees who are on our side. Call the Ghouls, and the Boggles, the Ogres and the Minotaurs. Call the Cruels, the Hags, the Spectres, and the people of the Toadstools. We will fight. What? Have I not still my wand? Will not their ranks turn into stone even as they come on? Be off quickly, I have a little thing to finish here while you are away."

The great brute bowed its head, turned, and galloped away.

"Now!" she said, "we have no table — let me see. We had better put it against the trunk of a tree."

Edmund found himself being roughly forced to his feet. Then the dwarf set him with his back against a tree and bound him fast. He saw the Witch take off her outer mantle. Her arms were bare underneath it and terribly white. Because they were so very white he could see them, but he could not see much else, it was so dark in this valley under the dark trees.

"Prepare the victim," said the Witch. And the dwarf undid Edmund's collar and folded back his shirt at the neck. Then he took Edmund's hair and pulled his head back so that he had to raise his chin. After that Edmund heard a strange noise – whizz – whizz – whizz. For a moment he couldn't think what

it was. Then he realized. It was the sound of a knife being sharpened.

At that very moment he heard loud shouts from every direction – a drumming of hoofs and a beating of wings – a scream from the Witch – confusion all round him. And then he found he was being untied. Strong arms were round him and he heard big, kind voices saying things like –

"Let him lie down – give him some wine – drink this – steady now – you'll be all right in a minute."

Then he heard the voices of people who were not talking to him but to one another. And they were saying things like "Who's got the Witch?" "I thought you had her." "I didn't see her after I knocked the knife out of her hand – I was after the dwarf – do you mean to say she's escaped?" "– A chap can't mind everything at once – what's that? Oh, sorry, it's only an old stump!" But just at this point Edmund went off in a dead faint.

Presently the centaurs and unicorns and deer and birds (they were of course the rescue party which Aslan had sent in the last chapter) all set off to go back to the Stone Table, carrying Edmund with them. But if they could have seen what happened in that valley after they had gone, I think they might have been surprised.

It was perfectly still and presently the moon grew bright; if you had been there you would have seen the moonlight shining on an old tree-stump and on a fair-sized boulder. But if you had gone on looking you would gradually have begun to think there was something odd about both the stump and the boulder. And next you would have thought that the stump did look really remarkably like a little fat man crouching on the ground. And if you had watched long enough you would have seen the stump walk across to the boulder and the boulder sit up and begin talking to the stump; for in reality the stump and the boulder were simply the Witch and the dwarf. For it was part of her magic that she could make things look like what they aren't, and she had the presence of mind to do so at the very moment when the knife was knocked out of her hand. She had kept hold of her wand, so it had been kept safe, too.

When the other children woke up next morning (they had been sleeping on piles of cushions in the pavilion) the first thing they heard — from Mrs Beaver — was that their brother had been rescued and brought into camp late last night; and was at that moment with Aslan. As soon as they had breakfasted they all went out, and there they saw Aslan and Edmund walking together in the dewy grass, apart from the rest of the court. There is no need to tell you (and no one ever heard) what Aslan was saying, but it was a conversation which Edmund never forgot. As the others drew nearer Aslan turned to meet them, bringing Edmund with him.

"Here is your brother," he said, "and — there is no need to talk to him about what is past."

Edmund shook hands with each of the others and said to each of them in turn, "I'm sorry," and everyone said, "That's all right." And then everyone wanted very hard to say something which would make it quite clear that they were all friends with him again — something ordinary and natural — and of course no one could think of anything in the world to say. But before they had time to feel really awkward one of the leopards approached Aslan and said,

"Sire, there is a messenger from the enemy who craves audience."

"Let him approach," said Aslan.

The leopard went away and soon returned leading the Witch's dwarf.

"What is your message, Son of Earth?" asked Aslan.

"The Queen of Narnia and Empress of the Lone Islands desires a safe conduct to come and speak with you," said the dwarf, "on a matter which is as much to your advantage as to hers."

"Queen of Narnia, indeed!" said Mr Beaver. "Of all the cheek —"

"Peace, Beaver," said Aslan. "All names will soon be restored to their proper owners. In the meantime we will not dispute about them. Tell your mistress, Son of Earth, that I grant her safe conduct on condition that she leaves her wand behind her at that great oak."

This was agreed to and two leopards went back with the dwarf to see that the conditions were properly carried out. "But supposing she turns the two leopards into stone?" whispered Lucy to Peter. I think the same idea had occurred to the leopards themselves; at any rate, as they walked off their fur was all standing up on their backs and their tails were bristling — like a cat's when it sees a strange dog.

"It'll be all right," whispered Peter in reply. "He wouldn't send them if it weren't."

A few minutes later the Witch herself walked out on to the top of the hill and came straight across and stood before Aslan. The three children who had not seen her before felt shudders running down their backs at the sight of her face; and there were low growls among all the animals present. Though it was bright sunshine everyone felt suddenly cold. The only two people present who seemed to be quite at their ease were Aslan and the Witch herself. It was the oddest thing to see those two faces — the golden face and the dead-white face — so close together. Not that the Witch looked Aslan exactly in his eyes; Mrs Beaver particularly noticed this.

"You have a traitor there, Aslan," said the Witch. Of course everyone present knew that she meant Edmund. But Edmund had got past thinking about himself after all he'd been through and after the talk he'd had that morning. He just went on looking at Aslan. It didn't seem to matter what the Witch said.

"Well," said Aslan. "His offence was not against you."

"Have you forgotten the Deep Magic?" asked the Witch.

"Let us say I have forgotten it," answered Aslan gravely. "Tell us of this Deep Magic."

"Tell you?" said the Witch, her voice growing suddenly shriller. "Tell you what is written on that very Table of Stone which stands beside us? Tell you what is written in letters deep as a spear is long on the fire-stones on the Secret Hill? Tell you what is engraved on the sceptre of the Emperor-beyond-the-Sea? You at least know the Magic which the Emperor put into Narnia at the very beginning. You know that every traitor belongs to me as my lawful prey and that for every treachery I have a right to a kill."

"Oh," said Mr Beaver. "So *that's* how you came to imagine yourself a queen — because you were the Emperor's hangman. I see."

"Peace, Beaver," said Aslan, with a very low growl.

"And so," continued the Witch, "that human creature is mine. His life is forfeit to me. His blood is my property."

"Come and take it then," said the Bull with the man's head in a great bellowing voice.

"Fool," said the Witch with a savage smile that was almost a snarl, "do you really think your master can rob me of my rights by mere force? He knows the Deep Magic better than that. He knows that unless I have blood as the Law says all Narnia will be overturned and perish in fire and water."

"It is very true," said Aslan, "I do not deny it."

"Oh, Aslan!" whispered Susan in the Lion's ear, "can't we – I mean, you won't, will you? Can't we do something about the Deep Magic? Isn't there something you can work against it?"

"Work against the Emperor's Magic?" said Aslan, turning to her with something like a frown on his face. And nobody ever made that suggestion to him again.

Edmund was on the other side of Aslan, looking all the time at Aslan's face. He felt a choking feeling and wondered if he ought to say something; but a moment later he felt that he was not expected to do anything except to wait, and do what he was told.

"Fall back, all of you," said Aslan, "and I will talk to the Witch alone."

They all obeyed. It was a terrible time this – waiting and wondering while the Lion and the Witch talked earnestly together in low voices. Lucy said, "Oh, Edmund!" and began to cry. Peter stood with

his back to the others looking out at the distant sea.
The Beavers stood holding each other's paws with
their heads bowed. The centaurs stamped uneasily
with their hoofs. But everyone became perfectly still
in the end, so that you noticed even small sounds like
a bumble-bee flying past, or the birds in the forest
down below them, or the wind rustling the leaves.
And still the talk between Aslan and the White Witch
went on.

At last they heard Aslan's voice, "You can all come

back," he said. "I have settled the matter. She has
renounced the claim on your brother's blood." And
all over the hill there was a noise as if everyone had
been holding their breath and had now begun breathing again, and then a murmur of talk.

The Witch was just turning away with a look of
fierce joy on her face when she stopped and said,

"But how do I know this promise will be kept?"

"Haa-a-arrh!" roared Aslan, half rising from his throne; and his great mouth opened wider and wider and the roar grew louder and louder, and the Witch, after staring for a moment with her lips wide apart, picked up her skirts and fairly ran for her life.

CHAPTER FOURTEEN

THE TRIUMPH OF THE WITCH

As soon as the Witch had gone Aslan said, "We must move from this place at once, it will be wanted for other purposes. We shall encamp tonight at the Fords of Beruna."

Of course everyone was dying to ask him how he had arranged matters with the witch; but his face was stern and everyone's ears were still ringing with the sound of his roar and so nobody dared.

After a meal, which was taken in the open air on the hill-top (for the sun had got strong by now and dried the grass), they were busy for a while taking the pavilion down and packing things up. Before two o'clock they were on the march and set off in a north-easterly direction, walking at an easy pace for they had not far to go.

During the first part of the journey Aslan explained to Peter his plan of campaign. "As soon as she has finished her business in these parts," he said, "the Witch and her crew will almost certainly fall back to her House and prepare for a siege. You may or may not be able to cut her off and prevent her from reaching it." He then went on to outline two plans of battle — one for fighting the Witch and her people in the wood and another for assaulting her castle. And all the time he was advising Peter how to conduct the operations, saying things like, "You must put your Centaurs in such and such a place" or "You must post scouts to see that she doesn't do so-and-so," till at last Peter said,

"But you will be there yourself, Aslan."

"I can give you no promise of that," answered the Lion. And he continued giving Peter his instructions.

For the last part of the journey it was Susan and Lucy who saw most of him. He did not talk very much and seemed to them to be sad.

It was still afternoon when they came down to a place where the river valley had widened out and the river was broad and shallow. This was the Fords of Beruna and Aslan gave orders to halt on this side of the water. But Peter said,

"Wouldn't it be better to camp on the far side – for fear she should try a night attack or anything?"

Aslan, who seemed to have been thinking about something else, roused himself with a shake of his magnificent mane and said, "Eh? What's that?" Peter said it all over again.

"No," said Aslan in a dull voice, as if it didn't matter. "No. She will not make an attack to-night." And then he sighed deeply. But presently he added, "All the same it was well thought of. That is how a soldier ought to think. But it doesn't really matter." So they proceeded to pitch their camp.

Aslan's mood affected everyone that evening. Peter was feeling uncomfortable too at the idea of fighting the battle on his own; the news that Aslan might not be there had come as a great shock to him. Supper that evening was a quiet meal. Everyone felt how different it had been last night or even that morning. It was as if the good times, having just begun, were already drawing to their end.

This feeling affected Susan so much that she

couldn't get to sleep when she went to bed. And after she had lain counting sheep and turning over and over she heard Lucy give a long sigh and turn over just beside her in the darkness.

"Can't you get to sleep either?" said Susan.

"No," said Lucy. "I thought you were asleep. I say, Susan!"

"What?"

"I've a most horrible feeling — as if something were hanging over us."

"Have you? Because, as a matter of fact, so have I."

"Something about Aslan," said Lucy. "Either some dreadful thing is going to happen to him, or something dreadful that he's going to do."

"There's been something wrong with him all afternoon," said Susan. "Lucy! What was that he said about not being with us at the battle? You don't think he could be stealing away and leaving us tonight, do you?"

"Where is he now?" said Lucy. "Is he here in the pavilion?"

"I don't think so."

"Susan! let's go outside and have a look round. We might see him."

"All right. Let's," said Susan; "we might just as well be doing that as lying awake here."

Very quietly the two girls groped their way among the other sleepers and crept out of the tent. The moonlight was bright and everything was quite still except for the noise of the river chattering over the stones. Then Susan suddenly caught Lucy's arm and said, "Look!" On the far side of the camping ground, just where the trees began, they saw the Lion slowly walking away from them into the wood. Without a word they both followed him.

He led them up the steep slope out of the river valley and then slightly to the right — apparently by the very same route which they had used that afternoon in coming from the Hill of the Stone Table. On and on he led them, into dark shadows and out into pale moonlight, getting their feet wet with the heavy dew. He looked somehow different from the Aslan they knew. His tail and his head hung low and he walked slowly as if he were very, very tired. Then, when they were crossing a wide open place where there where no shadows for them to hide in, he stopped and looked round. It was no good trying to run away so they came towards him. When they were closer he said,

"Oh, children, children, why are you following me?"

"We couldn't sleep," said Lucy — and then felt sure that she need say no more and that Aslan knew all they had been thinking.

"Please, may we come with you — wherever you're going?" asked Susan.

"Well —" said Aslan, and seemed to be thinking. Then he said, "I should be glad of company tonight. Yes, you may come, if you will promise to stop when I tell you, and after that leave me to go on alone."

"Oh, thank you, thank you. And we will," said the two girls.

Forward they went again and one of the girls walked on each side of the Lion. But how slowly he walked! And his great, royal head drooped so that his nose nearly touched the grass. Presently he stumbled and gave a low moan.

"Aslan! Dear Aslan!" said Lucy, "what is wrong? Can't you tell us?"

"Are you ill, dear Aslan?" asked Susan.

"No," said Aslan. "I am sad and lonely. Lay your hands on my mane so that I can feel you are there and let us walk like that."

And so the girls did what they would never have dared to do without his permission, but what they had longed to do ever since they first saw him — buried their cold hands in the beautiful sea of fur and stroked it and, so doing, walked with him. And presently they saw that they were going with him up the slope of the hill on which the Stone Table stood. They went up at the side where the trees came furthest up, and when they got to the last tree (it was one that had some bushes about it) Aslan stopped and said,

"Oh, children, children. Here you must stop. And whatever happens, do not let yourselves be seen. Farewell."

And both the girls cried bitterly (though they hardly knew why) and clung to the Lion and kissed his mane and his nose and his paws and his great, sad eyes. Then he turned from them and walked out on to the top of the hill. And Lucy and Susan, crouching in the bushes, looked after him, and this is what they saw.

A great crowd of people were standing all round the Stone Table and though the moon was shining many of them carried torches which burned with

evil-looking red flames and black smoke. But such people! Ogres with monstrous teeth, and wolves, and bull-headed men; spirits of evil trees and poisonous plants; and other creatures whom I won't describe because if I did the grown-ups would probably not let you read this book – Cruels and Hags and Incubuses, Wraiths, Horrors, Efreets, Sprites, Orknies, Wooses, and Ettins. In fact here were all those who were on the Witch's side and whom the Wolf had summoned at her command. And right in the middle, standing by the Table, was the Witch herself.

A howl and a gibber of dismay went up from the creatures when they first saw the great Lion pacing towards them, and for a moment even the Witch seemed to be struck with fear. Then she recovered herself and gave a wild fierce laugh.

"The fool!" she cried. "The fool has come. Bind him fast."

Lucy and Susan held their breaths waiting for Aslan's roar and his spring upon his enemies. But it never came. Four Hags, grinning and leering, yet also (at first) hanging back and half afraid of what they had to do, had approached him. "Bind him, I say!" repeated the White Witch. The Hags made a dart at him and shrieked with triumph when they found that he made no resistance at all. Then others – evil dwarfs and apes – rushed in to help them, and between them they rolled the huge Lion over on his back and tied all his four paws together, shouting and cheering as if they had done something brave, though, had the Lion chosen, one of those paws could have been the death of them all. But he made no noise, even when the enemies, straining and tugging, pulled the cords so tight that they cut into his flesh. Then they began to drag him towards the Stone Table.

"Stop!" said the Witch. "Let him first be shaved."

Another roar of mean laughter went up from her followers as an ogre with a pair of shears came forward and squatted down by Aslan's head. Snip-snip-snip went the shears and masses of curling gold began to fall to the ground. Then the ogre stood back and the children, watching from their hiding-place, could see the face of Aslan looking all small and different without its mane. The enemies also saw the difference.

"Why, he's only a great cat after all!" cried one.

"Is *that* what we were afraid of?" said another.

And they surged round Aslan, jeering at him, saying things like "Puss, Puss! Poor Pussy," and "How many mice have you caught today, Cat?" and "Would you like a saucer of milk, Pussums?"

"Oh, how *can* they?" said Lucy, tears streaming down her cheeks. "The brutes, the brutes!" for now that the first shock was over the shorn face of Aslan looked to her braver, and more beautiful, and more patient than ever.

"Muzzle him!" said the Witch. And even now, as they worked about his face putting on the muzzle, one bite from his jaws would have cost two or three of them their hands. But he never moved. And this seemed to enrage all that rabble. Everyone was at him now. Those who had been afraid to come near him even after he was bound began to find their courage, and for a few minutes the two girls could not even see him — so thickly was he surrounded by the whole crowd of creatures kicking him, hitting him, spitting on him, jeering at him.

At last the rabble had had enough of this. They began to drag the bound and muzzled Lion to the Stone Table, some pulling and some pushing. He was so huge that even when they got him there it took all their efforts to hoist him on to the surface of it. Then there was more tying and tightening of cords.

"The cowards! The cowards!" sobbed Susan. "Are they *still* afraid of him, even now?"

When once Aslan had been tied (and tied so that he was really a mass of cords) on the flat stone, a hush fell on the crowd. Four Hags, holding four torches, stood at the corners of the Table. The Witch bared her arms as she had bared them the previous night when it had been Edmund instead of Aslan. Then she began to whet her knife. It looked to the children, when the gleam of the torchlight fell on it, as if the knife were made of stone, not of steel, and it was of a strange and evil shape.

As last she drew near. She stood by Aslan's head. Her face was working and twitching with passion, but his looked up at the sky, still quiet, neither angry nor afraid, but a little sad. Then, just before she gave the blow, she stooped down and said in a quivering voice,

"And now, who has won? Fool, did you think that by all this you would save the human traitor? Now I will kill you instead of him as our pact was and so the Deep Magic will be appeased. But when you are dead what will prevent me from killing him as well? And who will take him out of my hand *then*? Understand that you have given me Narnia forever, you have lost your own life and you have not saved his. In that knowledge, despair and die."

The children did not see the actual moment of the killing. They couldn't bear to look and had covered their eyes.

CHAPTER FIFTEEN

DEEPER MAGIC FROM BEFORE THE DAWN OF TIME

WHILE the two girls still crouched in the bushes with their hands over their faces, they heard the voice of the Witch calling out,

"Now! Follow me all and we will set about what remains of this war! It will not take us long to crush the human vermin and the traitors now that the great Fool, the great Cat, lies dead."

At this moment the children were for a few seconds in very great danger. For with wild cries and a noise of skirling pipes and shrill horns blowing, the whole of that vile rabble came sweeping off the hill-top and down the slope right past their hiding-place. They felt the Spectres go by them like a cold wind and they felt the ground shake beneath them under the galloping feet of the Minotaurs; and overhead there went a flurry of foul wings and a blackness of vultures and giant bats. At any other time they would have trembled with fear; but now the sadness and shame and horror of Aslan's death so filled their minds that they hardly thought of it.

As soon as the wood was silent again Susan and Lucy crept out onto the open hill-top. The moon was getting low and thin clouds were passing across her, but still they could see the shape of the Lion lying dead in his bonds. And down they both knelt in the wet grass and kissed his cold face and stroked his beautiful fur – what was left of it – and cried till they could cry no more. And then they looked at each other and held each other's hands for mere loneliness and cried again; and then again were silent. At last Lucy said,

"I can't bear to look at that horrible muzzle. I wonder could we take if off?"

So they tried. And after a lot of working at it (for their fingers were cold and it was now the darkest part of the night) they succeeded. And when they saw his face without it they burst out crying again and kissed it and fondled it and wiped away the blood and the foam as well as they could. And it was all more lonely and hopeless and horrid than I know how to describe.

"I wonder could we untie him as well?" said Susan presently. But the enemies, out of pure spitefulness, had drawn the cords so tight that the girls could make nothing of the knots.

I hope no one who reads this book has been quite as miserable as Susan and Lucy were that night; but if you have been — if you've been up all night and cried till you have no more tears left in you — you will know that there comes in the end a sort of quietness. You feel as if nothing was ever going to happen again. At any rate that was how it felt to these two. Hours and hours seemed to go by in this dead calm, and they hardly noticed that they were getting colder and colder. But at last Lucy noticed two other things. One was that the sky on the east side of the hill was a little less dark than it had been an hour ago. The other was some tiny movement going on in the grass at her feet. At first she took no interest in this. What did it matter? Nothing mattered now! But at last she saw that whatever-it-was had begun to move up the upright stones of the Stone Table. And now whatever-they-were were moving about on Aslan's body. She peered closer. They were little grey things.

"Ugh!" said Susan from the other side of the Table. "How beastly! There are horrid little mice crawling over him. Go away, you little beasts." And she raised her hand to frighten them away.

"Wait!" said Lucy, who had been looking at them more closely still. "Can you see what they're doing?"

Both girls bent down and stared.

"I do believe —" said Susan. "But how queer! They're nibbling away at the cords!"

"That's what I thought," said Lucy. "I think they're friendly mice. Poor little things — they don't realize he's dead. They think it'll do some good untying him."

It was quite definitely lighter by now. Each of the
girls noticed for the first time the white face of the
other. They could see the mice nibbling away; dozens
and dozens, even hundreds, of little field mice. And at
last, one by one, the ropes were all gnawed through.

The sky in the east was whitish by now and the
stars were getting fainter – all except one very big one

low down on the eastern horizon. They felt colder
than they had been all night. The mice crept away
again.

The girls cleared away the remains of the gnawed
ropes. Aslan looked more like himself without them.
Every moment his dead face looked nobler, as the
light grew and they could see it better.

In the wood behind them a bird gave a chuckling
sound. It had been so still for hours and hours that it
startled them. Then another bird answered it. Soon
there were birds singing all over the place.

It was quite definitely early morning now, not late
night.

"I'm so cold," said Lucy.

"So am I," said Susan. "Let's walk about a bit."

They walked to the eastern edge of the hill and looked down. The one big star had almost disappeared. The country all looked dark grey, but beyond, at the very end of the world, the sea showed pale. The sky began to turn red. They walked to and fro more times than they could count between the dead Aslan and the eastern ridge, trying to keep warm; and oh, how tired their legs felt. Then at last, as they stood for a moment looking out towards the sea and Cair Paravel (which they could now just make out) the red turned to gold along the line where the sea and the sky met and very slowly up came the edge of the sun. At that moment they heard from behind them a loud noise — a great cracking, deafening noise as if a giant had broken a giant's plate.

"What's that?" said Lucy, clutching Susan's arm.

"I — I feel afraid to turn round," said Susan; "something awful is happening."

"They're doing something worse to *Him*," said Lucy. "Come on!" And she turned, pulling Susan round with her.

The rising of the sun had made everything look so different — all colours and shadows were changed — that for a moment they didn't see the important thing. Then they did. The Stone Table was broken into two pieces by a great crack that ran down it from end to end; and there was no Aslan.

"Oh, oh, oh!" cried the two girls, rushing back to the Table.

"Oh, it's *too* bad," sobbed Lucy; "they might have left the body alone."

"Who's done it?" cried Susan. "What does it mean? Is it magic?"

"Yes!" said a great voice behind their backs. "It is more magic." They looked round. There, shining in the sunrise, larger than they had seen him before,

shaking his mane (for it had apparently grown again) stood Aslan himself.

"Oh, Aslan!" cried both the children, staring up at him, almost as much frightened as they were glad.

"Aren't you dead then, dear Aslan?" said Lucy.

"Not now," said Aslan.

"You're not – not a – ?" asked Susan in a shaky voice. She couldn't bring herself to say the word *ghost*. Aslan stooped his golden head and licked her forehead. The warmth of his breath and a rich sort of smell that seemed to hang about his hair came all over her.

"Do I look it?" he said.

"Oh, you're real, you're real! Oh, Aslan!" cried Lucy, and both girls flung themselves upon him and covered him with kisses.

"But what does it all mean?" asked Susan when they were somewhat calmer.

"It means," said Aslan, "that though the Witch knew the Deep Magic, there is a magic deeper still which she did not know. Her knowledge goes back only to the dawn of time. But if she could have looked a little further back, into the stillness and the darkness before Time dawned, she would have read there a different incantation. She would have known that when a willing victim who had committed no treachery was killed in a traitor's stead, the Table would crack and Death itself would start working backwards. And now —"

"Oh yes. Now?" said Lucy, jumping up and clapping her hands.

"Oh, children," said the Lion, "I feel my strength coming back to me. Oh, children, catch me if you can!" He stood for a second, his eyes very bright, his limbs quivering, lashing himself with his tail. Then he made a leap high over their heads and landed on the other side of the Table. Laughing, though she didn't know why, Lucy scrambled over it to reach him. Aslan leaped again. A mad chase began. Round and round the hill-top he led them, now hopelessly out of their reach, now letting them almost catch his tail, now diving between them, now tossing them in the air with his huge and beautifully velveted paws and catching them again, and now stopping unexpectedly so that all three of them rolled over together in a happy laughing heap of fur and arms and legs. It was such a romp as no one has ever had except in Narnia; and whether it was more like playing with a thunderstorm or playing with a kitten Lucy could never make up her mind. And the funny thing was that when all three finally lay together panting in the sun the girls no longer felt in the least tired or hungry or thirsty.

"And now," said Aslan presently, "to business. I feel I am going to roar. You had better put your fingers in your ears."

And they did. And Aslan stood up and when he opened his mouth to roar his face became so terrible that they did not dare to look at it. And they saw all the trees in front of him bend before the blast of his roaring as grass bends in a meadow before the wind. Then he said,

"We have a long journey to go. You must ride on me." And he crouched down and the children climbed on to his warm, golden back, and Susan sat first, holding on tightly to his mane and Lucy sat behind holding on tightly to Susan. And with a great heave he rose underneath them and then shot off, faster than any horse could go, down hill and into the thick of the forest.

That ride was perhaps the most wonderful thing that happened to them in Narnia. Have you ever had a gallop on a horse? Think of that; and then take away the heavy noise of the hoofs and the jingle of the bits and imagine instead the almost noiseless padding of the great paws. Then imagine instead of the black or grey or chestnut back of the horse the soft roughness of golden fur, and the mane flying back in the wind. And then imagine you are going about twice as fast as the fastest racehorse. But this is a mount that doesn't need to be guided and never grows tired. He rushes on and on, never missing his footing, never hesitating, threading his way with perfect skill between tree trunks, jumping over bush and briar and the smaller streams, wading the larger, swimming the largest of all. And you are riding not on a road nor in a park nor even on the downs, but right across Narnia, in spring, down solemn avenues of beech and across sunny glades of oak, through wild orchards of snow-white cherry trees, past roaring waterfalls and mossy rocks and echoing caverns, up windy slopes alight with gorse bushes, and across the shoulders of heathery mountains and along giddy ridges and down, down, down again into wild valleys and out into acres of blue flowers.

It was nearly midday when they found themselves looking down a steep hillside at a castle – a little toy castle it looked from where they stood – which seemed to be all pointed towers. But the Lion was rushing down at such a speed that it grew larger every moment and before they had time even to ask themselves what it was they were already on a level with it. And now it no longer looked like a toy castle but rose frowning in front of them. No face looked over the battlements and the gates were fast shut. And Aslan, not at all slacking his pace, rushed straight as a bullet towards it.

"The Witch's home!" he cried. "Now, children, hold tight."

Next moment the whole world seemed to turn

upside down, and the children felt as if they had left their insides behind them; for the Lion had gathered himself together for a greater leap than any he had yet made and jumped — or you may call it flying rather than jumping — right over the castle wall. The two girls, breathless but unhurt, found themselves tumbling off his back in the middle of a wide stone courtyard full of statues.

CHAPTER SIXTEEN

WHAT HAPPENED ABOUT
THE STATUES

"WHAT an extraordinary place!" cried Lucy. "All those stone animals — and people too! It's — it's like a museum."

"Hush," said Susan, "Aslan's doing something."

He was indeed. He had bounded up to the stone lion and breathed on him. Then without waiting a moment he whisked round — almost as if he had been a cat chasing its tail — and breathed also on the stone dwarf, which (as you remember) was standing a few feet from the lion with his back to it. Then he pounced on a tall stone dryad which stood beyond the dwarf, turned rapidly aside to deal with a stone rabbit on his right, and rushed on to two centaurs. But at that moment Lucy said,

"Oh, Susan! Look! Look at the lion."

I expect you've seen someone put a lighted match to a bit of newspaper which is propped up in a grate against an unlit fire. And for a second nothing seems to have happened; and then you notice a tiny streak of flame creeping along the edge of the newspaper. It was like that now. For a second after Aslan had breathed upon him the stone lion looked just the same. Then a tiny streak of gold began to run along his white marble back — then it spread — then the colour seemed to lick all over him as the flame licks all over a bit of paper — then, while his hindquarters were still obviously stone, the lion shook his mane and all the heavy, stone folds rippled into living hair. Then he opened a great red mouth, warm and living, and gave a prodigious yawn. And now his hind legs had come to life. He lifted one of them and scratched himself. Then, having caught sight of Aslan, he went bounding after him and frisking round him whimpering with delight and jumping up to lick his face.

Of course the children's eyes turned to follow the lion; but the sight they saw was so wonderful that they soon forgot about *him*. Everywhere the statues were coming to life. The courtyard looked no longer like a museum; it looked more like a zoo. Creatures were running after Aslan and dancing round him till he was almost hidden in the crowd. Instead of all that deadly white the courtyard was now a blaze of colours; glossy chestnut sides of centaurs, indigo horns of unicorns, dazzling plumage of birds, reddy-brown of foxes, dogs and satyrs, yellow stockings and crimson hoods of dwarfs; and the birch-girls in silver, and the beech-girls in fresh, transparent green, and the larch-girls in green so bright that it was almost yellow. And instead of the deadly silence the whole place rang with the sound of happy roarings, brayings, yelpings, barkings, squealings, cooings, neighings, stampings, shouts, hurrahs, songs and laughter.

"Oh!" said Susan in a different tone. "Look! I wonder – I mean, is it safe?"

Lucy looked and saw that Aslan had just breathed on the feet of the stone giant.

"It's all right!" shouted Aslan joyously. "Once the feet are put right, all the rest of him will follow."

"That wasn't exactly what I meant," whispered

Susan to Lucy. But it was too late to do anything
about it now even if Aslan would have listened to her.
The change was already creeping up the Giant's legs.
Now he was moving his feet. A moment later he lifted
his club off his shoulder, rubbed his eyes and said,

"Bless me! I must have been asleep. Now! Where's
that dratted little Witch that was running about on
the ground. Somewhere just by my feet it was." But
when everyone had shouted up to him to explain
what had really happened, and when the Giant had
put his hand to his ear and got them to repeat it all
again so that at last he understood, then he bowed
down till his head was no further off than the top of a
haystack and touched his cap repeatedly to Aslan,
beaming all over his honest ugly face. (Giants of any
sort are now so rare in England and so few giants are
good-tempered that ten to one you have never seen a
giant when his face is beaming. It's a sight well worth
looking at.)

"Now for the inside of this house!" said Aslan.
"Look alive, everyone. Up stairs and down stairs and
in my lady's chamber! Leave no corner unsearched.
You never know where some poor prisoner may be
concealed."

And into the interior they all rushed and for several
minutes the whole of that dark, horrible, fusty old
castle echoed with the opening of windows and with
everyone's voices crying out at once, "Don't forget
the dungeons – Give us a hand with this door! –
Here's another little winding stair – Oh! I say. Here's
a poor kangaroo. Call Aslan – Phew! How it smells in
here – Look out for trap-doors – Up here! There are a

whole lot more on the landing!" But the best of all was when Lucy came rushing upstairs shouting out,

"Aslan! Aslan! I've found Mr Tumnus. Oh, do come quick."

A moment later Lucy and the little Faun were holding each other by both hands and dancing round and round for joy. The little chap was none the worse for having been a statue and was of course very interested in all she had to tell him.

But at last the ransacking of the Witch's fortress was ended. The whole castle stood empty with every door and window open and the light and the sweet spring air flooding into all the dark and evil places which needed them so badly. The whole crowd of liberated statues surged back into the courtyard. And it was then that someone (Tumnus, I think) first said,

"But how are we going to get out?" for Aslan had got in by a jump and the gates were still locked.

"That'll be all right," said Aslan; and then, rising on his hind-legs, he bawled up at the Giant. "Hi! You up there," he roared. "What's your name?"

"Giant Rumblebuffin, if it please your honour," said the Giant, once more touching his cap.

"Well then, Giant Rumblebuffin," said Aslan, "just let us out of this, will you?"

"Certainly, your honour. It will be a pleasure," said Giant Rumblebuffin. "Stand well away from the gates, all you little 'uns." Then he strode to the gate himself and bang – bang – bang – went his huge club. The gates creaked at the first blow, cracked at the second, and shivered at the third. Then he tackled the towers on each side of them and after a few minutes

of crashing and thudding both the towers and a good
bit of the wall on each side went thundering down in
a mass of hopeless rubble; and when the dust cleared
it was odd, standing in that dry, grim, stony yard, to
see through the gap all the grass and waving trees and
sparkling streams of the forest, and the blue hills
beyond that and beyond them the sky.

"Blowed if I ain't all in a muck sweat," said the
Giant, puffing like the largest railway engine. "Comes
of being out of condition. I suppose neither of you
young ladies has such a thing as a pocket-
handkerchee about you?"

"Yes, I have," said Lucy, standing on tip-toes and
holding her handkerchief up as far as she could reach.

"Thank you, Missie," said Giant Rumblebuffin,
stooping down. Next moment Lucy got rather a
fright for she found herself caught up in mid-air
between the Giant's finger and thumb. But just as she
was getting near his face he suddenly started and
then put her gently back on the ground muttering,
"Bless me! I've picked up the little girl instead. I beg
your pardon, Missie, I thought you *was* the
handkerchee!"

"No, no," said Lucy laughing, "here it is!" This
time he managed to get it but it was only about the
same size to him that a saccharine tablet would be to
you, so that when she saw him solemnly rubbing it to
and fro across his great red face, she said, "I'm afraid
it's not much use to you, Mr Rumblebuffin."

"Not at all. Not at all," said the giant politely.
"Never met a nicer handkerchee. So fine, so handy.
So – I don't know how to describe it."

"What a nice giant he is!" said Lucy to Mr Tumnus.

"Oh yes," replied the Faun. "All the Buffins always were. One of the most respected of all the giant families in Narnia. Not very clever, perhaps (I never knew a giant that was), but an old family. With traditions, you know. If he'd been the other sort she'd never have turned him into stone."

At this point Aslan clapped his paws together and called for silence.

"Our day's work is not yet over," he said, "and if the Witch is to be finally defeated before bed-time we must find the battle at once."

"And join in, I hope, sir!" added the largest of the Centaurs.

"Of course," said Aslan. "And now! Those who can't keep up — that is, children, dwarfs, and small animals — must ride on the backs of those who can — that is, lions, centaurs, unicorns, horses, giants and eagles. Those who are good with their noses must come in front with us lions to smell out where the battle is. Look lively and sort yourselves."

And with a great deal of bustle and cheering they did. The most pleased of the lot was the other lion who kept running about everywhere pretending to be very busy but really in order to say to everyone he met. "Did you hear what he said? *Us Lions.* That means him and me. *Us Lions.* That's what I like about Aslan. No side, no stand-off-ishness. *Us Lions.* That meant him and me." At least he went on saying this till Aslan had loaded him up with three dwarfs,

one dryad, two rabbits, and a hedgehog. That
steadied him a bit.

When all were ready (it was a big sheep-dog who
actually helped Aslan most in getting them sorted into
their proper order) they set out through the gap in the
castle wall. At first the lions and dogs went nosing
about in all directions. But then suddenly one great
hound picked up the scent and gave a bay. There was
no time lost after that. Soon all the dogs and lions and
wolves and other hunting animals were going at full
speed with their noses to the ground, and all the
others, streaked out for about half a mile behind
them, were following as fast as they could. The noise
was like an English fox-hunt only better because
every now and then with the music of the hounds was
mixed the roar of the other lion and sometimes the far
deeper and more awful roar of Aslan himself. Faster
and faster they went as the scent became easier and
easier to follow. And then, just as they came to the
last curve in a narrow, winding valley, Lucy heard
above all these noises another noise – a different one,
which gave her a queer feeling inside. It was a noise of
shouts and shrieks and of the clashing of metal
against metal.

Then they came out of the narrow valley and at
once she saw the reason. There stood Peter and
Edmund and all the rest of Aslan's army fighting
desperately against the crowd of horrible creatures
whom she had seen last night; only now, in the
daylight, they looked even stranger and more evil and
more deformed. There also seemed to be far more of
them. Peter's army – which had their backs to her –

looked terribly few. And there were statues dotted all over the battlefield, so apparently the Witch had been using her wand. But she did not seem to be using it now. She was fighting with her stone knife. It was Peter she was fighting — both of them going at it so hard that Lucy could hardly make out what was happening; she only saw the stone knife and Peter's sword flashing so quickly that they looked like three knives and three swords. That pair were in the centre. On each side the line stretched out. Horrible things were happening wherever she looked.

"Off my back, children," shouted Aslan. And they both tumbled off. Then with a roar that shook all Narnia from the western lamp-post to the shores of the eastern sea the great beast flung himself upon the White Witch. Lucy saw her face lifted towards him for one second with an expression of terror and amazement. Then Lion and Witch had rolled over together but with the Witch underneath; and at the same moment all war-like creatures whom Aslan had led from the Witch's house rushed madly on the enemy lines, dwarfs with their battleaxes, dogs with teeth, the Giant with his club (and his feet also crushed dozens of the foe), unicorns with their horns, centaurs with swords and hoofs. And Peter's tired army cheered, and the newcomers roared, and the enemy squealed and gibbered till the wood re-echoed with the din of that onset.

CHAPTER SEVENTEEN

THE HUNTING OF THE WHITE STAG

THE battle was all over a few minutes after their arrival. Most of the enemy had been killed in the first charge of Aslan and his companions; and when those who were still living saw that the Witch was dead they either gave themselves up or took to flight. The next thing that Lucy knew was that Peter and Aslan were shaking hands. It was strange to her to see Peter looking as he looked now – his face was so pale and stern and he seemed so much older.

"It was all Edmund's doing, Aslan," Peter was saying. "We'd have been beaten if it hadn't been for him. The Witch was turning our troops into stone right and left. But nothing would stop him. He fought his way through three ogres to where she was just turning one of your leopards into a statue. And when he reached her he had sense to bring his sword smashing down on her wand instead of trying to go for her directly and simply getting made a statue himself for his pains. That was the mistake all the rest were making. Once her wand was broken we began to have some chance – if we hadn't lost so many already. He was terribly wounded. We must go and see him."

They found Edmund in charge of Mrs Beaver a little way back from the fighting line. He was covered with blood, his mouth was open, and his face a nasty green colour.

"Quick, Lucy," said Aslan.

And then, almost for the first time, Lucy remembered the precious cordial that had been given her for a Christmas present. Her hands trembled so much that she could hardly undo the stopper, but she managed it in the end and poured a few drops into her brother's mouth.

"There are other people wounded," said Aslan while she was still looking eagerly into Edmund's pale face and wondering if the cordial would have any result.

"Yes, I know," said Lucy crossly. "Wait a minute."

"Daughter of Eve," said Aslan in a graver voice, "others also are at the point of death. Must *more* people die for Edmund?"

"I'm sorry, Aslan," said Lucy, getting up and going with him. And for the next half-hour they were busy – she attending to the wounded while he restored those who had been turned into stone. When at last she was free to come back to Edmund she found him standing on his feet and not only healed of his wounds but looking better than she had seen him look – oh, for ages; in fact ever since his first term at that horrid school which was where he had begun to go wrong. He had become his real old self again and could look you in the face. And there on the field of battle Aslan made him a knight.

"Does he know," whispered Lucy to Susan, "what Aslan did for him? Does he know what the arrangement with the Witch really was?"

"Hush! No. Of course not," said Susan.

"Oughtn't he to be told?" said Lucy.

"Oh, surely not," said Susan. "It would be too awful for him. Think how you'd feel if you were he."

"All the same I think he ought to know," said Lucy. But at that moment they were interrupted.

That night they slept where they were How Aslan provided food for them all I don't know; but somehow or other they found themselves all sitting down on the grass to a fine high tea at about eight o'clock. Next day they began marching eastward down the

side of the great river. And the next day after that, at about teatime, they actually reached the mouth. The castle of Cair Paravel on its little hill towered up above them; before them were the sands, with rocks and little pools of salt water, and seaweed, and the smell of the sea and long miles of bluish-green waves breaking for ever and ever on the beach. And oh, the cry of the sea-gulls! Have you heard it? Can you remember?

That evening after tea the four children all managed to get down to the beach again and get their shoes and stockings off and feel the sand between their toes. But next day was more solemn. For then, in the Great Hall of Cair Paravel — that wonderful hall with the ivory roof and the west wall hung with peacock's feathers and the eastern door which looks towards the sea, in the presence of all their friends and to the sound of trumpets, Aslan solemnly crowned them and led them to the four thrones amid deafening shouts of, "Long Live King Peter! Long Live Queen Susan! Long Live King Edmund! Long Live Queen Lucy!"

"Once a king or queen in Narnia, always a king or queen. Bear it well, Sons of Adam! Bear it well, Daughters of Eve!" said Aslan.

And through the eastern door, which was wide open, came the voices of the mermen and the mermaids swimming close to the shore and singing in honour of their new Kings and Queens.

So the children sat on their thrones and sceptres were put into their hands and they gave rewards and honours to all their friends, to Tumnus the Faun, and to the Beavers, and Giant Rumblebuffin, to the leopards, and the good centaurs, and the good dwarfs, and to the lion. And that night there was a great feast in Cair Paravel, and revelry and dancing, and gold flashed and wine flowed, and answering to the music inside, but stranger, sweeter, and more piercing, came the music of the sea people.

But amidst all these rejoicings Aslan himself quietly slipped away. And when the Kings and Queens noticed that he wasn't there they said nothing about it. For Mr Beaver had warned them, "He'll be coming and going," he had said. "One day you'll see him and another you won't. He doesn't like being tied down – and of course he has other countries to attend to. It's quite all right. He'll often drop in. Only you mustn't press him. He's wild, you know. Not like a *tame* lion."

And now, as you see, this story is nearly (but not quite) at an end. These two Kings and two Queens governed Narnia well, and long and happy was their reign. At first much of their time was spent in seeking out the remnants of the White Witch's army and destroying them, and indeed for a long time there would be news of evil things lurking in the wilder parts of the forest – a haunting here and a killing there, a glimpse of a werewolf one month and a rumour of a hag the next. But in the end all that foul brood was stamped out. And they made good laws and kept the peace and saved good trees from being unnecessarily cut down, and liberated young dwarfs and young satyrs from being sent to school, and generally stopped busybodies and interferers and encouraged ordinary people who wanted to live and let live. And they drove back the fierce giants (quite a different sort from Giant Rumblebuffin) on the north of Narnia when these ventured across the frontier. And they entered into friendship and alliance with countries beyond the sea and paid them visits of state and received visits of state from them. And they themselves grew and changed as the years passed over them. And Peter became a tall and deep-chested man and a great warrior, and he was called King Peter the Magnificent. And Susan grew into a tall and gracious woman with black hair that fell almost to her feet and the kings of the countries beyond the sea began to send ambassadors asking for her hand in marriage. And she was called Susan the Gentle. Edmund was a graver and quieter man than Peter, and great in council and judgement. He was called King Edmund the Just. But as for Lucy, she was always gay and golden-haired, and all princes in those parts desired her to be their Queen, and her own people called her Queen Lucy the Valiant.

So they lived in great joy and if ever they remembered their life in this world it was only as one remembers a dream. And one year it fell out that Tumnus (who was a middle-aged Faun by now and beginning to be stout) came down river and brought them news that the White Stag had once more appeared in his parts – the White Stag who would give you wishes if you caught him. So these two Kings and two Queens with the principal members of their court, rode a-hunting with horns and hounds in the Western Woods to follow the White Stag. And they had not hunted long before they had a sight of him. And he led them a great pace over rough and smooth and through thick and thin, till the horses of all the courtiers were tired out and these four were still following. And they saw the stag enter into a thicket where their horses could not follow. Then said King Peter (for they talked in quite a different style now, having been Kings and Queens for so long), "Fair Consorts, let us now alight from our horses and follow this beast into the thicket; for in all my days I never hunted a nobler quarry."

"Sir," said the others, "even so let us do."

So they alighted and tied their horses to trees and went on into the thick wood on foot. And as soon as they had entered it Queen Susan said,

"Fair friends, here is a great marvel, for I seem to see a tree of iron."

"Madam," said King Edmund, "if you look well

upon it you shall see it is a pillar of iron with a lantern set on the top thereof."

"By the Lion's Mane, a strange device," said King Peter, "to set a lantern here where the trees cluster so thick about it and so high above it that if it were lit it should give light to no man!"

"Sir," said Queen Lucy. "By likelihood when this post and this lamp were set here there were smaller trees in the place, or fewer, or none. For this is a young wood and the iron post is old." And they stood looking upon it. Then said King Edmund,

"I know not how it is, but this lamp on the post worketh upon me strangely. It runs in my mind that I have seen the like before; as it were in a dream, or in the dream of a dream."

"Sir," answered they all, "it is even so with us also."

"And more," said Queen Lucy, "for it will not go out of my mind that if we pass this post and lantern either we shall find strange adventures or else some great change of our fortunes."

"Madam," said King Edmund, "the like foreboding stirreth in my heart also."

"And in mine, fair brother," said King Peter.

"And in mine too," said Queen Susan. "Wherefore by my counsel we shall lightly return to our horses and follow this White Stag no further."

"Madam," said King Peter, "therein I pray thee to have me excused. For never since we four were Kings and Queens in Narnia have we set our hands to any high matter, as battles, quests, feats of arms, acts of justice, and the like, and then given over; but always what we have taken in hand, the same we have achieved."

"Sister," said Queen Lucy, "my royal brother speaks rightly. And it seems to me we should be shamed if for any fearing or foreboding we turned back from following so noble a beast as now we have in chase."

"And so say I," said King Edmund. "And I have such desire to find the signification of this thing that I would not by my good will turn back for the richest jewel in all Narnia and all the islands."

"Then in the name of Aslan," said Queen Susan, "if ye will all have it so, let us go on and take the adventure that shall fall to us."

So these Kings and Queens entered the thicket, and before they had gone a score of paces they all remembered that the thing they had seen was called a lamp-post, and before they had gone twenty more they noticed that they were making their way not through branches but through coats. And next moment they all came tumbling out of a wardrobe door into the empty room, and they were no longer Kings and Queens in their hunting array but just Peter, Susan, Edmund and Lucy in their old clothes. It was the same day and the same hour of the day on which they had all gone into the wardrobe to hide. Mrs Macready and the visitors were still talking in the passage; but luckily they never came into the empty room and so the children weren't caught.

And that would have been the very end of the story if it hadn't been that they felt they really must explain to the Professor why four of the coats out of his wardrobe were missing. And the Professor, who was a very remarkable man, didn't tell them not to be silly or not to tell lies, but believed the whole story. "No," he said, "I don't think it will be any good trying to go back through the wardrobe door to get the coats. You won't get into Narnia again by *that* route. Nor would the coats be much use by now if you did! Eh? What's that? Yes, of course you'll get back to Narnia again some day. Once a King in Narnia, always a King in Narnia. But don't go trying to use the same route twice. Indeed, don't *try* to get there at all. It'll happen when you're not looking for it. And don't talk too much about it even among yourselves. And don't mention it to anyone else unless you find that they've had adventures of the same sort themselves. What's that? How will you know? Oh, you'll *know* all right. Odd things they say – even their looks - will let the secret out. Keep your eyes open. Bless me, what *do* they teach them at these schools?

And that is the very end of the adventure of the wardrobe. But if the Professor was right it was only the beginning of the adventures of Narnia.

The Horse and His Boy

Mt. Pire

Anva

narrow gorge

D E S E R

Rock

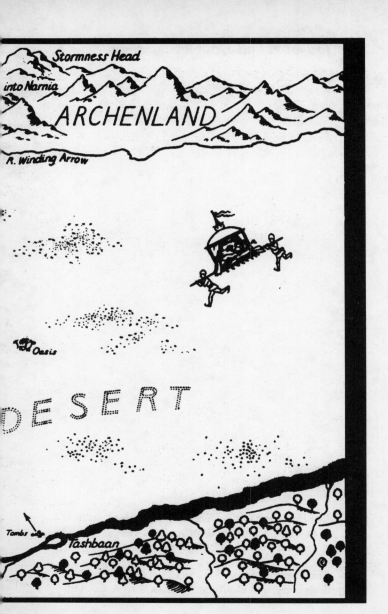

To David and Douglas Gresham

The Horse and His Boy was first published
in Great Britain by Geoffrey Bles 1954
First published by Collins 1980

CHAPTER ONE

HOW SHASTA SET OUT ON HIS
TRAVELS

THIS is the story of an adventure that happened in Narnia and Calormen and the lands between, in the Golden Age when Peter was High King in Narnia and his brother and his two sisters were King and Queens under him.

In those days, far south in Calormen on a little creek of the sea, there lived a poor fisherman called Arsheesh, and with him there lived a boy who called him Father. The boy's name was Shasta. On most days Arsheesh went out in his boat to fish in the morning, and in the afternoon he harnessed his donkey to a cart and loaded the cart with fish and went a mile or so southward to the village to sell it. If it had sold well he would come home in a moderately good temper and say nothing to Shasta, but if it had sold badly he would find fault with him and perhaps beat him. There was always something to find fault with for Shasta had plenty of work to do, mending and washing the nets, cooking the supper, and cleaning the cottage in which they both lived.

Shasta was not at all interested in anything that lay south of his home because he had once or twice been to the village with Arsheesh and he knew that there was nothing very interesting there. In the village he only met other men who were just like his father — men with long, dirty robes, and wooden shoes turned up at the toe, and turbans on their heads, and beards, talking to one another very slowly about things that sounded dull. But he was very interested in everything that lay to the North because no one ever went that way and he was never allowed to go there himself. When he was sitting out of doors mending the

nets, and all alone, he would often look eagerly to the
North. One could see nothing but a grassy slope running
up to a level ridge and beyond that the sky with perhaps a
few birds in it.

Sometimes if Arsheesh was there Shasta would say, "O
my Father, what is there beyond that hill?" And then if the
fisherman was in a bad temper he would box Shasta's ears
and tell him to attend to his work. Or if he was in a peaceable mood he would say, "O my son, do not allow your
mind to be distracted by idle questions. For one of the
poets has said, 'Application to business is the root of pros-
perity, but those who ask questions that do not concern
them are steering the ship of folly towards the rock of
indigence'."

Shasta thought that beyond the hill there must be some
delightful secret which his father wished to hide from him.
In reality, however, the fisher...an talked like this because
he didn't know what lay to the North. Neither did he care.
He had a very practical mind.

One day there came from the South a stranger who was
unlike any man that Shasta had seen before. He rode upon
a strong dappled horse with flowing mane and tail and his
stirrups and bridle were inlaid with silver. The spike of a
helmet projected from the middle of his silken turban and
he wore a shirt of chain mail. By his side hung a curving
scimitar, a round shield studded with bosses of brass hung
at his back, and his right hand grasped a lance. His face
was dark, but this did not surprise Shasta because all the
people of Calormen are like that; what did surprise him
was the man's beard which was dyed crimson, and curled
and gleaming with scented oil. But Arsheesh knew by the
gold on the stranger's bare arm that he was a Tarkaan or
great lord, and he bowed kneeling before him till his beard
touched the earth and made signs to Shasta to kneel also.

The stranger demanded hospitality for the night which of course the fisherman dared not refuse. All the best they had was set before the Tarkaan for supper (and he didn't think much of it) and Shasta, as always happened when the fisherman had company, was given a hunk of bread and turned out of the cottage. On these occasions he usually slept with the donkey in its little thatched stable. But it was

much too early to go to sleep yet, and Shasta, who had
never learned that it is wrong to listen behind doors, sat
down with his ear to a crack in the wooden wall of the cottage to hear what the grown-ups were talking about. And
this is what he heard.

"And now, O my host," said the Tarkaan, "I have a
mind to buy that boy of yours."

"O my master," replied the fisherman (and Shasta knew
by the wheedling tone the greedy look that was probably
coming into his face as he said it), "what price could induce
your servant, poor though he is, to sell into slavery his only
child and his own flesh? Has not one of the poets said,
'Natural affection is stronger than soup and offspring more
precious than carbuncles?'"

"It is even so," replied the guest dryly. "But another poet
has likewise said, "He who attempts to deceive the judicious is already baring his own back for the scourge." Do
not load your aged mouth with falsehoods. This boy is
manifestly no son of yours, for your cheek is as dark as
mine but the boy is fair and white like the accursed but
beautiful barbarians who inhabit the remote North."

"How well it was said," answered the fisherman, "that
Swords can be kept off with shields but the Eye of Wisdom
pierces through every defence! Know then, O my formid-
able guest, that because of my extreme poverty I have never
married and have no child. But in that same year in which
the Tisroc (may he live for ever) began his august and
beneficent reign, on a night when the moon was at her full,
it pleased the gods to deprive me of my sleep. Therefore I
arose from my bed in this hovel and went forth to the
beach to refresh myself with looking upon the water and
the moon and breathing the cool air. And presently I heard
a noise as of oars coming to me across the water and then,
as it were, a weak cry. And shortly after, the tide brought

to the land a little boat in which there was nothing but a man lean with extreme hunger and thirst who seemed to have died but a few moments before (for he was still warm), and an empty water-skin, and a child, still living. "Doubtless," said I, "these unfortunates have escaped from the wreck of a great ship, but by the admirable designs of the gods, the elder has starved himself to keep the child alive and has perished in sight of land." Accordingly, remembering how the gods never fail to reward those who befriend the destitute, and being moved by compassion (for your servant is a man of tender heart) –"

"Leave out all these idle words in your own praise," interrupted the Tarkaan. "It is enough to know that you took the child – and have had ten times the worth of his daily bread out of him in labour, as anyone can see. And now tell me at once what price you put on him, for I am wearied with your loquacity."

"You yourself have wisely said," answered Arsheesh, "that the boy's labour has been to me of inestimable value. This must be taken into account in fixing the price. For if I sell the boy I must undoubtedly either buy or hire another to do his work."

"I'll give you fifteen crescents for him," said the Tarkaan.

"Fifteen!" cried Arsheesh in a voice that was something between a whine and a scream. "Fifteen! For the prop of my old age and the delight of my eyes! Do not mock my grey beard, Tarkaan though you be. My price is seventy."

At this point Shasta got up and tiptoed away. He had heard all he wanted, for he had often listened when men were bargaining in the village and knew how it was done. He was quite certain that Arsheesh would sell him in the end for something much more than fifteen crescents and much less than seventy, but that he and the Tarkaan would take hours in getting to an agreement.

You must not imagine that Shasta felt at all as you and I would feel if we had just overheard our parents talking about selling us for slaves. For one thing, his life was already little better than slavery; for all he knew, the lordly stranger on the great horse might be kinder to him than Arsheesh. For another, the story about his own discovery in the boat had filled him with excitement and with a sense of relief. He had often been uneasy because, try as he might, he had never been able to love the fisherman, and he knew that a boy ought to love his father. And now, apparently, he was no relation to Arsheesh at all. That took a great weight off his mind. "Why, I might be anyone!" he thought. "I might be the son of a Tarkaan myself — or the son of the Tisroc (may he live for ever) — or of a god!"

He was standing out in the grassy place before the cottage while he thought these things. Twilight was coming on apace and a star or two was already out, but the remains of the sunset could still be seen in the west. Not far away the stranger's horse, loosely tied to an iron ring in the wall of the donkey's stable, was grazing. Shasta strolled over to it and patted its neck. It went on tearing up the grass and took no notice of him.

Then another thought came into Shasta's mind. "I wonder what sort of a man that Tarkaan is," he said out loud. "It would be splendid if he was kind. Some of the slaves in a great lord's house have next to nothing to do. They wear lovely clothes and eat meat every day. Perhaps he'd take me to the wars and I'd save his life in a battle and then he'd set me free and adopt me as his son and give me a palace and a chariot and a suit of armour. But then he might be a horrid cruel man. He might send me to work on the fields in chains. I wish I knew. How can I know? I bet this horse knows, if only he could tell me."

The Horse had lifted its head. Shasta stroked its smooth-as-satin nose and said, "I wish *you* could talk, old fellow."

And then for a second he thought he was dreaming, for quite distinctly, though in a low voice, the Horse said, "But I can."

Shasta stared into its great eyes and his own grew almost as big, with astonishment.

"How ever did *you* learn to talk?" he asked.

"Hush! Not so loud," replied the Horse. "Where I come from, nearly all the animals talk."

"Wherever is that?" asked Shasta.

"Narnia," answered the Horse. "The happy land of Narnia — Narnia of the heathery mountains and the thymy downs, Narnia of the many rivers, the plashing glens, the mossy caverns and the deep forests ringing with the hammers of the Dwarfs. Oh the sweet air of Narnia! An hour's life there is better than a thousand years in Calormen." It ended with a whinny that sounded very like a sigh.

"How did you get here?" said Shasta.

"Kidnapped," said the Horse. "Or stolen, or captured — whichever you like to call it. I was only a foal at the time. My mother warned me not to range the Southern slopes, into Archenland and beyond, but I wouldn't heed her. And by the Lion's Mane I have paid for my folly. All these years I have been a slave to humans, hiding my true nature and pretending to be dumb and witless like *their* horses."

"Why didn't you tell them who you were?"

"Not such a fool, that's why. If they'd once found out I could talk they would have made a show of me at fairs and guarded me more carefully than ever. My last chance of escape would have been gone."

"And why —" began Shasta, but the Horse interrupted him.

"Now look," it said, "we mustn't waste time on idle questions. You want to know about my master the Tarkaan Anradin. Well, he's bad. Not too bad to me, for a war horse costs too much to be treated very badly. But you'd better be lying dead tonight than go to be a human slave in his house tomorrow."

"Then I'd better run away," said Shasta, turning very pale.

"Yes, you had," said the Horse. "But why not run away with me?"

"Are you going to run away too?" said Shasta.

"Yes, if you'll come with me," answered the Horse. "This is the chance for both of us. You see if I run away without a rider, everyone who sees me will say "Stray horse" and be after me as quick as he can. With a rider I've a chance to get through. That's where you can help me. On the other hand, you can't get very far on those two silly legs of yours (what absurd legs humans have!) without being overtaken. But on me you can outdistance any other horse in this country. That's where I can help you. By the way, I suppose you know how to ride?"

"Oh yes, of course," said Shasta. "At least, I've ridden the donkey."

"Ridden the *what*?" retorted the Horse with extreme contempt. (At least, that is what he meant. Actually it came out in a sort of neigh — "Ridden the wha-ha-ha-ha-ha." Talking horses always become more horsy in accent when they are angry.)

"In other words," it continued, "you *can't* ride. That's a drawback. I'll have to teach you as we go along. If you can't ride, can you fall?"

"I suppose anyone can fall," said Shasta.

"I mean can you fall and get up again without crying and mount again and fall again and yet not be afraid of falling?"

"I – I'll try," said Shasta. "Poor little beast," said the Horse in a gentler tone. "I forget you're only a foal. We'll make a fine rider of you in time. And now – we mustn't start until those two in the hut are asleep. Meantime we can make our plans. My Tarkaan is on his way North to the great city, to Tashbaan itself and the court of the Tisroc –"

"I say," put in Shasta in rather a shocked voice, "oughtn't you to say 'May he live for ever'?"

"Why?" asked the Horse. "I'm a free Narnian. And why should I talk slaves' and fools' talk? I don't want him to live for ever, and I know that he's not going to live for ever whether I want him to or not. And I can see you're from the free North too. No more of this Southern jargon between you and me! And now, back to our plans. As I said, my human was on his way North to Tashbaan."

"Does that mean we'd better go to the South?"

"I think not," said the Horse. "You see, he thinks I'm dumb and witless like his other horses. Now if I really were, the moment I got loose I'd go back home to my stable and paddock; back to his palace which is two days' journey South. That's where he'll look for me. He'd never dream of my going on North on my own. And anyway he will probably think that someone in the last village who saw him ride through has followed us to here and stolen me."

"Oh hurrah!" said Shasta. "Then we'll go North. I've been longing to go to the North all my life."

"Of course you have," said the Horse. "That's because of the blood that's in you. I'm sure you're true Northern stock. But not too loud. I should think they'd be asleep soon now."

"I'd better creep back and see," suggested Shasta.

"That's a good idea," said the Horse. "But take care you're not caught."

It was a good deal darker now and very silent except for the sound of the waves on the beach, which Shasta hardly noticed because he had been hearing it day and night as long as he could remember. The cottage, as he approached it, showed no light. When he listened at the front there was no noise. When he went round to the only window, he could hear, after a second or two, the familiar noise of the old fisherman's squeaky snore. It was funny to think that if all went well he would never hear it again. Holding his breath and feeling a little bit sorry, but much less sorry than he was glad, Shasta glided away over the grass and went to the donkey's stable, groped along to a place he knew where the key was hidden, opened the door and found the Horse's saddle and bridle which had been locked up there for the night. He bent forward and kissed the donkey's nose. "I'm sorry we can't take *you*," he said.

"There you are at last," said the Horse when he got back to it. "I was beginning to wonder what had become of you."

"I was getting your things out of the stable," replied Shasta. "And now, can you tell me how to put them on?"

For the next few minutes Shasta was at work, very cautiously to avoid jingling, while the Horse said things like, "Get that girth a bit tighter," or "You'll find a buckle lower down," or "You'll need to shorten those stirrups a good bit." When all was finished it said:

"Now; we've got to have reins for the look of the thing, but you won't be using them. Tie them to the saddle-bow: very slack so that I can do what I like with my head. And, remember — you are not to touch them."

"What are they for, then?" asked Shasta.

"Ordinarily they are for directing me," replied the Horse. "But as I intend to do all the directing on this journey, you'll please keep your hands to yourself. And there's another thing. I'm not going to have you grabbing my mane."

"But I say," pleaded Shasta. "If I'm not to hold on by the reins or by your mane, what *am* I to hold on by?"

"You hold on with your knees," said the Horse. "That's the secret of good riding. Grip my body between your knees as hard as you like; sit straight up, straight as a poker; keep your elbows in. And by the way, what did you do with the spurs?"

"Put them on my heels, of course," said Shasta. "I do know that much."

"Then you can take them off and put them in the saddle-bag. We may be able to sell them when we get to Tashbaan. Ready? And now I think you can get up."

"Ooh! You're a dreadful height," gasped Shasta after his first, and unsuccessful, attempt.

"I'm a horse, that's all," was the reply. "Anyone would think I was a haystack from the way you're trying to climb up me! There, that's better. Now sit *up* and remember what I told you about your knees. Funny to think of me who has led cavalry charges and won races having a potato-sack like you in the saddle! However, off we go." It chuckled, not unkindly.

And it certainly began their night journey with great caution. First of all it went just south of the fisherman's cottage to the little river which there ran into the sea, and took care to leave in the mud some very plain hoof-marks pointing South. But as soon as they were in the middle of the ford it turned upstream and waded till they were about a hundred yards farther inland than the cottage.Then it selected a nice gravelly bit of bank which would take no footprints and came out on the Northern side. Then, still at a walking pace, it went Northward till the cottage, the one tree, the donkey's stable, and the creek – everything, in fact, that Shasta had ever known – had sunk out of sight in the grey summer-night darkness. They had been going up-hill and now were at the top of the ridge – that ridge which had always been the boundary of Shasta's known world. He could not see what was ahead except that it was all open and grassy. It looked endless: wild and lonely and free.

"I say!" observed the Horse. "What a place for a gallop, eh!"

"Oh don't let's," said Shasta. "Not yet. I don't know how to – please, Horse. I don't know your name."

"Breehy-hinny-brinny-hoohy-hah," said the Horse.

"I'll never be able to say that," said Shasta. "Can I call you Bree?"

"Well, if it's the best you can do, I suppose you must," said the Horse. "And what shall I call you?"

"I'm called Shasta."

"H'm," said Bree. "Well, now, there's a name that's *really* hard to pronounce. But now about this gallop. It's a good deal easier than trotting if you only knew, because you don't have to rise and fall. Grip with your knees and keep your eyes straight ahead between my ears. Don't look at the ground. If you think you're going to fall just grip harder and sit up straighter. Ready? Now: for Narnia and the North."

CHAPTER TWO

A WAYSIDE ADVENTURE

IT was nearly noon on the following day when Shasta was wakened by something warm and soft moving over his face. He opened his eyes and found himself staring into the long face of a horse; its nose and lips were almost touching his. He remembered the exciting events of the previous night and sat up. But as he did so he groaned.

"Ow, Bree," he gasped. "I'm so sore. All over. I can hardly move."

"Good morning, small one," said Bree. "I was afraid you might feel a bit stiff. It can't be the falls. You didn't have more than a dozen or so, and it was all lovely, soft springy turf that must have been almost a pleasure to fall on. And the only one that might have been nasty was broken by that gorse bush. No: it's the riding itself that comes hard at first. What about breakfast? I've had mine."

"Oh bother breakfast. Bother everything," said Shasta. "I tell you I can't move." But the horse nuzzled at him with its nose and pawed him gently with a hoof till he had to get up. And then he looked about him and saw where they were. Behind them lay a little copse. Before them the turf, dotted with white flowers, sloped down to the brow of a cliff. Far below them, so that the sound of the breaking waves was very faint, lay the sea. Shasta had never seen it from such a height and never seen so much of it before, nor dreamed how many colours it had. On either hand the coast stretched away, headland after headland, and at the points you could see the white foam running up the rocks but making no noise because it was so far off. There were gulls flying overhead and the heat shivered on the ground; it was a blazing day. But what Shasta chiefly noticed was the air. He couldn't think what was missing, until at last he realized that there was no smell of fish in it. For of course, neither in the cottage nor among the nets, had he ever been away from that smell in his life. And this new air was so delicious, and all his old life seemed so far away, that he forgot for a moment about his bruises and his aching muscles and said:

"I say, Bree, didn't you say something about breakfast?"

"Yes, I did," answered Bree. "I think you'll find something in the saddle-bags. They're over there on that tree where you hung them up last night – or early this morning, rather."

They investigated the saddle-bags and the results were cheering – a meat pasty, only slightly stale, a lump of dried figs and another lump of green cheese, a little flask of wine, and some money; about forty crescents in all, which was more than Shasta had ever seen.

While Shasta sat down – painfully and cautiously – with his back against a tree and started on the pasty, Bree had a few more mouthfuls of grass to keep him company.

"Won't it be stealing to use the money?" asked Shasta.

"Oh," said the Horse, looking up with its mouth full of grass, "I never thought of that. A free horse and a talking horse mustn't steal, of course. But I think it's all right. We're prisoners and captives in enemy country. That money is booty, spoil. Besides, how are we to get any food for you without it? I suppose, like all humans, you won't eat natural food like grass and oats."

"I can't."

"Ever tried?"

"Yes, I have. I can't get it down at all. You couldn't either if you were me."

"You're rum little creatures, you humans," remarked Bree.

When Shasta had finished his breakfast (which was by

far the nicest he had ever eaten), Bree said, "I think I'll have a nice roll before we put on that saddle again." And he proceeded to do so. "That's good. That's very good," he said, rubbing his back on the turf and waving all four legs in the air. "You ought to have one too, Shasta," he snorted. "It's most refreshing."

But Shasta burst out laughing and said, "You do look funny when you're on your back!"

"I look nothing of the sort," said Bree. But then suddenly he rolled round on his side, raised his head and looked hard at Shasta, blowing a little.

"Does it really look funny?" he asked in an anxious voice.

"Yes, it does," replied Shasta. "But what does it matter?"

"You don't think, do you," said Bree, "that it might be a thing *talking* horses never do — a silly, clownish trick I've learned from the dumb ones? It would be dreadful to find, when I get back to Narnia, that I've picked up a lot of low, bad habits. What do you think, Shasta? Honestly, now. Don't spare my feelings. Should you think the real, free horses — the talking kind — do roll?"

"How should I know? Anyway I don't think I should bother about it if I were you. We've got to get there first. Do you know the way?"

"I know my way to Tashbaan. After that comes the desert. Oh, we'll manage the desert somehow, never fear. Why, we'll be in sight of the Northern mountains then. Think of it! To Narnia and the North! Nothing will stop us then. But I'd be glad to be past Tashbaan. You and I are safer away from cities."

"Can't we avoid it?"

"Not without going a long way inland, and that would take us into cultivated land and main roads; and I wouldn't know the way. No, we'll just have to creep along the coast. Up here on the downs we'll meet nothing but sheep and rabbits and gulls and a few shepherds. And by the way, what about starting?"

Shasta's legs ached terribly as he saddled Bree and climbed into the saddle, but the Horse was kindly to him and went at a soft pace all afternoon. When evening twilight came they dropped by steep tracks into a valley and found a village. Before they got into it Shasta dismounted and entered it on foot to buy a loaf and some onions and radishes. The Horse trotted round by the fields in the dusk and met Shasta at the far side. This became their regular plan every second night.

These were great days for Shasta, and every day better than the last as his muscles hardened and he fell less often. Even at the end of his training Bree still said he sat like a bag of flour in the saddle. "And even if it was safe, young 'un, I'd be ashamed to be seen with you on the main road." But in spite of his rude words Bree was a patient teacher. No one can teach riding so well as a horse. Shasta learned to trot, to canter, to jump, and to keep his seat even when Bree pulled up suddenly or swung unexpectedly to the left or the right – which, as Bree told him, was a thing you might have to do at any moment in a battle. And then of course Shasta begged to be told of the battles and wars in which Bree had carried the Tarkaan. And Bree would tell of forced marches and the fording of swift rivers, of charges and of fierce fights between cavalry and cavalry when the war horses fought as well as the men, being all fierce stallions, trained to bite and kick, and to rear at the right moment so that the horse's weight as well as the rider's would come down on a enemy's crest in the stroke of sword or battleaxe. But Bree did not want to talk about the wars as often as Shasta wanted to hear about them. "Don't speak of them, youngster," he would say. "They were only the Tisroc's wars and I fought in them as a slave and a dumb beast. Give me the Narnian wars where I shall fight as a free Horse among my own people! Those will be wars worth talking about. Narnia and the North! Bra-ha-ha! Broo hoo!"

Shasta soon learned, when he heard Bree talking like that, to prepare for a gallop.

After they had travelled on for weeks and weeks past more bays and headlands and rivers and villages than Shasta could remember, there came a moonlit night when they started their journey at evening, having slept during the day. They had left the downs behind them and were crossing a wide plain with a forest about half a mile away on their left. The sea, hidden by low sandhills, was about the same distance on their right. They had jogged along for about an hour, sometimes trotting and sometimes walking, when Bree suddenly stopped.

"What's up?" said Shasta.

"S-s-ssh!" said Bree, craning his neck round and twitching his ears. "Did you hear something? Listen."

"It sounds like another horse — between us and the wood," said Shasta after he had listened for about a minute.

"It *is* another horse," said Bree. "And that's what I don't like."

"Isn't it probably just a farmer riding home late?" said Shasta with a yawn.

"Don't tell me!" said Bree. "*That's* not a farmer's riding. Nor a farmer's horse either. Can't you tell by the sound? That's quality, that horse is. And it's being ridden by a real horseman. I tell you what it is, Shasta. There's a Tarkaan under the edge of that wood. Not on his war horse — it's too light for that. On a fine blood mare, I should say."

"Well, it's stopped now, whatever it is," said Shasta.

"You're right," said Bree. "And why should he stop just when we do? Shasta, my boy, I do believe there's someone shadowing us at last."

"What shall we do?" said Shasta in a lower whisper than before. "Do you think he can see us as well as hear us?"

"Not in this light so long as we stay quite still," answered Bree. "But look! There's a cloud coming up. I'll wait till that gets over the moon. Then we'll get off to our right as quietly as we can, down to the shore. We can hide among the sandhills if the worst comes to the worst."

They waited till the cloud covered the moon and then, first at a walking pace and afterwards at a gentle trot, made for the shore.

The cloud was bigger and thicker than it had looked at first and soon the night grew very dark. Just as Shasta was saying to himself, "We must be nearly at those sandhills by now," his heart leaped into his mouth because an appalling noise had suddenly risen up out of the darkness ahead; a long snarling roar, melancholy and utterly savage. Instantly Bree swerved round and began galloping inland again as fast as he could gallop.

"What is it?" gasped Shasta.

"Lions!" said Bree, without checking his pace or turning his head.

After that there was nothing but sheer galloping for some time. At last they splashed across a wide, shallow stream and Bree came to a stop on the far side. Shasta noticed that he was trembling and sweating all over.

"That water may have thrown the brute off our scent," panted Bree when he had partly got his breath again. "We can walk for a bit now."

As they walked Bree said, "Shasta, I'm ashamed of myself. I'm just as frightened as a common, dumb Calormene horse. I am really. I don't feel like a Talking Horse at all. I don't mind swords and lances and arrows but I can't bear – those creatures. I think I'll trot for a bit."

About a minute later, however, he broke into a gallop again, and no wonder. For the roar broke out again, this time on their left from the direction of the forest.

"Two of them," moaned Bree.

When they had galloped for several minutes without any further noise from the lions Shasta said, "I say! That other horse is galloping beside us now. Only a stone's throw away."

"All the b-better," panted Bree. "Tarkaan on it – will have a sword – protect us all."

"But, Bree!" said Shasta. "We might just as well be killed by lions as caught. Or *I* might. They'll hang me for horse-stealing." He was feeling less frightened of lions than Bree because he had never met a lion; Bree had.

Bree only snorted in answer but he did sheer away to his right. Oddly enough the other horse seemed also to be sheering away to the left, so that in a few seconds the space between them had widened a good deal. But as soon as it did so there came two more lions' roars, immediately after one another, one on the right and the other on the left, the horses began drawing nearer together. So, apparently, did the lions. The roaring of the brutes on each side was horribly close and they seemed to be keeping up with the galloping horses quite easily. Then the cloud rolled away. The moonlight, astonishingly bright, showed up everything almost as if it were broad day. The two horses and two riders were galloping neck to neck and knee to knee just as if they were in a race. Indeed Bree said (afterwards) that a finer race had never been seen in Calormen.

Shasta now gave himself up for lost and began to wonder whether lions killed you quickly or played with you as a cat plays with a mouse and how much it would hurt. At the same time (one sometimes does this at the most frightful moments) he noticed everything. He saw that the other rider was a very small, slender person, mail-clad (the moon shone on the mail) and riding magnificently. He had no beard.

Something flat and shining was spread out before them. Before Shasta had time even to guess what it was there was

a great splash and he found his mouth half full of salt water. The shining thing had been a long inlet of the sea. Both horses were swimming and the water was up to Shasta's knees. There was an angry roaring behind them and looking back Shasta saw a great, shaggy, and terrible shape crouched on the water's edge; but only one. "We must have shaken off the other lion," he thought.

The lion apparently did not think its prey worth a wetting; at any rate it made no attempt to take the water in pursuit. The two horses, side by side, were now well out into the middle of the creek and the opposite shore could be clearly seen. The Tarkaan had not yet spoken a word. "But he will," thought Shasta. "As soon as we have landed. What am I to say? I must begin thinking out a story."

Then, suddenly, two voices spoke at his side.

"Oh, I *am* so tired," said the one. "Hold your tongue, Hwin, and don't be a fool," said the other.

"I'm dreaming," thought Shasta. "I could have sworn that other horse spoke."

Soon the horses were no longer swimming but walking and soon with a great sound of water running off their sides and tails and with a great crunching of pebbles under eight hoofs, they came out on the farther beach of the inlet. The Tarkaan, to Shasta's surprise, showed no wish to ask questions. He did not even look at Shasta but seemed anxious to urge his horse straight on. Bree, however, at once shouldered himself in the other horse's way.

"Broo-hoo-hah!" he snorted. "Steady there! I *heard* you, I did. There's no good pretending, Ma'am. *I* heard you. You're a Talking Horse, a Narnian horse just like me."

"What's it got to do with you if she is?" said the strange rider fiercely, laying hand on sword-hilt. But the voice in which the words were spoken had already told Shasta something.

"Why, it's only a girl!" he exclaimed.

"And what business is it of yours if I am *only* a girl?" snapped the stranger. "You're probably only a boy: a rude, common little boy — a slave probably, who's stolen his master's horse."

"That's all *you* know," said Shasta.

"He's not a thief, little Tarkheena," said Bree. "At least, if there's been any stealing, you might just as well say *I* stole *him*. And as for its not being my business, you wouldn't expect me to pass a lady of my own race in this strange country without speaking to her? It's only natural I should."

"I think it's very natural too," said the mare.

"I wish you'd held your tongue, Hwin," said the girl. "Look at the trouble you've got us into."

"I don't know about trouble," said Shasta. "You can clear off as soon as you like. We shan't keep you."

"No, you shan't," said the girl.

"What quarrelsome creatures these humans are," said Bree to the mare. "They're as bad as mules. Let's try to talk a little sense. I take it, ma'am, your story is the same as mine? Captured in early youth — years of slavery among the Calormenes?"

"Too true, sir," said the mare with a melancholy whinny.

"And now, perhaps — escape?"

"Tell him to mind his own business, Hwin," said the girl.

"No, I won't, Aravis," said the mare putting her ears back. "This is my escape just as much as yours. And I'm sure a noble war-horse like this is not going to betray us. We are trying to escape, to get to Narnia."

"And so, of course, are we," said Bree. "Of course you guessed that at once. A little boy in rags riding (or trying to ride) a war-horse at dead of night couldn't mean anything but an escape of some sort. And, if I may say so, a high-born Tarkheena riding alone at night — dressed up in her brother's armour — and very anxious for everyone to mind their own business and ask her no questions — well, if that's not fishy, call me a cob!"

"All right then," said Aravis. "You've guessed it. Hwin and I are running away. We are trying to get to Narnia. And now, what about it?"

"Why, in that case, what is to prevent us all going together?" said Bree. "I trust, Madam Hwin, you will accept such assistance and protection as I may be able to give you on the journey?"

"Why do you keep talking to my horse instead of to me?" asked the girl.

"Excuse me, Tarkheena," said Bree (with just the slightest backward tilt of his ears), "but that's Calormene talk. We're free Narnians, Hwin and I, and I suppose, if you're running away to Narnia, you want to be one too. In that case Hwin isn't *your* horse any longer. One might just as well say you're *her* human."

The girl opened her mouth to speak and then stopped. Obviously she had not quite seen it in that light before.

"Still," she said after a moment's pause, "I don't know that there's so much point in all going together. Aren't we more likely to be noticed?"

"Less," said Bree; and the mare said, "Oh do let's. I should feel much more comfortable. We're not even certain of the way. I'm sure a great charger like this knows far more than we do."

"Oh come on, Bree," said Shasta, "and let them go their own way. Can't you see they don't want us?"

"We do," said Hwin.

"Look here," said the girl. "I don't mind going with *you*, Mr War-Horse, but what about this boy? How do I know he's not a spy?"

"Why don't you say at once that you think I'm not good enough for you?" said Shasta.

"Be quiet, Shasta," said Bree. "The Tarkheena's question is quite reasonable. I'll vouch for the boy, Tarkheena. He's been true to me and a good friend. And he's certainly either a Narnian or an Archenlander."

"All right, then. Let's go together." But she didn't say anything to Shasta and it was obvious that she wanted Bree, not him.

"Splendid!" said Bree. "And now that we've got the water between us and those dreadful animals, what about you two humans taking off our saddles and our all having a rest and hearing one another's stories."

Both the children unsaddled their horses and the horses had a little grass and Aravis produced rather nice things to eat from her saddle-bag. But Shasta sulked and said No thanks, and that he wasn't hungry. And he tried to put on what he thought very grand and stiff manners, but as a fisherman's hut is not usually a good place for learning grand manners, the result was dreadful. And he half knew that it wasn't a success and then became sulkier and more awkward than ever. Meanwhile the two horses were getting on splendidly. They remembered the very same places in Narnia — "the grasslands up above Beaversdam" and found that they were some sort of second cousins once removed. This made things more and more uncomfortable for the humans until at last Bree said, "And now, Tarkheena, tell us your story. And don't hurry it — I'm feeling comfortable now."

Aravis immediately began, sitting quite still and using a rather different tone and style from her usual one. For in Calormen, story-telling (whether the stories are true or made up) is a thing you're taught, just as English boys and girls are taught essay-writing. The difference is that people want to hear the stories, whereas I never heard of anyone who wanted to read the essays.

CHAPTER THREE

AT THE GATES OF TASHBAAN

"My name," said the girl at once, "is Aravis Tarkheena and I am the only daughter of Kidrash Tarkaan, the son of Rishti Tarkaan, the son of Kidrash Tarkaan, the son of Ilsombreh Tisroc, the son of Ardeeb Tisroc who was descended in a right line from the god Tash. My father is the lord of the province of Calavar and is one who has the right of standing on his feet in his shoes before the face of Tisroc himself (may he live for ever). My mother (on whom be the peace of the gods) is dead and my father has married another wife. One of my brothers has fallen in battle against the rebels in the far west and the other is a child. Now it came to pass that my father's wife, my step-mother, hated me, and the sun appeared dark in her eyes as long as I lived in my father's house. And so she persuaded my father to promise me in marriage to Ahoshta Tarkaan. Now this Ahoshta is of base birth, though in these latter years he has won the favour of the Tisroc (may he live for ever) by flattery and evil counsels, and is now made a Tarkaan and the lord of many cities and is likely to be chosen as the Grand Vizier when the present Grand Vizier dies. Moreover he is at least sixty years old and has a hump on his back and his face resembles that of an ape. Nevertheless my father, because of the wealth and power of this Ahoshta, and being persuaded by his wife, sent messengers offering me in marriage, and the offer was favourably accepted and Ahoshta sent word that he would marry me this very year at the time of high summer.

"When this news was brought to me the sun appeared dark in my eyes and I laid myself on my bed and wept for a day. But on the second day I rose up and washed my face and caused my mare Hwin to be saddled and took with me a sharp dagger which my brother had carried in the western wars and rode out alone. And when my father's house was out of sight and I was come to a green open place in a certain wood where there were no dwellings of men, I dismounted from Hwin my mare and took out the dagger. Then I parted my clothes where I thought the readiest way lay to my heart and I prayed to all the gods that as soon as I was dead I might find myself with my brother. After that I shut my eyes and my teeth and prepared to drive the dagger into my heart. But before I had done so, this mare spoke with the voice of one of the daughters of men and said, "O my mistress, do not by any means destroy yourself, for if you live you may yet have good fortune but all the dead are dead alike."

"I didn't say it half so well as that," muttered the mare.

"Hush, Ma'am, hush," said Bree, who was thoroughly enjoying the story. "She's telling it in the grand Calormene manner and no story-teller in a Tisroc's court could do it better. Pray go on, Tarkheena."

"When I heard the language of men uttered by my mare," continued Aravis, "I said to myself, the fear of death has disordered my reason and subjected me to delusions. And I became full of shame for none of my lineage ought to fear death more than the biting of a gnat. Therefore I addressed myself a second time to the stabbing, but Hwin came near to me and put her head in between me and the dagger and discoursed to me most excellent reasons and rebuked me as a mother rebukes her daughter. And now my wonder was so great that I forgot about killing myself and about Ahoshta and said, 'O my mare, how have you learned to speak like one of the daughters of men?' And Hwin told me what is known to all this company, that in Narnia there are beasts that talk, and how she herself was stolen from thence when she was a little foal. She told me also of the woods and waters of Narnia and the castles and the great ships, till I said, 'In the name of Tash and Azaroth and Zardeenah Lady of the Night, I have a great wish to be in that country of Narnia.' 'O my mistress,' answered the mare, 'if you were in Narnia you would be happy, for in that land no maiden is forced to marry against her will.'

"And when we had talked together for a great time hope returned to me and I rejoiced that I had not killed myself. Moreover it was agreed between Hwin and me that we should steal ourselves away together and we planned it in this fashion. We returned to my father's house and I put on my gayest clothes and sang and danced before my father and pretended to be delighted with the marriage which he had prepared for me. Also I said to him, 'O my father and O the delight of my eyes, give me your licence and permission to go with one of my maidens alone for three days into the woods to do secret sacrifices to Zardeenah, Lady of the Night and of Maidens, as is proper and customary for damsels when they must bid farewell to the service of Zardeenah and prepare themselves for marriage.' And he answered, 'O my daughter and O the delight of my eyes, so shall it be.'

"But when I came out from the presence of my father I went immediately to the oldest of his slaves, his secretary, who had dandled me on his knees when I was a baby and loved me more than the air and the light. And I swore him to be secret and begged him to write a certain letter for me. And he wept and implored me to change my resolution but in the end he said, 'To hear is to obey,' and did all my will. And I sealed the letter and hid it in my bosom."

"But what was in the letter?" asked Shasta.

"Be quiet, youngster," said Bree. "You're spoiling the story. She'll tell us all about the letter in the right place. Go on, Tarkheena."

"Then I called the maid who was to go with me to the woods and perform the rites of Zardeenah and told her to

wake me very early in the morning. And I became merry
with her and gave her wine to drink; but I had mixed such
things in her cup that I knew she must sleep for a night and a
day. As soon as the household of my father had committed
themselves to sleep I arose and put on an armour of my
brother's which I always kept in my chamber in his memory.
I put into my girdle all the money I had and certain choice
jewels and provided myself also with food, and saddled the
mare with my own hands and rode away in the second
watch of the night. I directed my course not to the woods
where my father supposed that I would go but north and
east to Tashbaan.

"Now for three days and more I knew that my father
would not seek me, being deceived by the words I had said to
him. And on the fourth day we arrived at the city of Azim
Balda. Now Azim Balda stands at the meeting of many
roads and from it the posts of the Tisroc (may he live for
ever) ride on swift horses to every part of the empire: and it
is one of the rights and privileges of the greater Tarkaans to
send messages by them. I therefore went to the Chief of the
Messengers in the House of Imperial Posts in Azim Balda
and said, 'O dispatcher of messages, here is a letter from my
uncle Ahoshta Tarkaan to Kidrash Tarkaan lord of Calavar.
Take now these five crescents and cause it to be sent to him.'
And the Chief of the Messengers said, 'To hear is to obey.'

"This letter was feigned to be written by Ahoshta and this
was the signification of the writing: 'Ahoshta Tarkaan to
Kidrash Tarkaan, salutation and peace. In the name of Tash
the irresistible, the inexorable. Be it known to you that as I
made my journey towards your house to perform the con-
tract of marriage between me and your daughter Aravis
Tarkheena, it pleased fortune and the gods that I fell in with
her in the forest when she had ended the rites and sacrifices
of Zardeenah according to the custom of maidens. And

when I learned who she was, being delighted with her beauty and discretion, I became inflamed with love and it appeared to me that the sun would be dark to me if I did not marry her at once. Accordingly I prepared the necessary sacrifices and married your daughter the same hour that I met her and have returned with her to my own house. And we both pray and charge you to come hither as speedily as you may that we may be delighted with your face and speech; and also that you may bring with you the dowry of my wife, which, by reason of my great charges and expenses, I require without delay. And because thou and I are brothers I assure myself that you will not be angered by the haste of my marriage which is wholly occasioned by the great love I bear your daughter. And I commit you to the care of all the gods.'

"As soon as I had done this I rode on in all haste from Azim Balda, fearing no pursuit and expecting that my father, having received such a letter, would send messages to Ahoshta or go to him himself, and that before the matter was discovered I should be beyond Tashbaan. And that is the pith of my story until this very night when I was chased by lions and met you at the swimming of the salt water."

"And what happened to the girl – the one you drugged?" asked Shasta.

"Doubtless she was beaten for sleeping late," said Aravis coolly. "But she was a tool and spy of my stepmother's. I am very glad they should beat her."

"I say, that was hardly fair," said Shasta.

"I did not do any of these things for the sake of pleasing *you*," said Aravis.

"And there's another thing I don't understand about that story," said Shasta. "You're not grown up, I don't believe you're any older than I am. I don't believe you're as old. How could you be getting married at your age?"

Aravis said nothing, but Bree at once said, "Shasta, don't display your ignorance. They're always married at that age in the great Tarkaan families."

Shasta turned very red (though it was hardly light enough for the others to see this) and felt snubbed. Aravis asked Bree for his story. Bree told it, and Shasta thought that he put in a great deal more than he needed about the falls and the bad riding. Bree obviously thought it very funny, but Aravis did not laugh. When Bree had finished they all went to sleep.

Next day all four of them, two horses and two humans, continued their journey together. Shasta thought it had been much pleasanter when he and Bree were on their own. For now it was Bree and Aravis who did nearly all the talking. Bree had lived a long time in Calormen and had always been among Tarkaans and Tarkaans' horses, and so of course he knew a great many of the same people and places that Aravis knew. She would always be saying things like, "But if you were at the fight of Zulindreh you would have seen my cousin Alimash," and Bree would answer, "Oh, yes, Alimash, he was only captain of the chariots, you know. I don't quite hold with chariots or the kind of horses who draw chariots. That's not real cavalry. But he is a worthy nobleman. He filled my nosebag with sugar after the taking of Teebeth." Or else Bree would say, "I was down at the lake of Mezreel that summer," and Aravis would say, "Oh, Mezreel! I had a friend there, Lasaraleen Tarkheena. What a delightful place it is. Those gardens, and the Valley of the Thousand Perfumes!" Bree was not in the least trying to leave Shasta out of things, though Shasta sometimes nearly thought he was. People who know a lot of the same things can hardly help talking about them, and if you're there you can hardly help feeling that you're out of it.

Hwin the mare was rather shy before a great war-horse like Bree and said very little. And Aravis never spoke to Shasta at all if she could help it.

Soon, however, they had more important things to think of. They were getting near Tashbaan. There were more, and larger, villages, and more people on the roads. They now did nearly all their travelling by night and hid as best they could during the day. And at every halt they argued and argued about what they were to do when they reached Tashbaan. Everyone had been putting off this difficulty, but now it could be put off no longer. During these discussions Aravis became a little, a very little, less unfriendly to Shasta; one usually gets on better with people when one is making plans than when one is talking about nothing in particular.

Bree said the first thing now to do was to fix a place where they would all promise to meet on the far side of Tashbaan even if, by any ill luck, they got separated in passing the city. He said the best place would be the Tombs of the Ancient Kings on the very edge of the desert. "Things like great stone bee-hives," he said, "you can't possibly miss them. And the best of it is that none of the Calormenes will go near them because they think the place is haunted by ghouls and are afraid of it." Aravis asked if it wasn't really haunted by ghouls. But Bree said he was a free Narnian horse and didn't believe in these Calormene tales. And then Shasta said he wasn't a Calormene either and didn't care a straw about these old stories of ghouls. This wasn't quite true. But it rather impressed Aravis (though at the moment it annoyed her too) and of course she said she didn't mind any number of ghouls either. So it was settled that the Tombs should be their assembly place on the other side of Tashbaan, and everyone felt they were getting on very well till Hwin humbly pointed out that the real problem was not where they should go when they had got through Tashbaan but how they were to get through it.

"We'll settle that tomorrow, Ma'am," said Bree. "Time for a little sleep now."

But it wasn't easy to settle. Aravis's first suggestion was that they should swim across the river below the city during the night and not go into Tashbaan at all. But Bree had two reasons against this. One was that the river-mouth was very wide and it would be far too long a swim for Hwin to do, especially with a rider on her back. (He thought it would be too long for himself too, but he said much less about that). The other was that it would be full of shipping and of course anyone on the deck of a ship who saw two horses swimming past would be almost certain to be inquisitive.

Shasta thought they should go up the river above Tashbaan and cross it where it was narrower. But Bree explained that there were gardens and pleasure houses on both banks of the river for miles and that there would be Tarkaans and Tarkheenas living in them and riding about the roads and having water parties on the river. In fact it would be the most likely place in the world for meeting someone who would recognize Aravis or even himself.

"We'll have to have a disguise," said Shasta.

Hwin said it looked to her as if the safest thing was to go right through the city itself from gate to gate because one was less likely to be noticed in the crowd. But she approved of the idea of disguise as well. She said, "Both the humans will have to dress in rags and look like peasants or slaves. And all Aravis's armour and our saddles and things must be made into bundles and put on our backs, and the children must pretend to drive us and people will think we're only pack-horses."

"My dear Hwin!" said Aravis rather scornfully. "As if anyone could mistake Bree for anything but a war-horse however you disguised him!"

"I should think not, indeed," said Bree, snorting and letting his ears go ever so little back.

"I know it's not a *very* good plan," said Hwin. "But I think it's our only chance. And we haven't been groomed for ages and we're not looking quite ourselves (at least, I'm sure I'm not). I do think if we get well plastered with mud and go along with our heads down as if we're tired and lazy — and don't lift our hooves hardly at all — we might not be noticed. And our tails ought to be cut shorter: not neatly, you know, but all ragged."

"My dear Madam," said Bree. "Have you pictured to yourself how very disagreeable it would be to arrive in Narnia in *that* condition?"

"Well," said Hwin humbly (she was a very sensible mare), "the main thing is to get there."

Though nobody much liked it, it was Hwin's plan which had to be adopted in the end. It was a troublesome one and involved a certain amount of what Shasta called stealing, and Bree called "raiding". One farm lost a few sacks that evening and another lost a coil of rope the next: but some tattered old boy's clothes for Aravis to wear had to be fairly bought and paid for in a village. Shasta returned with them in triumph just as evening was closing in. The others were waiting for him among the trees at the foot of a low range of wooded hills which lay right across their path. Everyone was feeling excited because this was the last hill; when they reached the ridge at the top they would be looking down on Tashbaan. "I do wish we were safely past it," muttered Shasta to Hwin. "Oh I do, I do," said Hwin fervently.

That night they wound their way through the woods up to the ridge by a wood-cutter's track. And when they came out of the woods at the top they could see thousands of lights in the valley down below them. Shasta had had no notion of what a great city would be like and it frightened him. They had their supper and the children got some sleep. But the horses woke them very early in the morning.

The stars were still out and the grass was terribly cold and wet, but daybreak was just beginning, far to their right across the sea. Aravis went a few steps away into the wood and came back looking odd in her new, ragged clothes and carrying her real ones in a bundle. These, and her armour and shield and scimitar and the two saddles and the rest of the horses' fine furnishings were put into the sacks. Bree and Hwin had already got themselves as dirty and bedraggled as they could and it remained to shorten their tails. As the only tool for doing this was Aravis's scimitar, one of the packs had to be undone again in order to get it out. It was a longish job and rather hurt the horses.

"My word!" said Bree, "if I wasn't a Talking Horse what a lovely kick in the face I could give you! I thought you were going to cut it, not pull it out. That's what it feels like."

But in spite of semi-darkness and cold fingers all was done in the end, the big packs bound on the horses, the rope halters (which they were now wearing instead of bridles and reins) in the children's hands, and the journey began.

"Remember," said Bree. "Keep together if we possibly

can. If not, meet at the Tombs of the Ancient Kings, and whoever gets there first must wait for the others."

"And remember," said Shasta. "Don't you two horses forget yourselves and start *talking*, whatever happens."

CHAPTER FOUR

SHASTA FALLS IN WITH THE NARNIANS

AT first Shasta could see nothing in the valley below him but a sea of mist with a few domes and pinnacles rising from it; but as the light increased and the mist cleared away he saw more and more. A broad river divided itself into two streams and on the island between them stood the city of Tashbaan, one of the wonders of the world. Round the very edge of the island, so that the water lapped against the stone, ran high walls strengthened with so many towers that he soon gave up trying to count them. Inside the walls the island rose in a hill and every bit of that hill, up to the Tisroc's palace and the great temple of Tash at the top, was completely covered with buildings – terrace above terrace, street above street, zigzag roads or huge flights of steps bordered with orange trees and lemon trees, roof-gardens, balconies, deep archways, pillared colonnades, spires, battlements, minarets, pinnacles. And when at last the sun rose out of the sea and the great silver-plated dome of the temple flashed back its light, he was almost dazzled.

"Get on, Shasta," Bree kept saying.

The river banks on each side of the valley were such a mass of gardens that they looked at first like forest, until you got closer and saw the white walls of innumerable houses peeping out from beneath the trees. Soon after that, Shasta noticed a delicious smell of flowers and fruit. About fifteen minutes later they were down among them, plodding on a level road with white walls on each side and trees bending over the walls.

"I say," said Shasta in an awed voice. "This is a wonderful place!"

"I daresay," said Bree. "But I wish we were safely through

it and out at the other side. Narnia and the North!"

At that moment a low, throbbing noise began which gradually swelled louder and louder till the whole valley seemed to be swaying with it. It was a musical noise, but so strong and solemn as to be a little frightening.

"That's the horns blowing for the city gates to be open,"

said Bree. "We shall be there in a minute. Now, Aravis, do droop your shoulders a bit and step heavier and try to look less like a princess. Try to imagine you've been kicked and cuffed and called names all your life."

"If it comes to that," said Aravis, "what about you drooping your head a bit more and arching your neck a bit less and trying to look less like a war-horse?"

"Hush," said Bree. "Here we are."

And they were. They had come to the river's edge and the road ahead of them ran along a many-arched bridge. The water danced brightly in the early sunlight; away to their right nearer the river's mouth, they caught a glimpse of ships' masts. Several other travellers were before them on the bridge, mostly peasants driving laden donkeys and mules or carrying baskets on their heads. The children and horses joined the crowd.

"Is anything wrong?" whispered Shasta to Aravis, who had an odd look on her face.

"Oh it's all very well for *you*," whispered Aravis rather savagely. "What would *you* care about Tashbaan? But I ought to be riding in on a litter with soldiers before me and slaves behind, and perhaps going to a feast in the Tisroc's palace (may he live for ever) — not sneaking in like this. It's different for you."

Shasta thought all this very silly.

At the far end of the bridge the walls of the city towered high above them and the brazen gates stood open in the gateway which was really wide but looked narrow because it was so very high. Half a dozen soldiers, leaning on their spears, stood on each side. Aravis couldn't help thinking, "They'd all jump to attention and salute me if they knew whose daughter I am." But the others were only thinking of how they'd get through and hoping the soldiers would not ask any questions. Fortunately they did not. But one of them picked a carrot out of a peasant's basket and threw it at Shasta with a rough laugh, saying:

"Hey! Horse-boy! You'll catch it if your master finds you've been using his saddle-horse for pack work."

This frightened him badly for of course it showed that no one who knew anything about horses would mistake Bree for anything but a charger.

"It's my master's orders, so there!" said Shasta. But it would have been better if he had held his tongue for the soldier gave him a box on the side of his face that nearly knocked him down and said, "Take that, you young filth, to teach you how to talk to freemen." But they all slunk into the city without being stopped. Shasta cried only a very little; he was used to hard knocks.

Inside the gates Tashbaan did not at first seem so splendid as it had looked from a distance. The first street was narrow and there were hardly any windows in the walls on each side. It was much more crowded than Shasta had expected: crowded partly by the peasants (on their way to market) who had come in with them, but also with watersellers, sweetmeat sellers, porters, soldiers, beggars, ragged children, hens, stray dogs, and bare-footed slaves. What you would chiefly have noticed if you had been there was the smells, which came from unwashed people, unwashed dogs, scent, garlic, onions, and the piles of refuse which lay everywhere.

Shasta was pretending to lead but it was really Bree, who knew the way and kept guiding him by little nudges with his nose. They soon turned to the left and began going up a steep hill. It was much fresher and pleasanter, for the road was bordered by trees and there were houses only on the right side; on the other they looked out over the roofs of houses in the lower town and could see some way up the river. Then they went round a hairpin bend to their right and continued rising. They were zigzagging up to the centre of Tashbaan. Soon they came to finer streets. Great statues of the gods and heroes of Calormen – who are mostly impressive rather than agreeable to look at – rose on shining pedestals. Palm trees and pillared arcades cast shadows over the burning pavements. And through the arched gateways of many a palace Shasta caught sight of green branches, cool fountains, and smooth lawns. It must be nice inside, he thought.

At every turn Shasta hoped they were getting out of the crowd, but they never did. This made their progress very slow, and every now and then they had to stop altogether. This usually happened because a loud voice shouted out "Way, way, way, for the Tarkaan", or "for the Tarkheena", or "for the fifteenth Vizier", "or for the Ambassasor", and everyone in the crowd would crush back against the walls;

and above their heads Shasta would sometimes see the great lord or lady for whom all the fuss was being made, lolling upon a litter which four or even six gigantic slaves carried on their bare shoulders. For in Tashbaan there is only one traffic regulation, which is that everyone who is less important has to get out of the way for everyone who is more important; unless you want a cut from a whip or punch from the butt end of a spear.

It was in a splendid street very near the top of the city (the Tisroc's palace was the only thing above it) that the most disastrous of these stoppages occurred.

"Way! Way! Way!" came the voice. "Way for the White Barbarian King, the guest of the Tisroc (may he live for ever)! Way for the Narnian lords."

Shasta tried to get out of the way and to make Bree go back. But no horse, not even a Talking Horse from Narnia, backs easily. And a woman with a very edgy basket in her hands, who was just behind Shasta, pushed the basket hard against his shoulders, and said, "Now then! Who are you shoving!" And then someone else jostled him from the side and in the confusion of the moment he lost hold of Bree. And then the whole crowd behind him became so stiffened and packed tight that he couldn't move at all. So he found himself, unintentionally, in the first row and had a fine sight of the party that was coming down the street.

It was quite unlike any other party they had seen that day. The crier who went before it shouting "Way, way!" was the only Calormene in it. And there was no litter; everyone was on foot. There were about half a dozen men and Shasta had never seen anyone like them before. For one thing, they were all as fair-skinned as himself, and most of them had fair hair. And they were not dressed like men of Calormen. Most of them had legs bare to the kneee. Their tunics were of fine, bright, hardy colours – woodland green, or gay yellow, or fresh blue. Instead of turbans they wore steel or silver caps, some of them set with jewels, and one with little wings on each side of it. A few were bare-headed. The swords at their sides were long and straight, not curved like Calormene scimitars. And instead of being grave and mysterious like most Calormenes, they walked with a swing and let their arms and shoulders go free, and chatted and laughed. One was whistling. You could see that they were ready to be friends with anyone who was friendly and didn't give a fig for anyone who wasn't. Shasta thought he had never seen anything so lovely in his life.

But there was not time to enjoy it for at once a really dreadful thing happened. The leader of the fair-headed men suddenly pointed at Shasta, cried out, "There he is! There's our runaway!" and seized him by the shoulder. Next moment he gave Shasta a smack – not a cruel one to make you cry but a sharp one to let you know you are in disgrace – and added, shaking:

"Shame on you, my lord! Fie for shame! Queen Susan's eyes are red with weeping because of you. What! Truant for a whole night! Where have you been?"

Shasta would have darted under Bree's body and tried to make himself scarce in the crowd if he had had the least chance; but the fair-haired men were all round him by now and he was held firm.

Of course his first impulse was to say that he was only poor Arsheesh the fisherman's son and that the foreign lord must have mistaken him for someone else. But then, the very last thing he wanted to do in that crowded place was to start explaining who he was and what he was doing. If he started on that, he would soon be asked where he had got his horse from, and who Aravis was – and then, goodbye to any chance of getting through Tashbaan. His next impulse was to look at Bree for help. But Bree had no intention of letting all the crowd know that he could talk, and stood looking just as stupid as a horse can. As for Aravis, Shasta did not even dare to look at her for fear of drawing attention. And there was no time to think, for the leader of the Narnians said at once:

"Take one of his little lordship's hands, Peridan, of your courtesy, and I'll take the other. And now, on. Our royal sister's mind will be greatly eased when she sees our young scapegrace safe in our lodging."

And so, before they were half-way through Tashbaan, all their plans were ruined, and without even a chance to say good-bye to the others Shasta found himself being marched off among strangers and quite unable to guess what might be going to happen next. The Narnian King – for Shasta began to see by the way the rest spoke to him that he must be a king – kept on asking him questions; where he had been, how he had got out, what he had done with his clothes, and didn't he know that he had been very naughty. Only the king called it "naught" instead of naughty.

And Shasta said nothing in answer, because he couldn't think of anything to say that would not be dangerous.

"What! All mum?" asked the king. "I must plainly tell you, prince, that this hangdog silence becomes one of your blood even less than the scape itself. To run away might pass for a boy's frolic with some spirit in it. But the king's son of Archenland should avouch his deed; not hang his head like a Calormene slave."

This was very unpleasant, for Shasta felt all the time that this young king was the very nicest kind of grown-up and would have liked to make a good impression on him.

The strangers led him – held tightly by both hands – along a narrow street and down a flight of shallow stairs and then up another to a wide doorway in a white wall with two tall, dark cypress trees, one on each side of it. Once through the arch, Shasta found himself in a courtyard which was also a garden. A marble basin of clear water in the centre was kept continually rippling by the fountain that fell into it. Orange trees grew round it out of smooth grass, and the four white walls which surrounded the lawn were covered with climbing roses. The noise and dust and crowding of the streets seemed suddenly far away. He was led rapidly across the garden and then into a dark doorway. The crier remained outside. After that they took him along a corridor, where the stone floor felt beautifully cool to his hot feet, and up some stairs. A moment later he found himself blinking in the light of a big, airy room with wide open windows, all looking North so that no sun came in. There was a carpet on the floor more wonderfully coloured than anything he had ever seen and his feet sank down into it as if he were treading in thick moss. All round the walls there were low sofas with rich cushions on them, and the room seemed to be full of people; very queer people some of them, thought Shasta. But he had no time to think of that before the most beautiful lady he had ever seen rose from her place and threw her arms round him and kissed him, saying:

"Oh Corin, Corin, how could you? And thou and I such close friends ever since thy mother died. And what should I have said to thy royal father if I came home without thee? Would have been a cause almost of war between Archenland and Narnia which are friends time out of mind. It was naught, playmate, very naught of thee to use us so."

"Apparently," thought Shasta to himself, "I'm being mistaken for a prince of Archenland, wherever that is. And these must be the Narnians. I wonder where the real Corin is?" But these thoughts did not help him say anything out loud.

"Where hast been, Corin?" said the lady, her hands still on Shasta's shoulders.

"I — I don't know," stammered Shasta.

"There it is, Susan," said the King. "I could get no tale out of him, true or false."

"Your Majesties! Queen Susan! King Edmund!" said a voice: and when Shasta turned to look at the speaker he nearly jumped out of his skin with surprise. For this was one of these queer people whom he had noticed out of the corner of his eye when he first came into the room. He was about the same height as Shasta himself. From the waist upwards he was like a man, but his legs were hairy like a goat's, and shaped like a goat's and he had goat's hooves and a tail. His skin was rather red and he had curly hair and a short pointed beard and two little horns. He was in fact a Faun, which is a creature Shasta had never seen a picture of or even heard of. And if you've read a book called *The Lion, the Witch and the Wardrobe* you may like to know that this was the very same Faun, Tumnus by name, whom Queen Susan's sister Lucy had met on the very first day when she found her way into Narnia. But he was a good deal older now for by this time Peter and Susan and Edmund and Lucy had been Kings and Queens of Narnia for several years.

"Your Majesties," he was saying, "His little Highness has had a touch of the sun. Look at him! He is dazed. He does not know where he is."

Then of course everyone stopped scolding Shasta and asking him questions and he was made much of and laid on a sofa and cushions were put under his head and he was given iced sherbet in a golden cup to drink and told to keep very quiet.

Nothing like this had ever happened to Shasta in his life before. He had never even imagined lying on anything so comfortable as that sofa or drinking anything so delicious as that sherbet. He was still wondering what had happened to the others and how on earth he was going to escape and meet them at the Tombs, and what would happen when the real Corin turned up again. But none of these worries seemed so pressing now that he was comfortable. And perhaps, later on, there would be nice things to eat!

Meanwhile the people in that cool airy room were very interesting. Besides the Faun there were two Dwarfs (a kind of creature he had never seen before) and a very large Raven.

The rest were all humans; grown-ups, but young, and all of them, both men and women, had nicer faces and voices than most Calormenes. And soon Shasta found himself taking an interest in the conversation. "Now, Madam," the King was saying to Queen Susan (the lady who had kissed Shasta). "What think you? We have been in this city fully three weeks. Have you yet settled in your mind whether you will marry this dark-faced lover of yours, this Prince Rabadash, or no?"

The lady shook her head. "No, brother," she said, "not for all the jewels in Tashbaan." ("Hullo!" thought Shasta. "Although they're king and queen, they're brother and sister, not married to one another.")

"Truly, sister," said the King, "I should have loved you the less if you had taken him. And I tell you that at the first coming of the Tisroc's ambassadors into Narnia to treat of this marriage, and later when the Prince was our guest at Cair Paravel, it was a wonder to me that ever you could find it in your heart to show him so much favour."

"That was my folly, Edmund," said Queen Susan, "of which I cry you mercy. Yet when he was with us in Narnia, truly this Prince bore himself in another fashion than he does now in Tashbaan. For I take you all to witness what marvellous feats he did in that great tournament and hastilude which our brother the High King made for him, and how meekly and courteously he consorted with us the space of seven days. But here, in his own city, he has shown another face."

"Ah!" croaked the Raven. "It is an old saying: see the bear in his own den before you judge of his conditions."

"That's very true, Sallowpad," said one of the Dwarfs. "And another is, Come, live with me and you'll know me."

"Yes," said the King. "We have now seen him for what he is: that is, a most proud, bloody, luxurious, cruel, and self-pleasing tryant."

"Then in the name of Aslan," said Susan, "let us leave Tashbaan this very day."

"There's the rub, sister," said Edmund. "For now I must open to you all that has been growing in my mind these last two days and more. Peridan, of your courtesy look to the door and see that there is no spy upon us. All well? So. For now we must be secret."

Everyone had begun to look very serious. Queen Susan jumped up and ran to her brother. "Oh, Edmund," she cried. "What is it? There is something dreadful in your face."

CHAPTER FIVE

PRINCE CORIN

"MY dear sister and very good Lady," said King Edmund, "you must now show your courage. For I tell you plainly we are in no small danger."

"What is it, Edmund?" asked the Queen.

"It is this," said Edmund. "I do not think we shall find it easy to leave Tashbaan. While the Prince had hope that you would take him, we were honoured guests. But by the Lion's Mane, I think that as soon as he has your flat denial we shall be no better than prisoners."

One of the Dwarfs gave a low whistle.

"I warned your Majesties, I warned you," said Sallowpad the Raven. "Easily in but not easily out, as the lobster said in the lobster pot!"

"I have been with the Prince this morning," continued Edmund. "He is little used (more's the pity) to having his will crossed. And he is very chafed at your long delays and doubtful answers. This morning he pressed very hard to know your mind. I put it aside – meaning at the same time to diminish his hopes – with some light common jests about women's fancies, and hinted that his suit was likely to be cold. He grew angry and dangerous. There was a sort of threatening, though still veiled under a show of courtesy, in every word he spoke."

"Yes," said Tumnus. "And when I supped with the Grand Vizier last night, it was the same. He asked me how I like Tashbaan. And I (for I could not tell him I hated every stone of it and I would not lie) told him that now, when high summer was coming on, my heart turned to the cool woods and dewy slopes of Narnia. He gave a smile that meant no good and said, 'There is nothing to hinder you from dancing there again, little goatfoot; *always provided you leave us in exchange a bride for our prince.'*"

"Do you mean he would make me his wife by force?" exclaimed Susan.

"That's my fear, Susan," said Edmund. "Wife: or slave which is worse."

"But how can he? Does the Tisroc think our brother the High King would suffer such an outrage?"

"Sire," said Peridan to the King. "They would not be so mad. Do they think there are no swords and spears in Narnia?"

"Alas," said Edmund. "My guess is that the Tisroc has very small fear of Narnia. We are a little land. And little lands on the borders of a great empire were always hateful to the lords of the great empire. He longs to blot them out, gobble them up. When first he suffered the Prince to come to Cair Paravel as your lover, sister, it may be that he was only seeking an occasion against us. Most likely he hopes to make one mouthful of Narnia and Archenland both."

"Let him try," said the second Dwarf. "At sea we are as big as he is. And if he assaults us by land, he has the desert to cross."

"True, friend," said Edmund. "But is the desert a sure defence? What does Sallowpad say?"

"I knew that desert well," said the Raven. "For I have flown above it far and wide in my younger days," (you may be sure that Shasta pricked up his ears at this point). "And this is certain; that if the Tisroc goes by the great oasis he can never lead a great army across it into Archenland. For though they could reach the oasis by the end of their first day's march, yet the springs there would be too little for the thirst of all those soldiers and their beasts. But there is another way."

Shasta listened more attentively still.

"He that would find that way," said the Raven, "must start from the Tombs of the Ancient Kings and ride northwest so that the double peak of Mount Pire is always straight ahead of him. And so, in a day's riding or a little more, he shall come to the head of a stony valley, which is so narrow that a man might be within a furlong of it a thousand times and never know that it was there. And looking down this valley he will see neither grass nor water nor anything else good. But if he rides on down it he will come to a river and can ride by the water all the way into Archenland."

"And do the Calormenes know of this Western way?" asked the Queen.

"Friends, friends," said Edmund, "what is the use of all this discourse? We are not asking whether Narnia or Calormen would win if war arose between them. We are asking how to save the honour of the Queen and our own lives out of this devilish city. For though my brother, Peter the High King, defeated the Tisroc a dozen times over, yet long before that day our throats would be cut and the Queen's grace would be the wife, or more likely, the slave, of this prince."

"We have our weapons, King," said the first Dwarf. "And this is a reasonably defensible house."

"As to that," said the King, "I do not doubt that every one of us would sell our lives dearly in the gate and they would not come at the Queen but over our dead bodies. Yet we should be merely rats fighting in a trap when all's said."

"Very true," croaked the Raven. "These last stands in a house make good stories, but nothing ever came of them. After their first few repulses the enemy always set the house on fire."

"I am the cause of all this," said Susan, bursting into tears. "Oh, if only I had never left Cair Paravel. Our last happy day was before those ambassadors came from Calormen. The Moles were planting an orchard for us . . . oh . . . oh."

And she buried her face in her hands and sobbed.

"Courage, Su, courage," said Edmund. "Remember – but what is the matter with *you*, Master Tumnus?" For the Faun was holding both his horns with his hands as if he were trying to keep his head on by them and writhing to and fro as if he had a pain in his inside.

"Don't speak to me, don't speak to me," said Tumnus. "I'm thinking. I'm thinking so that I can hardly breathe. Wait, wait, do wait."

There was a moment's puzzled silence and then the Faun looked up, drew a long breath, mopped its forehead and said:

"The only difficulty is how to get down to our ship – with some stores, too – without being seen and stopped."

"Yes," said a Dwarf dryly. "Just as the beggar's only difficulty about riding is that he has no horse."

"Wait, wait," said Mr Tumnus impatiently. "All we need is some pretext for going down to our ship today and taking stuff on board."

"Yes," said King Edmund doubtfully.

"Well, then," said the Faun, "how would it be if your majesties bade the Prince to a great banquet to be held on board our own galleon, the *Spendour Hyaline*, tomorrow night? And let the message be worded as graciously as the Queen can contrive without pledging her honour: so as to give the Prince a hope that she is weakening."

"This is very good counsel, Sire," croaked the Raven.

"And then," continued Tumnus excitedly, "everyone will expect us to be going down to the ship all day, making preparations for our guests. And let some of us go to the bazaars and spend every minim we have at the fruiterers and the sweetmeat sellers and the wine merchants, just as we would if we were really giving a feast. And let us order magicians and jugglers and dancing girls and flute players, all to be on board tomorrow night."

"I see, I see," said King Edmund, rubbing his hands.

"And then," said Tumnus, "we'll all be on board tonight. And as soon as it is quite dark —"

"Up sails and out oars —!" said the King.

"And so to sea," cried Tumnus, leaping up and beginning to dance.

"And our nose Northward," said the first Dwarf.

"Running for home! Hurrah for Narnia and the North!" said the other.

"And the Prince waking next morning and finding his birds flown!" said Peridan, clapping his hands.

"Oh Master Tumnus, dear Master Tumnus," said the Queen, catching his hands and swinging with him as he danced. "You have saved us all."

"The Prince will chase us," said another lord, whose name Shasta had not heard.

"That's the least of my fears," said Edmund. "I have seen all the shipping in the river and there's no tall ship of war nor swift galley there. I wish he may chase us! For the *Splendour Hyaline* could sink anything he has to send after her — if we were overtaken at all."

"Sire," said the Raven. "You shall hear no better plot than the Faun's though we sat in council for seven days. And now, as we birds say, nests before eggs. Which is as much as to say, let us all take our food and then at once be about our business."

Everyone arose at this and the doors were opened and the lords and the creatures stood aside for the King and Queen to go out first. Shasta wondered what he ought to do, but Mr Tumnus said, "Lie there, your Highness, and I will bring you up a little feast to yourself in a few moments. There is no need for you to move until we are all ready to embark."

Shasta laid his head down again on the pillows and soon he was alone in the room.

"This is perfectly dreadful," thought Shasta. It never came into his head to tell these Narnians the whole truth and ask for their help. Having been brought up by a hard, close-fisted man like Arsheesh, he had a fixed habit of never telling

grown-ups anything if he could help it: he thought they would always spoil or stop whatever you were trying to do. And he thought that even if the Narnian King might be friendly to the two horses, because they were Talking Beasts of Narnia, he would hate Aravis, because she was a Calor-mene, and either sell her for a slave or send her back to her father. As for himself, "I simply daren't tell them I'm not Prince Corin *now*," thought Shasta. "I've heard all their plans. If they knew I wasn't one of themselves, they'd never let me out of this house alive. They'd be afraid I'd betray them to the Tisroc. They'd kill me. And if the real Corin turns up, it'll all come out, and they *will*!" He had, you see, no idea of how noble and free-born people behave.

"What am I to do? What am I to do?" he kept saying to

himself. "What – hullo, here comes that goaty little creature again."

The Faun trotted in, half dancing, with a tray in its hands which was nearly as large as itself. This he set on an inlaid table beside Shasta's sofa, and sat down himself on the carpeted floor with his goaty legs crossed.

"Now, princeling," he said. "Make a good dinner. It will be your last meal in Tashbaan."

It was a fine meal after the Calormene fashion. I don't know whether you would have liked it or not, but Shasta did. There were lobsters, and salad, and snipe stuffed with almonds and truffles, and a complicated dish made of chicken-livers and rice and raisins and nuts, and there were cool melons and gooseberry fools and mulberry fools, and every kind of nice thing that can be made with ice. There was also a little flagon of the sort of wine that is called "white" though it is really yellow.

While Shasta was eating, the good little Faun, who thought he was still dazed with sunstroke, kept talking to him about the fine times he would have when they all got home; about his good old father King Lune of Archenland and the little castle where he lived on the southern slopes of the pass. "And don't forget," said Mr Tumnus, "that you are promised your first suit of armour and your first war horse on your next birthday. And then your Highness will begin to learn how to tilt and joust. And in a few years, if all goes well, King Peter has promised your royal father that he himself will make you Knight at Cair Paravel. And in the meantime there will be plenty of comings and goings between Narnia and Archenland across the neck of the mountains. And of course you remember you have promised to come for a whole week to stay with me for the Summer Festival, and there'll be bonfires and all-night dances of Fauns and Dryads in the heart of the woods and, who knows? — we might see Aslan himself!"

When the meal was over the Faun told Shasta to stay quietly where he was. "And it wouldn't do you any harm to have a little sleep," he added. "I'll call you in plenty of time to get on board. And then, Home. Narnia and the North!"

Shasta had so enjoyed his dinner and all the things Tumnus had been telling him that when he was left alone his thoughts took a different turn. He only hoped now that the real Prince Corin would not turn up until it was too late and that he would be taken away to Narnia by ship. I am afraid he did not think at all of what might happen to the real Corin when he was left behind in Tashbaan. He was a little worried about Aravis and Bree waiting for him at the Tombs. But then he said to himself, "Well, how can I help it?" and, "Anyway, that Aravis thinks she's too good to go about with me, so she can jolly well go alone," and at the same time he couldn't help feeling that it would be much nicer going to Narnia by sea than toiling across the desert.

When he had thought all this he did what I expect you would have done if you had been up very early and had a long walk and a great deal of excitement and then a very good meal, and were lying on a sofa in a cool room with no noise in it except when a bee came buzzing in through the wide open windows. He fell asleep.

What woke him was a loud crash. He jumped up off the

sofa, staring. He saw at once from the mere look of the room
– the lights and shadows all looked different – that he must
have slept for several hours. He saw also what had made the
crash: a costly porcelain vase which had been standing on
the window-sill lay on the floor broken into about thirty
pieces. But he hardly noticed all these things. What he did

notice was two hands gripping the window-sill from
outside. They gripped harder and harder (getting white at
the knuckles) and then up came a head and a pair of
shoulders. A moment later there was a boy of Shasta's own
age sitting astride the sill with one leg hanging down inside
the room.

Shasta had never seen his own face in a looking-glass.
Even if he had, he might not have realized that the other
boy was (at ordinary times) almost exactly like himself.
At the moment this boy was not particularly like anyone
for he had the finest black eye you ever saw, and a
tooth missing, and his clothes (which must have been
splendid ones when he put them on) were torn and dirty,

and there was both blood and mud on his face.

"Who are you?" said the boy in a whisper.

"Are you Prince Corin?" said Shasta.

"Yes, of course," said the other. "But who are you?"

"I'm nobody, nobody in particular, I mean," said Shasta. "King Edmund caught me in the street and mistook me for you. I suppose we must look like one another. Can I get out the way you've got in?"

"Yes, if you're any good at climbing," said Corin. "But why are you in such a hurry? I say: we ought to be able to get some fun out of this being mistaken for one another."

"No, no," said Shasta. "We must change places at once. It'll be simply frightful if Mr Tumnus comes back and finds us both here. I've had to pretend to be you. And you're starting tonight – secretly. And where were you all this time?"

"A boy in the street made a beastly joke about Queen Susan," said Prince Corin, "so I knocked him down. He ran howling into a house and his big brother came out. So I knocked the big brother down. Then they all followed me until we ran into three old men with spears who are called the Watch. So I fought the Watch and they knocked me down. It was getting dark by now. Then the Watch took me along to lock me up somewhere. So I asked them if they'd like a stoup of wine and they said they didn't mind if they did. Then I took them to a wine shop and got them some and they all sat down and drank till they feel asleep. I thought it was time for me to be off so I came out quietly and then I found the first boy – the one who had started all the trouble – still hanging about. So I knocked him down again. After that I climbed up a pipe on to the roof of a house and lay quiet till it began to get light this morning. Ever since that I've been finding my way back. I say, is there anything to drink?"

"No, I drank it," said Shasta. "And now, show me how

you got in. There's not a minute to lose. You'd better lie down on the sofa and pretend — but I forgot. It'll be no good with all those bruises and black eye. You'll just have to tell them the truth, once I'm safely away."

"What else did you think I'd be telling them?" asked the Prince with a rather angry look. "And who are *you*?"

"There's no time," said Shasta in a frantic whisper. "I'm a Narnian, I believe; something Northern anyway. But I've been brought up all my life in Calormen. And I'm escaping: across the desert; with a talking Horse called Bree. And now, quick! How do I get away?"

"Look," said Corin. "Drop from this window on to the roof of the verandah. But you must do it lightly, on your toes, or someone will hear you. Then along to your left and you can get up to the top of that wall if you're any good at all as a climber. Then along the wall to the corner. Drop onto the rubbish heap you will find outside, and there you are."

"Thanks," said Shasta, who was already sitting on the sill. The two boys were looking into each other's faces and suddenly found that they were friends.

"Good-bye," said Corin. "And *good* luck. I do hope you get safe away."

"Good-bye," said Shasta. "I say, you have been having some adventures."

"Nothing to yours," said the Prince. "Now drop; lightly — I say," he added as Shasta dropped. "I hope we meet in Archenland. Go to my father King Lune and tell him you're a friend of mine. Look out! I hear someone coming."

CHAPTER SIX

SHASTA AMONG THE TOMBS

SHASTA ran lightly along the roof on tiptoes. It felt hot to his bare feet. He was only a few seconds scrambling up the wall at the far end and when he got to the corner he found himself looking down into a narrow, smelly street, and there was a rubbish heap against the outside of the wall just as Corin had told him. Before jumping down he took a rapid glance round him to get his bearings. Apparently he had now come over the crown of the island-hill on which Tashbaan is built. Everything sloped away before him, flat roofs below flat roofs, down to the towers and battlements of the city's Northern wall. Beyond that was the river and beyond the river a short slope covered with gardens. But beyond that again there was something he had never seen the like of – a great yellowish-grey thing, flat as a calm sea, and stretching for miles. On the far side of it were huge blue things, lumpy but with jagged edges, and some of them with white tops. "The desert! the mountains!" thought Shasta.

He jumped down on to the rubbish and began trotting along downhill as fast as he could in the narrow lane, which soon brought him into a wider street where there were more people. No one bothered to look at a little ragged boy running along on bare feet. Still, he was anxious and uneasy till he turned a corner and there saw the city gate in front of him. Here he was pressed and jostled a bit, for a good many other people were also going out; and on the bridge beyond the gate the crowd became quite a slow procession, more like a queue than a crowd. Out there, with clear running water on each side, it was deliciously fresh after the smell and heat and noise of Tashbaan.

When once Shasta had reached the far end of the bridge he

found the crowd melting away; everyone seemed to be going either to the left or right along the river bank. He went straight ahead up a road that did not appear to be much used, between gardens. In a few paces he was alone, and a few more brought him to the top of the slope. There he stood and stared. It was like coming to the end of the world for all the grass stopped quite suddenly a few feet before him and the sand began: endless level sand like on a sea shore but a bit rougher because it was never wet. The mountains, which now looked further off than before, loomed ahead. Greatly to his relief he saw, about five minutes' walk away on his left, what must certainly be the Tombs, just as Bree had described them; great masses of mouldering stone shaped like gigantic bee-hives, but a little narrower. They looked very black and grim, for the sun was now setting right behind them.

He turned his face West and trotted towards the Tombs. He could not help looking out very hard for any sign of his friends, though the setting sun shone in his face so that he could see hardly anything. "And anyway," he thought, "of course they'll be round on the far side of the farthest Tomb, not this side where anyone might see them from the city."

There were about twelve Tombs, each with a low arched doorway that opened into absolute blackness. They were dotted about in no kind of order, so that it took a long time, going round this one and going round that one, before you could be sure that you had looked round every side of every tomb. This was what Shasta had to do. There was nobody there.

It was very quiet here out on the edge of the desert; and now the sun had really set.

Suddenly from somewhere behind him there came a terrible sound. Shasta's heart gave a great jump and he had to bite his tongue to keep himself from screaming. Next moment he realized what it was: the horns of Tashbaan blowing for the closing of the gates. "Don't be a silly little coward," said Shasta to himself. "Why, it's only the same noise you heard this morning." But there is a great difference between a noise heard letting you in with your friends in the morning, and a noise heard alone at nightfall, shutting

you out. And now that the gates were shut he knew there was no chance of the others joining him that evening. "Either they're shut up in Tashbaan for the night," thought Shasta, "or else they've gone on without me. It's just the sort of thing that Aravis would do. But Bree wouldn't. Oh, he wouldn't.—now, would he?"

In this idea about Aravis Shasta was once more quite wrong. She was proud and could be hard enough but she was as true as steel and would never have deserted a companion, whether she liked him or not.

Now that Shasta knew he would have to spend the night alone (it was getting darker every minute) he began to like the look of the place less and less. There was something very uncomfortable about those great, silent shapes of stone. He had been trying his hardest for a long time not to think of ghouls: but he couldn't keep it up any longer.

"Ow! Ow! Help!" he shouted suddenly, for at that very moment he felt something touch his leg. I don't think anyone can be blamed for shouting if something comes up from behind and touches him; not in such a place and at such a time, when he is frightened already. Shasta at any rate was too frightened to run. Anything would be better than being chased round and round the burial places of the Ancient Kings with something he dared not look at behind him. Instead, he did what was really the most sensible thing he could do. He looked round; and his heart almost burst with relief. What had touched him was only a cat.

The light was too bad now for Shasta to see much of the cat except that it was big and very solemn. It looked as if it might have lived for long, long years among the Tombs, alone. Its eyes made you think it knew secrets it would not tell.

"Puss, puss," said Shasta. "I suppose you're not a *talking* cat."

The cat stared at him harder than ever. Then it started walking away, and of course Shasta followed it. It led him right through the tombs and out on the desert side of them. There it sat down bolt upright with its tail curled round its feet and its face set towards the desert and towards Narnia and the North, as still as if it were watching for some enemy. Shasta lay down beside it with his back against the cat and his face towards the Tombs, because if one is nervous there's nothing like having your face towards the danger and having something warm and solid at your back. The sand wouldn't have seemed very comfortable to you, but Shasta had been sleeping on the ground for weeks and hardly noticed it. Very soon he fell asleep, though even in his dreams he went on wondering what had happened to Bree and Aravis and Hwin.

He was wakened suddenly by a noise he had never heard before. "Perhaps it was only a nightmare," said Shasta to himself. At the same moment he noticed that the cat had gone from his back, and he wished it hadn't. But he lay quite still without even opening his eyes because he felt sure he would be more frightened if he sat up and looked round at the Tombs and the loneliness: just as you or I might lie still with the clothes over our heads. But then the noise came again – a harsh, piercing cry from behind him out of the desert. Then of course he had to open his eyes and sit up.

The moon was shining brightly. The Tombs – far bigger and nearer than he had thought they would be – looked grey in the moonlight. In fact, they looked horribly like huge people, draped in grey robes that covered their heads and faces. They were not at all nice things to have near you when spending a night alone in a strange place. But the noise had come from the opposite side, from the desert. Shasta had to turn his back on the Tombs (he didn't like that much) and stare out across the level sand. The wild cry rang out again.

"I hope it's not more lions," thought Shasta. It was in fact not very like the lion's roars he had heard on the night when they met Hwin and Aravis, and was really the cry of a jackal. But of course Shasta did not know this. Even if he had known, he would not have wanted very much to meet a jackal.

The cries rang out again and again. "There's more than one of them, whatever they are," thought Shasta. "And they're coming nearer."

I suppose that if he had been an entirely sensible boy he would have gone back through the Tombs nearer to the river where there were houses, and wild beasts would be less likely to come. But then there were (or he thought there were) the ghouls. To go back through the Tombs would mean going past those dark openings in the Tombs; and what might come out of them? It may have been silly, but Shasta felt he would rather risk the wild beasts. Then, as the cries came nearer and nearer, he began to change his mind.

He was just going to run for it when suddenly, between him and the desert, a huge animal bounded into view. As the moon was behind it, it looked quite black, and Shasta did not know what it was, except that it had a very big, shaggy head and went on four legs. It did not seem to have noticed Shasta, for it suddenly stopped, turned its head towards the desert and let out a roar which re-echoed through the Tombs and seemed to shake the sand under Shasta's feet. The cries of the other creatures suddenly stoppd and he thought he could hear feet scampering away. Then the great beast turned to examine Shasta.

"It's a lion, I know it's a lion," thought Shasta. "I'm done. I wonder will it hurt much. I wish it was over. I wonder does anything happen to people after they're dead. O-o-oh! Here it comes!" And he shut his eyes and his teeth tight.

But instead of teeth and claws he only felt something warm lying down at his feet. And when he opened his eyes he said, "Why, it's not nearly as big as I thought! It's only half the size. No, it isn't even quarter the size. I do declare it's only the cat!! I must have dreamed all that about its being as big as a horse."

And whether he really had been dreaming or not, what was now lying at his feet, and staring him out of countenance with its big, green, unwinking eyes, was the cat; though certainly one of the largest cats he had ever seen.

"Oh, Puss," gasped Shasta. "I *am* so glad to see you again. I've been having such horrible dreams." And he at once lay down again, back to back with the cat as they had been at the beginning of the night. The warmth from it spread all over him.

"I'll never do anything nasty to a cat again as long as I live," said Shasta, half to the cat and half to himself. "I did once, you know. I threw stones at a half-starved mangy old stray. Hey! Stop that." For the cat had turned round and given him a scratch. "None of that," said Shasta. "It isn't as if you could understand what I'm saying." Then he dozed off.

Next morning when he woke, the cat was gone, the sun was already up, and the sand hot. Shasta, very thirsty, sat up and rubbed his eyes. The desert was blindingly white and, though there was a murmur of noises from the city behind him, where he sat everything was perfectly still. When he looked a little left and west, so that the sun was not in his eyes, he could see the mountains on the far side of the desert, so sharp and clear that they looked only a stone's throw away. He particularly noticed one blue height that divided into two peaks at the top and decided that it must be Mount Pire. "That's our direction, judging by what the Raven said," he thought, "so I'll just make sure of it, so as not to waste any time when the others turn up." So he made a good, deep straight furrow with his foot pointing exactly to Mount Pire.

The next job, clearly, was to get something to eat and drink. Shasta trotted back through the Tombs – they looked quite ordinary now and he wondered how he could ever have been afraid of them – and down into the cultivated land by the river's side. There were a few people about but not very many, for the city gates had been open several hours and the early morning crowds had already gone in. So he had no diffculty in doing a little "raiding" (as Bree called it). It involved a climb over a garden wall and the results were three oranges, a melon, a fig or two, and a pomegranate. After that, he went down to the river bank, but not too near the bridge, and had a drink. The water was so nice that he took off his hot, dirty clothes and had a dip; for of course Shasta, having lived on the shore all his life, had learned to swim almost as soon as he had learned to walk. When he came out he lay on the grass looking across the water at Tashbaan – all the splendour and strength and glory of it. But that made him remember the dangers of it too. He suddenly realized that the others might have reached the Tombs while he was bathing ("and gone on without me, as likely as not"), so he dressed in a fright and tore back at such a speed that he was all hot and thirsty when he arrived and so the good of his bathe was gone.

Like most days when you are alone and waiting for something this day seemed about a hundred hours long. He had plenty to think of, of course, but sitting alone, just thinking, is pretty slow. He thought a good deal about the Narnians and especially about Corin. He wondered what had happened when they discovered that the boy who had been lying on the sofa and hearing all their secret plans wasn't really Corin at all. It was very unpleasant to think of all those nice people imagining him a traitor.

But as the sun slowly, slowly climbed up to the top of the sky and then slowly, slowly began going downwards to the West, and no one came and nothing at all happened, he began to get more and more anxious. And of course he now realized that when they arranged to wait for one another at the Tombs no one had said anything about How Long. He couldn't wait here for the rest of his life! And soon it would be dark again, and he would have another night just like last night. A dozen different plans went through his head, all wretched ones, and at last he fixed on the worst plan of all. He decided to wait till it was dark and then go back to the river and steal as many melons as he could carry and set out

for Mount Pire alone, trusting for his direction to the line
he had drawn that morning in the sand. It was a crazy idea
and if he had read as many books as you have about
journeys over deserts he would never have dreamed of it.
But Shasta had read no books at all.

Before the sun set something did happen. Shasta was
sitting in the shadow of one of the Tombs when he looked
up and saw two horses coming towards him. Then his heart
gave a great leap, for he recognized them as Bree and Hwin.
But the next moment his heart went down into his toes
again. There was no sign of Aravis. The Horses were being
led by a strange man, an armed man pretty handsomely
dressed like an upper slave in a great family. Bree and Hwin
were no longer got up like pack-horses, but saddled and
bridled. And what could it all mean? "It's a trap," thought
Shasta. "Somebody has caught Aravis and perhaps they've
tortured her and she's given the whole thing away. They
want me to jump out and run up and speak to Bree and then
I'll be caught too! And yet if I don't, I may be losing my only
chance to meet the others. Oh I do wish I knew what had
happened." And he skulked behind the Tomb, looking out
every few minutes, and wondering which was the least
dangerous thing to do.

CHAPTER SEVEN

ARAVIS IN TASHBAAN

WHAT had really happened was this. When Aravis saw Shasta hurried away by the Narnians and found herself alone with two horses who (very wisely) wouldn't say a word, she never lost her head even for a moment. She grabbed Bree's halter and stood still, holding both the horses; and though her heart was beating as hard as a hammer, she did nothing to show it. As soon as the Narnian lords had passed she tried to move on again. But before she could take a step, another crier ("Bother all these people" thought Aravis) was heard shouting out, "Way, way, way! Way for the Tarkheena Lasaraleen!" and immediately, following the crier, came four armed slaves and then four bearers carrying a litter which was all a-flutter with silken curtains and all a-jingle with silver bells and which scented the whole street with perfumes and flowers. After the litter, female slaves in beautiful clothes, and then a few grooms, runners, pages, and the like. And now Aravis made her first mistake.

She knew Lasaraleen quite well — almost as if they had been at school together — because they had often stayed in the same houses and been to the same parties. And Aravis couldn't help looking up to see what Lasaraleen looked like now that she was married and a very great person indeed.

It was fatal. The eyes of the two girls met. And immediately Lasaraleen sat up in the litter and burst out at the top of her voice.

"Aravis! What on earth are you doing here? Your father—"

There was not a moment to lose. Without a second's delay Aravis let go the Horses, caught the edge of the litter, swung herself up beside Lasaraleen and whispered furiously in her ear.

"Shut up! Do you hear! Shut up. You must hide me. Tell your people —"

"But darling —" began Lasaraleen in the same loud voice. (She didn't in the least mind making people stare; in fact she rather liked it.)

"Do what I tell you or I'll never speak to you again," hissed Aravis. "Please, please be quick, Las. It's frightfully important. Tell your people to bring those two horses along. Pull all the curtains of the litter and get away somewhere where I can't be found. And do *hurry*."

"All right, darling," said Lasaraleen in her lazy voice. "Here. Two of you take the Tarkheena's horses." (This was

to the slaves.) "And now home. I say, darling, do you think
we really want the curtains drawn on a day like this? I mean
to say —"

But Aravis had already drawn the curtains, enclosing
Lasaraleen and herself in a rich and scented, but rather
stuffy, kind of tent.

"I mustn't be seen," she said. "My father doesn't know
I'm here. I'm running away."

"My dear, how perfectly thrilling," said Lasaraleen. "I'm
dying to hear all about it. Darling, you're sitting on my
dress. Do you mind? That's better. It is a new one. Do you
like it? I got it at —"

"Oh, Las, do be serious," said Aravis. "Where is my
father?"

"Didn't you know?" said Lasaraleen. "He's here, of
course. He came to town yesterday and is asking about you
everywhere. And to think of you and me being here together
and his not knowing anything about it! It's the funniest
thing I ever heard." And she went off into giggles. She
always had been a terrible giggler, as Aravis now
remembered.

"It isn't funny at all," she said. "It's dreadfully serious.
Where can you hide me?"

"No difficulty at all, my dear girl," said Lasaraleen. "I'll
take you home. My husband's away and no one will see you.
Phew! It's not much fun with the curtains drawn. I want to
see people. There's no point in having a new dress on if one's
to go about shut up like this."

"I hope no one heard you when you shouted out to me
like that," said Aravis.

"No, no, of course, darling," said Lasaraleen
absentmindedly. "But you haven't even told me yet what
you think of the dress."

"Another thing," said Aravis. "You must tell your people

to treat those two horses very respectfully. That's part of the secret. They're really Talking Horses from Narnia."

"Fancy!" said Lasaraleen. "How exciting! And oh, darling, have you seen the barbarian queen from Narnia? She's staying in Tashbaan at present. They say Prince Rabadash is madly in love with her. There have been the most wonderful parties and hunts and things all this last fortnight. I can't see that she's so very pretty myself. But some of the Narnian *men* are lovely. I was taken out on a river party the day before yesterday, and I was wearing my—"

"How shall we prevent your people telling everyone that you've got a visitor—dressed like a beggar's brat—in your house? It might so easily get round to my father."

"Now don't keep on fussing, there's a dear," said Lasaraleen. "We'll get you some proper clothes in a moment. And here we are!"

The bearers had stopped and the litter was being lowered. When the curtains had been drawn Aravis found that she was in a courtyard-garden very like the one that Shasta had been taken into a few minutes earlier in another part of the city. Lasaraleen would have gone indoors at once but Aravis reminded her in a frantic whisper to say something to the slaves about not telling anyone of their mistress's strange visitor.

"Sorry, darling, it had gone right out of my head," said Lasareleen. "Here. All of you. And you, doorkeeper. No one is to be let out of the house today. And anyone I catch talking about this young lady will be first beaten to death and then burned alive and after that be kept on bread and water for six weeks. There."

Although Lasaraleen had said she was dying to hear Aravis's story, she showed no sign of really wanting to hear it at all. She was, in fact, much better at talking than at listening. She insisted on Aravis having a long and luxurious bath (Calormene baths are famous) and then dressing her up in the finest clothes before she would let her explain anything. The fuss she made about choosing the dresses nearly drove Aravis mad. She remembered now that Lasaraleen had always been like that, interested in clothes and parties

and gossip. Aravis had always been more interested in bows and arrows and horses and dogs and swimming. You will guess that each thought the other silly. But when at last they were both seated after a meal (it was chiefly of the whipped cream and jelly and fruit and ice sort) in a beautiful pillared room (which Aravis would have liked better if Lasaraleen's spoiled pet monkey hadn't been climbing about it all the time) Lasaraleen at last asked her why she was running away from home.

When Aravis had finished telling her story, Lasaraleen said, "But, darling, why *don't* you marry Ahoshta Tarkaan? Everyone's crazy about him. My husband says he is beginning to be one of the greatest men in Calormen. He has just been made Grand Vizier now old Axartha has died. Didn't you know?"

"I don't care. I can't stand the sight of him," said Aravis.

"But, darling, only think! Three palaces, and one of them that beautiful one down on the lake at Ilkeen. Positively ropes of pearls, I'm told. Baths of asses' milk. And you'd see such a lot of *me*."

"He can keep his pearls and palaces as far as I'm concerned," said Aravis.

"You always *were* a queer girl, Aravis," said Lasaraleen. "What more *do* you want?"

In the end, however, Aravis managed to make her friend believe that she was in earnest and even to discuss plans. There would be no difficulty now about getting the two horses out of the North gate and then on to the Tombs. No one would stop or question a groom in fine clothes leading a war horse and a lady's saddle horse down to the river, and Lasaraleen had plenty of grooms to send. It wasn't so easy to decide what to do about Aravis herself. She suggested that she could be carried out in the litter with the curtains drawn. But Lasaraleen told her that litters were only used in the city and the sight of one going out through the gate would be certain to lead to questions.

When they had talked for a long time – and it was all the longer because Aravis found it hard to keep her friend to the point – at last Lasaraleen clapped her hands and said, "Oh, I have an idea. There is *one* way of getting out of the city without using the gates. The Tisroc's garden (may he live for ever!) runs right down to the water and there is a little water-door. Only for the palace people of course – but then you know, dear (here she tittered a little) we almost *are* palace people. I say, it is lucky for you that you came to *me*. The dear Tisroc (may he live for ever!) is *so* kind. We're asked to the palace almost every day and it is like a second home. I love all the dear princes and princesses and I positively *adore* Prince Rabadash. I might run in and see any of the palace ladies at any hour of the day or night. Why shouldn't I slip in with you, after dark, and let you out by the water-door? There are always a few punts and things tied up outside it. And even if we were caught –"

"All would be lost," said Aravis.

"Oh darling, don't get so excited," said Lasaraleen. "I was going to say, even if we were caught everyone would only say it was one of my mad jokes. I'm getting quite well known for them. Only the other day – do listen, dear, this is frightfully funny –"

"I meant, all would be lost *for me*," said Aravis a little sharply.

"Oh – ah – yes – I *do* see what you mean, darling. Well, can you think of any better plan?"

Aravis couldn't, and answered, "No. We'll have to risk it. When can we start?"

"Oh, not tonight," said Lasaraleen. "Of course not tonight. There's a great feast on tonight (I must start getting my hair done for it in a few minutes) and the whole place will be a blaze of lights. And such a crowd too! It would have to be tomorrow night."

This was bad news for Aravis, but she had to make the best of it. The afternoon passed very slowly and it was a relief when Lasaraleen went out to the banquet, for Aravis was very tired of her giggling and her talk about dresses and parties, weddings and engagements and scandals. She went to bed early and that part she did enjoy: it was so nice to have pillows and sheets again.

But the next day passed very slowly. Lasaraleen wanted to go back on the whole arrangement and kept on telling Aravis that Narnia was a country of perpetual snow and ice inhabited by demons and sorcerers, and she was mad to think of going there. "And with a peasant boy, too!" said Lasaraleen. "Darling, think of it! It's not Nice." Aravis had thought of it a good deal, but she was so tired of Lasaraleen's silliness by now that, for the first time, she began to think that travelling with Shasta was really rather more fun than fashionable life in Tashbaan. So she only replied, "You forget that I'll be nobody, just like him, when we get to Narnia. And anyway, I promised."

"And to think," said Lasaraleen, almost crying, "that if only you had sense you could be the wife of a Grand Vizier!" Aravis went away to have a private word with the horses.

"You must go with a groom a little before sunset down to the Tombs," she said. "No more of those packs. You'll be saddled and bridled again. But there'll have to be food in Hwin's saddle-bags and a full water-skin behind yours, Bree. The man has orders to let you both have a good long drink at the far side of the bridge."

"And then, Narnia and the North!" whispered Bree. "But what if Shasta is not at the Tombs."

"Wait for him of course," said Aravis. "I hope you've been quite comfortable."

"Never better stabled in my life," said Bree. "But if the husband of that tittering Tarkheena friend of yours is paying his head groom to get the best oats, then I think the head groom is cheating him."

Aravis and Lasaraleen had supper in the pillared room.

About two hours later they were ready to start. Aravis was dressed to look like a superior slave-girl in a great house and wore a veil over her face. They had agreed that if any questions were asked Lasaraleen would pretend that Aravis was a slave she was taking as a present to one of the princesses.

The two girls went out on foot. A very few minutes

brought them to the palace gates. Here there were of course soldiers on guard but the officer knew Lasaraleen quite well and called his men to attention and saluted. They passed at once into the Hall of Black Marble. A fair number of courtiers, slaves and others were still moving about here but this only made the two girls less conspicuous. They passed on into the Hall of Pillars and then into the Hall of Statues and down the colonnade, passing the great beaten-copper doors of the throne room. It was all magnificent beyond description; what they could see of it in the dim light of the lamps.

Presently they came out into the garden-court which sloped downhill in a number of terraces. On the far side of that they came to the Old Palace. It had already grown almost quite dark and they now found themselves in a maze of corridors lit only by occasional torches fixed in brackets to the walls. Lasaraleen halted at a place where you had to go either left or right.

"Go on, do go on," whispered Aravis, whose heart was beating terribly and who still felt that her father might run into them at any corner.

"I'm just wondering . . ." said Lasaraleen. "I'm not absolutely sure which way we go from here. I *think* it's the left. Yes, I'm almost sure it's the left. What fun this is!"

They took the left hand way and found themselves in a passage that was hardly lighted at all and which soon began going down steps.

"It's all right," said Lasaraleen. "I'm sure we're right now. I remember these steps." But at that moment a moving light appeared ahead. A second later there appeared from round a distant corner, the dark shapes of two men walking backwards and carrying tall candles. And of course it is only before royalties that people walk backwards. Aravis felt Lasaraleen grip her arm – that sort of sudden grip which is almost a pinch and which means that the person who is gripping you is very frightened indeed. Aravis thought it odd that Lasaraleen should be so afraid of the Tisroc if he were really such a friend of hers, but there was no time to go on thinking. Lasaraleen was hurrying her back to the top of the steps, on tiptoes, and groping wildly along the wall.

"Here's a door," she whispered. "Quick."

They went in, drew the door very softly behind them, and found themselves in pitch darkness. Aravis could hear by Lasaraleen's breathing that she was terrified.

"Tash preserve us!" whispered Lasaraleen. "What *shall* we do if he comes in here. Can we hide?"

There was a soft carpet under their feet. They groped forward into the room and blundered on to a sofa.

"Let's lie down behind it," whimpered Lasaraleen. "Oh, I *do* wish we hadn't come."

There was just room between the sofa and the curtained wall and the two girls got down. Lasaraleen managed to get the better position and was completely covered. The upper part of Aravis's face stuck out beyond the sofa, so that if anyone came into that room with a light and happened to look in exactly the right place they would see her. But of course, because she was wearing a veil, what they saw would not at once look like a forehead and a pair of eyes. Aravis shoved desperately to try to make Lasaraleen give her a little more room. But Lasaraleen, now quite selfish in her panic, fought back and pinched her feet. They gave it up and lay still, panting a little. Their own breath semed dreadfully noisy, but there was no other noise.

"Is it safe?" said Aravis at last in the tiniest possible whisper.

"I – I – *think* so," began Lasaraleen. "But my poor nerves –" and then came the most terrible noise they could have heard at that moment: the noise of the door opening. And then came light. And because Aravis couldn't get her head any further in behind the sofa, she saw everything.

First came the two slaves (deaf and dumb, as Aravis rightly guessed, and therefore used at the most secret councils) walking backwards and carrying the candles. They took up their stand one at each end of the sofa. This was a good thing, for of course it was now harder for anyone to see Aravis once a slave was in front of her and she was looking between his heels. Then came an old man, very fat, wearing a curious pointed cap by which she immediately knew that he was the Tisroc. The least of the jewels with which he was covered was worth more than all the clothes and weapons of the Narnian lords put together: but he was so fat and such a mass of frills and pleats and bobbles and buttons and tassels and talismans that Aravis couldn't help thinking the Narnian fashions (at any rate for men) looked nicer. After him came a tall young man with a feathered and jewelled turban on his head and an ivory-sheathed scimitar at his side. He seemed very excited and his eyes and teeth flashed fiercely in the candlelight. Last of all came a little hump-backed, wizened old man in whom she recognized with a shudder the new Grand Vizier and her own betrothed husband, Ahoshta Tarkaan himself.

As soon as all three had entered the room and the door was shut, the Tisroc seated himself on the divan with a sigh of contentment, the young man took his place, standing before him, and the Grand Vizier got down on his knees and elbows and laid his face flat on the carpet.

CHAPTER EIGHT

IN THE HOUSE OF THE TISROC

"OH-my-father-and-oh-the-delight-of-my-eyes," began the young man, muttering the words very quickly and sulkily and not at all as if the Tisroc *were* the delight of his eyes. "May you live for ever, but you have utterly destroyed me. If you had given me the swiftest of the galleys at sunrise when I first saw that the ship of the accursed barbarians was gone from her place I would perhaps have overtaken them. But you persuaded me to send first and see if they had not merely moved round the point into better anchorage. And now the whole day has been wasted. And they are gone – gone – out of my reach! The false jade, the –" and here he added a great many descriptions of Queen Susan which would not look at all nice in print. For of course this young man was Prince Rabadash and of course the false jade was Susan of Narnia.

"Compose yourself, O my son," said the Tisroc. "For the departure of guests makes a wound that is easily healed in the heart of a judicious host."

"But I *want* her," cried the Prince. "I must have her. I shall die if I do not get her – false, proud, black-hearted daughter of a dog that she is! I cannot sleep and my food has no savour and my eyes are darkened because of her beauty. I must have the barbarian queen."

"How well it was said by a gifted poet," observed the Vizier, raising his face (in a somewhat dusty condition) from the carpet, "that deep draughts from the fountain of reason are desirable in order to extinguish the fire of youthful love."

This seemed to exasperate the Prince. "Dog," he shouted, directing a series of well-aimed kicks at the hindquarters of the Vizier, "do not dare to quote the poets to me. I have had maxims and verses flung at me all day and I can endure them no more." I am afraid Aravis did not feel at all sorry for the Vizier.

The Tisroc was apparently sunk in thought, but when, after a long pause, he noticed what was happening, he said tranquilly:

"My son, by all means desist from kicking the venerable and enlightened Vizier: for as a costly jewel retains its value even if hidden in a dung-hill, so old age and discretion are to be respected even in the vile persons of our subjects. Desist therefore, and tell us what you desire and propose."

"I desire and propose, O my father," said Rabadash, "that you immediately call out your invincible armies and invade the thrice-accursed land of Narnia and waste it with fire and sword and add it to your illimitable empire, killing their High King and all of his blood except the queen Susan. For I must have her as my wife, though she shall learn a sharp lesson first."

"Understand, O my son," said the Tisroc, "that no words you can speak will move me to open war against Narnia."

"If you were not my father, O ever-living Tisroc," said the Prince, grinding his teeth, "I should say that was the word of a coward."

"And if you were not my son, O most inflammable Rabadash," replied his father, "your life would be short and your death slow when you had said it." (The cool, placid voice in which he spoke these words made Aravis's blood run cold.)

"But why, O my father," said the Prince – this time in a much more respectful voice, "why should we think twice about punishing Narnia any more than about hanging an idle slave or sending a worn-out horse to be made into dog's-meat? It is not the fourth size of one of your least provinces. A thousand spears could conquer it in five weeks. It is an unseemly blot on the skirts of your empire."

"Most undoubtedly," said the Tisroc. "These little barbarian countries that call themselves *free* (which is as much as to say, idle, disordered, and unprofitable) are hateful to the gods and to all persons of discernment."

"Then why have we suffered such a land as Narnia to remain thus long unsubdued?"

"Know, O enlightened Prince," said the Grand Vizier, "that until the year in which your exalted father began his salutary and unending reign, the land of Narnia was covered with ice and snow and was moreover ruled by a most powerful enchantress."

"This I know very well, O loquacious Vizier," answered the Prince. "But I know also that the enchantress is dead. And the ice and snow have vanished, so that Narnia is now wholesome, fruitful, and delicious."

"And this change, O most learned Prince, has doubtless been brought to pass by the powerful incantations of those wicked persons who now call themselves kings and queens of Narnia."

"I am rather of the opinion," said Rabadash, "that it has

come about by the alteration of the stars and the operation of natural causes."

"All this," said the Tisroc, "is a question for the disputations of learned men. I will never believe that so great an alteration, and the killing of the old enchantress, were effected without the aid of strong magic. And such things are to be expected in that land, which is chiefly inhabited by demons in the shape of beasts that talk like men, and monsters that are half man and half beast. It is commonly reported that the High King of Narnia (whom may the gods utterly reject) is supported by a demon of hideous aspect and irresistible maleficence who appears in the shape of a Lion. Therefore the attacking of Narnia is a dark and doubtful enterprise, and I am determined not to put my hand out farther than I can draw it back."

"How blessed is Calormen," said the Vizier, popping up his face again, "on whose ruler the gods have been pleased to bestow prudence and circumspection! Yet as the irrefutable and sapient Tisroc has said it is very grievous to be constrained to keep our hands off such a dainty dish as Narnia. Gifted was that poet who said —" but at this point Ahoshta noticed an impatient movement of the Prince's toe and became suddenly silent.

"It is very grievous," said the Tisroc in his deep, quiet voice. "Every morning the sun is darkened in my eyes, and every night my sleep is the less refreshing, because I remember that Narnia is still free."

"O my father," said Rabadash. "How if I show you a way by which you can stretch out your arm to take Narnia and yet draw it back unharmed if the attempt prove unfortunate?"

"If you can show me that, O Rabadash," said the Tisroc, "you will be the best of sons."

"Hear then, O father. This very night and in this hour I

will take but two hundred horse and ride across the desert. And it shall seem to all men that you know nothing of my going. On the second morning I shall be at the gates of King Lune's castle of Anvard in Archenland. They are at peace with us and unprepared and I shall take Anvard before they have bestirred themselves. Then I will ride through the pass above Anvard and down through Narnia to Cair Paravel. The High King will not be there; when I left them he was already preparing a raid against the giants on his northern border. I shall find Cair Paravel, most likely with open gates, and ride in. I shall exercise prudence and courtesy and spill as little Narnian blood as I can. And what then remains but to sit there till the *Splendour Hyaline* puts in, with Queen Susan on board, catch my strayed bird as she sets foot ashore, swing her into the saddle, and then, ride, ride, ride back to Anvard?"

"But is it not probable, O my son," said the Tisroc, "that at the taking of the woman either King Edmund or you will lose his life?"

"They will be a small company," said Rabadash, "and I will order ten of my men to disarm and bind him: restraining my vehement desire for his blood so that there shall be no deadly cause of war between you and the High King."

"And how if the *Splendour Hyaline* is at Cair Paravel before you?"

"I do not look for that with these winds, O my father."

"And lastly, O my resourceful son," said the Tisroc, "you have made clear how all this might give you the barbarian woman, but not how it helps me to the over-throwing of Narnia."

"O my father, can it have escaped you that though I and my horsemen will come and go through Narnia like an arrow from a bow, yet we shall have Anvard for ever? And when you hold Anvard you sit in the very gate of Narnia, and your garrison in Anvard can be increased by little and little till it is a great host."

"It is spoken with understanding and foresight. But how do I draw back my arm if all this miscarries?"

"You shall say that I did it without your knowledge and against your will, and without your blessing, being constrained by the violence of my love and the impetuosity of youth."

"And how if the High King then demands that we send back the barbarian woman, his sister?"

"O my father, be assured that he will not. For though the fancy of a woman has rejected this marriage, the High King Peter is a man of prudence and understanding who will in no way wish to lose the high honour and advantage of being allied to our House and seeing his nephew and grand nephew on the throne of Calormen."

"He will not see that if I live for ever as is no doubt your wish," said the Tisroc in an even drier voice than usual.

"And also, O my father and O the delight of my eyes," said the Prince, after a moment of awkward silence, "we shall write letters as if from the Queen to say that she loves me and has no desire to return to Narnia. For it is well known that women are as changeable as weathercocks. And even if they do not wholly believe the letters, they will not dare to come to Tashbaan in arms to fetch her."

"O enlightened Vizier," said the Tisroc, "bestow your wisdom upon us concerning this strange proposal."

"O eternal Tisroc," answered Ahosta, "the strength of paternal affection is not unknown to me and I have often heard that sons are in the eyes of their fathers more precious than carbuncles. How then shall I dare freely to unfold to you my mind in a matter which may imperil the life of this exalted Prince?"

"Undoubtedly you will dare," replied the Tisroc.

"Because you will find that the dangers of not doing so are at least equally great."

"To hear is to obey," moaned the wretched man. "Know then, O most reasonable Tisroc, in the first place, that the danger of the Prince is not altogether so great as might appear. For the gods have withheld from the barbarians the light of discretion, as that their poetry is not, like ours, full of choice apophthegms and useful maxims, but is all of love and war. Therefore nothing will appear to them more noble and admirable than such a mad enterprise as this of – ow!" For the Prince, at the word "mad", had kicked him again.

"Desist, O my son," said the Tisroc. "And you, estimable Vizier, whether he desists or not, by no means allow the flow of your eloquence to be interrupted. For nothing is more suitable to persons of gravity and decorum than to endure minor inconveniences with constancy."

"To hear is to obey," said the Vizier, wriggling himself round a little so as to get his hinder parts further away from Rabadash's toe. "Nothing, I say, will seem as pardonable, if not estimable, in their eyes as this – er – hazardous attempt, especially because it is undertaken for the love of a woman. Therefore, if the Prince by misfortune fell into their hands, they would assuredly not kill him. Nay, it may even be, that though he failed to carry off the queen, yet the sight of his great valour and of the extremity of his passion might incline her heart to him."

"That is a good point, old babbler," said Rabadash. "Very good, however it came into your ugly head."

"The praise of my masters is the light of my eyes," said Ahoshta. "And secondly, O Tisroc, whose reign must and shall be interminable, I think that with the aid of the gods it is very likely that Anvard will fall into the Prince's hands. And if so, we have Narnia by the throat."

There was a long pause and the room became so silent

that the two girls hardly dared to breathe. At last the Tisroc spoke.

"Go, my son," he said. "And do as you have said. But expect no help nor countenance from me. I will not avenge you if you are killed and I will not deliver you if the barbarians cast you into prison. And if, either in success or failure, you shed a drop more than you need of Narnian noble blood and open war arises from it, my favour shall never fall upon you again and your next brother shall have

your place in Calormen. Now go. Be swift, secret, and fortunate. May the strength of Tash the inexorable, the irresistible be in your sword and lance."

"To hear is to obey," cried Rabadash, and after kneeling for a moment to kiss his father's hands he rushed from the room. Greatly to the disappointment of Aravis, who was now horribly cramped, the Tisroc and Vizier remained.

"O Vizier," said the Tisroc, "is it certain that no living soul knows of this council we three have held here tonight?"

"O my master," said Ahoshta, "it is not possible that any

should know. For that very reason I proposed, and you in your wisdom agreed, that we should meet here in the Old Palace where no council is ever held and none of the household has any occasion to come."

"It is well," said the Tisroc. "If any man knew, I would see to it that he died before an hour had passed. And do you also, O prudent Vizier, forget it. I sponge away from my own heart and from yours all knowledge of the Prince's plans. He is gone without my knowledge or my consent, I know not whither, because of his violence and the rash and disobedient disposition of youth. No man will be more

astonished than you and I to hear that Anvard is in his hands."

"To hear is to obey," said Ahoshta.

"That is why you will never think even in your secret heart that I am the hardest hearted of fathers who thus send my first-born son on an errand so likely to be his death; pleasing as it must be to you who do not love the Prince. For I see into the bottom of your mind."

"O impeccable Tisroc," said the Vizier. "In comparison with you I love neither the Prince nor my own life nor bread nor water nor the light of the sun."

"Your sentiments," said the Tisroc, "are elevated and correct. I also love none of these things in comparison with the glory and strength of my throne. If the Prince succeeds, we have Archenland, and perhaps hereafter Narnia. If he fails — I have eighteen other sons and Rabadash, after the manner of the eldest sons of kings, was beginning to be dangerous. More than five Tisrocs in Tashbaan have died before their time because their eldest sons, enlightened princes, grew tired of waiting for their throne. He had better cool his blood abroad than boil it in inaction here. And now, O excellent Vizier, the excess of my paternal anxiety inclines me to sleep. Command the musicians to my chamber. But before you lie down, call back the pardon we wrote for the third cook. I feel within me the manifest prognostics of indigestion."

"To hear is to obey," said the Grand Vizier. He crawled backwards on all fours to the door, rose, bowed, and went out. Even then the Tisroc remained seated in silence on the divan till Aravis almost began to be afraid that he had dropped asleep. But at last with a great creaking and sighing he heaved up his enormous body, signed to the slaves to precede him with the lights, and went out. The door closed behind him, the room was once more totally dark, and the two girls could breathe freely again.

CHAPTER NINE

ACROSS THE DESERT

"How dreadful! How perfectly dreadful!" whimpered Lasaraleen. "Oh darling, I *am* so frightened. I'm shaking all over. Feel me."

"Come on," said Aravis, who was trembling herself. "They've gone back to the new palace. Once we're out of this room we're safe enough. But it's wasted a terrible time. Get me down to that water-gate as quick as you can."

"Darling, how *can* you?" squeaked Lasaraleen. "I can't do anything – not now. My poor nerves! No: we must just lie still a bit and then go back."

"Why back?" asked Aravis.

"Oh, you don't understand. You're so unsympathetic," said Lasaraleen, beginning to cry. Aravis decided it was no occasion for mercy.

"Look here!" she said, catching Lasaraleen and giving her a good shake. "If you say another word about going back, and if you don't start taking me to that water-gate at once – do you know what I'll do? I'll rush out into that passage and scream. Then we'll both be caught."

"But we shall both be k-k-killed!" said Lasaraleen. "Didn't you hear what the Tisroc (may he live for ever) said?"

"Yes, and I'd sooner be killed than married to Ahosht. So come *on*."

"Oh you *are* unkind," said Lasaraleen. "And I in such a state!"

But in the end she had to give in to Aravis. She led the way down the steps they had already descended, and along another corridor and so finally out into the open air. They were now in the palace garden which sloped down in terraces to the city wall. The moon shone brightly. One of the drawbacks about adventures is that when you come to the most beautiful places you are often too anxious and hurried to appreciate them; so that Aravis (though she remembered them years later) had only a vague impression of grey lawns, quietly bubbling fountains, and the long black shadows of cypress trees.

When they reached the very bottom and the wall rose frowning above them, Lasaraleen was shaking so that she could not unbolt the gate. Aravis did it. There, at last, was the river, full of reflected moonlight, and a little landing stage and a few pleasure boats.

"Good-bye," said Aravis, "and thank you. I'm sorry if I've been a pig. But think what I'm flying from!"

"Oh Aravis darling," said Lasaraleen. "Won't you change your mind? Now that you've seen what a very great man Ahoshta is!"

"Great man!" said Aravis. "A hideous grovelling slave who flatters when he's kicked but treasures it all up and hopes to get his own back by egging on that horrible Tisroc to plot his son's death. Faugh! I'd sooner marry my father's scullion than a creature like that."

"Oh Aravis, Aravis! How can you say such dreadful things; and about the Tisroc (may he live for ever) too. It must be right if *he's* going to do it!"

"Good-bye," said Aravis, "and I thought your dresses lovely. And I think your house is lovely too. I'm sure you'll have a lovely life — though it wouldn't suit me. Close the door softly behind me."

She tore herself away from her friend's affectionate embraces, stepped into a punt, cast off, and a moment later was out in midstream with a huge real moon overhead and a huge reflected moon down, deep down, in the river. The air was fresh and cool and as she drew near the farther bank she heard the hooting of an owl. "Ah! That's better!" thought Aravis. She had always lived in the country and had hated every minute of her time in Tashbaan.

When she stepped ashore she found herself in darkness for the rise of the ground, and the trees, cut off the moonlight. But she managed to find the same road that Shasta had found, and came just as he had done to the end of the grass and the beginning of the sand, and looked (like him) to her left and saw the big, black Tombs. And now at last, brave girl though she was, her heart quailed. Supposing the others weren't there! Supposing the ghouls were! But she stuck out her chin (and a little bit of her tongue too) and went straight towards them.

But before she had reached them she saw Bree and Hwin and the groom.

"You can go back to your mistress now," said Aravis (quite forgetting that he couldn't, until the city gates opened next morning). "Here is money for your pains."

"To hear is to obey," said the groom, and at once set off at a remarkable speed in the direction of the city. There was no need to tell him to make haste: he also had been thinking a good deal about ghouls.

For the next few seconds Aravis was busy kissing the noses and patting the necks of Hwin and Bree just as if they were quite ordinary horses.

"And here comes Shasta! Thanks be to the Lion!" said Bree.

Aravis looked round, and there, right enough, was Shasta who had come out of hiding the moment he saw the groom going away.

"And now," said Aravis. "There's not a moment to lose." And in hasty words she told them about Rabadash's expedition.

"Treacherous hounds!" said Bree, shaking his mane and

stamping with his hoof. "An attack in time of peace, without defiance sent! But we'll grease his oats for him. We'll be there before he is."

"Can we?" said Aravis, swinging herself into Hwin's saddle. Shasta wished he could mount like that.

"Brooh-hoo!" snorted Bree. "Up you get, Shasta. Can we! And with a good start too!"

"He said he was going to start at once," said Aravis.

"That's how humans talk," said Bree. "But you don't get a company of two hundred horse and horsemen watered and victualled and armed and saddled and started all in a minute. Now: what's our direction? Due North?

"No," said Shasta. "I know about that. I've drawn a line. I'll explain later. Bear a bit to our left, both you horses. Ah — here it is!"

"Now," said Bree. "All that about galloping for a day and a night, like in stories, can't really be done. It must be walk and trot: but brisk trots and short walks. And whenever we walk you two humans can slip off and walk too. Now. Are you ready, Hwin? Off we go. Narnia and the North!"

At first it was delightful. The night had now been going on for so many hours that the sand had almost finished giving back all the sun-heat it had received during the day, and the air was cool, fresh, and clear. Under the moonlight the sand, in every direction and as far as they could see, gleamed as if it were smooth water or a great silver tray. Except for the noise of Bree's and Hwin's hoofs there was not a sound to be heard. Shasta would nearly have fallen asleep if he had not had to dismount and walk every now and then.

This seemed to last for hours. Then there came a time when there was no longer any moon. They seemed to ride in the dead darkness for hours and hours. And after that there came a moment when Shasta noticed that he could see Bree's neck and head in front of him a little more clearly than before; and slowly, very slowly, he began to notice the vast grey flatness on every side. It looked absolutely dead, like something in a dead world; and Shasta felt quite terribly tired and noticed that he was getting cold and that his lips were dry. And all the time the squeak of the leather, the jingle of the bits, and the noise of the hoofs – not *Propputty-propputty* as it would be on a hard road, but *Thubbudy-thubbudy* on the dry sand.

At last, after hours of riding, far away on his right there came a single long streak of paler grey, low down on the horizon. Then a streak of red. It was the morning at last, but without a single bird to sing about it. He was glad of the walking bits now, for he was colder than ever.

Then suddenly the sun rose and everything changed in a moment. The grey sand turned yellow and twinkled as if it was strewn with diamonds. On their left the shadows of Shasta and Hwin and Bree and Aravis, enormously long, raced beside them. The double peak of Mount Pire, far ahead, flashed in the sunlight and Shasta saw they were a little out of the course. "A bit left, a bit left," he sang out. Best of all, when you looked back, Tashbaan was already small and remote. The Tombs were quite invisible: swallowed up in that single, jagged-edged hump which was the city of the Tisroc. Everyone felt better.

But not for long. Though Tashbaan looked very far away when they first saw it, it refused to look any further away as they went on. Shasta gave up looking back at it, for it only gave him the feeling that they were not moving at all. Then the light became a nuisance. The glare of the sand made his eyes ache: but he knew he mustn't shut them. He must screw them up and keep on looking ahead at Mount Pire and shouting out directions. Then came the heat. He noticed it for the first time when he had to dismount and walk: as he slipped down to the sand the heat from it struck up into his face as if from the opening of an oven door. Next time it was worse. But the third time, as his bare feet touched the sand he screamed with pain and got one foot back in the stirrup and the other half over Bree's back before you could have said knife.

"Sorry, Bree," he gasped. "I can't walk. It burns my feet." "Of course!" panted Bree. "Should have thought of that myself. Stay on. Can't be helped."

"It's all right for *you*," said Shasta to Aravis who was walking beside Hwin. "You've got shoes on."

Aravis said nothing and looked prim. Let's hope she didn't mean to, but she did.

On again, trot and walk and trot, jingle-jingle-jingle, squeak-squeak-squeak, smell of hot horse, smell of hot self, blinding glare, headache. And nothing at all different for mile after mile. Tashbaan would never look any further away. The mountains would never look any nearer. You felt this had been going on for always — jingle-jingle-jingle, squeak-squeak-squeak, smell of hot horse, smell of hot self.

Of course one tried all sorts of games with oneself to try to make the time pass: and of course they were all no good. And one tried very hard not to think of drinks — iced sherbet in a palace in Tashbaan, clear spring water tinkling with a dark earthy sound, cold, smooth milk just creamy enough and not too creamy — and the harder you tried not to think, the more you thought.

At last there was something different — a mass of rock sticking up out of the sand about fifty yards long and thirty feet high. It did not cast much shadow, for the sun was now very high, but it cast a little. Into that shade they crowded. There they ate some food and drank a little water. It is not easy giving a horse a drink out of a skin bottle, but Bree and Hwin were clever with their lips. No one had anything like enough. No one spoke. The Horses were flecked

with foam and their breathing was noisy. The children were
pale.

After a very short rest they went on again. Same noises,
same smells, same glare, till at last their shadows began to
fall on their right, and then got longer and longer till they
seemed to stretch out to the Eastern end of the world. Very
slowly the sun drew nearer to the Western horizon. And
now at last he was down and, thank goodness, the merciless
glare was gone, though the heat coming up from the sand
was still as bad as ever. Four pairs of eyes were looking out
eagerly for any sign of the valley that Sallowpad the Raven
had spoken about. But, mile after mile, there was nothing
but level sand. And now the day was quite definitely done,
and most of the stars were out, and still the Horses

thundered on and the children rose and sank in their saddles, miserable with thirst and weariness. Not till the moon had risen did Shasta – in the strange, barking voice of someone whose mouth is perfectly dry – shout out:

"There it is!"

There was no mistaking it now. Ahead, and a little to their right, there was at last a slope: a slope downward and hum-mocks of rock on each side. The Horses were far too tired to speak but they swung round towards it and in a minute or

two they were entering the gully. At first it was worse in there than it had been out in the open desert, for there was a breathless stuffiness between the rocky walls and less moonlight. The slope continued steeply downwards and the rocks on either hand rose to the height of cliffs. Then they began to meet vegetation – prickly cactus-like plants and coarse grass of the kind that would prick your fingers. Soon the horse-hoofs were falling on pebbles and stones instead of sand. Round every bend of the valley – and it had many bends – they looked eagerly for water. The Horses were nearly at the end of their strength now, and Hwin, stumbling and panting, was lagging behind Bree. They were almost in despair before at last they came to a little muddiness and a tiny trickle of water through softer and better grass. And the trickle became a brook, and the brook became a stream with bushes on each side, and the stream became a river and there came (after more disappointments than I could possibly describe) a moment when Shasta, who had been in a kind of doze, suddenly realized that Bree had stopped and found himself slipping off. Before them a little cataract of water poured into a broad pool: and both the Horses were already in the pool with their heads down, drinking, drinking, drinking. "O-o-oh," said Shasta and plunged in – it was about up to his knees – and stooped his head right into the cataract. It was perhaps the loveliest moment in his life.

It was about ten minutes later when all four of them (the two children wet nearly all over) came out and began to notice their surroundings. The moon was now high enough to peep down into the valley. There was soft grass on both sides of the river, and beyond the grass, trees and bushes sloped up to the bases of the cliffs. There must have been some wonderful flowering shrubs hidden in that shadowy undergrowth for the whole glade was full of the coolest and most delicious smells. And out of the darkest recess among the trees there came a sound Shasta had never heard before – a nightingale.

Everyone was much too tired to speak or to eat. The Horses, without waiting to be unsaddled, lay down at once. So did Aravis and Shasta.

About ten minutes later the careful Hwin said, "But we mustn't go to sleep. We've got to keep ahead of that Rabadash."

"No," said Bree very slowly. "Mustn't go sleep. Just a little rest."

Shasta knew (for a moment) that they would all go to sleep if he didn't get up and do something about it, and felt that he ought to. In fact he decided that he would get up and persuade them to go on. But presently; not yet: not just yet . . .

Very soon the moon shone and the nightingale sang over two horses and two human children, all fast asleep.

It was Aravis who awoke first. The sun was already high in the heavens and the cool morning hours were already wasted. "It's my fault," she said to herself furiously as she jumped up and began rousing the others. "One wouldn't expect Horses to keep awake after a day's work like that, even if they *can* talk. And of course that Boy wouldn't; he's had no decent training. But *I* ought to have known better."

The others were dazed and stupid with the heaviness of their sleep.

"Heigh-ho — broo-hoo," said Bree. "Been sleeping in my saddle, eh? I'll never do that again. Most uncomfortable—"

"Oh come on, come on," said Aravis. "We've lost half the morning already. There isn't a moment to spare."

"A fellow's got to have a mouthful of grass," said Bree.

I'm afraid we can't wait," said Aravis.

"What's the terrible hurry?" said Bree. "We've crossed the desert, haven't we?"

"But we're not in Archenland yet," said Aravis. "And we've got to get there before Rabadash."

"Oh, we must be miles ahead of him," said Bree. "Haven't we been coming a shorter way? Didn't that Raven friend of yours say this was a short cut, Shasta?"

"He didn't say anything about *shorter*," answered Shasta. "He only said *better*, because you got to a river this way. If the oasis is due North of Tashbaan, then I'm afraid this may be longer."

"Well I can't go on without a snack," said Bree. "Take my bridle off, Shasta."

"P-please," said Hwin, very shyly, "I feel just like Bree that I *can't* go on. But when Horses have humans (with spurs and things) on their backs, aren't they often made to go on when they're feeling like this? and then they find they can. I m-mean — oughtn't we to be able to do even more, now that we're free. It's all for Narnia."

"I think, Ma'am," said Bree very crushingly, "that I know a little more about campaigns and forced marches and what a horse can stand than you do."

To this Hwin made no answer, being, like most highly bred mares, a very nervous and gentle person who was easily put down. In reality she was quite right, and if Bree had had a Tarkaan on his back at that moment to make him go on, he would have found that he was good for several hours' hard going. But one of the worst results of being a slave and being forced to do things is that when there is no one to force you any more you find you have almost lost the power of forcing yourself.

So they had to wait while Bree had a snack and a drink, and of course Hwin and the children had a snack and a drink too. It must have been nearly eleven o'clock in the morning before they finally got going again. And even then Bree took things much more gently than yesterday. It was really Hwin, though she was the weaker and more tired of the two, who set the pace.

The valley itself, with its brown, cool river, and grass and moss and wild flowers and rhododendrons, was such a pleasant place that it made you want to ride slowly.

CHAPTER TEN

THE HERMIT OF THE
SOUTHERN MARCH

AFTER they had ridden for several hours down the valley, it widened out and they could see what was ahead of them. The river which they had been following here joined a broader river, wide and turbulent, which flowed from their left to their right, towards the east. Beyond this new river a delightful country rose gently in low hills, ridge beyond ridge, to the Northern Mountains themselves. To the right there were rocky pinnacles, one or two of them with snow clinging to the ledges. To the left, pine-clad slopes, frowning cliffs, narrow gorges, and blue peaks stretched away as far as the eye could reach. He could no longer make out Mount Pire. Straight ahead the mountain range sank to a wooded saddle which of course must be the pass from Archenland into Narnia.

"Broo-hoo-hoo, the North, the green North!" neighed Bree: and certainly the lower hills looked greener and fresher than anything that Aravis and Shasta, with their southern-bred eyes, had ever imagined. Spirits rose as they clattered down to the water's-meet of the two rivers.

The eastern-flowing river, which was pouring from the higher mountains at the western end of the range, was far too swift and too broken with rapids for them to think of swimming it; but after some casting about, up and down the bank, they found a place shallow enough to wade. The roar and clatter of water, the great swirl against the horses' fetlocks, the cool, stirring air and the darting dragon-flies, filled Shasta with a strange excitement.

"Friends, we are in Archenland!" said Bree proudly as he splashed and churned his way out on the Northern bank.

"I think that river we've just crossed is called the Winding Arrow."

"I hope we're in time," murmured Hwin.

Then they began going up, slowly and zigzagging a good deal, for the hills were steep. It was all open park-like country with no roads or houses in sight. Scattered trees, never thick enough to be a forest, were everywhere. Shasta, who had lived all his life in an almost tree-less grassland, had never seen so many or so many kinds. If you had been there you would probably have known (he didn't) that he was seeing oaks, beeches, silver birches, rowans, and sweet chestnuts. Rabbits scurried away in every direction as they advanced, and presently they saw a whole herd of fallow deer making off among the trees.

"Isn't it simply glorious!" said Aravis.

At the first ridge Shasta turned in the saddle and looked back. There was no sign of Tashbaan; the desert, unbroken except by the narrow green crack which they had travelled down, spread to the horizon.

"Hullo!" he said suddenly. "What's that!"

"What's what?" said Bree, turning round. Hwin and Aravis did the same.

"That," said Shasta, pointing. "It looks like smoke. Is it a fire?"

"Sand-storm, I should say," said Bree.

"Not much wind to raise it," said Aravis.

"Oh!" exclaimed Hwin. "Look! There are things flashing in it. Look! They're helmets — and armour. And it's moving: moving this way."

"By Tash!" said Aravis. "It's the army. It's Rabadash."

"Oh course it is," said Hwin. "Just what I was afraid of. Quick! We must get to Anvard before it." And without another word she whisked round and began galloping

North. Bree tossed his head and did the same.

"Come *on*, Bree, come on," yelled Aravis over her shoulder.

The race was very gruelling for the Horses. As they topped each ridge they found another valley and another ridge beyond it; and though they knew they were going in more or less the right direction, no one knew how far it was to Anvard. From the top of the second ridge Shasta looked back again. Instead of a dust-cloud well out in the desert he now saw a black, moving mass, rather like ants, on the far bank of the Winding Arrow. They were doubtless looking for a ford.

"They're on the river!" he yelled wildly.

"Quick! Quick!" shouted Aravis. "We might as well not have come at all if we don't reach Anvard in time. Gallop, Bree, gallop. Remember you're a war-horse."

It was all Shasta could do to prevent himself from shouting out similar instructions; but he thought, "The poor chap's doing all he can already," and held his tongue. And certainly both Horses were doing, if not all they could, all they thought they could; which is not quite the same thing. Bree had caught up with Hwin and they thundered side by side over the turf. It didn't look as if Hwin could possibly keep it up much longer.

At that moment everyone's feelings were completely altered by a sound from behind. It was not the sound they had been expecting to hear — the noise of hoofs and jingling armour, mixed, perhaps, with Calormene battle-cries. Yet Shasta knew it at once. It was the same snarling roar he had heard that moonlit night when they first met Aravis and Hwin. Bree knew it too. His eyes gleamed red and his ears lay flat back on his skull. And Bree now discovered that he had not really been going as fast — not quite as fast — as he could. Shasta felt the change at once. Now they were really going all out. In a few seconds they were well ahead of Hwin.

"It's not fair," thought Shasta. "I *did* think we'd be safe from lions here!"

He looked over his shoulder. Everything was only too clear. A huge tawny creature, its body low to the ground, like a cat streaking across the lawn to a tree when a strange dog has got into the garden, was behind them. And it was nearer every second and half second.

He looked forward again and saw something which he

did not take in, or even think about. Their way was barred by a smooth green wall about ten feet high. In the middle of that wall there was a gate, open. In the middle of the gateway stood a tall man dressed, down to his bare feet, in a robe coloured like autumn leaves, leaning on a straight staff. His beard fell almost to his knees.

Shasta saw all this in a glance and looked back again. The lion had almost got Hwin now. It was making snaps at her hind legs, and there was no hope now in her foam-flecked, wide-eyed face.

"Stop," bellowed Shasta in Bree's ear. "Must go back. Must help!"

Bree always said afterwards that he never heard, or never understood this; and as he was in general a very truthful horse we must accept his word.

Shasta slipped his feet out of the stirrups, slid both his legs over the left side, hesitated for one hideous hundredth of a second, and jumped. It hurt horribly and nearly winded him; but before he knew how it hurt him he was staggering back to help Aravis. He had never done anything like this in his life before and hardly knew why he was doing it now.

One of the most terrible noises in the world, a horse's scream, broke from Hwin's lips. Aravis was stooping low over Hwin's neck and seemed to be trying to draw her sword. And now all three – Aravis, Hwin, and the lion – were almost on top of Shasta. Before they reached him the lion rose on its hind legs, larger than you would have believed a lion could be, and jabbed at Aravis with its right paw. Shasta could see all the terrible claws extended. Aravis screamed and reeled in the saddle. The lion was tearing her shoulders. Shasta, half mad with horror, managed to lurch towards the brute. He had no weapon, not even a stick or a stone. He shouted out, idiotically, at the lion as one would at a dog. "Go home! Go home!" For a fraction of a second he was staring right into its wide-opened, raging mouth. Then, to his utter astonishment, the lion, still on its hind legs, checked itself suddenly, turned head over heels, picked itself up, and rushed away.

Shasta did not for a moment suppose it had gone for good. He turned and raced for the gate in the green wall which, now for the first time, he remembered seeing. Hwin, stumbling and nearly fainting, was just entering the gate: Aravis still kept her seat but her back was covered with blood.

"Come in, my daughter, come in," the robed and bearded man was saying, and then "Come in, my son" as Shasta panted up to him. He heard the gate closed behind him; and the bearded stranger was already helping Aravis off her horse.

They were in a wide and perfectly circular enclosure, protected by a high wall of green turf. A pool of perfectly still water, so full that the water was almost exactly level with the ground, lay before him. At one end of the pool, completely overshadowing it with its branches, there grew the hugest and most beautiful tree that Shasta had ever seen. Beyond the pool was a little low house of stone roofed with deep and ancient thatch. There was a sound of bleating and over at the far side of the enclosure there were some goats. The level ground was completely covered with the finest grass.

"Are — are — are you," panted Shasta. "Are you King Lune of Archenland?"

The old man shook his head. "No," he replied in a quiet voice, "I am the Hermit of the Southern March. And now, my son, waste no time on questions, but obey. This damsel is wounded. Your horses are spent. Rabadash is at this moment finding a ford over the Winding Arrow. If you run now, without a moment's rest, you will still be in time to warn King Lune."

Shasta's heart fainted at these words for he felt he had no strength left. And he writhed inside at what seemed the cruelty and unfairness of the demand. He had not yet learned that if you do one good deed your reward usually is to be set to do another and harder and better one. But all he said out loud was:

"Where is the King?"

The Hermit turned and pointed with his staff. "Look," he said. "There is another gate, right opposite to the one you entered by. Open it and go straight ahead: always straight ahead, over level or steep, over smooth or rough, over dry or wet. I know by my art that you will find King Lune straight ahead. But run, run: always run."

Shasta nodded his head, ran to the northern gate and disappeared beyond it. Then the Hermit took Aravis, whom he had all this time been supporting with his left arm, and half led, half carried her into the house. After a long time he came out again.

"Now, cousins," he said to the Horses. "It is your turn."

Without waiting for an answer – and indeed they were too exhausted to speak – he took the bridles and saddles off both of them. Then he rubbed them both down, so well that a groom in a King's stable could not have done it better.

"There, cousins," he said, "dismiss it all from your minds and be comforted. Here is water and there is grass. You shall have a hot mash when I have milked my other cousins, the goats."

"Sir," said Hwin, finding her voice at last, "will the Tarkheena live? Has the lion killed her?"

"I who know many present things by my art," replied the Hermit with a smile, "have yet little knowledge of things future. Therefore I do not know whether any man or woman or beast in the whole world will be alive when the sun sets tonight. But be of good hope. The damsel is likely to live as long as any of her age."

When Aravis came to herself she found that she was lying on her face on a low bed of extraordinary softness in a cool, bare room with walls of undressed stone. She couldn't understand why she had been laid on her face; but when she tried to turn and felt the hot, burning pains all over her back, she remembered, and realized why. She couldn't understand what delightfully springy stuff the bed was made of, because it was made of heather (which is the best bedding) and heather was a thing she had never seen or heard of.

The door opened and the Hermit entered, carrying a large wooden bowl in his hand. After carefully setting this down, he came to the bedside, and asked:

"How do you find yourself, my daughter?"

"My back is very sore, father," said Aravis, "but there is nothing else wrong with me."

He knelt beside her, laid his hand on her forehead, and felt her pulse.

"There is no fever," he said. "You will do well. Indeed there is no reason why you should not get up tomorrow. But now, drink this."

He fetched the wooden bowl and held it to her lips. Aravis couldn't help making a face when she tasted it, for goats' milk is rather a shock when you are not used to it. But she was very thirsty and managed to drink it all and felt better when she had finished.

"Now, my daughter, you may sleep when you wish," said the Hermit. "For your wounds are washed and dressed and though they smart they are no more serious than if they had been the cuts of a whip. It must have been a very strange lion; for instead of catching you out of the saddle and getting his teeth into you, he has only drawn his claws across your back. Ten scratches: sore, but not deep or dangerous."

"I say!" said Aravis. "I *have* had luck."

"Daughter," said the Hermit, "I have now lived a hundred and nine winters in this world and have never yet met any such thing as Luck. There is something about all this that I do not understand: but if ever we need to know it, you may be sure that we shall."

"And what about Rabadash and his two hundred horse?" asked Aravis.

"They will not pass this way, I think," said the Hermit. "They must have found a ford by now well to the east of us. From there they will try to ride straight to Anvard."

"Poor Shasta!" said Aravis. "Has he far to go? Will he get there first?"

"There is good hope of it," said the old man.

Aravis lay down again (on her side this time) and said, "Have I been asleep for a long time? It seems to be getting dark."

The Hermit was looking out of the only window, which faced north. "This is not the darkness of night," he said presently. "The clouds are falling down from Stormness Head. Our foul weather always comes from there in these parts. There will be thick fog tonight."

Next day, except for her sore back, Aravis felt so well that after breakfast (which was porridge and cream) the Hermit said she could get up. And of course she at once went out to speak to the Horses. The weather had changed and the whole of that green enclosure was filled, like a great green cup, with sunlight. It was a very peaceful place, lonely and quiet.

Hwin at once trotted across to Aravis and gave her a horse-kiss.

"But where's Bree?" said Aravis when each had asked after the other's health and sleep.

"Over there," said Hwin, pointing with her nose to the far side of the circle. "And I wish you'd come and talk to him. There's something wrong, I can't get a word out of him."

They strolled across and found Bree lying with his face towards the wall, and though he must have heard them coming, he never turned his head or spoke a word.

"Good morning, Bree," said Aravis. "How are you this morning?"

Bree muttered something that no one could hear.

"The Hermit says that Shasta probably got to King Lune in time," continued Aravis, "so it looks as if all our troubles are over. Narnia, at last, Bree!"

"I shall never see Narnia," said Bree in a low voice.

"Aren't you well, Bree dear?" said Aravis.

Bree turned round at last, his face mournful as only a horse's can be.

"I shall go back to Calormen," he said.

"What?" said Aravis. "Back to slavery!"

"Yes," said Bree. "Slavery is all I'm fit for. How can I ever show my face among the free Horses of Narnia? – I who left a mare and a girl and a boy to be eaten by lions while I galloped all I could to save my own wretched skin!"

"We all ran as hard as we could," said Hwin.

"Shasta didn't!" snorted Bree. "At least he ran in the right direction: ran *back*. And that is what shames me most of all. I, who called myself a war-horse and boasted of a hundred fights, to be beaten by a little human boy – a child, a mere foal, who had never held a sword nor had any good nurture or example in his life!"

"I know," said Aravis. "I felt just the same. Shasta was marvellous. I'm just as bad as you, Bree. I've been snubbing him and looking down on him ever since you met us and now he turns out to be the best of us all. But I think it would be better to stay and say we're sorry than to go back to Calormen."

"It's all very well for you," said Bree. "You haven't disgraced yourself. But I've lost everything."

"My good Horse," said the Hermit, who had approached them unnoticed because his bare feet made so little noise on that sweet, dewy grass. "My good Horse, you've lost nothing but your self-conceit. No, no, cousin. Don't put back your ears and shake your mane at me. If you are really so humbled as you sounded a minute ago, you must learn to listen to sense. You're not quite the great Horse you had come to think, from living among poor dumb horses. Of course you were braver and cleverer than *them*. You could hardly help being that. It doesn't follow that you'll be anyone very special in Narnia. But as long as you know you're nobody special, you'll be a very decent sort of Horse, on the whole, and taking one thing with another. And now, if you and my other four-footed cousin will come round to the kitchen door we'll see about the other half of that mash."

CHAPTER ELEVEN

THE UNWELCOME
FELLOW TRAVELLER

WHEN Shasta went through the gate he found a slope of grass and a little heather running up before him to some trees. He had nothing to think about now and no plans to make: he had only to run, and that was quite enough. His limbs were shaking, a terrible stitch was beginning in his side, and the sweat that kept dropping into his eyes blinded them and made them smart. He was unsteady on his feet too, and more than once he nearly turned his ankle on a loose stone.

The trees were thicker now than they had yet been and in the more open spaces there was bracken. The sun had gone in without making it any cooler. It had become one of those hot, grey days when there seem to be twice as many flies as usual. Shasta's face was covered with them; he didn't even try to shake them off – he had too much else to do.

Suddenly he heard a horn – not a great throbbing horn like the horns of Tashbaan but a merry call, Ti-ro-to-to-ho! Next moment he came out into a wide glade and found himself in a crowd of people.

At least, it looked a crowd to him. In reality there were about fifteen or twenty of them, all gentlemen in green hunting-dress, with their horses; some in the saddle and some standing by their horses' heads. In the centre someone was holding the stirrup for a man to mount. And the man he was holding it for was the jolliest, fat, apple-cheeked, twinkling-eyed King you could imagine.

As soon as Shasta came in sight this King forgot all about mounting his horse. He spread out his arms to Shasta, his face lit up, and he cried out in a great, deep voice that seemed to come from the bottom of his chest:

"Corin! My son! And on foot, and in rags! What –"

"No," panted Shasta, shaking his head. "Not Prince Corin. I – I – know I'm like him . . . saw his Highness in Tashbaan . . . sent his greetings."

The King was staring at Shasta with an extraordinary expression on his face.

"Are you K-King Lune?" gasped Shasta. And then, without waiting for an answer, "Lord King – fly – Anvard – shut the gates – enemies upon you – Rabadash and two hundred horse."

"Have you assurance of this, boy?" asked one of the other gentlemen.

"My own eyes," said Shasta. "I've seen them. Raced them all the way from Tashbaan."

"On foot?" said the gentleman, raising his eyebrows a little.

"Horses – with the Hermit," said Shasta.

"Question him no more, Darrin," said King Lune. "I see truth in his face. We must ride for it, gentlemen. A spare horse there, for the boy. You can ride fast, friend?"

For answer Shasta put his foot in the stirrup of the horse which had been led towards him and a moment later he was in the saddle. He had done it a hundred times with

Bree in the last few weeks, and his mounting was very different now from what it had been on that first night when Bree had said that he climbed up a horse as if he were climbing a haystack.

He was pleased to hear the Lord Darrin say to the King, "The boy has a true horseman's seat, Sire. I'll warrant there's noble blood in him."

"His blood, aye, there's the point," said the King. And he stared hard at Shasta again with that curious expression, almost a hungry expression, in his steady, grey eyes.

But by now the whole party was moving off at a brisk canter. Shasta's seat was excellent but he was sadly puzzled what to do with his reins, for he had never touched the reins while he was on Bree's back. But he looked very carefully out of the corners of his eyes to see what the others were doing (as some of us have done at parties when we weren't quite sure which knife or fork we were meant to use) and tried to get his fingers right. But he didn't dare to try really directing the horse; he trusted it would follow the rest. The horse was of course an ordinary horse, not a Talking Horse; but it had quite wits enough to realize that the strange boy on its back had no whip and no spurs and was not really master of the situation. That was why Shasta soon found himself at the tail end of the procession.

Even so, he was going pretty fast. There were no flies now and the air in his face was delicious. He had got his breath back too. And his errand had succeeded. For the first time since the arrival at Tashbaan (how long ago it seemed!) he was beginning to enjoy himself.

He looked up to see how much nearer the mountain tops had come. To his disappointment he could not see them at all: only a vague greyness, rolling down towards them. He had never been in mountain country before and was surprised. "It's a cloud," he said to himself, "a cloud coming down. I see. Up here in the hills one is really in the sky. I shall see what the inside of a cloud is like. What fun! I've often wondered." Far away on his left and a little behind him, the sun was getting ready to set.

They had come to a rough kind of road by now and were making very good speed. But Shasta's horse was still the last of the lot. Once or twice when the road made a bend (there was now continuous forest on each side of it) he lost sight of the others for a second or two.

Then they plunged into the fog, or else the fog rolled

over them. The world became grey. Shasta had not realized
how cold and wet the inside of a cloud would be; nor how
dark. The grey turned to black with alarming speed.

Someone at the head of the column winded the horn
every now and then, and each time the sound came from a
little farther off. He couldn't see any of the others now, but
of course he'd be able to as soon as he got round the next
bend. But when he rounded it he still couldn't see them. In
fact he could see nothing at all. His horse was walking
now. "Get on, Horse, get on," said Shasta. Then came the
horn, very faint. Bree had always told him that he must
keep his heels well turned out, and Shasta had got the idea
that something very terrible would happen if he dug his
heels into a horse's sides. This seemed to him an occasion
for trying it. "Look here, Horse," he said, "if you don't
buck up, do you know what I'll do? I'll dig my heels into
you. I really will." The horse, however, took no notice of
this threat. So Shasta settled himself firmly in the saddle,
gripped with his knees, clenched his teeth, and punched
both the horse's sides with his heels as hard as he could.

The only result was that the horse broke into a kind of
pretence of a trot for five or six paces and then subsided
into a walk again. And now it was quite dark and they
seemed to have given up blowing that horn. The only
sound was a steady drip-drip from the branches of the
trees.

"Well, I suppose even a walk will get us somewhere
sometime," said Shasta to himself. "I only hope I shan't
run into Rabadash and his people."

He went on for what seemed a long time, always at a
walking pace. He began to hate that horse, and he was also
beginning to feel very hungry.

Presently he came to a place where the road divided into
two. He was just wondering which led to Anvard when he

was startled by a noise from behind him. It was the noise of trotting horses. "Rabadash!" thought Shasta. He had no way of guessing which road Rabadash would take. "But if I take one," said Shasta to himself, "he *may* take the other: and if I stay at the cross-roads I'm *sure* to be caught." He dismounted and led his horse as quickly as he could along the right-hand road.

The sound of the cavalry grew rapidly nearer and in a minute or two Shasta realized that they were at the cross-roads. He held his breath, waiting to see which way they would take.

There came a low word of command "Halt!" then a moment of horsey noises — nostrils blowing, hoofs pawing, bits being champed, necks being patted. Then a voice spoke.

"Attend, all of you," it said. "We are now within a furlong of the castle. Remember your orders. Once we are in Narnia, as we should be by sunrise, you are to kill as little as possible. On this venture you are to regard every drop of Narnian blood as more precious than a gallon of your own. On *this* venture, I say. The gods will send us a happier hour and then you must leave nothing alive between Cair Paravel and the Western Waste. But we are not yet in Narnia. Here in Archenland it is another thing. In the assault on this castle of King Lune's, nothing matters but speed. Show your mettle. It must be mine within an hour. And if it is, I give it all to you. I reserve no booty for myself. Kill me every barbarian male within its walls, down to the child that was born yesterday, and everything else is yours to divide as you please — the women, the gold, the jewels, the weapons, and the wine. The man that I see hanging back when we come to the gates shall be burned alive. In the name of Tash the irresistible, the inexorable — forward!"

With a great cloppitty-clop the column began to move, and Shasta breathed again. They had taken the other road.

Shasta thought they took a long time going past, for though he had been talking and thinking about "two hundred horse" all day, he had not realized how many they really were. But at last the sound died away and once more he was alone amid the drip-drip from the trees.

He now knew the way to Anvard but of course he could not now go there: that would only mean running into the arms of Rabadash's troopers. "What on earth am I to do?" said Shasta to himself. But he remounted his horse and continued along the road he had chosen, in the faint hope of finding some cottage where he might ask for shelter and a meal. He had thought, of course, of going back to Aravis and Bree and Hwin at the hermitage, but he couldn't because by now he had not the least idea of the direction.

"After all," said Shasta, "this road is bound to get to somewhere."

But that all depends on what you mean by somewhere. The road kept on getting to somewhere in the sense that it got to more and more trees, all dark and dripping, and to colder and colder air. And strange, icy winds kept blowing the mist past him though they never blew it away. If he had been used to mountain country he would have realized that this meant he was now very high up – perhaps right at the top of the pass. But Shasta knew nothing about mountains.

"I *do* think," said Shasta, "that I must be the most unfortunate boy that ever lived in the whole world. Everything goes right for everyone except me. Those Narnian lords and ladies got safe away from Tashbaan; I was left behind. Aravis and Bree and Hwin are all as snug as anything with that old Hermit: of course I was the one who was sent on. King Lune and his people must have got safely into the castle and shut the gates long before Rabadash arrived, but I get left out."

And being very tired and having nothing inside him, he felt so sorry for himself that the tears rolled down his cheeks.

What put a stop to all this was a sudden fright. Shasta discovered that someone or somebody was walking beside him. It was pitch dark and he could see nothing. And the Thing (or Person) was going so quietly that he could hardly hear any footfalls. What he could hear was breathing. His invisible companion seemed to breathe on a very large scale, and Shasta got the impression that it was a very large creature. And he had come to notice this breathing so gradually that he had really no idea how long it had been there. It was a horrible shock.

It darted into his mind that he had heard long ago that there were giants in these Northern countries. He bit his lip in terror. But now that he really had something to cry about, he stopped crying.

The Thing (unless it was a Person) went on beside him so very quietly that Shasta began to hope he had only imagined it. But just as he was becoming quite sure of it, there suddenly came a deep, rich sigh out of the darkness beside him. That couldn't be imagination! Anyway, he had felt the hot breath of that sigh on his chilly left hand.

If the horse had been any good – or if he had known how to get any good out of the horse – he would have risked everything on a breakaway and a wild gallop. But he knew he couldn't make that horse gallop. So he went on at a walking pace and the unseen companion walked and breathed beside him. At last he could bear it no longer.

"Who are you?" he said, scarcely above a whisper.

"One who has waited long for you to speak," said the Thing. Its voice was not loud, but very large and deep.

"Are you – are you a giant?" asked Shasta.

"You might call me a giant," said the Large Voice. "But I am not like the creatures you call giants."

"I can't see you at all," said Shasta, after staring very hard. Then (for an even more terrible idea had come into his head) he said, almost in a scream, "You're not – not something *dead*, are you? Oh please – please do go away. What harm have I ever done you? Oh, I am the unluckiest person in the whole world!"

Once more he felt the warm breath of the Thing on his hand and face. "There," it said, "that is not the breath of a ghost. Tell me your sorrows."

Shasta was a little reassured by the breath: so he told how he had never known his real father or mother and had been brought up sternly by the fisherman. And then he told the story of his escape and how they were chased by lions and forced to swim for their lives; and of all their dangers in Tashbaan and about his night among the tombs and how the beasts howled at him out of the desert. And he told about the heat and thirst of their desert journey and how they were almost at their goal when another lion chased them and wounded Aravis. And also, how very long it was since he had had anything to eat.

"I do not call you unfortunate," said the Large Voice.

"Don't you think it was bad luck to meet so many lions?" said Shasta.

"There was only one lion," said the Voice.

"What on earth do you mean? I've just told you there were at least two the first night, and –"

"There was only one: but he was swift of foot."

"How do you know?"

"I was the lion." And as Shasta gaped with open mouth and said nothing, the Voice continued. "I was the lion who forced you to join with Aravis. I was the cat who comforted you among the houses of the dead. I was the lion who drove the jackals from you while you slept. I was the lion who gave the Horses the new strength of fear for the last mile so that you should reach King Lune in time. And I was the lion you do not remember who pushed the boat in which you lay, a child near death, so that it came to shore where a man sat, wakeful at midnight, to receive you."

"Then it was you who wounded Aravis?"

"It was I."

"But what for?"

"Child," said the Voice, "I am telling you your story, not hers. I tell no one any story but his own."

"Who *are* you?" asked Shasta.

"Myself," said the Voice, very deep and low so that the earth shook: and again "Myself", loud and clear and gay: and then the third time "Myself", whispered so softly you could hardly hear it, and yet it seemed to come from all round you as if the leaves rustled with it.

Shasta was no longer afraid that the Voice belonged to something that would eat him, nor that it was the voice of a ghost. But a new and different sort of trembling came over him. Yet he felt glad too.

The mist was turning from black to grey and from grey to white. This must have begun to happen some time ago, but while he had been talking to the Thing he had not been noticing anything else. Now, the whiteness around him became a shining whiteness; his eyes began to blink. Somewhere ahead he could hear birds singing. He knew the night was over at last. He could see the mane and ears and head of his horse quite easily now. A golden light fell on them from the left. He thought it was the sun.

He turned and saw, pacing beside him, taller than the horse, a Lion. The horse did not seem to be afraid of it or else could not see it. It was from the Lion that the light came. No one ever saw anything more terrible or beautiful.

Luckily Shasta had lived all his life too far south in Calormen to have heard the tales that were whispered in Tashbaan about a dreadful Narnian demon that appeared in the form of a lion. And of course he knew none of the true stories about Aslan, the great Lion, the son of the Emperor-over-the-sea, the King above all High Kings in Narnia. But after one glance at the Lion's face he slipped out of the saddle and fell at its feet. He couldn't say anything but then he didn't want to say anything, and he knew he needn't say anything.

The High King above all kings stooped towards him. Its mane, and some strange and solemn perfume that hung about the mane, was all round him. It touched his forehead with its tongue. He lifted his face and their eyes met. Then instantly the pale brightness of the mist and the fiery brightness of the Lion rolled themselves together into a swirling glory and gathered themselves up and disappeared. He was alone with the horse on a grassy hillside under a blue sky. And there were birds singing.

CHAPTER TWELVE

SHASTA IN NARNIA

"WAS it all a dream?" wondered Shasta. But it couldn't have been a dream for there in the grass before him he saw the deep, large print of the Lion's front right paw. It took one's breath away to think of the weight that could make a footprint like that. But there was something more remarkable than the size about it. As he looked at it, water had already filled the bottom of it. Soon it was full to the brim, and then overflowing, and a little stream was running downhill, past him, over the grass.

Shasta stooped and drank – a very long drink – and then dipped his face in and splashed his head. It was extremely cold, and clear as glass, and refreshed him very much. After that he stood up, shaking the water out of his ears and flinging the wet hair back from his forehead, and began to take stock of his surroundings.

Apparently it was still very early morning. The sun had only just risen, and it had risen out of the forests which he saw low down and far away on his right. The country which he was looking at was absolutely new to him. It was a green valley-land dotted with trees through which he caught the gleam of a river that wound away roughly to the North-West. On the far side of the valley there were high and even rocky hills, but they were lower than the mountains he had seen yesterday. Then he began to guess where he was. He turned and looked behind him and saw that the slope on which he was standing belonged to a range of far higher mountains.

"I see," said Shasta to himself. "Those are the big mountains between Archenland and Narnia. I was on the other side of them yesterday. I must have come through the pass in the night. What luck that I hit it! – at least it wasn't luck at all really, it was *Him*. And now I'm in Narnia."

He turned and unsaddled his horse and took off its bridle – "Though you *are* a perfectly horrid horse," he said. It took no notice of this remark and immediately began eating grass. That horse had a very low opinion of Shasta.

"I wish I could eat grass!" thought Shasta. "It's no good going back to Anvard, it'll all be besieged. I'd better get lower down into the valley and see if I can get anything to eat."

So he went on downhill (the thick dew was cruelly cold to his bare feet) till he came into a wood. There was a kind of track running through it and he had not followed this for many minutes when he heard a thick and rather wheezy voice saying to him.

"Good morning, neighbour."

Shasta looked round eagerly to find the speaker and presently saw a small, prickly person with a dark face who had just come out from among the trees. At least, it was small for a person but very big indeed for a hedgehog, which was what it was.

"Good morning," said Shasta. "But I'm not a neighbour. In fact I'm a stranger in these parts."

"Ah?" said the Hedgehog inquiringly.

"I've come over the mountains – from Archenland, you know."

"Ah, Archenland," said the Hedgehog. "That's a terrible long way. Never been there myself."

"And I think, perhaps," said Shasta, "someone ought to be told that there's an army of savage Calormenes attacking Anvard at this very moment."

"You don't say so!" answered the Hedgehog. "Well, think of that. And they do say that Calormen is hundreds and thousands of miles away, right at the world's end, across a great sea of sand."

"It's not nearly as far as you think," said Shasta. "And oughtn't something to be done about this attack on Anvard? Oughtn't your High King to be told?"

"Certain sure, something ought to be done about it," said the Hedgehog. "But you see I'm just on my way to bed for a good day's sleep. Hullo, neighbour!"

The last words were addressed to an immense biscuit-coloured rabbit whose head had just popped up from somewhere beside the path. The Hedgehog immediately told the Rabbit what it had just learned from Shasta. The Rabbit agreed that this was very remarkable news and that somebody ought to tell someone about it with a view to doing something.

And so it went on. Every few minutes they were joined by other creatures, some from the branches overhead and some from little underground houses at their feet, till the party consisted of five rabbits, a squirrel, two magpies, a goat-foot faun, and a mouse, who all talked at the same time and all agreed with the Hedgehog. For the truth was that in that golden age when the Witch and the Winter had gone and Peter the High King ruled at Cair Paravel, the smaller woodland people of Narnia were so safe and happy that they were getting a little careless.

Presently, however, two more practical people arrived in the little wood. One was a Red Dwarf whose name appeared to be Duffle. The other was a stag, a beautiful lordly creature with wide liquid eyes, dappled flanks and legs so thin and graceful that they looked as if you could break them with two fingers.

"Lion alive!" roared the Dwarf as soon as he had heard the news. "And if that's so, why are we all standing still, chattering? Enemies at Anvard! News must be sent to Cair Paravel at once. The army must be called out. Narnia must go to the aid of King Lune."

"Ah!" said the Hedgehog. "But you won't find the High King at the Cair. He's away to the North trouncing those giants. And talking of giants, neightbours, that puts me in mind –"

"Who'll take our message?" interrupted the Dwarf. "Anyone here got more speed than me?"

"I've got speed," said the Stag. "What's my message? How many Calormenes?"

"Two hundred: under Prince Rabadash. And –" But the Stag was already away – all four legs off the ground at once, and in a moment its white stern had disappeared among the remoter trees.

"Wonder where he's going," said a Rabbit. "He won't find the High King at Cair Paravel, you know."

"He'll find Queen Lucy," said Duffle. "And then – hullo! What's wrong with the Human? It looks pretty green. Why, I do believe it's quite faint. Perhaps it's mortal hungry. When did you last have a meal, youngster?"

"Yesterday morning," said Shasta weakly.

"Come on, then, come on," said the Dwarf, at once throwing his thick little arms round Shasta's waist to support him. "Why, neighbours, we ought all to be ashamed of ourselves! You come with me, lad. Breakfast! Better than talking."

With a great deal of bustle, muttering reproaches to itself, the Dwarf half led and half supported Shasta at a great speed further into the wood and a little downhill. It was a longer walk than Shasta wanted at that moment and his legs had begun to feel very shaky before they came out from the trees on to bare hillside. There they found a little house with a smoking chimney and an open door, and as they came to the doorway Duffle called out,

"Hey, brothers! A visitor for breakfast."

And immediately, mixed with a sizzling sound, there came to Shasta a simply delightful smell. It was one he had never smelled in his life before, but I hope you have. It was, in fact, the smell of bacon and eggs and mushrooms all frying in a pan.

"Mind your head, lad," said Duffle a moment too late, for Shasta had already bashed his forehead against the low lintel of the door. "Now," continued the Dwarf, "sit you down. The table's a bit low for you, but then the stool's low too. That's right. And here's porridge – and here's a jug of cream – and here's a spoon."

By the time Shasta had finished his porridge, the Dwarf's two brothers (whose names were Rogin and Bricklethumb) were putting the dish of bacon and eggs and mushrooms, and the coffee pot and the hot milk, and the toast, on the table.

It was all new and wonderful to Shasta for Calormene

food is quite different. He didn't even know what the slices of brown stuff were, for he had never seen toast before. He didn't know what the yellow soft thing they smeared on the toast was, because in Calormen you nearly always get oil instead of butter. And the house itself was quite different from the dark, frowsty, fish-smelling hut of Arsheesh and from the pillared and carpeted halls in the palaces of Tashbaan. The roof was very low, and everything was made of wood, and there was a cuckoo-clock and a red-and-white checked table-cloth and a bowl of wild flowers and little curtains on the thick-paned windows. It was also rather troublesome having to use dwarf cups and plates and knives and forks. This meant that helpings were very small, but then there were a great many helpings, so that Shasta's plate or cup was being filled every moment, and every moment the Dwarfs themselves were saying, "Butter please", or "Another cup of coffee," or "I'd like a few more mushrooms," or "What about frying another egg or so?" And when at last they had all eaten as much as they possibly could the three Dwarfs drew lots for who would do the washing-up, and Rogin was the unlucky one. Then Duffle and Bricklethumb took Shasta outside to a bench which ran against the cottage wall, and they all stretched out their legs and gave a great sigh of contentment and the two Dwarfs lit their pipes. The dew was off the grass now and the sun was warm; indeed, if there hadn't been a light breeze, it would have been too hot.

"Now, Stranger," said Duffle, "I'll show you the lie of the land. You can see nearly all South Narnia from here, and we're rather proud of the view. Right away on your left, beyond those near hills, you can just see the Western Mountains. And that round hill away on your right is called the Hill of the Stone Table. Just beyond –"

But at that moment he was interrupted by a snore from Shasta who, what with his night's journey and his excellent breakfast, had gone fast asleep. The kindly Dwarfs, as soon as they noticed this, began making signs to each other not to wake him, and indeed did so much whispering and nodding and getting up and tiptoeing away that they certainly would have waked him if he had been less tired.

He slept pretty well nearly all day but woke up in time for supper. The beds in that house were all too small for him but they made him a fine bed of heather on the floor, and he never stirred nor dreamed all night. Next morning they had just finished breakfast when they heard a shrill, exciting sound from outside.

"Trumpets!" said all the Dwarfs, as they and Shasta all came running out.

The trumpets sounded again: a new noise to Shasta, not huge and solemn like the horns of Tashbaan nor gay and merry like King Lune's hunting horn, but clear and sharp and valiant. The noise was coming from the woods to the East, and soon there was a noise of horse-hoofs mixed with it. A moment later the head of the column came into sight.

First came the Lord Peridan on a bay horse carrying the great banner of Narnia — a red lion on a green ground. Shasta knew him at once. Then came three people riding abreast, two on great chargers and one on a pony. The two on the chargers were King Edmund and a fair-haired lady with a very merry face who wore a helmet and a mail shirt and carried a bow across her shoulder and a quiver full of arrows at her side. ("The Queen Lucy," whispered Duffle.) But the one on the pony was Corin. After that came the main body of the army: men on ordinary horses, men on Talking Horses (who didn't mind being ridden on proper occasions, as when Narnia went to war), centaurs, stern, hard-bitten bears, great Talking Dogs, and last of all six giants. For there are good giants in Narnia. But though he knew they were on the right side Shasta at first could hardly bear to look at them; there are some things that take a lot of getting used to.

Just as the King and Queen reached the cottage and the Dwarfs began making low bows to them, King Edmund called out,

"Now, friends! Time for a halt and a morsel!" and at once there was a great bustle of people dismounting and haversacks being opened and conversation beginning when Corin came running up to Shasta and seized both his hands and cried,

"What! *You* here! So you got through all right? I *am* glad. Now we shall have some sport. And isn't it luck! We only got into harbour at Cair Paravel yesterday morning and the very first person who met us was Chervy the Stag with all this news of an attack on Anvard. Don't you think —"

"Who is your Highness's friend?" said King Edmund who had just got off his horse.

"Don't you see, Sire?" said Corin. "It's my double: the boy you mistook me for at Tashbaan."

"Why, so he is your double," exclaimed Queen Lucy. "As like as two twins. This is a marvellous thing."

"Please, your Majesty," said Shasta to King Edmund, "I was no traitor, really I wasn't. And I couldn't help hearing your plans. But I'd never have dreamed of telling them to your enemies."

"I know now that you were no traitor, boy," said King Edmund, laying his hand on Shasta's head. "But if you would not be taken for one, another time try not to hear what's meant for other ears. But all's well."

After that there was so much bustle and talk and coming and going that Shasta for a few minutes lost sight of Corin and Edmund and Lucy. But Corin was the sort of boy whom one is sure to hear of pretty soon and it wasn't very long before Shasta heard King Edmund saying in a loud voice:

"By the Lion's Mane, prince, this is too much! Will your Highness never be better? You are more of a heart's-scald than our whole army together! I'd as lief have a regiment of hornets in my command as you."

Shasta wormed his way through the crowd and there saw Edmund, looking very angry indeed, Corin looking a little ashamed of himself, and a strange Dwarf sitting on the ground making faces. A couple of fauns had apparently just been helping it out of its armour.

"If I had but my cordial with me," Queen Lucy was saying, "I could soon mend this. But the High King has so strictly charged me not to carry it commonly to the wars and to keep it only for great extremities!"

What had happened was this. As soon as Corin had

spoken to Shasta, Corin's elbow had been plucked by a Dwarf in the army called Thornbut.

"What is it, Thornbut?" Corin had said.

"Your Royal Highness," said Thornbut, drawing him aside, "our march today will bring us through the pass and right to your royal father's castle. We may be in battle before night."

"I know," said Corin. "Isn't it splendid!"

"Splendid or not," said Thornbut, "I have the strictest orders from King Edmund to see to it that your Highness is not in the fight. You will be allowed to see it, and that's treat enough for your Highness's little years."

"Oh what nonsense!" Corin burst out. "Of course I'm going to fight. Why, the Queen Lucy's going to be with the archers."

"The Queen's grace will do as she pleases," said Thornbut. "But you are in my charge. Either I must have your solemn and princely word that you'll keep your pony beside mine – not half a neck ahead – till I give your

Highness leave to depart: or else – it is his Majesty's word – we must go with our wrists tied together like two prisoners."

"I'll knock you down if you try to bind me," said Corin.

"I'd like to see your Highness do it," said the Dwarf.

That was quite enough for a boy like Corin and in a second he and the Dwarf were at it hammer and tongs. It would have been an even match for, though Corin had longer arms and more height, the Dwarf was older and tougher. But it was never fought out (that's the worst of fights on a rough hillside) for by very bad luck Thornbut trod on a loose stone, came flat down on his nose, and found when he tried to get up that he had sprained his ankle: a real excruciating sprain which would keep him from walking or riding for at least a fortnight.

"See what your Highness has done," said King Edmund. "Deprived us of a proved warrior on the very edge of battle."

"I'll take his place, Sire," said Corin.

"Pshaw," said Edmund. "No one doubts your courage. But a boy in battle is a danger only to his own side."

At that moment the King was called away to attend to something else, and Corin, after apologizing handsomely to the Dwarf, rushed up to Shasta and whispered,

"Quick. There's a spare pony now, and the Dwarf's armour. Put it on before anyone notices."

"What for?" said Shasta.

"Why, so that you and I can fight in the battle of course! Don't you want to?"

"Oh – ah, yes, of course," said Shasta. But he hadn't been thinking of doing so at all, and began to get a most uncomfortable prickly feeling in his spine.

"That's right," said Corin. "Over your head. Now the sword-belt. But we must ride near the tail of the column and keep as quiet as mice. Once the battle begins everyone will be far too busy to notice us."

CHAPTER THIRTEEN

THE FIGHT AT ANVARD

BY about eleven o'clock the whole company was once more on the march, riding westward with the mountains on their left. Corin and Shasta rode right at the rear with the Giants immediately in front of them. Lucy and Edmund and Peridan were busy with their plans for the battle and though Lucy once said, "But where is his goosecap Highness?" Edmund only replied, "Not in the front, and that's good news enough. Leave well alone."

Shasta told Corin most of his adventures and explained that he had learned all his riding from a horse and didn't really know how to use the reins. Corin instructed him in this, besides telling him all about their secret sailing from Tashbaan.

"And where is the Queen Susan?"

"At Cair Paravel," said Corin. "She's not like Lucy, you know, who's as good as a man, or at any rate as good as a boy. Queen Susan is more like an ordinary grown-up lady. She doesn't ride to the wars, though she is an excellent archer."

The hillside path which they were following became narrower all the time and the drop on their right hand became steeper. At last they were going in single file along the edge of a precipice and Shasta shuddered to think that he had done the same last night without knowing it. "But of course," he thought, "I was quite safe. That is why the Lion kept on my left. He was between me and the edge all the time."

Then the path went left and south away from the cliff and there were thick woods on both sides of it and they went steeply up and up into the pass. There would have

been a splendid view from the top if it were open ground
but among all those trees you could see nothing — only,
every now and then, some huge pinnacle of rock above the
tree-tops, and an eagle or two wheeling high up in the blue
air.

"They smell battle," said Corin, pointing at the birds.
"They know we're preparing a feed for them."

Shasta didn't like this at all.

When they had crossed the neck of the pass and come a
good deal lower they reached more open ground and from
here Shasta could see all Archenland, blue and hazy, spread
out below him and even (he thought) a hint of the desert
beyond it. But the sun, which had perhaps two hours or so
to go before it set, was in his eyes and he couldn't make
things out distinctly.

Here the army halted and spread out in a line, and there
was a great deal of rearranging. A whole detachment of
very dangerous-looking Talking Beasts whom Shasta had
not noticed before and who were mostly of the cat kind
(leopards, panthers, and the like) went padding and growling to take up their positions on the left. The giants were
ordered to the right, and before going there they all took
off something they had been carrying on their backs and
sat down for a moment. Then Shasta saw that what they
had been carrying and were now putting on were pairs of
boots: horrid, heavy, spiked boots which came up to their
knees. Then they sloped their huge clubs over their
shoulders and marched to their battle position. The archers, with Queen Lucy, fell to the rear and you could first
see them bending their bows and then hear the twang-
twang as they tested the strings. And wherever you looked
you could see people tightening girths, putting on helmets,
drawing swords, and throwing cloaks to the ground. There
was hardly any talking now. It was very solemn and very

dreadful. "I'm in for it now — I really am in for it now," thought Shasta. Then there came noises far ahead: the sound of many men shouting and a steady thud-thud-thud.

"Battering ram," whispered Corin. "They're battering the gate."

Even Corin looked quite serious now.

"Why doesn't King Edmund get *on?*" he said. "I can't stand this waiting about. Chilly too."

Shasta nodded: hoping he didn't look as frightened as he felt.

The trumpet at last! On the move now — now trotting — the banner streaming out in the wind. They had topped a low ridge now, and below them the whole scene suddenly opened out; a little, many-towered castle with its gate towards them. No moat, unfortunately, but of course the gate shut and the portcullis down. On the walls they could see, like little white dots, the faces of the defenders. Down below, about fifty of the Calormenes, dismounted, were steadily swinging a great tree trunk against the gate. But at once the scene changed. The main bulk of Rabadash's men had been on foot ready to assault the gate. But now he had seen the Narnians sweeping down from the ridge. There is no doubt those Calormenes are wonderfully trained. It seemed to Shasta only a second before a whole line of the enemy were on hoseback again, wheeling round to meet them, swinging towards them.

And now a gallop. The ground between the two armies grew less every moment. Faster, faster. All swords out now, all shields up to the nose, all prayers said, all teeth clenched. Shasta was dreadfully frightened. But it suddenly came into his head, "If you funk this, you'll funk every battle all your life. Now or never."

But when at last the two lines met he had really very little idea of what happened. There was a frightful confusion

and an appalling noise. His sword was knocked clean out
of his hand pretty soon. And he'd got the reins tangled
somehow. Then he found himself slipping. Then a spear
came straight at him and as he ducked to avoid it he rolled
right off his horse, bashed his left knuckles terribly against
someone else's armour, and then —

But it is no use trying to describe the battle from Shasta's
point of view; he understood too little of the fight in
general and even of his own part in it. The best way I can
tell you what really happened is to take you some miles
away to where the Hermit of the Southern March sat gazing into the smooth pool beneath the spreading tree, with
Bree and Hwin and Aravis beside him.

For it was in this pool that the Hermit looked when he
wanted to know what was going on in the world outside
the green walls of his hermitage. There, as in a mirror, he
could see, at certain times, what was going on in the streets
of cities far farther south than Tashbaan, or what ships
were putting into Redhaven in the remote Seven Isles, or
what robbers or wild beasts stirred in the great Western
forests between Lantern Waste and Telmar. And all this
day he had hardly left his pool, even to eat or drink, for he
knew that great events were on foot in Archenland. Aravis

and the Horses gazed into it too. They could see it was a magic pool: instead of reflecting the tree and the sky it revealed cloudy and coloured shapes moving, always moving, in its depths. But they could see nothing clearly. The Hermit could and from time to time he told them what he saw. A little while before Shasta rode into his first battle, the Hermit had begun speaking like this:

"I see one – two – three eagles wheeling in the gap by Stormness Head. One is the oldest of all the eagles. He would not be out unless battle was at hand. I see him wheel to and fro, peering down sometimes at Anvard and sometimes to the east, behind Stormness. Ah – I see now what Rabadash and his men have been so busy at all day. They have felled and lopped a great tree and they are now coming out of the woods carrying it as a ram. They have learned something from the failure of last night's assult. He would have been wiser if he had set his men to making ladders: but it takes too long and he is impatient. Fool that he is! He ought to have ridden back to Tashbaan as soon as the first attack failed, for his whole plan depended on speed and surprise. Now they are bringing their ram into position. King Lune's men are shooting hard from the walls. Five Calormenes have fallen: but not many will. They have their shields above their heads. Rabadash is giving his orders now. With him are his most trusted lords, fierce Tarkaans from the eastern provinces. I can see their faces. There is Corradin of Castle Tormunt, and Azrooh, and Chlamash, and Ilgamuth of the twisted lip, and a tall Tarkaan with a crimson beard –"

"By the Mane, my old master Anradin!" said Bree.

"S-s-sh," said Aravis.

"Now the ram has started. If I could hear as well as see, what a noise that would make! Stroke after stroke: and no gate can stand it for ever. But wait! Something up by

Stormness has scared the birds. They're coming out in
masses. And wait again . . . I can't see yet . . . ah! Now I
can. The whole ridge, up on the east, is black with horsemen. If only the wind would catch that standard and
spread it out. They're over the ridge now, whoever they
are. Aha! I've seen the banner now. Narnia, Narnia! It's
the red lion. They're in full career down the hill now. I can
see King Edmund. There's a woman behind among the
archers. Oh! –"

"What is it?" asked Hwin breathlessly.

"All his Cats are dashing out from the left of the line."

"Cats?" said Aravis.

"Great cats, leopards and such," said the Hermit
impatiently. "I see, I see. The Cats are coming round in a
circle to get at the horses of the dismounted men. A good
stroke. The Calormene horses are mad with terror already.
Now the Cats are in among them. But Rabadash has reformed his line and has a hundred men in the saddle.
They're riding to meet the Narnians. There's only a
hundred yards between the two lines now. Only fifty. I can
see King Edmund, I can see the Lord Peridan. There are
two mere children in the Narnian line. What can the King
be about to let them into battle? Only ten yards – the lines
have met. The Giants on the Narnian right are doing
wonders . . . but one's down . . . shot through the eye, I
suppose. The centre's all in a muddle. I can see more on the
left. There are the two boys again. Lion alive! one is Prince
Corin. The other, like him as two peas. It's your little
Shasta. Corin is fighting like a man. He's killed a
Calormene. I can see a bit of the centre now. Rabadash
and Edmund almost met then, but the press has separated
them –"

"What about Shasta?" said Aravis.

"Oh the fool!" groaned the Hermit. "Poor, brave little

fool. He knows nothing about this work. He's making no use at all of his shield. His whole side's exposed. He hasn't the faintest idea what to do with his sword. Oh, he's remembered it now. He's waving it wildly about . . . nearly cut his own pony's head off, and he will in a moment if he's not careful. It's been knocked out of his hand now. It's mere murder sending a child into the battle; he can't live five minutes. Duck, you fool – oh, he's down."

"Killed?" asked three voices breathlessly.

"How can I tell?" said the Hermit. "The Cats have done their work. All the riderless horses are dead or escaped now: no retreat for the Calormenes on *them*. Now the Cats are turning back into the main battle. They're leaping on the rams-men. The ram is down. Oh, good! good! The gates are opening from the inside: there's going to be a sortie. The first three are out. It's King Lune in the middle: the brothers Dar and Darrin on each side of him. Behind them are Tran and Shar and Cole with his brother Colin. There are ten – twenty – nearly thirty of them out by now. The Calormen line is being forced back upon them. King Edmund is dealing marvellous strokes. He's just slashed Corradin's head off. Lots of Calormenes have thrown down their arms and are running for the woods. Those that remain are hard pressed. The Giants are closing in on the right – Cats on the left – King Lune from their rear. The Calormenes are a little knot now, fighting back to back. Your Tarkaan's down, Bree. Lune and Azrooh are fighting hand to hand; the King looks like winning – the King is keeping it up well – the King has won. Azrooh's down. King Edmund's down – no, he's up again: he's at it with Rabadash. They're fighting in the very gate of the castle. Several Calormenes have surrendered. Darrin has killed Ilgamuth. I can't see what's happened to Rabadash. I think he's dead, leaning against the castle wall, but I don't know.

Chlamash and King Edmund are still fighting but the battle is over everywhere else. Chlamash has surrendered. The battle *is* over. The Calormenes are utterly defeated."

When Shasta fell off his horse he gave himself up for lost. But horses, even in battle, tread on human beings very much less than you would suppose. After a very horrible ten minutes or so Shasta realized suddenly that there were no longer any horses stamping about in the immediate

neighbourhood and that the noise (for there were still a good many noises going on) was no longer that of a battle. He sat up and stared about him. Even he, little as he knew of battles, could soon see that the Archenlanders and Narnians had won. The only living Calormenes he could see were prisoners, the castle gates were wide open, and King Lune and King Edmund were shaking hands across the battering ram. From the circle of lords and warriors around them there arose a sound of breathless and excited, but obviously cheerful conversation. And then, suddenly, it all united and swelled into a great roar of laughter.

Shasta picked himself up, feeling uncommonly stiff, and ran towards the sound to see what the joke was. A very curious sight met his eyes. The unfortunate Rabadash appeared to be suspended from the castle walls. His feet, which were about two feet from the ground, were kicking wildly. His chain-shirt was somehow hitched up so that it was horribly tight under the arms and came half way over his face. In fact he looked just as a man looks if you catch him in the very act of getting into a stiff shirt that is a little too small for him. As far as could be made out afterwards (and you may be sure the story was well talked over for many a day) what happened was something like this. Early in the battle one of the Giants had made an unsuccessful stamp at Rabadash with his spiked boot: unsuccessful because it didn't crush Rabadash, which was what the Giant had intended, but not quite useless because one of the spikes tore the chain mail, just as you or I might tear an ordinary shirt. So Rabadash, by the time he encountered Edmund at the gate, had a hole in the back of his hauberk. And when Edmund pressed him back nearer and nearer to the wall, he jumped up on a mounting block and stood there raining down blows on Edmund from above. But then, finding that this position, by raising him above the heads of everyone else, made him a mark for every arrow from the Narnian bows, he decided to jump down again. And he meant to look and sound — no doubt for a moment he *did* look and sound — very grand and very dreadful as he jumped, crying, "The bolt of Tash falls from above." But he had to jump sideways because the crowd in front of him left him no landing place in that direction. And then, in the neatest way you could wish, the tear in the back of his hauberk caught on a hook in the wall. (Ages ago this hook had had a ring in it for tying horses to.) And there he found himself, like a piece of washing hung up to dry, with everyone laughing at him.

"Let me down, Edmund," howled Rabadash. "Let me down and fight me like a king and a man; or if you are too great a coward to do that, kill me at once."

"Certainly," began King Edmund, but King Lune interrupted.

"By your Majesty's good leave," said King Lune to Edmund. "Not so." Then turning to Rabadash he said, "Your royal Highness, if you had given that challenge a week ago, I'll answer for it there was no one in King Edmund's dominion, from the High King down to the smallest Talking Mouse, who would have refused it. But by attacking our castle of Anvard in time of peace without defiance sent, you have proved yourself no knight, but a traitor, and one rather to be whipped by the hangman than to be suffered to cross swords with any person of honour. Take him down, bind him, and carry him within till our pleasure is further known."

Strong hands wrenched Rabadash's sword from him and he was carried away into the castle, shouting, threatening, cursing, and even crying. For though he could have faced torture he couldn't bear being made ridiculous. In Tashbaan everyone had always taken him seriously.

At that momemt Corin ran up to Shasta, seized his hand and started dragging him towards King Lune. "Here he is, Father, here he is," cried Corin.

"Aye, and here *thou* art, at last," said the King in a very gruff voice. "And hast been in the battle, clean contrary to your obedience. A boy to break a father's heart! At your age a rod to your breech were fitter than a sword in your fist, ha!" But everyone, including Corin, could see that the King was very proud of him.

"Chide him no more, Sire, if it please you," said Lord

Darrin. "His Highness would not be your son if he did not inherit your conditions. It would grieve your Majesty more if he had to be reproved for the opposite fault."

"Well, well," grumbled the King. "We'll pass it over for this time. And now —"

What came next surprised Shasta as much as anything that had ever happened to him in his life. He found himself suddenly embraced in a bear-like hug by King Lune and kissed on both cheeks. Then the King set him down again and said, "Stand here together, boys, and let all the court see you. Hold up your heads. Now, gentlemen, look on them both. Has any man any doubts?"

And still Shasta could not understand why everyone stared at him and at Corin nor what all the cheering was about.

CHAPTER FOURTEEN

HOW BREE BECAME A WISER HORSE

WE must now return to Aravis and the Horses. The Hermit, watching his pool, was able to tell them that Shasta was not killed or even seriously wounded, for he saw him get up and saw how affectionately he was greeted by King Lune. But as he could only see, not hear, he did not know what anyone was saying and, once the fighting had stopped and the talking had begun, it was not worth while looking in the pool any longer.

Next morning, while the Hermit was indoors, the three of them discussed what they should do next.

"I've had enough of this," said Hwin. "The Hermit has been very good to us and I'm very much obliged to him I'm sure. But I'm getting as fat as a pet pony, eating all day and getting no exercise. Let's go on to Narnia."

"Oh not today, Ma'am," said Bree. "I wouldn't hurry things. Some other day, don't you think?"

"We must see Shasta first and say good-bye to him – and – and apologize," said Aravis.

"Exactly!" said Bree with great enthusiasm. "Just what I was going to say."

"Oh, of course," said Hwin. "I expect he is in Anvard. Naturally we'd look in on him and say good-bye. But that's on our way. And why shouldn't we start at once? After all, I thought it was Narnia we all wanted to get to?"

"I suppose so," said Aravis. She was beginning to wonder what exactly she would do when she got there and was feeling a little lonely.

"Of course, of course," said Bree hastily. "But there's no need to rush things, if you know what I mean."

"No, I don't know what you mean," said Hwin. "Why don't you want to go?"

"M-m-m, broo-hoo," muttered Bree. "Well, don't you see, Ma'am – it's an important occasion – returning to one's country – entering society – the best society – it is so essential to make a good impression – not perhaps looking quite ourselves, yet, eh?"

Hwin broke out into a horse-laugh. "It's your tail, Bree! I see it all now. You want to wait till your tail's grown again! And we don't even know if tails are worn long in Narnia. Really, Bree, you're as vain as that Tarkheena in Tashbaan!"

"You *are* silly, Bree," said Aravis.

"By the Lion's Mane, Tarkheena, I'm nothing of the sort," said Bree indignantly. "I have a proper respect for myself and for my fellow horses, that's all."

"Bree," said Aravis, who was not very interested in the cut of his tail, "I've been wanting to ask you something for a long time. Why do you keep on swearing *By the Lion* and *By the Lion's Mane*? I thought you hated lions."

"So I do," answered Bree. "But when I speak of *the* Lion of course I mean Aslan, the great deliverer of Narnia who drove away the Witch and the Winter. All Narnians swear by *him*."

"But is he a lion?"

"No, no, of course not," said Bree in a rather shocked voice.

"All the stories about him in Tashbaan say he is," replied Aravis. "And if he isn't a lion why do you call him a lion?"

"Well, you'd hardly understand that at your age," said Bree. "And I was only a little foal when I left so I don't quite fully understand it myself."

(Bree was standing with his back to the green wall while

he said this, and the other two were facing him. He was talking in rather a superior tone with his eyes half shut; that was why he didn't see the changed expression in the faces of Hwin and Aravis. They had good reason to have open mouths and staring eyes; because while Bree spoke they saw an enormous lion leap up from outside and balance itself on the top of the green wall; only it was a brighter yellow and it was bigger and more beautiful and more alarming than any lion they had ever seen. And at once it jumped down inside the wall and began approaching Bree from behind. It made no noise at all. And Hwin and Aravis couldn't make any noise themselves, no more than if they were frozen.)

"No doubt," continued Bree, "when they speak of him as a Lion they only mean he's as strong as a lion or (to our enemies, of course) as fierce as a lion. Or something of that kind. Even a little girl like you, Aravis, must see that it would be quite absurd to suppose he is a *real* lion. Indeed it would be disrespectful. If he was a lion he'd have to be a Beast just like the rest of us. Why!" (and here Bree began to laugh) "If he was a lion he'd have four paws, and a tail, and *Whiskers*! . . . Aie, ooh, hoo-hoo! Help!"

For just as he said the word *Whiskers* one of Aslan's had actually tickled his ear. Bree shot away like an arrow to the other side of the enclosure and there turned; the wall was too high for him to jump and he could fly no farther. Aravis and Hwin both started back. There was about a second of intense silence.

Then Hwin, though shaking all over, gave a strange little neigh, and trotted across to the Lion.

"Please," she said, "you're so beautiful. You may eat me if you like. I'd sooner be eaten by you than fed by anyone else."

"Dearest daughter," said Aslan, planting a lion's kiss on

her twitching, velvet nose, "I knew you would not be long in coming to me. Joy shall be yours."

Then he lifted his head and spoke in a louder voice.

"Now, Bree," he said, "you poor, proud frightened Horse, draw near. Nearer still, my son. Do not dare not to dare. Touch me. Smell me. Here are my paws, here is my tail, these are my whiskers. I am a true Beast."

"Aslan," said Bree in a shaken voice, "I'm afraid I must be rather a fool."

"Happy the Horse who knows that while he is still young. Or the Human either. Draw near, Aravis my daughter. See! My paws are velveted. You will not be torn this time."

"This time, sir?" said Aravis.

"It was I who wounded you," said Aslan. "I am the only lion you met in all your journeyings. Do you know why I tore you?"

"No, sir."

"The scratches on your back, tear for tear, throb for throb, blood for blood, were equal to the stripes laid on the back of your stepmother's slave because of the drugged sleep you cast upon her. You needed to know what it felt like."

"Yes, sir. Please –"

"Ask on, my dear," said Aslan.

"Will any more harm come to her by what I did?"

"Child," said the Lion, "I am telling you your story, not hers. No one is told any story but their own." Then he shook his head and spoke in a lighter voice.

"Be merry, little ones," he said. "We shall meet soon again. But before that you will have another visitor." Then in one bound he reached the top of the wall and vanished from their sight.

Strange to say, they felt no inclination to talk to one

another about him after he had gone. They all moved
slowly away to different parts of the quiet grass and there
paced to and fro, each alone, thinking.

About half an hour later the two Horses were summoned to the back of the house to eat something nice that the
Hermit had got ready for them and Aravis, still walking
and thinking, was startled by the harsh sound of a trumpet
outside the gate.

"Who is there?" asked Aravis.

"His Royal Highness Prince Cor of Archenland," said a
voice from outside.

Aravis undid the door and opened it, drawing back a
little way to let the strangers in.

Two soldiers with halberds came first and took their
stand at each side of the entry. Then followed a herald, and
the trumpeter.

"His Royal Highness Prince Cor of Archenland desires
an audience of the Lady Aravis," said the Herald. Then he
and the trumpeter drew aside and bowed and the soldiers
saluted and the Prince himself came in. All his attendants
withdrew and closed the gate behind them.

The Prince bowed, and a very clumsy bow for a Prince it
was. Aravis curtsied in the Calormene style (which is not at
all like ours) and did it very well because, of course, she
had been taught how. Then she looked up and saw what
sort of person this Prince was.

She saw a mere boy. He was bare-headed and his fair
hair was encircled with a very thin band of gold, hardly
thicker than a wire. His upper tunic was of white cambric,
as fine as a handkerchief, so that the bright red tunic
beneath it showed through. His left hand, which rested on
his enamelled sword hilt, was bandaged.

Aravis looked twice at his face before she gasped and
said, "Why! It's Shasta!"

Shasta all at once turned very red and began speaking very quickly. "Look here, Aravis," he said, "I do hope you won't think I'm got up like this (and the trumpeter and all) to try to impress you or make out that I'm different or any rot of that sort. Because I'd far rather have come in my old clothes, but they're burnt now, and my father said —"

"Your father?" said Aravis.

"Apparently King Lune is my father," said Shasta. "I might really have guessed it. Corin being so like me. We were twins, you see. Oh, and my name isn't Shasta, it's Cor."

"Cor is a nicer name than Shasta," said Aravis.

"Brothers' names run like that in Archenland," said Shasta (or Prince Cor as we must now call him). "Like Dar and Darrin, Cole and Colin and so on."

"Shasta — I mean Cor," said Aravis. "No, shut up. There's something I've got to say at once. I'm sorry I've been such a pig. But I did change before I knew you were a Prince, honestly I did: when you went back, and faced the Lion."

"It wasn't really going to kill you at all, that Lion," said Cor.

"I know," said Aravis, nodding. Both were still and solemn for a moment as each saw that the other knew about Aslan.

Suddenly Aravis remembered Cor's bandaged hand. "I say!" she cried, "I forgot! You've been in a battle. Is that a wound?"

"A mere scratch," said Cor, using for the first time a rather lordly tone. But a moment later he burst out laughing and said, "If you want to know the truth, it isn't a proper wound at all. I only took the skin off my knuckles just as any clumsy fool might do without going near a battle."

"Still you were in the battle," said Aravis. "It must have been wonderful."

"It wasn't at all like what I thought," said Cor.

"But Sha – Cor, I mean – you haven't told me anything yet about King Lune and how he found out who you were."

"Well, let's sit down," said Cor. "For it's rather a long story. And by the way, Father's an absolute brick. I'd be just as pleased – or very nearly – at finding he's my father even if he wasn't a king. Even though Education and all sorts of horrible things are going to happen to me. But you want the story. Well, Corin and I were twins. And about a week after we were both born, apparently, they took us to a wise old Centaur in Narnia to be blessed or something. Now this Centaur was a prophet as a good many Centaurs are. Perhaps you haven't seen any Centaurs yet? There were some in the battle yesterday. Most remarkable people, but I can't say I feel quite at home with them yet. I say, Aravis, there are going to be a lot of things to get used to in these Northern countries."

"Yes, there are," said Aravis. "But get on with the story."

"Well, as soon as he saw Corin and me, it seems this Centaur looked at me and said, A day will come when that boy will save Archenland from the deadliest danger in which ever she lay. So of course my Father and Mother were very pleased. But there was someone present who wasn't. This was a chap called the Lord Bar who had been Father's Lord Chancellor. And apparently he'd done something wrong – *bezzling* or some word like that – I didn't understand that part very well – and Father had had to dismiss him. But nothing else was done to him and he was allowed to go on living in Archenland. But he must have been as bad as he could be, for it came out afterwards he had been in the pay of the Tisroc and had sent a lot of secret information to Tashbaan. So as soon as he heard I was going to save Archenland from a great danger he decided I must be put out of the way. Well, he succeeded in kidnapping me (I don't exactly know how) and rode away down the Winding Arrow to the coast. He'd had everything prepared and there was a ship manned with his own followers lying ready for him and he put out to sea with me on board. But Father got wind of it, though not quite in time, and was after him as quickly as he could. The Lord

Bar was already at sea when Father reached the coast, but not out of sight. And Father was embarked in one of his own warships within twenty minutes.

"It must have been a wonderful chase. They were six days following Bar's galleon and brought her to battle on the seventh. It was a great sea-fight (I heard a lot about it yesterday evening) from ten o'clock in the morning till sunset. Our people took the ship in the end. But I wasn't there. The Lord Bar himself had been killed in the battle. But one of his men said that, early that morning, as soon as he saw he was certain to be overhauled, Bar had given me to one of his knights and sent us both away in the ship's boat. And that boat was never seen again. But of course that was the same boat that Aslan (he seems to be at the back of all the stories) pushed ashore at the right place for Arsheesh to pick me up. I wish I knew that knight's name, for he must have kept me alive and starved himself to do it."

"I suppose Aslan would say that was part of someone else's story," said Aravis.

"I was forgetting that," said Cor.

"And I wonder how the prophecy will work out," said Aravis, "and what the great danger is that you're to save Archenland from."

"Well," said Cor rather awkwardly, "they seem to think I've done it already."

Aravis clapped her hands. "Why, of course!" she said. "How stupid I am. And how wonderful! Archenland can never be in much greater danger than it was when Rabadash had crossed the Arrow with his two hundred horse and you hadn't yet got through with your message. Don't you feel proud?"

"I think I feel a bit scared," said Cor.

"And you'll be living at Anvard now," said Aravis rather wistfully.

"Oh!" said Cor, "I'd nearly forgotten what I came about. Father wants you to come and live with us. He says there's been no lady in the court (they call it the court, I don't know why) since Mother died. Do, Aravis. You'll like Father – and Corin. They're not like me; they've been properly brought up. You needn't be afraid that –"

"Oh stop it," said Aravis, "or we'll have a real fight. Of course I'll come."

"Now let's go and see the Horses," said Cor.

There was a great and joyous meeting between Bree and Cor, and Bree, who was still in a rather subdued frame of mind, agreed to set out for Anvard at once: he and Hwin would cross into Narnia on the following day. All four bade an affectionate farewell to the Hermit and promised that they would soon visit him again. By about the middle of the morning they were on their way. The Horses had expected that Aravis and Cor would ride, but Cor explained that except in war, where everyone must do what he can do best, no one in Narnia or Archenland ever dreamed of mounting a Talking Horse.

This reminded poor Bree again of how little he knew about Narnian customs and what dreadful mistakes he might make. So while Hwin strolled along in a happy dream, Bree got more nervous and more self-conscious with every step he took.

"Buck up, Bree," said Cor. "It's far worse for me than for you. You aren't going to be *educated*. I shall be learning reading and writing and heraldry and dancing and history and music while you'll be galloping and rolling on the hills of Narnia to your heart's content."

"But that's just the point," groaned Bree. "*Do* Talking Horses roll? Supposing they don't? I can't bear to give it up. What do you think, Hwin?"

"I'm going to roll anyway," said Hwin. "I don't suppose any of them will care two lumps of sugar whether you roll or not."

"Are we near that castle?" said Bree to Cor.

"Round the next bend," said the Prince.

"Well," said Bree, "I'm going to have a good one now: it may be the last. Wait for me a minute."

It was five minutes before he rose again, blowing hard and covered with bits of bracken.

"Now I'm ready," he said in a voice of profound gloom. "Lead on, Prince Cor, Narnia and the North."

But he looked more like a horse going to a funeral than a long-lost captive returning to home and freedom.

CHAPTER FIFTEEN

RABADASH THE RIDICULOUS

THE next turn of the road brought them out from among the trees and there, across green lawns, sheltered from the north wind by the high wooded ridge at its back, they saw the castle of Anvard. It was very old and built of a warm, reddish-brown stone.

Before they had reached the gate King Lune came out to meet them, not looking at all like Aravis's idea of a king and wearing the oldest of old clothes; for he had just come from making a round of the kennels with his Huntsman and had only stopped for a moment to wash his doggy hands. But the bow with which he greeted Aravis as he took her hand would have been stately enough for an Emperor.

"Little lady," he said, "we bid you very heartily welcome. If my dear wife were still alive we could make you better cheer but could not do it with a better will. And I am sorry that you have had misfortunes and been driven from your father's house, which cannot but be a grief to you. My son Cor has told me about your adventures together and all your valour."

"It was he who did all that, Sir," said Aravis. "Why, he rushed at a lion to save me."

"Eh, what's that?" said King Lune, his face brightening. "I haven't heard that part of the story."

Then Aravis told it. And Cor, who had very much wanted the story to be known, though he felt he couldn't tell it himself, didn't enjoy it so much as he had expected, and indeed felt rather foolish. But his father enjoyed it very much indeed and in the course of the next few weeks told it to so many people that Cor wished it had never happened.

Then the King turned to Hwin and Bree and was just as polite to them as to Aravis, and asked them a lot of questions about their families and where they had lived in Narnia before they had been captured. The Horses were rather tongue-tied for they weren't yet used to being talked to as equals by Humans – grown-up Humans, that is. They didn't mind Aravis and Cor.

Presently Queen Lucy came out from the castle and joined them and King Lune said to Aravis, "My dear, here is a loving friend of our house, and she has been seeing that your apartments are put to rights for you better than I could have done it."

"You'd like to come and see them, wouldn't you?" said Lucy, kissing Aravis. They liked each other at once and soon went away together to talk about Aravis's bedroom and Aravis's boudoir and about getting clothes for her, and all the sort of things girls do talk about on such an occasion.

After lunch, which they had on the terrace (it was cold birds and cold game pie and wine and bread and cheese), King Lune ruffled up his brow and heaved a sigh and said, "Heigh-ho! We have still that sorry creature Rabadash on our hands, my friends, and must needs resolve what to do with him."

Lucy was sitting on the King's right and Aravis on his left. King Edmund sat at one end of the table and the Lord Darrin faced him at the other. Dar and Peridan and Cor and Corin were on the same side as the King.

"Your Majesty would have a perfect right to strike off his head," said Peridan. "Such an assault as he made puts him on a level with assassins."

"It is very true," said Edmund. "But even a traitor may mend. I have known one that did." And he looked very thoughtful.

"To kill this Rabadash would go near to raising war with the Tisroc," said Darrin.

"A fig for the Tisroc," said King Lune. "His strength is in numbers and numbers will never cross the desert. But I have no stomach for killing men (even traitors) in cold blood. To have cut his throat in the battle would have eased my heart mightily: but this is a different thing."

"By my counsel," said Lucy, "your Majesty shall give him another trial. Let him go free on strait promise of fair dealing in the future. It may be that he will keep his word."

"Maybe Apes will grow honest, Sister," said Edmund. "But, by the Lion, if he breaks it again, may it be in such time and place that any of us could swap off his head in clean battle."

"It shall be tried," said the King: and then to one of the attendants, "Send for the prisoner, friend."

Rabadash was brought before them in chains. To look at him anyone would have supposed that he had passed the night in a noisome dungeon without food or water; but in reality he had been shut up in quite a comfortable room and provided with an excellent supper. But as he was sulking far too furiously to touch the supper and had spent the whole night stamping and roaring and cursing, he naturally did not now look his best.

"Your royal Highness needs not to be told," said King Lune, "that by the law of nations as well as by all reasons of prudent policy, we have as good right to your head as ever one mortal man had against another. Nevertheless, in consideration of your youth and the ill nurture, devoid of all gentilesse and courtesy, which you have doubtless had in the land of slaves and tyrants, we are disposed to set you free, unharmed, on these conditions: first, that –"

"Curse you for a barbarian dog!" spluttered Rabadash. "Do you think I will even hear your conditions? Faugh!

You talk very largely of nurture and I know not what. It's easy, to a man in chains, ha! Take off these vile bonds, give me a sword, and let any of you who dares then debate with me."

Nearly all the lords sprang to their feet, and Corin shouted:

"Father! Can I *box* him? Please."

"Peace! Your Majesties! My Lords!" said King Lune. "Have we no more gravity among us than to be so chafed by the taunt of a pajock? Sit down, Corin, or shalt leave the table. I ask your Highness again, to hear our conditions."

"I hear no conditions from barbarians and sorcerers," said Rabadash. "Not one of you dare touch a hair of my head. Every insult you have heaped on me shall be paid with oceans of Narnian and Archenlandish blood. Terrible shall the vengeance of the Tisroc be: even now. But kill me, and the burnings and torturings in these northern lands shall become a tale to frighten the world a thousand years hence. Beware! Beware! Beware! The bolt of Tash falls from above!"

"Does it ever get caught on a hook half-way?" asked Corin.

"Shame, Corin," said the King. "Never taunt a man save when he is stronger than you: then, as you please."

"Oh you foolish Rabadash," sighed Lucy.

Next moment Cor wondered why everyone at the table had risen and was standing perfectly still. Of course he did the same himself. And then he saw the reason. Aslan was among them though no one had seen him coming. Rabadash started as the immense shape of the Lion paced softly in between him and his accusers.

"Rabadash," said Aslan. "Take heed. Your doom is very near, but you may still avoid it. Forget your pride (what have you to be proud of?) and your anger (who has done you wrong?) and accept the mercy of these good kings."

Then Rabadash rolled his eyes and spread out his mouth into a horrible, long mirthless grin like a shark, and wagged his ears up and down (anyone can learn how to do this if they take the trouble). He had always found this very effective in Calormen. The bravest had trembled when he made these faces, and ordinary people had fallen to the floor, and sensitive people had often fainted. But what Rabadash hadn't realized is that it is very easy to frighten people who know you can have them boiled alive the moment you give the word. The grimaces didn't look at all alarming in Archenland; indeed Lucy only thought Rabadash was going to be sick.

"Demon! Demon! Demon!" shrieked the Prince. "I know you. You are the foul fiend of Narnia. You are the enemy of the gods. Learn who *I* am, horrible phantasm. I am descended from Tash, the inexorable, the irresistible. the curse of Tash is upon you. Lightning in the shape of scorpions shall be rained on you. The mountains of Narnia shall be ground into dust. The –"

"Have a care, Rabadash," said Aslan quietly. "The doom is nearer now: it is at the door: it has lifted the latch."

"Let the skies fall," shrieked Rabadash. "Let the earth gape! Let blood and fire obliterate the world! But be sure I will never desist till I have dragged to my palace by her hair the barbarian queen, the daughter of dogs, the –"

"The hour has struck," said Aslan: and Rabadash saw, to his supreme horror, that everyone had begun to laugh.

They couldn't help it. Rabadash had been wagging his ears all the time and as soon as Aslan said, "The hour has struck!" the ears began to change. They grew longer and more pointed and soon were covered with grey hair. And

while everyone was wondering where they had seen ears
like that before, Rabadash's face began to change too. It
grew longer, and thicker at the top and larger eyed, and the
nose sank back into the face (or else the face swelled out
and became all nose) and there was hair all over it. And his
arms grew longer and came down in front of him till his
hands were resting on the ground: only they weren't hands,
now, they were hoofs. And he was standing on all fours,
and his clothes disappeared, and everyone laughed louder
and louder (because they couldn't help it) for now what
had been Rabadash was, simply and unmistakably, a
donkey. The terrible thing was that his human speech
lasted just a moment longer than his human shape, so that
when he realized the change that was coming over him, he
screamed out:

"Oh, not a Donkey! Mercy! If it were even a horse – e'en
– a hor – eeh – auh, eeh-auh." And so the words died away
into a donkey's bray.

"Now hear me, Rabadash," said Aslan. "Justice shall be
mixed with mercy. You shall not always be an Ass."

At this of course the Donkey twitched its ears forward –
and that also was so funny that
everybody laughed all the more. They
tried not to, but they tried in vain.

"You have appealed to Tash," said
Aslan. "And in the temple of Tash you
shall be healed. You must stand before
the altar of Tash in Tashbaan at the great
Autumn Feast this year and there, in the
sight of all Tashbaan, your ass's shape
will fall from you and all men will know
you for Prince Rabadash. But as long as
you live, if ever you go more than ten
miles away from the great temple in

Tashbaan you shall instantly become again as you now are. And from that second change there will be no return."

There was a short silence and then they all stirred and looked at one another as if they were waking from sleep. Aslan was gone. But there was a brightness in the air and on the grass, and a joy in their hearts, which assured them that he had been no dream: and anyway, there was the donkey in front of them.

King Lune was the kindest-hearted of men and on seeing his enemy in this regrettable condition he forgot all his anger.

"Your royal Highness," he said. "I am most truly sorry that things have come to this extremity. Your Highness will bear witness that it was none of our doing. And of course we shall be delighted to provide your Highness with shipping back to Tashbaan for the – er – treatment which Aslan has prescribed. You shall have every comfort which your Highness's situation allows: the best of the cattle-boats – the freshest carrots and thistles –"

But a deafening bray from the Donkey and a well-aimed kick at one of the guards made it clear that these kindly offers were ungratefully received.

And here, to get him out of the way, I'd better finish off the story of Rabadash. He (or it) was duly sent back by boat to Tashbaan and brought into the temple of Tash at the great Autumn Festival, and then he became a man again. But of course four or five thousand people had seen the transformation and the affair could not possibly be hushed up. And after the old Tisroc's death when Rabadash became Tisroc in his place he turned out the most peaceable Tisroc Calormen had ever known. This was because, not daring to go more than ten miles from Tashbaan, he could never go on a war himself: and he didn't want his Tarkaans to win fame in the wars at his expense, for that is the way Tisrocs get overthrown. But though his reasons were selfish, it made things much more comfortable for all the smaller countries round Calormen. His own peole never forgot that he had been a donkey. During his reign, and to his face, he was called Rabadash the Peacemaker, but after his death and behind his back he was called Rabadash the Ridiculous, and if you look him up in a good History of Calormen (try the local library) you will find him under that name. And to this day in Calormene schools, if you do anything unusually stupid, you are very likely to be called "a second Rabadash".

Meanwhile at Anvard everyone was very glad that he had been disposed of before the real fun began, which was a grand feast held that evening on the lawn before the castle, with dozens of lanterns to help the moonlight. And the wine flowed and tales were told and jokes were cracked, and then silence was made and the King's poet with two fiddlers stepped out into the middle of the circle. Aravis and Cor prepared themselves to be bored, for the only poetry they knew was the Calormene kind, and you know now what that was like. But at the very first scrape of the fiddles a rocket seemed to go up inside their heads, and the poet sang the great old lay of Fair Olvin and how he fought the Giant Pire and turned him into stone (and that is the origin of Mount Pire — it was a two-headed Giant) and won the Lady Liln for his bride; and when it was over they wished it was going to begin again. And though Bree couldn't sing he told the story of the fight at Zalindreh. And Lucy told again (they had all, except Aravis and Cor, heard it many times but they all wanted it again) the tale of the Wardrobe and how she and King Edmund and Queen Susan and Peter the High King had first come into Narnia.

And presently, as was certain to happen sooner or later,

King Lune said it was time for young people to be in bed. "And tomorrow, Cor," he added, "shalt come over all the castle with me and see the estres and mark all its strength and weakness: for it will be thine to guard when I'm gone."

"But Corin will be the King then, Father," said Cor.

"Nay, lad," said King Lune, "thou art my heir. The crown comes to thee."

"But I don't want it," said Cor. "I'd far rather —"

"'Tis no question what thou wantest, Cor, nor I either. 'Tis in the course of law."

"But if we're twins we must be the same age."

"Nay," said the King with a laugh. "One must come first. Art Corin's elder by full twenty minutes. And his better too, let's hope, though that's no great mastery." And he looked at Corin with a twinkle in his eyes.

"But, Father, couldn't you make whichever you like to be the next King?"

"No. The king's under the law, for it's the law makes him a king. Hast no more power to start away from thy crown than any sentry from his post."

"Oh dear," said Cor. "I don't want to at all. And Corin — I am most dreadfully sorry. I never dreamed my turning up was going to chisel you out of your kingdom."

"Hurrah! Hurrah!" said Corin. "I shan't have to be King. I shan't have to be King. I'll always be a prince. It's princes have all the fun."

"And that's truer than thy brother knows, Cor," said King Lune. "For this is what it means to be a king: to be first in every desperate attack and last in every desperate retreat, and when there's hunger in the land (as must be now and then in bad years) to wear finer clothes and laugh louder over a scantier meal than any man in your land."

When the two boys were going upstairs to bed Cor again

asked Corin if nothing could be done about it. And Corin said:

"If you say another word about it, I'll – I'll knock you down."

It would be nice to end the story by saying that after that the two brothers never disagreed about anything again, but I am afraid it would not be true. In reality they quarrelled and fought just about as often as any other two boys would, and all their fights ended (if they didn't begin) with Cor getting knocked down. For though, when they had both grown up and become swordsmen, Cor was the more dangerous man in battle, neither he nor anyone else in the North Countries could ever equal Corin as a boxer. That was how he got his name of Corin Thunder-Fist; and how he performed his great exploit against the Lapsed Bear of Stormness, which was really a Talking Bear but had gone back to Wild Bear habits. Corin climbed up to its lair on the Narnian side of Stormness one winter day when the snow was on the hills and boxed it without a time-keeper for thirty-three rounds. And at the end it couldn't see out of its eyes and became a reformed character.

Aravis also had many quarrels (and, I'm afraid, even fights) with Cor, but they always made it up again: so that years later, when they were grown up, they were so used to quarrelling and making it up again that they got married so as to go on doing it more conveniently. And after King Lune's death they made a good King and Queen of Archenland and Ram the Great, the most famous of all the kings of Archenland, was their son. Bree and Hwin lived happily to a great age in Narnia and both got married but not to one another. And there weren't many months in which one or both of them didn't come trotting over the pass to visit their friends at Anvard.